DECLAN RUSH

MACABRE TROPHIES

DECLAN RUSH

MACABRE TROPHIES

DARK WATERS BOOKS
mystery · thriller · fantasy · fiction · crime noir

Paperback ISBN: 979-8-9865676-4-8
Ebook ISBN: 979-8-9865676-7-9
Library of Congress Control Number: 2023931955

For Jimbo...

PROLOGUE
SANDY POINT, CAPE COD

TUESDAY

Anthony Medeiros wore a wide grin as he marked off his calendar with a red "X." It was finally here — the day after Labor Day. The 70-year-old retired history teacher giggled like a child on Christmas as he gathered his fishing gear. As clichéd as it sounded to Anthony and all the other locals of Sandy Point, Cape Cod, the day after Labor Day was Christmas.

"Pointers," as they were known, could finally reclaim their town, and that meant Anthony could also reclaim his favorite jetty and pull in a few keepers before bass season ended.

Yes, the idiots are gone, he grinned, tossing a dozen thawed-out silver pogies into his bait bucket.

Sandy Point was two towns: summer and winter. The summer town would appear and balloon moments after the last school bell rang on a sticky, June afternoon. That balloon hovered over the Pointers for a couple of months and finally popped when the Sunday papers arrived with those glossy back-to-school circulars.

Time to pack up the car, idiots!

He opened the screen door with his back while balancing his pole, tackle box, and bucket. His crooked frame paused for a minute, savoring the warmth from the early evening sun falling on his shoulders.

He chuckled lightly.

They probably thought that Sandy Point turned to ice the day after Labor Day.

They were the "summer people," the idiots. There were all types of summer people and the locals secretly hated most of them. Sure, Pointers smiled when confused tourists asked questions like, "Where's the bridge to Martha's Vineyard?" Or mimicked, "Where can I get some good chowdah?"

As painful as it was to offer those smiles, there was a reason to give them. Tourists loved handing over lots of green paper in Sandy Point. They'd hand it over for anything with Cape Cod stamped on it, even recycled Coke bottles filled with sand. That's why the locals put up with the tourists, and ironically, it wasn't their departure that was privately celebrated. At least their dollars lined the Pointers' pockets, keeping them warm during the sweater months.

Anthony whistled no particular tune as he headed for Sea Glass Beach. It would take him ten minutes, and as he strolled along, he thought of the other types of Summer People — the homeowners. They were the ones he was happy to see go. They didn't care about preserving the natural beauty of the landscape. Instead, they made The Point their summer sandbox, kicking up that sand with crane scoops and bulldozers so they could build their monstrosities. He knew if they continued to mold their Sandy Point castles, in twenty years, his town would just be another bustling suburb.

No regard for nature.

They didn't care what they were doing to the Cape, and to Anthony, they only summered in Sandy Point for material to chirp about at holiday cocktail parties up in the city.

There were three types of homeowners: The WASPS, the Jews, and the Irish. The first two were from the money suburbs of Boston — Wellesley, Weston, and Newton.

Every summer day was always the same routine for those women. They packed coolers with turkey sandwiches and Cokes for the kids — TaB soda and chicken salad for themselves. They'd meet around nine to stake their beach chair camp.

Swimming lessons for the kids while the tribe of sun worshippers settled in for the long day ahead. For the next seven hours, the tribe dug their feet into the sand, soaked up the sun while the kids ran wild. The young ones snapped towels at one another and raced for the ice cream man, while the bored teenagers harassed the lifeguard about his penis size until he'd finally storm over to the circle of chairs for help. But the worshippers either thought their kids were "cute," or they were too busy gossiping about the unfortunate tribal member who hadn't made it to the beach. Usually, they wouldn't even glance up at the angry lifeguard. Instead, they'd keep their eyes closed, faces poised to the heavens, each one secretly hoping the Sun God would bless them with those extra rays, so they would glow brighter at that night's barbecue.

What the hell were they all thinking? Another five minutes and I'll be at an empty beach without any of them there. How could they live their lives like that? Playing a role.

Anthony thought about the men and their routine, which he found just as pathetic. A Bloody Mary with breakfast, 18 holes, a business deal, and a quick stop at the 19th allowing just enough time for an early evening dip before the neighborhood cookout. Time to man the grill and feed sweet blender drinks to the wives so later that night they could go groping far beyond the tan line.

And then there were the Irish.

Oh, the Irish!

He chuckled, thinking about them. They were similar except when it came to money. The Irish were still playing Triple-A ball. They came from the lace curtain neighborhoods of Milton, Watertown, and Canton, and the Venetian blind counties of Dorchester and good ol' paddy whacky, Southie. They tried to imitate their upper-class neighbors but couldn't quite pull it off. They also had wise-ass kids who harassed the lifeguards, but not by pointing out small penises, God forbid. And it wasn't because of the myth. No, any kind of sex talk would get the kids a stinging slap in front of the entire beach from their freckle-speckled mothers.

For the men, a stop at the 19th lasted as long as it took to play all 18. As for the cookout, they never bothered making sweet drinks for their wives. Unless she wanted to get knocked up, a drink with a pink umbrella floating in it wasn't going to get any Irish broad into bed. So, the Irish continued playing through the 19th using vodka or whiskey as their putter. Or sometimes both.

Pathetic is the word — Anthony shook his head, but then smiled, spotting the tumbling waves in the distance. He turned his hearing aid off.

Silence.

His smile broadened. He wouldn't have to see or hear any of them for another nine months.

A slight pain near his heart suddenly halted his thoughts. He put down half of his gear in order to massage his chest, tapping one of his brown dotted hands against his fish-stained Boston Bruins sweatshirt. Licking his lips, he tried to identify the sour taste that had formed on the back of his tongue.

Deep breaths.

Tapping harder, the pain faded for a second. But a quick jolt then stabbed his heart. The stinging charge made him drop the rest of his gear, bait sliding out of the bucket onto the dirt path next to Beach Street. The dead eye of a fish stared up at him as he tapped harder. Taps turned to solid punches against his chest until the pain finally subsided.

"Wooooo," he let out a sigh of relief trying to remember if he had taken his pills. Ever since his dear Marie passed on two years before, he was always forgetting his pills. He took the damn things when he'd remember, but it was Marie who had kept him on the clock.

That was her job in life, keeping me on track. She was a master at it.

He missed how she used to chide him about his poor heart and his unhealthy eating habits.

The pills?

He pondered the question for a minute, shook his head, and was pretty sure he had taken them after he had breakfast with some of the guys at the diner. He remembered what he had eaten, a Portuguese omelet with extra linguica. It was now beating him up. Reaching into his jeans pocket, he pulled out a pack of Rolaids and popped two into his mouth.

Anthony mumbled up at the sky, "Sorry, Marie, but, honey, I couldn't resist."

Feeling better, he gave a playful shrug and squatted to pick up the bait, but then stopped. His eye caught two people on the beach. He was a good 100 yards away. Needing the cataract operation he kept delaying, he couldn't make out who they were. With his hands, he shielded the remaining sun and squinted. He could see a man and a little boy. Father and son. They both had fishing poles and gear and were headed straight for Anthony's jetty. The father was several yards ahead of the son and turned around every few steps, motioning for his son to hurry up. The boy stumbled in the sand, his little legs working overtime to catch up. Anthony wasn't angry that they were about to steal his favorite spot. High tide wasn't for a while. Anyway, his plan was to watch the pink sun fall behind the surf and enjoy the tranquility of the beach before baiting his hook. He could do that from where he was and still take in the scene in front of him.

They had to be Pointers and the father must know the tide charts, so he couldn't be after fish. He was probably just going to teach his son the basics. Father and son time.

He thought of his own boy. Memories unexpectedly began rolling in with the surf. He spent countless summers teaching Tony how to swim and fish. To enjoy nature. They were buddies, good buddies. On those nippy October nights, when they tried to catch the last keeper to fill the freezer, they would warm each other by chuckling over bad jokes. He turned from the beach and allowed himself to ride one of those memories. Tony was twelve and it was a night of endless casts.

"Hey, Dad. Two cannibals were eating a clown when one turned to the other. What did he ask him?"

"I don't know, pal."

"Does this taste funny to you?"

Their laughter echoed across the beach that night, but then his boy got older. Never mind jokes, now they didn't even exchange birthday cards.

What happened? Anthony asked himself. He really didn't have to ask. He knew it was his fault. He let them grow apart, and as Marie had told him, he was too much of a stubborn old "Portagee" to admit it. He loved the simple life The Point had to offer and was furious when his son picked the suit and tie lifestyle of New York City. Was the Cape not good enough for Tony? Or the real question: was it Anthony's life that wasn't good enough?

Deep down, Anthony knew it was his own baggage. He always felt like a lesser person for never leaving the Cape — teaching history, not making it. That was the real reason he hated the summer people. Jealousy. Having the minor heart scare and thinking of Marie, topped with the father and son scene on the beach, made him realize time was running out.

I can go fishing tomorrow. But tonight, I'm going to call my boy. Time to go home.

He felt like he had zoned out for a while. He wiped his moist eyes and turned back to give one last admiring glance at the scene on the beach.

A blast of adrenaline shot through him.

WHAT THE...

For half a second, he thought it wasn't real. It couldn't be. Then he knew it was real. But it made no sense. He had to stop it! Now! He tried to yell, but the shock and terror of the sight clamped his throat shut.

Run, his mind hollered, *Stop it! Stop it now!*

Anthony sprinted toward the beach, but only made it a few yards when the cutting pain ripped his heart knocking him to the ground. His eyes filled with burning tears as he tried to spit out the grass and dirt, gagging while the realization hit him.

The pills!

They were being filled. He hadn't taken them. His heart was exploding, but in those last few seconds, it wasn't his life that passed before Anthony Medeiros's eyes.

No, it was the horrifying act on the beach. That was the sight he would be taking with him to the grave.

His last thought was: *If only I had taken my pills, maybe I could've stopped it!*

And maybe, just maybe, the retired schoolteacher was right, and if he had taken his pills, it may have never begun. But it did.

CHAPTER 1

JUNE 7, 2004

MONDAY

J.T. O'ROURKE

Seventy-seven miles. That's all it was from Boston to Sandy Point, Cape Cod, and as I sped along 495 South, I wondered if that was far enough for a change of scenery. Hell, I needed one. Of course, my coworkers and friends thought I was — and I quote — "fucking crazy" for quitting my job. They were probably right. I was feeling pretty crazy these days, and I must've been, because I was giving up Ben Franklins for the unknown. For the past eight years, I had been head bartender at Tilt the Jar, the hottest Irish pub in Kenmore Square. Sure, I hadn't just quit some high-powered law firm to open a bed and breakfast, or some crap like that, but at 34, my wit and loyalty to my patrons had already made me somewhat of a legend in the Boston bar world. Many said I was more popular than the Sox players who came in after a game now and then to pound a few down. I'm certainly not bragging. People will always rub your back if they know there's a chance you might slide them a free beer, but I was pretty good at what I did. God didn't bless the Irish with big dicks, but he did grace them with big personalities. And I used mine.

One could say J.T. O'Rourke was a regular Sam Malone and, like Sam, I decided to shut the doors to Cheers and move on, if you will.

But did Sam move on in that last episode? I asked myself, laughing at my inner dialogue before flicking my blinker to pass an SUV covered with Martha's Vineyard bumper stickers.

Why the hell am I doing this again? I shifted gears, glancing over at the tiny soccer mom who commandeered her black tank with one hand while using the other to blindly swat behind her. I couldn't see the fighting kids in the back seat, but I really didn't have to. My three sisters and I had dodged the flailing hand many times.

"Okay, why the hell am I doing this?" I repeated, thinking of the events that had pushed me over the edge. It was a couple of weeks back, after I had worked a double. It had been a routine day, opening the oak doors so the barflies could flutter in. They nursed a couple of Bloodies followed by Black and Tans while reading their Heralds for an hour or two, before stepping it up with vodka tonics and Jack and Cokes. Then it was slur time featuring the same tired arguments over their favorite dead movie stars and theories on the Kennedy curse.

Around four, when they flew out on half wings, as if on cue, a group of pasty-faced Harvard silver spoons stumbled in to celebrate "Jonathan's 21st Birthday." They fed birthday boy candy-ass shots and patted his back after every slam of the glass. For the first five, Jonathan was "the man." But then he got loud. Too loud. An 11 on drunk volume. I had to turn him down. I don't know if that's what pissed me off or that he was also wearing one of those foam rubber trucker hats tilted to the side like he was Ashton Kutcher searching for some B-list celebrity to punk. I hated that stuff. As I grabbed our bottom shelf tequila, I wondered what truckers thought when they encountered models and Ivy League punks parading around in their garb. I bet they hated that shit too and speaking of punks — it was closing time for them. Time to punk the birthday boy.

I poured Jonathan a Prairie Dog shot, compliments of the bar — Happy Birthday!

He studied it like a beaker in a chemistry lab. After several seconds, he took a deep breath and threw it back. And then two seconds later, he threw it back up, painting the floor orange to the sounds of gut-wrenching laughter from his buddies. And then he heaved again, after I told him that a Prairie Dog was tequila and Tabasco sauce, and in some bars known as a Prairie Fire. Either name — it bit and burned him; his friends carried him out of The Jar like he was an injured Pats player. When I sprinkled sawdust on the puke, I knew I had been part of my own little *Good Will Hunting* moment, but I didn't care.

How do you like them apples?

My workday finally ended with a group of 30 beer bellies getting shit faced, wearing bachelor party T-shirts. They were harmless drunks, hugging the groom constantly, screaming, "Bart, I love you man!"

Even though I've had thousands of days like that, and they could get very annoying, that shift wasn't what made me quit. It was after I locked the oak doors, restocked the bar, poured myself a pint, plodded up the back stairwell to my one-room apartment, and turned on the tube.

The music from *CHiPs* was playing. I glanced down at my watch — 3:05 a.m. I realized I was catching the opening of the show, so I threw off my sweat-drenched work polo, grabbed some Ben and Jerry's, a spoon, and collapsed into my Archie Bunker chair.

Chomping on my Chunky Monkey while washing it down with my pint of Guinness, I watched Ponch give his characteristic toothy grin to a van of Lakers cheerleaders. That's when a loud crash changed my life.

No, it wasn't another 20-car collision on the LA freeway. It was something in my apartment. One of the pictures hanging on my wall fell to the floor breaking the frame, glass showering everywhere. After I placed the noise, I hesitated for a moment to check out the van of Lakers girls. It seemed Ponch was going to have more luck with them than I was from my La-Z-Boy, so I got up and headed to the closet. I grabbed a broom and dustpan and was about to sweep up the glass when I saw two words staring up at me: BOSTON COLLEGE. It wasn't a picture that had fallen; it was my B.C. degree. I was extremely proud of that degree because it took me seven years of night school to get it. I must've served a million drinks, so I could hang that piece of paper. And man, had I come close to quitting a few times. More than a few... But I never gave up and my night school professors had never given up on me either. That night, as I swept up the glass, I remembered what Father Shea, the Dean of the Night School, had said to me.

"J.T., you're going to make wonderful contributions to this world."

I thought about that while I dumped the glass into the wastebasket. I had what my Irish Lit Professor said happened to many of the characters in Joyce's *Dubliners* — an epiphany. It hit me. It hit me hard. My eyes lowered to the new ripple forming in the gut that was already spilling over my belt. I was becoming a fat, double-chinned, Irish bachelor who served up drinks to last call and beyond and then watched bad '80s cop shows. Seriously depressing. I didn't want to spend the next 35 years doing that. Doing nothing. I wanted to use my degree. I didn't care how corny it sounded, I wanted to contribute. That's when I went to the top drawer of my bureau. I riffled through old cell phone bills, a few take out menus, and even a couple of cocktail napkins decorated with flowery handwriting and 617 area codes — the bartender's version of the black book — until I finally spotted the business card. I studied it for a minute and then placed it against the light on my nightstand.

Like most nights, I didn't sleep. I sprawled along my windowsill staring down at the lonely delivery trucks unloading fresh bread and newspapers and waited for the sun to rise over the CITGO sign. When it finally did, I got up and grabbed the card. I stared at the numbers and then the phone for a long while, reminiscent of the days of calling for a date in the eighth grade. Except this wasn't about pizza and a movie. This was about my life. But then I realized my life still was pizza and a movie, so I said, "Fuck it," and made the call. During the 10-minute conversation I found out the offer was still available, and I'd be heading for a new beginning in Sandy Point, Cape Cod.

"Well, thank God that frame did fall," I laughed out loud, spotting two long-haired blondes in a purple convertible in front of me. I slid over to the left lane and accelerated until I was beside them. I tried to casually turn my head to sneak a peek. I guess there was nothing casual about it. They were waiting. They mockingly waved as their silicone balloons also greeted me, busting out of their matching yellow tops.

"Girls Gone Wild on the Cape," I mused and, unfazed at getting caught, I jokingly tilted my shades at them, *Risky Business* style. I figured I was dating myself, but apparently, they had TBS or Netflix because they loved it. They returned teasing smiles and blew kisses, but then they pointed to my car roof. I knew what they were asking. It was 80 degrees, and I was driving a convertible, a black Cabriolet I borrowed from a waitress at The Jar, but I had the top up.

I tugged on my tie, gestured to my hair and shrugged at them. The silicone sisters flashed me their "You-poor-boy-you-have-to-work" looks before slowing down to let me pass. I had been tempted to drive with the top down, especially since the car was going to be picked up the following day. But I wanted to make a good first impression. So, the top stayed up and my hair stayed straight. Of course, I didn't look straight. I was driving a Cabriolet, a chick car — "Not that there's anything wrong with that."

God, I love *Seinfeld*.

And there wasn't anything wrong with it as far as I was concerned. My best friend, Frannie Fitzgerald, was gay. Best damn wingman I ever had. God, I missed him.

Anyway, I had already received surly stares from many male drivers, and a few minutes after the party balloons floated past, beeping goodbye, a green Jeep pulled up beside me. Three teens wearing straight-from-the-box baseball caps swung their heads over in hopes of checking out the girl driver. I responded with a sympathetic shrug.

One of the teens, with the face of a bulldog, sitting in the back seat, shook his head in disgust when he saw me. It was easy to figure out the kids came from the land of the loaded.

Bulldog Face wore a Concord-Carlisle High School T-shirt, the colors matching the several maroon and gold bumper stickers decorating the Jeep. He cradled a ball in the pouch of his lacrosse stick and stared me down. He leaned over to his friends, said something, and then pointed at me, laughing. I tried to ignore the young dickheads, but then Bulldog Face started yelling.

"Hey, nice car! Nice car! I'm talkin' to you."

I kept looking forward, my hands tightening on the steering wheel.

"Where you going? P-town?"

I thought of the bullies who used to jump Frannie, and the memory of me being one of them brought back the old shame and anger.

I blurted back, "Fuck you, asshole!" Real original.

"Fuck me? I bet you want to, but no! Fuck *you*!" Bulldog Face cocked his stick back and fired the ball at the Cabriolet. I heard and felt a loud thud on the driver's side door. Everyone was silent for a second.

"Fuck," I yelled realizing what just happened.

The driver stepped on the gas and chugged away, weaving in and out of traffic. I was bullshit and started to race after them. I would make those little bastards pay.

The speedometer needle rapidly bent to the right until it was hovering at 85, I was catching up to them. I laughed with maniacal anticipation. But then I spotted a vehicle with flashing lights up ahead. It was parked on the side of the road, and I remembered how everyone at the bar warned me about speed traps on 495 South. Thinking it was a cop, I slowed down immediately, but Bulldog Face and friends continued on at a steady clip, waving farewell middle fingers. I

11

knew they hadn't seen the lights, and I silently prayed for sweet justice. But, as I moved closer to the swirling lights, I realized they were yellow. And, as I passed the yellow van that was flashing the lights, I saw ten guys in orange jumpsuits carrying trash bags poking the ground with sticks.

"The drunks," I scoffed and thought of my own father, who had to pick up the trash too many times. I looked ahead. The Jeep was long gone. And as pissed off as I was at those kids, I knew by chasing them I was doing a Billy O'Rourke. I didn't want to be Billy O'Rourke, the retired drunk cop with the legendary temper. It was stamped on my DNA and took me several years to overcome it. I didn't ever want to be "that guy" again.

That was the other reason I left Boston. My father. He was back on the bottle. The month before, my old man had left his 90-day sobriety chip as a tip on the bar at the V.F.W. club and was back at it. Better than ever.

I had watched it all of my life, and I refused to watch it again. His show was getting old. I was pretty confident that his latest binge would be his swan song. In his mind, he had nothing to live for since my mother passed on from breast cancer two years earlier, and my three sisters cut him loose many blackouts and blowouts long ago.

All my ol' man had were retired cop buddies, and most of them were either dead or in the program, which meant they were dead to him. Of course, he still had me — his codependent son who was always there to clean up his puke and feed him buttered toast and ginger ale. Not this time.

When I found out he had another slip, I went looking for him, like the hundreds of times before. But this time when I found him in the local gin mill, drowning in a whiskey glass, clutching hopeless Keno tickets, I stood up to him. I told him I wasn't going to take it anymore. None of it. The lies. The shitty excuses. The puke. The verbal abuse. None of it!

His reaction was taken from one of his old scripts. He bawled his eyes out and recited his usual, "I miss your mother" drunk-a-logue. This time, I didn't stay for the closing scene. I walked to the door.

And, when I did, he blew up and hollered, "I may like a little drink now and then to blow off some steam. And, I may have yelled at the girls and you a bit, but I never laid a hand on you. Any of you! You can take that to the bank. Never."

I restrained myself and turned around slowly and said calmly, "It wasn't your hands that put Mom in the grave. It was your tongue."

I slammed the door behind me, knowing I had probably just put the final nail in my father's coffin. I was certain he'd spend the rest of the summer drinking himself to death.

Yep, I was definitely driving away from my past. I knew it and I didn't care. It was time. I was going to forget about it all, and a little asshole like Bulldog Face wasn't worth the trouble. No road rage for J.T. O'Rourke. I was going to enjoy the rest of the ride.

I flipped the radio to 88.7 WMVY, the Vineyard radio station. One of the flies had told me that when MVY came in on the dial, it was the unofficial sign that you were on Cape Cod. The station spit out nothing but static for a couple of minutes, but as soon as I spotted the Bourne Bridge, the sound became crystal clear, and the warm voice of Bob Marley brought a wide smile to my face. Cape Cod and Marley. Summer. I had taken a risk, but it wasn't like I had just accepted a job in Siberia. It was Cape Cod in the summer. I felt a change wash over me immediately. A cleansing feeling. Even though it was sunny, there was a light veil of fog blocking the bridge. It reminded me of some magical kingdom straight out of a picture book.

As the Cabriolet climbed over the bridge, the temperature dropped slightly, and I felt like Terence Mann about to enter the cornfield in *Field of Dreams*. The nervous, giddy excitement of the unknown overtook me as I tapped the horn to the music and then I spotted the rotary hedges that spelled "CAPE COD."

I even sang along with Marley, and I was not worrying about a thing.

I kept the Rastafarian's advice in my head for the next 20 minutes. And I softly repeated the lyrics to "Three Little Birds" after turning off the ignition and staring at the small white building with the black, bold lettering: SANDY POINT STANDARD TIMES.

I checked myself in the rearview mirror and sighed, "I hope you're right, Marley man."

With hardly any newspaper experience, I was about to take a job as a reporter for the *Sandy Point Standard Times*. I sighed again and prayed that 77 miles was far enough and that I had just left it all behind. Everything. Even the nightmare…

CHAPTER 2
SEPTEMBER 9, 1970

WEDNESDAY

MICHAEL DEVLIN

Officer Michael Devlin yawned, rubbing his eyes awake for a third time. He propped himself up in his cruiser, parked on the edge of the dock. His light blue eyes focused on the barely visible ocean in front of him. He was about to drift off again, when he spotted the small car ferry knifing through the darkness and quarter mile stretch of surf. It was headed for Oyster Island.

He had been living on the private island since he was six, but the sight of the first arriving ferry still amazed him. It always looked like the ferry was actually carrying the sun to the island.

His eyes grew heavier. Even though dawn was approaching, his shift was just beginning. He knew if he stayed in his cruiser any longer, those lids would shut like window shades in a thunderstorm, and he couldn't afford the reputation of a cop who sleeps on the job. Devlin stretched his bulky arms and savored another yawn before dragging his six-foot-three muscular frame out of the car.

"God, I'm exhausted," he grunted to himself, and leaned against the cruiser. He had good reason to be tired. In the last week, he had covered for practically everyone on the squad, and he knew why. The rent-a-cops had all gone home to their real jobs, and the new officer that had been able to blend in with the crowd was now visible. Twenty-five-year-old Officer Michael Devlin was back at being the low man on the Sandy Point Police Department totem pole — a rookie cop. From the Chief to the janitor, Devlin knew they would test him. He was a rookie and that's how it worked — a time honored tradition. You want respect? You have to earn it. Devlin knew the drill. He would have to prove to everyone on the force that he could be trusted before he was considered "true blue." The way a "rook" learned if he was finally one of them was an invitation to The Angry Fisherman for a beer after his shift. After five months on the force, Michael Devlin was still thirsty. And there was no telling when he'd get that pint. It was a test that might involve a few more extra details or a year or two of bullshit. He knew one way to make it an easier process — keep his trap shut, bite the inside of his cheek, and do whatever was asked.

Just like the army.

That hazing phase didn't last long. He spent his first four months nodding his head in the affirmative, but by the end of his tour, he was the one shouting orders. But that was Nam, not Sandy Point.

Ironically, he knew it was probably easier to gain acceptance thousands of miles away, squirming on his belly in a jungle while bullets whizzed by, than it would be breaking up pot parties behind the dunes of Sea Glass Beach. The reason was quite simple. In Nam they didn't care what your last name was or where you came from. All they cared about: when the time came, would you squeeze that trigger?

And he did. Many times. Maybe too many times.

The sun was wide-awake, and the ferry was about to dock. Devlin turned his head and arched his strong chin, glancing up at the mansion perched on the only hill of Oyster Island. That was the real reason he hadn't been asked to have that beer. It was his parents' house. Officer Devlin was a rich kid. But not just any rich kid. He was the son of Allan Devlin, one of New England's top defense attorneys — a man who was despised by almost every law enforcement agency from Cape Cod to the Berkshires and beyond. He was hated because he was the best. No one better. The cops caught the bad guys, and Allan Devlin set them free. So, how could any of them trust his son?

Devlin yawned one more time, knowing there would be more sleepless nights before he could prove he was not his father. Never would be.

"Hey there, Mikey!" Gerry Tadmor, the sixty-plus captain of the ferry yelled and waved from behind his one-man pilothouse.

"Hey, Cap!" Devlin returned the wave before heading over to the pylon that was attached to the dock. He planned on catching the rope in case Tadmor missed hooking the pylon. It was their routine even though the captain never missed.

Tadmor shifted his gears, and the ferry's engine rumbled, slowly gliding, rubbing, and squeaking against the dock pads. Devlin noticed Tadmor pointing over at a smiling young boy who was holding the rope. It was Devlin's paper-boy, Greggie. He remembered when he was that age and how the captain would let him try to lasso the dock. He smiled, too, remembering how he always failed.

"Officer Devlin, please don't catch the rope. I know I can do it." The eleven-year-old twirled the rope with his right hand, fixing his eyes on the target.

"Okay, I won't. But I'd throw it now if I were you." He didn't think the boy had a chance.

Greggie cranked his arm a couple of times before letting the rope fly. It barely caught the back of the pole. He loosened his grip, and it completely slid over.

Devlin shouted, "Great throw, Greggie!"

"Yes, sir. You're a natural seaman!" Captain Tadmor added.

"Thanks," Greggie tried to suppress a smile as he tied the rope to one of the cleats on the ferry while Tadmor tied up the other ones and then unhooked the chain to let off the only waiting car. It was Frank Williams' car.

"Good morning, Mr. Williams." Devlin threw a half wave, but stopped when he didn't get anything in return, just a look of anger mixed with confusion. The businessman who resembled Paul Newman then squealed off, almost driving over Devlin's foot.

"Jesus." Devlin uttered as he backed up.

"Don't mind him, Officer Devlin," Greggie shook his head, "He's a bit cranky. He told me he and his work partner had to drive all the way from New York last night. I guess they were on a business trip. I saw her drop him off at his car."

"Oh, really?" Devlin and Tadmor exchanged knowing looks as Greggie slung his newspaper bag over his shoulder, hopped on the banana seat, and clutched the high handlebars of his red Sting-Ray.

It wasn't New York that Frank Williams was returning from — it was his girl-friend's house. That wouldn't be a problem if there were no Mrs. Williams waiting at home. Half the town already knew about his affair with the Twiggy look-alike secretary from Sandy Point Oil who heated his nights.

That half kept it quiet — don't get into my business and I won't get into yours. The other half, the gossip queens who patrolled places like the cereal aisle of Lareby's Market, beauty parlor chairs, and church pews. They would know by noon, considering Greggie's father collected information for a living. Greg, Sr. owned the *Sandy Point Standard Times*. Frank Williams' expression now made sense to Devlin. The lies were wearing thin.

"Officer Devlin, do you want your paper now?" Greggie offered.

"No, that's okay. My Mom will want to read it with her breakfast."

Allan Devlin and his high-profile case in Boston would be spread all over page one. Not exactly Michael Devlin's kind of reading material.

"Okay. Well, have a good day, Officer Devlin. See you soon, Captain. And remember, you said I could try to go two for two at the Sandy Point dock." Greggie began to pedal, but stopped and turned back, "You know what? Some-day, I'm going to sail around the world and lasso them all."

Like being shot out of cannon, he zoomed off on his Sting-Ray.

"I hope he does," Tadmor said in thought, as he watched the boy for a minute and then perked up, pointing at the cruiser. "Mikey, bring her aboard."

Devlin nodded, jumped in, fired up the engine and drove up the loading ramp. He turned the key off while trying to stifle another yawn. He couldn't.

"Here," Tadmor handed him a Styrofoam cup of coffee through the window, "Another dawn to yawn shift, huh?"

"These days it's more like yawn to yawn," Devlin laughed, but hesitated at the offer. "I don't know how you do it every day, Cap."

"I do it 'cause it's my life. Now, take the damn cup while it's still hot. I knew you'd need it."

Devlin cradled the cup with both hands, blew the steam away, and took a small sip, "Thanks, Cap." He reached over for some quarters in the change holder, "How much do I owe you?"

Tadmor waved him off, "Can you believe Frank Williams?"

He left the question lingering in the salty breeze as he walked over, untied the ropes, and revved the ferry's engine. Devlin knew the cue. Captain Tadmor wanted to talk. He got out of the car, took a healthier sip, and made his way to the pilothouse. Tadmor shifted gears, pulling the ferry out of the slip.

Picking up on the conversation, the captain said, "I told the horny bastard he'd get caught. I mean, it's one thing to have an affair, but to have one when you live on an island. Stupid. Just plain stupid. Remember the old saying? 'You don't shit where you eat.' And speaking of shit, he gave me a ton of it. Said he was on time for the last run last night and I was already closed. You were on that boat. Did I leave early?"

"No. In fact, we left about ten minutes late. It was around 1:20 or so. God, that was only a few hours ago." Devlin took another sip, and it was now the perfect temperature. He gulped again, grabbed some change from his pocket and handed it to Tadmor.

"Here, Cap."

Again, he waved him off, "Mikey, can't a friend buy another friend a cup of Joe?"

"Cap, don't mean to be self-righteous, but when I put on this uniform, I don't want any freebies. Not even coffee. I don't want to pick up bad habits. You know what I mean?"

Tadmor laughed. "Well, you are self-righteous," but then put out his weathered hand, "but that's why you're such a good boy, Mikey. I guess I should start calling you Officer Devlin. I just wish I could've raised my Larry to be as honorable as you."

There is no easy way to approach a man who has a murderer for a son, so Devlin just put it out there. "How's he doing?"

The captain stared straight at Sandy Point looming on the horizon.

"Not good, Mikey. Not good at all."

He kept his eyes focused in front of him, "Y'know, Mikey, he's been doing his time up in Walpole. That's a bad crew up there. And you know how Larry can have a mouth on him. Well... He hasn't said... But... It's gotten back to me that, ah... he's been roughed up a bit."

Roughed up. The words translated in Devlin's head: raped.

Devlin nodded for him to continue.

"I was wondering if you knew when your dad would be done with that trial?"

"To be honest, I try not to talk with him about his work. And I've been busy and all."

"Oh," Tadmor looked briefly at him and went back into his tunnel stare. There was sadness in that one-word response that stung Devlin.

"You know, Cap, I was planning on calling him tonight, though. I'm sure he'd

18

help Larry either get a transfer or his own cell or something. I know he has been working on the transfer." Devlin hadn't planned on calling his old man, and he really didn't know if his father was working on a transfer or not. He felt sorry for Captain Tadmor, so he wanted to give him some hope. Even if that meant hearing his father go on about his latest trial — a "family man," bank president client accused of killing a prostitute.

A three-hundred-pound man bludgeoning a malnourished hooker with a hammer would be spun as self-defense. Hearing the boasting voice explain how it would be done would make Devlin sick, but he'd listen. Of course, the phone would be far away from his ear.

Captain Tadmor finally met his eyes.

"Thank you, Mikey. I appreciate it. I don't know what I'd ever do without your family's help. There would've been no way for me to afford a lawyer like your dad. He was a saint to take Larry's case pro bono like that. And, for Larry to only get involuntary manslaughter was an absolute miracle. Your father made that happen."

"I guess so," Devlin said plainly, thinking the piece of shit should be doing life for what he did. There was nothing involuntary about it.

Larry Tadmor had worked for a small-time bookie. One February night, he got drunk and went looking for a skinny, Northeastern freshman who had placed fifty bucks on the Huskies to win the Beanpot Hockey Tournament. Boston University won "the Pot" and Larry found the kid. He didn't have the money. Nine lethal stab wounds later, Larry Tadmor was crying self-defense. There was no question he would've been doing life if Allan Devlin hadn't been the puppeteer who pulled the strings on his golfing-buddy judge, a green prosecutor, and a mesmerized jury. And because of it, Larry would be out in a few years if he kept his nose clean. If Devlin really had his wish, though, Larry Tadmor would have that nose of his…

But he wasn't going to call his father for Larry Tadmor. He was going to do it for the friendly captain who had carted him over to Sandy Point ever since kindergarten, a man whose rust-colored hair was now white as a result of having a messed-up son.

Captain Tadmor inhaled a deep breath and shook his head, "Maybe if his mother hadn't died so early in his life, and maybe if I spent more…" He stopped, realizing that he was talking out loud about a question that pounded his brain with every whitecap of every crossing.

"Anyway, Mikey. Thank you. And thank your dad for me. He's a saint, I tell you."

SAINT. Devlin couldn't take that word anymore. He nodded before heading back to his cruiser. Behind the wheel for the rest of the ride, he watched the busy world of Sandy Point slowly develop from the early morning mist while thinking of Allan Devlin, the saint. He remembered a brief moment in his life when he actually gained some respect for his father. He was sixteen and was in a fight with his dad and called him every name he had learned in the locker room and his father just stood there and took it.

But then he said, "You're just a money whore. You don't care about justice."

His father's eyes filled up and he walked out of the kitchen, leaving his son standing there in shock. His father never cried, and he never left an argument. He was even more stunned when his mother, who hardly ever raised her voice hissed, "Michael, get your coat!"

Mrs. Devlin stormed outside, started the car, and pushed the door open, motioning for him to get in. She didn't say a word when she drove to the dock, or when she pulled the car onto the ferry, or when she bought two tickets to see *To Kill a Mockingbird*, the new movie everyone was buzzing about.

Devlin gazed straight ahead thinking about the impact that movie made on him that night. The windshield of his cruiser became a movie screen for his mind and the black and white scene appeared in front of him.

Jem, 11, sitting on the porch, face buried in his folded arms, trying to make sense of why an innocent man had just been convicted of rape, while Miss Maudie, the caring neighbor trying to make Jem understand the importance of his father, Atticus Finch, the Defense Attorney.

"Jem, there are some men in this world that are born to do our unpleasant jobs for us. Your father is one of them."

Thinking back on that night, Devlin remembered that after Miss Maudie recited those lines, he tried to give his mother a look to tell her he understood. But the theater was dark, so he reached for her hand. She accepted it and lightly patted it. He went home and apologized and even gave his father an awkward hug, a rare occurrence. But as the years went on, one by one, Miss Maudie's words vanished from his mind and the ones he shouted that night in the kitchen slowly crept back. Deep down, Devlin knew his father was a good man, who probably began his career intending to defend the "Tom Robinsons" of the world, but somewhere along the way, his Atticus Finch white suit got soiled.

Devlin glanced over at the passenger seat and stared long and hard at the navy blue hat with the brass badge attached to the front. He vowed that would never happen to him. Ever. His life's work would be to seek justice at all costs. Yeah, there'd be no stain on his hat.

"Mikey! Come on! You can go!" Tadmor shouted through cupped hands, shaking Devlin out of his trance. They were already docked, and there were three cars waiting in line to board. Devlin took a final sip of his coffee, crushed the cup, and threw it on the passenger's side floor. Then he keyed on his cruiser, squared his hat, saluted the captain, and drove off the ramp where he was greeted by the smells and sights of the mainland.

One of the scents was the aroma of freshly baked Portuguese bread and sticky buns wafting from Dave's Bakery. Every day, Devlin was tempted to spin the steering wheel for Dave's, but he always resisted because Dave's also made doughnuts. It was another part of the cop stereotype he vowed to avoid. Of course, some of his colleagues didn't share the same belief. As he passed, he noticed a cruiser parked out front, nestled between two yellow utility trucks.

"Jessie," Devlin mumbled.

Jessie Gordon was a fifteen-year veteran of the force. He tipped the scales at 290 pounds. Many joked that 280 was made up of jelly doughnuts. The other 10 was the shit in his head. Jessie Gordon was a fat shithead.

Devlin's cruiser turned onto Main Street and the smells of fried eggs and bacon penetrated his nostrils as he passed Pilgrim Diner. No Pilgrims ever owned or ate at "The Diner," but the name always drew in a few tourists who thought some of the ancestors of the Mayflower were actually in the back, flipping flapjacks. Devlin tried to eat at least one of his meals at "The Diner" once a day. It was a great place to take the pulse of what was going on in town because everyone went there — tourists and locals. Seeing the uniform, he felt, was a subconscious reminder to the patrons. He was also accessible if anyone had a problem. Of course, it was his way of justifying his love for their famous Portuguese omelets. In the end, when it came to the omelets, he knew he wasn't any better than Jessie.

But no omelets today, he already had his breakfast: a bowl of soggy cornflakes with a banana and a glass of OJ to wash it all down.

The red light stopped him at the corner of Main Street. As he waited, he glanced over, spotting Harold "Pop" Tucker unlocking POP'S TREATS & EATS. He tapped the horn lightly and startled Pop, who paused before turning around.

21

His blank squint turned into a full smile when he realized it was Devlin. Pop took a lollipop out of his mouth and waved it.

Devlin laughed. It wasn't even six-thirty and Pop was already sucking on a lollipop.

"That's why they call him Pop," Devlin waved back.

Pop loved his suckers and was always handing out free samples. He was in his late forties, but every time Devlin saw Pop, it brought him back to his childhood. Pop really hadn't changed much since Devlin was a kid. Maybe his potbelly. It was larger, but he still wore the same outfit every day: a white shirt, red suspenders, and dark blue jeans. He once told Devlin that he wore the same style of clothes because it was his persona. When kids saw him out in his red suspenders, they would instantly think of candy and toys. Pop was dead on. When Devlin was a kid, it always worked on him. Pop Tucker wasn't just a town character — he was also a shrewd businessman. He bought the store when he was 26, and he now had four more stores opened throughout the Cape. Plus, he had a former homecoming queen for a wife, a great little boy, Pop, Jr., and a sprawling mansion on Mackerel Beach, the richest section of Sandy Point. It was safe to say that the only real suckers were the ones who made fun of Pop Tucker's lollipops and red suspenders.

Everyone else knew better.

"Mikey, when are you going to come in for a visit?"

"Soon, Pop. Soon." Devlin yelled back as the light turned green. He slid his foot off the brake and the cruiser began to roll along.

Pop's big, brown, bushy eyebrows furrowed while he cupped his right hand to his mouth, "Just 'cause you're not a kid anymore, doesn't mean you can't still make those model airplanes."

Devlin laughed, tapping a "goodbye" on his horn. He was a grown man, and Pop Tucker was still trying to persuade him to spend his allowance. The man definitely could be persuasive, he thought, wondering how much of his piggy bank had contributed to building the estate on Mackerel Beach.

Must've been hundreds.

Devlin spent most of his youth hanging out in that store. All the kids did. Life was simple then. Life was good.

The cruiser turned onto Ocean Way. He had another half hour before his shift began, so he thought he'd take the beach road to the station. The sun was bright, and the waves were jumping onto the shoreline. He slowed down to watch two seagulls, busily picking at the sand in search of washed-up clams. Their persistence paid off. Each clutched a shell with their yellow bills, then flew above the beach wall, dropping the shellfish to the pavement like short order cooks preparing omelets. They swooped down, devoured their meals in seconds, and squawked in satisfaction before flying off to sea. He thought the gulls didn't look that much different from a couple eating quickly at The Diner, trying to get on the road and beat the traffic back to Boston. The Cape was filled with gulls. Some people hated them, thought they were scavengers. And they were. But Devlin loved them. To him, the gulls symbolized the Cape.

While huddled in the jungles of Nam, he didn't get much sleep. The times he did drift off though, it was the friendly shrieks of the gulls he would dream about. In those dreams, they would be flying above, calling down to Devlin as he walked along the dunes. He felt that they understood one another — that they were connected in some inexplicable way. He had only one feeling in those dreams: a feeling of peace. He zoned out for a moment realizing the two gulls were now gone and what remained was the rest of his memory from Nam — the times when he would wake up. He was always jarred to attention by other calls, the cries of death. There would never be another sound like it. He wondered if he ever would be able to shake those shrieks from his head.

"Probably not," he admitted. His memory was now like a dark path that should be avoided, but for some reason he was about to take it. The blood-soaked images were surfacing from the back of his mind.

The radio crackled.

At first, it confused him. Was he really back in Nam? Then the airways sounded with the three-packs-a-day voice.

It was Alice Harper, the department dispatcher, trying to locate Oscar 4.

When he heard that, he took a breath and shook the images out of his head, realizing he wasn't in Nam.

More like Mayberry!

Or at least that's how Alice Harper worked as a dispatcher. She really should've been a cast member on *The Andy Griffith Show* because she had no regard for protocol. And she really didn't care. She had been a dispatcher for 12 years and she wasn't going to change for anyone. Most of the cops loved her for it, thought she was entertaining in her own uninformed, sarcastic way. Devlin didn't like her act but kept quiet and tried to roll with it.

"Oscar-4, are you there?" Her voice was tired, as if she didn't expect an answer. And she didn't get one.

Devlin knew where Oscar-4 was, so he unhooked his radio and answered, "Oscar-9 responding for Oscar-4, over."

There was a pause before she answered, "Go ahead, Oscar-9."

"Oscar-4 is having a 10-48."

"A what?"

"10-48."

"I don't have that damn sheet on me. In English, Officer Devlin," her rasp commanded.

"Twelve years and she still needs the code sheet," Devlin barked to himself. *Well, if she's not going to be professional, why should I?*

He clicked back on, "Jessie's taking a coffee break. I saw his cruiser at Dave's Bakery."

"What else is new? That's all you had to say. Gee, that wasn't so hard, was it?"

She waited for him to respond when he didn't, she laughed. "Okay. Okay. Anyway, we have a report of a white male possibly lying unconscious near the path on the corner of Beach Street and Bevans Beach."

Bevans Beach was the original name for Sea Glass Beach. Alice was one of the few people who still called it that because she was a distant branch on the Bevans family tree. She even grabbed the microphone several times at Town Meeting the night the name change was debated. But the 'ayes' had it, and it was decided that Sea Glass Beach would attract a hell of a lot more tourists than a beach that was named after a bootlegger and notorious womanizer from the 1800s — Sea Captain Johnny Q. Bevans.

Devlin clicked back on and smirked, "Yeah, I can check it out. I'm about two minutes from Sea Glass Beach. Over."

There was a longer pause this time. "Yeah, over and out."

"Gotcha, Alice," he chuckled and flipped the toggle switch, awakening the siren and the blue and white lights. He figured that was probably all that was needed for the call. The cruiser raced over Beach View Hill. He had responded to around 20 calls that summer that dealt with that description. Every single one of them turned out to be passed-out hippies or college kids. All they ever needed was the siren, a couple of aspirin, and a nudge about not sleeping on the beach. After the cruiser propelled over the hill, he spotted a guy with long hair, wearing a tie-dye shirt and cut-off dungarees, waving at him — a hippie.

"I called that one." He cracked a smile in satisfaction. But when he screeched to a stop and turned off the siren, he noticed the grim expression on the hippie's face and the motionless body lying nearby. Devlin realized it might be a lot more serious than he had first anticipated, so he sprang out of the car.

"Police!"

"No shit, man." The hippie, who appeared to be in his twenties, looked at Devlin like he was stupid while taking a slow drag from his cigarette.

He's right, Devlin thought briefly, before recovering, "What happened? A friend of yours? Drugs?"

"It's always drugs with us, huh? No man. Check him out. He's an old one." The hippie pointed his dirty finger down at the man who was lying face down. There was a fishing pole and a tipped over bait bucket beside him. Chunks of bait and a couple of fish heads that were scattered nearby had already sounded the dinner bell for hundreds of black flies. From the man's white hair and fishing equipment, Devlin knew it wasn't a hippie. He also knew he didn't have to check the elderly man's pulse, but he crouched down anyway, pressing his two fingers against the cold neck. Nothing.

"I called 'cause I thought the old man might be passed out. But the more I look at him…"

"Yeah, he's dead."

"Wow, shit, man." The hippie moved back from the body as if he could actually catch death from it. He stepped back even farther after Devlin turned the corpse over to see the face.

Devlin gasped for a minute before blurting, "Mr. Medeiros!"

"You know him?"

"Yeah, he was my history teacher," he answered more to himself than to the hippie.

Devlin couldn't believe it. Just the day before, he had a long chat with Mr. Medeiros at the diner.

They both snapped their heads around when they heard a cruiser, with its siren running, barrel over the hill and squeal to a stop. Jessie Gordon's big gut bounced as he bounded out and attempted to run toward them.

"What's… ah ah, going… on?" Gordon was already out of breath.

"DOA. Mr. Medeiros." Devlin said.

Unfazed, Gordon shrugged, "They're like a thousand Medeiroses. Which one?"

"The history teacher." Devlin answered.

"No shit. Really?" Gordon almost brightened as he sauntered over and stared down at Mr. Medeiros before adding, "Well, he's dead alright. His heart probably finally gave out."

Devlin nodded, "Yeah."

Gordon chuckled, "Well, serves the cocksucker right for giving me a D in history."

Devlin wanted to punch him right then and there but restrained himself.

"Okay, I'll call for the meat wagon, and you," Gordon pointed his meaty stub at the hippie, "Get that shit bag's info."

Gordon turned, waddling toward the cruiser.

"Hey man, what the..." The hippie began, but Devlin raised his hand to stop him.

"I'm sorry about that. Officer Gordon has had a rough shift."

"Doing what? Sitting on that fat ass?"

He laughed, calming the hippie down.

"Okay," Devlin flipped open his pad and clicked his pen open. "First off, I need your name and address."

"Rainbow."

"Excuse me?"

"I go by the name 'Rainbow' to spread joy like a rainbow. As for where I am from, I'm really a spirit of the world. You know what I'm saying, man?"

"I know what you're saying," the word stuck in his throat for a minute, "Rainbow. Do you have a wallet?"

"Yes."

"May I please see it?"

Rainbow was reluctant, but Devlin looked down at Mr. Medeiros and back up at him. Rainbow reached into his shorts and pulled out a tattered brown wallet. Devlin went through it and found an Ohio license and an Ohio State University Library card, both issued to a Marvin T. Miller. He copied the information and handed it back.

"So, when did you find Mr. Medeiros?"

"About five or ten minutes before you. I thought he was passed out, so I went down the street to that bar called 'The Angry' something or other, but it was closed, so I used the pay phone and called you. Used my last dime to help."

'Til Daddy sends you your allowance, Devlin wanted to say, but kept scribbling.

"Okay, Marv… I mean, Rainbow. Where were you coming from?"

Rainbow reached into his front pocket, pulled out a crumpled-up piece of paper and handed it over.

Devlin could only make out some of the handwriting. It read: Come back tonight, 37 Maple Street. Love and Peace, …

The name was illegible.

"I can't read her name. What is it?"

Rainbow threw his butt on the ground, toed it out, and shrugged, "I don't remember…Wait… She's named after a month, April, or May, or something."

Free love lives on, Devlin thought, writing down the information.

"What matters," Rainbow pointed at Mr. Medeiros, "is that I made the call and here we are, connected by the death of an old man. Was he a good teacher?"

"Yes, he was. He also coached me in Pee Wee hockey," he said, thinking about how just the day before, Mr. Medeiros had urged him to go to college and become a teacher. He also had the nerve to say the reason Devlin hadn't gone was to spite his father.

Of course, the salty old bastard was probably correct, he thought, as he thanked Rainbow for doing his civic duty while trying to usher him away. Rainbow finally got the hint. He lit another cigarette, gave a half-wave, and strolled away with his head to the ground, but then stopped, and turned around.

"Hey, man, are you sure that guy died from a heart attack?"

"Well, we can't be sure until the ME takes a look. But it's a good bet. Why?"

"'Cause, there's a footprint over here." He pointed down in front of him.

"So?"

"It looks like someone stepped in blood."

Devlin rushed over and studied the area. His eyebrows arched when he saw the print, a small bloody footprint. He got down in push-up form and hovered above the print to get the best possible view without disturbing it. There was no question about it. It was a small bloody footprint. Studying the print, he thought it was a child or a woman's since it was so small.

"The wagon will be here soon," Gordon hollered over and added, "What are you doing push-ups for? You already did your tour." He laughed, sounding like hiccups.

Ignoring him, Devlin rose, wiped his hands on his pants and continued to follow more bloody prints that got bolder and bolder, but stopped when he approached the beach.

Makes sense, wind and sand would destroy the rest of the trail.

Gordon finally saw what Devlin was following, "Holy shit!"

Gordon followed but then stopped, yelling at Rainbow who was also trailing, "Stay back!"

Rainbow threw up don't-shoot-me hands. "Alright. Alright."

Gordon caught up to Devlin who was now on the beach wall surveying the sand.

"Those prints were headed from this direction, right, Jessie?"

"Yep." Gordon answered and pointed over at a jetty, "Look! Over there!"

Devlin tried to focus on it, but it was too far away. Whatever it was, it was lying beside the jetty. They both hopped off the wall onto the sand. Devlin's heart and legs pumped rapidly toward it with Gordon lumbering behind. Devlin could only guess. It was small. The bloody footprints were small. He could guess. But he didn't want to.

Please God, don't let it be a child.

He raced faster, and when he got there, he still didn't know if it was a corpse or carcass or what. Then he spotted the decapitated head. Both officers cupped their right hands over their noses as they stared down at the bloody heap. It was covered with thousands of swarming green flies methodically picking away. The sight baffled them.

Gordon broke the silence, "What the hell? Did... Do you think Medeiros did this?"

"I doubt it. The prints were leading to his body not from his body. But I have no idea."

They were quiet for a minute. Devlin's mind began to work.

Finally, Devlin nodded. "I don't know how the hell this is connected to Mr. Medeiros... if it is at all... I know I'm going to go grab the tape. 'Cause we're definitely dealing with some sort of weird crime scene here."

CHAPTER 3

SEPTEMBER 14, 1970

MONDAY

JUNIOR

Junior waited six long days before stealing out of the house to head for his Silent Place. It had felt like an eternity. But now the excitement coursed through his small body as he came to the foot of the woods. He hadn't waited because he was afraid of getting caught. He was always extremely careful. He'd lie in bed sometimes for hours, pretending he was asleep while his parents drank their rum and sang merrily before their laughter turned to endless rants and curses. It was after their cursing subsided and their bedroom door slammed shut that he would change into his clothes. Then he'd press his ear against his wall and wait until the squeaky noise in their room stopped and his father's shouts and his mother's loud moans became even louder snores. It was then that he knew it was safe to slide out of his window and creep along the backyard and head for his Silent Place. But for the past week he hadn't left his house for one simple reason — he could barely walk.

Two mornings after their fishing trip to Sea Glass Beach, his father woke him with the coal stove hand shovel, whacking it against Junior's chest and legs over and over again. On that morning, Junior wasn't able to contain the tears that formed, but as he entered the woods and thought of the beating, he was proud of himself for being able to hold in the painful sobs that should've accompanied those tears. It wasn't easy — his clenched teeth nearly bit off his inside cheek. It was his worst beating since the day of his eighth birthday. He learned that day that the more he cried, the more rage he would receive. So, he tried never to make a sound again. Not a peep. It was also his way of showing his father that in spite of his punishment, he still had some control of the situation even though the truth was the eleven-year-old boy had no power at all. He missed three days of school, something that never happened before. But even his father knew the bruises might draw attention. Junior winced his way through the following three days before his bathroom mirror revealed his purple bruised chest, legs, and ass were finally yellowing over. The color told him he was well enough to make his midnight journey to his secret hideaway, and now he was almost there.

Samoset Woods or just "The Place," as the locals called it, was the town's woods where he always thought differently. Maybe when he got there, he could figure it all out. He still didn't understand why he deserved the beating. And why his father ripped off his boots and ordered him never to talk to anyone about what happened on the beach? He had simply done what his father had dared him to do. And because of it, he received his worst beating ever. It made no sense. But not many things did.

My Silent Place will help me.

"Ah, almost there," he whispered to himself. He discovered the hideaway on that eighth birthday, when he ran away from home to hide his gift. He called it his Silent Place because it was the one spot where Junior could shut out the world. It was safe. His parents couldn't find him. No one could. He looked down at the large empty Mason jar he was carrying in one hand, and the bottle of rum stolen from his father in the other. The excitement gripped him. He picked up the pace and was getting more and more anxious. He wanted to be there... Now!!

It was there that he could think about that day on the beach. The deeper he invaded the woods, the more he took in his surroundings. The few remaining peepers and crickets hummed and chirped their final farewells to summer while the ocean growled and nipped at the cliffs hidden in the distance beyond the woods.

Junior stopped and closed his eyes momentarily, welcoming the subtle, ocean breeze that barely whistled through the trees and washed over him. He loved the stillness of the woods in the middle of the night. He also enjoyed the idea that every other eleven-year-old kid in Sandy Point was tucked away in bed sound asleep. Not Junior. Opening his eyes, he cackled while clutching the jar and bottle, prancing down the path in an exaggerated manner. He laughed at the thought that he was doing something no other kid could ever dream of doing. The town owned the miles of acres during the day, but at night the woods were his — Junior's Land — he called it. It was a power and privilege in his world that he wished he could bottle in one of his jars. Unfortunately, a part of him knew it was just a game, but it was his game and no one else was invited to play. He often continued the game at school.

Every year his new teacher commented, "You're one of the best students in class, but you always fall asleep. Why?"

"I'm sorry. It's just that I study all night because I want to attend college someday."

The word "attend" always got them. He sounded studious. The truth was, he had heard the same line on a TV show and just like in the show, it worked. Always.

An admiring smile from the teacher followed with, "Well, try to get some sleep."

The teachers liked him. And so did his classmates. He felt absolutely nothing for them. Nothing. They were part of his game. He was out to trick them, and he was tricking them all. Even his father. He was a man who played his own game every day with the Pointers. And that is how Junior learned to lie, by observing his father — he smiled, laughed at their jokes, listened to their boring stories, and they all loved him. But then his father would come home. He'd curse as he drank and mumbled his hatred for every one of them. In his early years, this disturbed Junior. Not anymore. Now it amused him. His father was able to fool so many people. In public he never touched a drop of alcohol or laid a hand on Junior. He was "Dad." He'd chat with the townspeople and tussle his son's hair. No one knew he was the meanest drunk around because no one knew he even drank. He'd drive off-Cape to buy his month's supply of booze, and he only had one drinking partner — Junior's mother. That is, when she was around.

Junior's mother was different. She didn't play the part. She never shunned the bar scene, and that was what many of his parents' arguments were about — her public drunkenness, and rumors that she was loose.

But that was what was so strange about the day on the beach.

31

It was the first time his father left the house drunk. And he was drunk. Blind drunk.

He told Junior to get the bait out of the freezer and load the pickup with the fishing gear because they were going to Sea Glass Beach. Chugging on his rum, he weaved the truck back and forth along the desolate beach road while shouting curses about Junior's mother.

He handed Junior the bottle and forced a long sip down his throat.

"It's time you be a man!"

Gagging and coughing, the boy's throat burned.

Senior laughed and bellowed, "That's the good man! There you go!"

Junior remembered how the rum swished around in his stomach and how he had felt a warm glow come to his face. And then he laughed. He liked it. A lot. And his father liked him for liking it, and they laughed together for the first time that he could remember. And then they headed for the beach.

"Stop!" Junior shouted into the night, turning off the picture in his mind. He knew he couldn't think about the beach until he got to his Silent Place. That was the deal he always made with himself when he wanted to think about the things that excited him.

The full moon slipped through the trees and gave him just enough light to sprint the final twenty yards until the trail came to a sudden stop. The path ended directly in front of a massive wall of razor sharp thorns. It was a briar patch that continued on for hundreds of yards to the foot of an ocean cliff. At least, that's what many people thought over the years as the worn path turned left and went on for miles. But, when he found the fortress of thorns that April night of his eighth birthday, it was more than just curiosity that drove him on to see if there was anything other than the cliff on the other side. It was an undying need for safety and shelter for not only him, but for the things he loved. He was searching for his own home to escape the terror his parents put him through almost every day, birthdays and holidays included.

On that night, Junior had been running away from home because of a gift his grandmother had sent him from Florida. He had never met his grandmother and was thrilled when the postman handed him the big, brown package with his name handwritten on it. It was the first gift he'd received from her. He knew he should wait until his parents got home, but the little boy couldn't hold in the urge. He raced into his room and ripped off the paper exposing the black case. Seconds later, he had the case open and was staring at a beautifully polished cranberry-colored violin. He held it in his hands, picked up the bow, and glided over the strings. He had never touched a violin before, and the screeching sound amazed him. It was harsh, but beautiful. He moved the bow back and forth again. Faster and faster. It grew louder and harsher almost like someone screaming at a high pitch. The sound brought him instant joy as he hummed along. But then the front door slammed, and he heard his father's heavy footsteps plodding down the hallway. The case was on the other side of the room, so there was no time to place the violin back. Junior rushed over to his bed and shoved it under his pillow.

The door swung open, and his father glared at him, "Did I hear a violin?"

He spotted the case and didn't wait for an answer. He moved slowly to the case, staring at it for several seconds. Junior prayed he wouldn't open it. He didn't. He ordered Junior to fasten the buckles shut.

He did. Senior picked up the unopened envelope that was lying beside the brown paper, ripped it open and scanned the letter. Junior could see the anger building in Senior's eyes. He then crumpled up the letter, placed it into his pocket, and pointed to the violin.

"Grab that and follow me!"

Junior did, and what happened after that he still couldn't comprehend. Senior ordered him to build a roaring fire in the fireplace that they never used. Junior didn't mind. He enjoyed lighting fires. But when the flames were jumping, his father pointed to the violin case and then to the fire, "Throw it in!"

Licking flames attacked the case while Senior tossed the letter on top and simply stated, "You will never play a violin in this house."

Senior then went down into the cellar to get a bottle of rum before he could see that the flames were destroying an empty case. It was after that bottle was consumed that Junior got his beating, and after that he knew he had to find a safe place for his violin. He wrapped it in an old beach towel and headed for the woods, and in those woods, he found the briar patch. He knew it was the perfect place, but as he gingerly made his way beyond the patch, the army of thorns stabbed his body. He quickly learned it wasn't the perfect place, but like any builder of a house, he'd make it one. That night he hid his violin in the hollow of a tree and for the rest of the spring he used gardening shears to pick off the thorns and sculpt a narrow path through the wiry web – one that only his eyes would be able to detect. When he finally made it through the maze, his Silent Place was even more beautiful than he'd dreamed. He thought the briar patch

33

would end at the cliff, but there were thirty yards of open, lush green grass before the patch continued another ten yards, stopping a few feet from the ocean cliff. He knew the wall of thorns that circled his Silent Place would always keep him safe.

Now, three years later, that small patch of lush green grass was Junior's real home. It was his Silent Place, and every time he came to it, he performed the same ritual. He placed the jar and the bottle down on a wooden plank that served as one of his three tables. There were different sizes and jars on each table, and he briefly thought that someday soon he should date and place them in the proper order. But not tonight. He rolled on the grass and let out a long breath that he had been holding forever. Comfort moved through his veins, and he smiled, moving his arms and legs back and forth, resembling a child making an angel in the snow. Doing this and hearing the ocean so close always soothed him and now, at complete ease, stared up at the white pin-shaped stars dotting the sky.

"Now," Junior paused and then ordered himself, "Now you can think about the beach." The picture instantly appeared before him. He was trudging through the sand trying to catch up to his father.

"Hur…eeees…up…" Senior slurred as he hollered and staggered on the jetty, "We're gonna miss high tide."

Junior knew high tide wasn't for another two or three hours, but he also knew to never correct his father, especially when he was drunk. He hustled to pick up the pace while his father beckoned him with his hand.

He expected a slap across his face when he climbed on the jetty, but instead, his father patted his head and cracked a smile, "The booze already got you, huh?"

"I guess so. Everything kinda feels… like slower."

Senior burst into laughter, "That's what it does. Slows down the world so you can enjoy it more."

He nodded, but then Senior's face clouded, "Or hate it more."

Senior turned around and stumbled from rock to rock, one hand carrying a fish bucket that contained another bottle of rum, and in the other, his pole and tackle box. There were four seagulls squawking annoyingly in his way. Junior thought for sure his father would lose his balance and fall. But he didn't.

"Get the hell outta here!" Senior kicked at the gulls, scaring them all away, except for one gull that tried to fly, but like a faulty plane, crash-landed in between a few rocks at the point of the jetty.

It looked like it had a broken wing, Junior thought, and then he realized his father was oblivious to the gull.

The man was actually talking to himself, "That whore. I'll teach her someday."

Then he snapped out of his thoughts. "Get over here with that bait!"

Junior rested his pole on one of the rocks and hustled over carrying the bait bucket and put it down. Senior took a long swig from his new bottle before crouching down and grabbing the bait from the bucket. He slapped the encased ice block of bait against the rock.

"Aww, hell," he growled, "It's frozen. Get my knife. Now!" he ordered. Junior hurried to the tackle box, pulled out a thin-bladed bait knife, and handed it to him.

"I thought I told you to get the bait out of the freezer." His glassy eyes cut.

Yeah, ten minutes before we left!

"I'm sorry. It's my fault."

The boy learned early on just to take the blame no matter what. Sometimes he got lucky, and it defused his father's anger.

"You're damn right it's your fault." The cold dark eyes studied Junior for a minute contemplating hitting him, but then he kneeled before the bait and attempted cutting some pogies loose from the ice.

While Senior grunted and cursed and cut away, Junior turned his attention back to the gull. It wasn't crying like a normal gull. It was screeching. It sounded so much like his violin.

Oh, how I love that sound!

He watched the bird, who, despite being in excruciating pain, tried to fly away. But every time, it would go only a few feet and, as if it were shot, stumble backward into the rocks.

"Aww, fuck!" Senior screamed.

Junior turned just in time to see the block of bait sliding along the jetty. The knife had slipped off the bait, catching his father's hand and slicing into his right index finger.

Senior cursed over and over again as he licked the blood that was trickling out.

Nervously, Junior asked, "Are you okay?"

Senior inspected the finger that was still bleeding, "Goddamn it!"

Junior edged closer and asked again, "Are you okay?"

Senior wiped it down the side of his jeans streaking a long thin line of blood and winced through a tight lip, "Shit, I've had worse."

Then he flashed Junior his other hand as a reminder. It was the one that was missing two fingers that he had told the boy a grenade had stolen from him in Korea.

"Now, where's that goddamn tackle box?" Senior seemed to be in a daze, so Junior hesitantly suggested, "Why don't you go home and put a bandage on it?"

"No!" Senior hollered, turning and placing his hands firmly on his son's shoulders, blood spilling in the process, "You and me are going to fish, like what other fathers and sons do. You know why?" His rum-soured breath almost knocked him out. Senior squeezed his shoulders, waiting for an answer.

"Why?"

"'Cause, I've got to get to know you. We have to become friends. Y'know why?"

Junior couldn't believe what he was hearing. It was the first time his father showed any interest in him.

"Why do we have to become friends?"

"'Cause your mother!"

Senior called his mother the worst word he could and the boy's face twisted with anger. He pushed the callous hands off his shoulders. He didn't know exactly what the word meant but he knew it was the worst thing you could call a woman.

"Don't call her..." he began, but Senior howled with laughter.

"That's a good boy, defending your mother and all, but we both know you hate her, too. I found a picture you drew of her. It was the one with an ax in her head."

If father had seen that picture, why hadn't I received a beating for drawing it?

"I thought it was pretty funny. Anyway, shit, she can't stand you. She always says to me the best part of you ended up on the sheets. You know what that means?"

The boy didn't know what it meant but answered, "I don't hate her." He had no idea what his father was saying but he thought he was supposed to stand up for his mother even though the picture illustrated the truth.

Senior's laughter died. "You have to understand something. We have to become friends because your mother is sleeping everybody in town. I heard even women now. So, it won't be long before she finds some dumb bastard who can't get enough of her and then she'll leave us. You see. Just you and me. Got it?" He was quiet for a moment, but then came alive again, "So go over there and get that tackle box, or I'll whip you right now!"

Junior shook with boiling hatred. He wanted to kill his father with his bare hands. While Senior turned swigging his rum, Junior stared at his back for a very long minute.

Maybe if I push him?

The man was drunk enough to lose his balance.

If I smashed his head against the rocks that might just do it. I wonder what his brain would look like.

The boy then realized it was just a fantasy and grabbed the tackle box. He handed it to his father, who in return, gave Junior the bottle and nodded for him to drink. The boy swallowed and welcomed another glow to his face while Senior rummaged through the multicolored lures, knives, and fishing line, until he came to the bottom of the box.

"There she is!" Senior exclaimed, pulling out the black-handled, silver, block-shaped knife.

"Old Heidi here will do the trick." He grinned, displaying the huge blade that flashed in the late evening sun.

The boy wasn't sure he should ask, but couldn't help himself, "Who's Old Heidi?"

"Shit, I never told you about Old Heidi?" The man shook his head for a moment, "I gotta be a better dad. That's a story I'll save for when we're drinking some night. Anyway…"

He admired the knife, "That's what I call her. Old Heidi."

Multiple squawking sounds interrupted them. Six gulls swooped down and landed on the jetty. A couple flew over to the wounded gull and the rest picked away at the frozen bait.

"Hey! Hey! I thought I told you to get the hell outta here!" Senior swung the large knife shooing them away. They squawked back with idle threats while flapping off to sea. All of the gulls took flight except for the wounded one. He tried to follow the flock, but just as before, he crashed in between the rocks. But this time, Senior noticed the gull.

"Why the hell are you still here?" He asked the gull, and Junior thought his father was actually waiting for an answer.

"It can't fly. I think it has a broken wing."

"Oh, yeah?" He smirked at Junior for a minute and then reached down, trying to pick the bird up. Junior knew that was a bad idea. The fear in the gull's screech hit a higher level and it moved its head frantically. The yellow beak lunged out and nipped his father's forearm.

"Fuck!" Senior said for the thousandth time, and then everything went from slow motion into high speed. Somehow his father grabbed the gull by its neck and cursed it while tossing it onto the jetty where it landed ten yards away. Then he jumped from rock to rock and kicked it like a football, sending it to the beach. The man cackled and stumbled a bit as he plunged off the jetty and onto the sand and yelled at the helpless gull that screeched in terror

"You want to mess with me? Is that it? You're nothing but a rat with wings. You piece of shit!" He wound up his boot again to end him, but then stopped, yelling over his shoulder, "Get me Old Heidi!"

Junior dashed over and grabbed the cleaver, while still trying to figure out what just happened. As he approached, Senior was still cursing at the gull with his back to the boy. The fantasy appeared again. But this time it felt real as the rage jumped up to his throat.

"You…" he began.

I could do it now! I could slice his head wide open. And if I get caught, I could say I was just protecting the gull. I could do it. Yes, I'm going to do it!

The boy fixated on his father's back but then heard, "Don't even think of it!"

"What?" Junior stopped, stunned.

Senior turned around grinning, "I know you want to kill me. But you have to kill that gull. That's your job. Got it?"

"Me?" Junior pointed the cleaver at himself.

The man pointed down to the gray and white bird that was now black and red, heaving "Yes. I'm going to teach you how to kill. If you want to kill me, you have to first learn how to kill." Senior walked over, raised his foot, and stamped on the gull's good wing, snapping it.

Junior thought it was such an interesting sound and how could anyone get tired of hearing it? It was the sound of approaching death and it intrigued him. He moved closer and looked at his father.

"Do it! You want to be a man? Someday you'll wanna be like me. For now, pretend it's me! Do it! Be a man!"

Junior drank in the sight of the dying gull. Its black eyes pleaded with him; the gull seemed to know that the boy had control of its fate. He had no hate for the gull, but he did have hate, and when his father said, "Pretend it's me," that opened the door to his simmering rage. It was now free to boil over. He was going to finish off the dying bird, and the gull knew it.

He raised the cleaver and the gull's eyes widened with a fear that was palpable — the inevitable fear of death. The gull desperately tried to move its head, but Junior brought the knife down with full power and fury. The razor sharp blade severed the gull's head cleanly shooting blood up onto his face.

Junior's tongue found it while his eyes blinked wildly. In the distance, he heard his father's voice, "Enough! Enough! Enough!"

But he couldn't stop. He didn't want to stop. He was in a frenzy slashing the carcass over and over again and hearing Senior's voice only made it worse. Because that gull was his father, and he wasn't going to stop until that voice was silent. He continued — chopping the gull's legs off then hacking at the stomach, sending bits of intestines spitting in the early fall night.

From out of nowhere, another far away voice broke his trance.

"Holy shit!" Senior pointed at an elderly man sprinting toward them. They both watched, not knowing what to do, but then the man plummeted to the ground face first.

"Get your shit and let's go!" Senior barked, the fear of getting caught sobering him immediately. Senior raced to grab his pole and tackle box.

But Junior didn't grab his gear. He wasn't listening. He was catching his breath while examining the carcass. He studied it for many seconds with a strange feeling of accomplishment.

He picked up something that was lying beside the bloody heap and stuffed it in his pocket. He admired his work and lingered, observing the gull's eyes. The terrified eyes now had a faraway look. The eyes had moved on.

I freed the gull and it's now flying to heaven!

What a wonderful gift I have given the gull!

The truck's engine revved, and Junior awoke from his satisfied trance. The boy knew he had to hurry, or his father would beat him. But then he thought of the man lying on the ground across the street.

Was he dead?

He had never seen a dead person before, and he wondered if the man's eyes would have that same faraway look.

Had he gone to heaven, too?

Junior had to find out. He sprinted across the street.

Senior waved frantically, "What are you doing?"

Junior closed in and could see the man was motionless. He didn't have to check to see if he was alive. No one slept on their face, especially with their eyes open. He crouched down and noticed that the eyes had that same faraway look.

Yes, the man is dead and flying to heaven with the gull.

He clapped his hands gleefully. A few seconds later, the out-of-control truck skidded to a stop.

Senior pushed open the door. "Get in!"

The boy jogged over, hopped in, and Senior slammed his foot on the accelerator.

"Was he dead?"

"Yes."

And flying to heaven!

Junior wanted to giggle.

"Thank Christ!" Senior reached for a half pint from under the seat and took three quick swigs. The boy wondered how his father would react, but being safe again, Senior's drunkenness resurfaced as he handed the half pint to Junior. "Drink deep, son. You just had your first kill! You made me proud. And you didn't even sing. I was taught to sing during it. Makes it easier."

Senior broke into a rousing rendition of "Goodnight Irene" while Junior sat back and listened, enjoying the fact his father was proud. He told himself he wouldn't enjoy the memory again until he got to his Silent Place. Then he would ponder it. Savor it.

Now, lying under the starry night, he was doing just that. He had savored every moment, except for one thing. He went over behind one of the tables where there was a wooden box. He opened it and pulled out the violin. Then, he walked over to the empty Mason jar and twisted the cover open. He reached into his coat pocket and pulled out the object from the beach. It was one of the gull's webbed feet. It was scaly and putrid.

What a comforting odor! How many kids have a gull's foot, a gull they had killed? Only me!

He placed the foot in the jar, closed it, and rested it beside several other jars.

The jars contained dead mice, rabbits, squirrels, and frogs. They all had their eyes intact except for the frogs. He detested frogs, so he had cut the eyes out of their sockets.

Frogs shouldn't go to heaven. Frogs shouldn't see God!

"I really do have to put the jars in order someday soon," he mused and thought again about his father. He may've been proud of his son, but he was wrong about one thing — Junior had been killing animals for years, but never with a large knife. The boy really enjoyed that. He wished he could've brought the gull's head.

Next kill!

He thought about the song of death the gull sang that day on the beach, and he tried to play it on the violin. He didn't need lessons, he realized, as he moved the bow over the strings harshly, making the violin scream exactly like the gull. The sound that came from dying animals — how he loved it! His pulse quickened, and he thought of the old man and his eyes.

What kind of sound did he make before he died? Could it have been any more enjoyable?

Another strange feeling mixed up his insides. He put his violin away before looking down at the bulge in his pants. The thought of screaming and people dying was making him hard.

The eleven-year-old boy lay back down under the starry night sky, occasionally glancing at his penis that was slowly softening. The feeling was unexplainable, and he wondered if being hard was a good thing or a bad thing.

For now, all he could do was wonder.

CHAPTER 4

JUNE 7, 2004

MONDAY

J.T.

"Goddamn it! Those bastards!" I snorted, inspecting the round orange dent in the middle of the driver's side door. The lacrosse ball had done more damage than I thought. At least, a couple of hundred bucks, I guessed.

"I really hope you don't use those kinds of words in your articles." A female's voice froze me.

Aww, shit.

I turned around slowly. An attractive woman in her early fifties with emerald eyes glared at me. I thought those eyes were about to shoot green lasers into my head, the embarrassment flowed red to my face. I tried to look down and noticed she was carrying a paper restaurant take-out bag.

"Oh, ah… I'm sorry, ma'am… it's… There were these kids, and I was driving and… Ah, I shouldn't have said…"

"I don't think your boss, Mr. Crocker, would like to hear you talk like that."

How did she know Mr. Crocker was my boss?

"You're right. I'm sorry…"

She held her stare a bit longer before her angry face spread into a smirk. She burst into continuous laughter. The laughter lasted several seconds, and I found myself joining her, even though I had no idea what the hell was so humorous.

Finally, catching her breath, she waved her free hand. "I'm sorry. I couldn't help myself. Boy, you're easy. I was just giving you a hard time."

I laughed again, this time out of relief.

"Did the nuns teach you?" She asked.

"No. I went to public school. But they taught my parents. Why?"

"You looked like I was going to wash your mouth out with soap or something."

"Oh." I said and thought how on target she was.

When I was a kid, my mother kept the nun's soap and water cure alive and well for any of the O'Rourke children who had a slip of the tongue. Of course, those were the days she wasn't in bed trying to sleep away her depression.

She pointed at the dent. "You're right. Whoever did this is a bastard. So, what happened, Mr. O'Rourke?"

"On my way to the Cape, some kid shot his lacrosse ball at me. It's not even my car. Wait, how did you know my name?"

"Not that difficult to figure out. Most guys go tie-less on the Cape in the summer, especially on a day like this. So, either you're going to a funeral or it's your first day on the job. I'm guessing it's your first day. Of course, there is one other reason: Mr. Crocker said you'd be coming. I'm his personal secretary, Mrs. Walsh." She laughed again and added, "Actually, I'm everyone's personal secretary."

Her laugh was infectious, and I liked her immediately.

I tugged on my tie, giving a Rodney Dangerfield shrug, "Well, what do you think, Mrs. Walsh? Is this too much?"

"You do look like a high school coach going to a sports banquet. Y'know, clearly uncomfortable. But the boss will appreciate it. Shows you care. By the end of the week, we'll have you in surf shirts and Tevas."

"Tevas?"

"Sandals. Wow, you are a city boy!" Mrs. Walsh tried pushing one of her frosted blonde locks off her face but was quickly losing grip of the bag.

"I suppose I am."

"Never mind that, Mr. O'Rourke. Are you going to stand there, or are you

43

going to help this old broad carry in the staff's lunch?" She offered me the bag, but I put one hand to the air while holding my laptop bag with the other.

"First of all, call me J.T. And second of all, I'd only help if I saw an old broad in front of me."

"Uh, oh. There's that famous Irish blarney. Actually, I had another term for it when I was married to Mr. Walsh. Now what was it?" She pretended to think for a minute. "Oh, yes. 'Bullshit.' Now take the bag and I'll grab your case."

Mrs. Walsh didn't wait for an answer but exchanged bags and walked in front of me toward the front door of the *Sandy Point Standard Times*. I watched admiringly, knowing she was a woman who was still confident in her sexuality.

She moved proudly in her cream colored jacket and matching skirt that swayed from side to side, slightly exposing her athletic legs. It may've been a little blarney, but it certainly was no bullshit — the woman still looked good, and I knew back in her day, she probably broke more than a few hearts, as well as bedposts.

She had long, blonde hair that she wore up. As I followed her into the building, I couldn't help but wonder if she still liked to let that hair down now and then.

"Get ready," she winked.

"Huh?" I asked, thinking: Did she read my mind?

When I turned around, I realized what she was talking about. A gaggle of gray heads almost tripped over one another, hustling down the hallway, barking their BLT and steak and cheese orders at me. I rested the bag on her desk and raised don't-shoot-me hands at them.

"Go now, while there's still time." Mocking the seriousness of an old adventure movie, she handed me my laptop bag and pointed. "Mr. Crocker will be back soon. His office is the first door on the right. You'll be safe there. Go now!"

I laughed and retreated down the hallway.

I shut the office door behind me and was tempted to walk around the small room and peruse his diplomas and pictures but decided it was more professional to rein in my curiosity and just take a seat and wait. As I settled into the uncomfortable old deck chair that looked to be salvaged from the bottom of the sea, I was feeling pretty good. If everyone was as cool as Mrs. Walsh, I was going to love my new job. A second later, I found out it was a fleeting thought.

The door swung open and an extremely short man in his early twenties rushed in and cracked an accusatory, "May, I help you?"

"Huh?"

"May I help you?" His tone was even sharper the second time around. I studied him briefly. And he was an easy study at that. I knew he must still watch TRL on MTV because he was wearing the V.J. bed-head hairstyle. At the bar, whenever I flipped past MTV, I always noticed the male Video Jockeys who thought they were so talented because they could utter, "Number three video" while also having their hair look like they had just awakened from a night of partying with the Hilton sisters.

My hair's a mess and I don't give a shit. I'm cool.

This guy was definitely an apostle from that school of thought and probably spent a couple of hours every morning in front of the mirror working the gel in angles.

All those times in high school when I slept through my alarm clock, I could've been a trendsetter if only I hadn't showered.

He was barely tall enough to reach the height requirement for the "big boy" rides at the county fair, and to compensate for his lack of height, it was obvious he spent many hours in the gym. He wore a blue Polo shirt one size too small to enhance the bulges in his arms and continued the tight clothing trick with his beige Dockers to show everyone he had a bulge somewhere else and that he also had an ass. By his tone and look, I quickly surmised that the guy was an ass.

"I'll ask you again. May I help you?"

"I don't think so. I'm here to see Mr. Crocker."

"Why?"

I could've just answered Napoleon, but I really didn't like him, so I said, "It's personal."

"Well, I'm Mr. Crocker's nephew, Norman Chadwick. I'm second in command."

"Second in command? What is this? Iraq?" I laughed, wondering if he practiced his name and rank in the mirror every morning after his gel treatment.

"I take care of the paper when he's not here. And he's not here right now. So, what can I do for you?"

I got up and extended my hand, "Well, I guess I should introduce myself then. Your uncle hired me. I'm J.T. O'Rourke."

He looked down at my hand for a second as if it were diseased and reluctantly shook it.

"Oh, yes. Now, I remember. Well, it's good to see you're presentable on your first day." He pointed at the tie before walking over to the desk.

I guess the tie does work.

Mumbling, he began rifling through the drawers. "I know he keeps it in here somewhere.

The man is so disorganized. When I take over this place, I swear... Oh, here we go."

He grabbed a manila folder and sat behind Mr. Crocker's desk. He took a piece of paper from the folder and read it to himself for a minute before looking up at me.

"Now, was it North Sandy Point deliveries we hired you for or West Sandy Point?" he asked.

Oh My God, he thinks I am a paperboy.

"Norm, I think you misunderstood me."

"It's Norman."

"Of course, it is," I grinned, thinking — I know I have seen this on some bad TV show.

But then I continued, "Your uncle hired me as a reporter."

"A what?"

"A tiger shark," I laughed at my inside joke before continuing my sarcasm, "A reporter, you know, for the paper. With a pen and a pad. A reporter. Someone who reports the news."

"When?" He shot up from the desk.

"A couple of weeks back."

"He didn't tell me about this. I have interviews lined up to give. He can't just hire you. He has to consult me on that kind of..."

"Consider yourself consulted." A voice from the doorway cut him off.

We both looked over to see Mr. Crocker. He was a visual contradiction of his age. From talking with him at the bar, I knew he was only in his mid-forties, but his full head of gray hair made him look older. Yet, his clothes were youthful, a white flowing button- down shirt, faded blue jeans, and brown boat shoes. He was fit looking and not much taller than Norman, but his wide, white-tooth smile made him seem larger than life.

"J.T., how the hell are you?" He walked over and shook my hand enthusiastically.

"Great, Mr. Crocker. Happy to be here."

"How was the ride?"

"A little adventurous but I'm…"

"I need to talk to you." Norman cut me off.

"I'm sorry, J.T. Can you wait out in the hall for just a minute?"

"Sure thing." I walked out and shut the door behind me.

Five minutes later, the door swung open. Norman stormed past me.

Mr. Crocker gave a friendly holler for me to come in and acted like nothing happened.

He was leaning back in his chair with his hands behind his head and his feet on the desk.

He motioned for me to sit in the deck chair.

"J.T., that chair you're sitting in. Guess where I got it."

"I was actually wondering that myself. I figured it must've come from the bottom of the sea. 'Cause, it's not that comfortable and kind of ugly, I gotta tell you."

"You're right. It's not comfortable. And you're not that far off about it coming from the bottom of the sea. When I was a kid, my buddy and I had a rowboat. We'd spend hours in it going along the shore searching for shipwrecks and treasure. That chair was the closest thing we ever found of any real value. On the back, in small lettering you can read that it came from a ship called *The Island Jumper*."

"Wow. How'd it sink?"

"Oh, when we were kids, we never knew. So, we had our own theories. A tidal wave struck it, or it was a cannonball from pirates, or we even thought a great whale like Moby Dick had devoured it… It wasn't until a couple of years later that I found out *The Island Jumper* wasn't a ship at all. It was a ferry from down Cape that ran booze cruises, and the most likely scenario is some drunk threw the chair overboard."

We laughed for a minute and Mr. Crocker added as if he were talking to himself, "I kind of wish I had never found that out."

I let him drift in thought but then he came back with a smile. "Kind of strange of me enjoying make-believe stories considering I'm in the truth telling business."

"I understand what you mean, though," I said. "It's like when you find out there's no Santa Claus. Takes away the joy of dreaming."

"What do you mean, there's no Santa Claus?"

"Whoops. Sorry."

"Okay, back to business. First thing's first — the Norman factor. I have to ask you: did you tell him how you and I met?"

"God no, Mr. Crocker. I consider being a bartender like being a priest. Seal of confession, you know what I mean?"

"Some might consider that analogy a little much, but in my case, you really hit it on the head. 'Cause if anyone finds out about that night last November, Norman might be running this paper."

"I don't get it. I mean, I know passing out in a bar is probably not one of your favorite highlights in life, but to lose the paper?" I asked, while thinking how hammered he had been when he came into the Jar and how I refused to serve him only to find him later passed out, covered in trash under a table.

Crocker kicked his feet off the desk and sat up in his chair, "You see, I've had a drinking problem for years, and in the last five, I've been working on it. Going to A.A. Doing the steps. All that shit. And I've been good. I'll go months without a drink. The problem is, I've had more slips than a Provincetown Drag Queen."

I laughed at his line until a flash of my old man banging back a shot then appeared.

"You see, my ol' man died when I was a kid, and my mother retired to Florida. She made my half-sister and me co-owners of the paper years ago. My sister and her husband have no interest in running it but their son, that jackass you just met, does. So, after my last binge, the one she knows about, I felt so guilty I had a legal agreement typed up stating that if I ever touched an ounce of booze again, I'd let him take over. Guilt was one reason. Motivation to quit drinking was the other. There is no way in hell I want Norman running this place, so I thought that was motivation enough. But... Well, when you found me under that table, I had literally pissed on that agreement."

"Your secret's safe with me. Why hire me and risk being found out?"

"That night when you found me, you could've done a number of things, the first, call the cops. But you didn't. You didn't tell anyone. You let me sleep it off on your couch. Me. A complete stranger. And the next morning you even made me breakfast. I don't think I ate it, but I remember sitting there thinking, 'This is one hell of a kid and the big guy in the sky has just given me one more chance. Maybe my last one. Don't screw it up, Crocker.' So, when you called to check on me and we got to talking and you mentioned how you wrote some articles for the B.C. paper, what's it called again?"

"The Heights."

"That's right." He snapped his fingers. "I said to myself, 'Here's my chance for some payback,' so I offered you the job. But you didn't take it, so I gave it to someone else. That was way back in November. But what's bizarre is, she quit last week, and you called the day after. Well, they say things do happen for a reason. Who knows? J.T., what made you call me months later, anyway?"

"Who knows?"

"Well, I'm glad to have you. Now, for my asshole nephew, if you could, nod and smile at him, but don't listen to a goddamn thing he says. I'll give you your assignments. Always come to me."

"No problem."

But if there were a problem, I'd find my own way of settling it. I made it a rule early in life to take care of it on the playground, not in the principal's office.

Crocker rose from his chair. "Today is probably the worst day to introduce you to everyone since it's a madhouse with the paper coming out tomorrow."

"Oh, yeah, Mr. Crocker, I never asked, how many times a week does it come out?"

"Will you please call me Greg or even just Crocker. I don't do that 'mister' stuff. Never have."

"Okay, Greg." I smiled and got up to follow him out the door.

He stopped before opening it. "And to answer your question, the paper comes out Tuesdays and Fridays. When I was a kid, it was actually a daily paper. That's why I'm in such great shape — from riding my bike all over town every day." He chuckled.

"Why did it stop being a daily?"

"That's a good segue for me to discuss my philosophy of how I run this place. In the mid-eighties, I made the decision to stop covering the national and regional news. I made that decision for a number of reasons. The most obvious was economic. *The Globe* and the *Herald's* distribution was now all across the Cape, and it was impossible to compete. Not to mention the *Cape Cod Times.* But to me, the more important reason was: I wanted to establish a clear identity for the paper. I wanted this to be a paper that wasn't always concerned about the big scoop."

"I don't get it?"

He laughed, "Let me rephrase that. Don't get me wrong: if the big scoop falls into our laps, we'll always cover it. My point is our paper tries to represent the positive things in life. We have our share of negative stories, but we try to balance them out. I mean, most of our stories come from chatting with an elderly customer in the checkout line at Lareby's Market, who mentions that her grand-daughter's dance recital is coming up. Or talking to the college lifeguard at the beach who brings up the fact that she broke the Division Three record for most goals in a field hockey game, or the President of the class of '74, who calls wanting you to cover the upcoming reunion, or even when you're cashing your check, and the bank teller brags that her son placed first in the eighth-grade science fair. You know, things like that. When we find out that kind of positive stuff, we write about it. That would never get mentioned in a city paper. You see, J.T., we're here to remind people every Tuesday and Friday that in this violent world, they still have a home with neighbors, friends, and family. A safe home, a community, and that community is Sandy Point. Okay, off my soapbox now. So, can you do a job like that, J.T.?"

Man, he was worked up, but I was also kind of moved by his Frank Capra *"It's A Wonderful Life"* outlook.

"Yes, Greg. I've been looking for a community like that for a while now. I feel like I might need one."

"I know."

"How do you know?"

"It's in the eyes. It's always in the eyes. There's a reason you left Boston. And there's a reason you are here. You might not know now, but you'll find the answer."

He sounded like some sort of soothsayer who had read my future from Tarot cards or tea leaves. And because of it, we were both quiet for a minute.

Then he returned to his chipper self and opened the door. "Okay then, now let's give you the five-minute tour."

We walked down the hall and around a corner to an open area that was littered with about a dozen desks. A few people were pecking away on their laptops, a couple chatting, and a few more hid behind their monitors, surfing the net while finishing up lunch. As we entered, they dropped what they were doing and assembled like soldiers called to attention and quickly formed a greeting line. There was an even ratio of men to women, but they all had one thing in common — the color of their hair. The majority were gray heads and those who didn't have gray hair, didn't have hair at all.

Greg began the introductions. I shook hands, smiling, forgetting names instantly as my mind wandered to the past. I had to remind myself that I was at the *Sandy Point Standard Times* and not back at J.F. O'Brien's Funeral Home on Dorchester Street. The old faces resembled a greeting line for a wake. I couldn't fight the memory.

When I was a kid, at least twice a week my father slapped the same gravy-stained blue clip-on tie on me, and then practically pulled my arm out of its socket while dragging me along the alphabet streets of Southie in search of what he called, "A Good Irish Wake."

We would go to wakes for retired cops, firefighters, relatives I didn't even know I had, and even brittle old ladies because my deeply religious father would state solemnly, "They have no one else."

What they did have was an open bar where roast beef-faced Irishmen could pay their respects. It wasn't until I grew out of the clip-on that I learned the real meaning, that a "Good Irish Wake" = free booze.

When I shook the last wrinkled hand, it suddenly dawned on me. Other than Norman, who I didn't think I'd be shooting pool with anytime soon, all the employees were old. Not one young person in the whole bunch. I knew I hadn't taken the job for the social benefits, but man, I thought, couldn't there be someone remotely close to my age? Never mind my age, how about close to my generation? That was one of the negatives I had forgotten to put on my list of cons. And it was a big one. Meeting women was what I had really loved about bartending at The Jar. Every night there was always the chance that "The One" would walk through those oak doors and sit at the barstool and gaze up at me. And so many times I thought she had. And, so many more times I was wrong. But, even if it wasn't "The One," there were always those snowy nights in February when one of the lonely, chubby waitresses would stay and do shots of Jager with me.

Greg showed me my desk while I glanced around the office, realizing I could only do shots of Metamucil with the women of this crew. But then I told myself I had to remember why I left Boston. It was those Jagermeister nights. Actually, it was the morning after those nights. The hangover sun would slash through the blinds, illuminating the husky waitress's thick, pale backside as I cursed myself, while at the same time praying for her to stop snoring, slip on her granny panties, and get out. It may sound harsh, but I wanted those days to be over, I thought, while placing my laptop bag on the desk.

"Oh, there's Harrison, I'll be right back." There was an annoyed edge to

Greg's voice and it was accented with a slight frown before he moved to the office entrance to talk with another gray-haired man. The man looked to be in his mid-seventies and was wearing tortoiseshell glasses that rested on his nose. He peered over at me a couple of times. They talked for a minute, and from Greg's sluggish body language, I got the feeling that whoever Harrison was, Greg didn't like him. I turned my attention back to the desk where I noticed a paper bag and a can of Coke. I thought it might be an old bag, but then I spotted a yellow post-it-note attached to it that read:

J.T. — Thought you might be hungry. Enjoy, SUNSHINE.

"Sunshine?" I said out loud.

"That's what we call Mrs. Walsh." Greg smiled as he approached with Harrison.

"You mean that's what you call her, Greggie." Harrison stressed the name, and I could see the tension attacking Greg's smile as he tried to ignore the comment.

"They stopped calling me Greggie a long time ago... J.T. O'Rourke, I'd like you to meet Paul Harrison. Paul is the columnist that I told you about when I met you in Boston."

My brain searched for a second and then it came to me — the night in the bar. After I picked Greg up from under the table and gave him some water, he spent the next ten minutes hurling drunken slurs at an empty stool beside him. The name he kept repeating in between the curses was Paul Harrison. The next morning, I asked him who Paul Harrison was, and he laughed it off saying he was just an asshole columnist who worked for his paper. I got the feeling there was more to it than that but didn't push it.

"Oh, yes," I put out my hand. "Greg has told me a lot about you."

Harrison squinted and shook my hand, scanning me up and down. He did it again and I realized it was a perpetual squint, almost making him look Asian.

He let go of my hand and pushed his glasses up. "Oh, he has. What did he say?"

"Just that I could learn a lot from a columnist like you."

"Bullshit."

"Excuse me?"

"You heard me. Bullshit. I'm a newspaperman and I learned to read people a long time ago. I know you're lying. And even if you weren't, I know Crocker here can't stand me. Isn't that right?" He turned to Greg.

"It's not that I can't stand you, it's just..."

Harrison stopped him with his hand. "I really don't give a shit. But just so we're all on the same page, Crocker hired you, right?"

"Yes."

"So, basically, you're his boy. So, you stay out of my way, and I'll stay out of yours."

My blood instantly boiled. I was pissed. Clearly, he was a bully, and he was coming out of the gate at me. I wasn't going to have any of that. I moved closer and laughed down in his wrinkled face.

"Welcome to the neighborhood. I guess you didn't bake me a cake then. First off, Mr. Harrison, I'm nobody's boy. Second, something to remember: always unzip your fly before you start marking your territory. 'Cause if you don't, you end up pissing on yourself. Got it?"

Harrison was taken aback and actually glanced down at his pants.

I turned to Greg. "Is there anyone else you want to introduce to me?"

Greg, who was stunned for a minute, came back to the moment. "Oh, yes. Ah, yes, one more person. Let's go this way."

I waited until we were in the hallway before I said anything.

"I'm sorry, but something you have to know is I don't back down to threats, especially when I've done nothing to deserve them. I mean, what the hell was that?"

"Don't apologize, J.T. If anything, I should apologize. Harrison's just been that way so long that it's too late to do anything about it."

"I don't know 'bout that. It's your paper. Why do you put up with him?"

"Tradition, for one. He's been here for thirty-nine years. Thank God, he's retiring in September, though. But also his column does sell papers. He's a great columnist, but a lousy reporter, because he always breaks the golden rule of journalism. You know what that is?"

"He picks subjective."

"Exactly. If he's reporting a story, he never reports it impartially. It drives me crazy. If it's a liquor license hearing for a restaurant, he'll side with the restaurant just to get a few lobster dinners. If it's about landscape companies vying for a special town contract, his article will be slanted toward the company that plows his driveway for free. It's unethical. A while back, I decided it was easier to give him a column, so that way people would know it's really his view being expressed. But occasionally, he still covers assignments when we're short-handed. That's why I hired you, to lighten our load, and he probably resents it."

We stopped at a white door with the word DARKROOM written on it in black magic marker.

"J.T., I know you haven't gotten off to the best start by meeting my nephew and now Harrison. But, believe me, everyone else is great. I think you'll hit it off with this last person I want you to meet." He gave a mischievous glance at me before knuckling the door.

"Echo, you in there?"

"Yeah. Is that you, Crockerman?" A female shouted from the other side.

"Yeah. I've got our new reporter here. I want you to meet him."

"No way!"

"What do you mean, no way?"

"I look like a grub. I'll meet him later."

"Miss Echo Landers, I've known you since you were eight, and I don't think anyone has ever described you that way."

"You're wrong. In the fourth grade, Candy Treem used to call me that and also 'barf face.' Give me like five minutes."

"Okay, five minutes and then we break down the door."

Laughter came from the darkroom and Greg turned back to me. "By the way, I wasn't able to get you that part-time landscaping job I promised. My friend hired a bunch of Brazilians for cheap. He also said he won't be doing much work on weekends. But the good news is I got you a bartending job at The Angry Fisherman if you want. Some serious money shifts."

"Cool." A part of me wanted to leave the bar world behind and I was looking forward to working outdoors and losing my Guinness chins and maybe even lacing up my boxing gloves again but bartending on the Cape in the summer was a no-brainer.

"All the info is at your place."

"My place? But I haven't found a place yet."

"I got you one. Right on the water."

"I can't afford anything on the water. I just need a one room…"

"Is free cheap enough?" He reached into his jeans and pulled out some keys and an envelope with directions. "Read them later."

I was about to react to the word "free" when the greatest distraction of my life appeared. I sheepishly smiled at the vision in front of me. I had expected another gray head, but what I was looking at had long raven hair tied up in a messy bun. She was either in her late twenties or early thirties.

I guess the P.C. term to describe her is "African-American," but her complexion was a shade lighter than Halle Berry's, showing she also had some white blood running through those veins. All I know was my Irish blood was flowing freely. I tried to be subtle as I continued checking her out. She wore a red flannel shirt that was unbuttoned halfway, exposing a white tank top that concealed large, shapely breasts. She also wore a pair of maroon, old lady, pointed glasses — the kind that look comical on everyone except a beautiful woman. She was that woman. The glasses gave her dark eyes a tinge of red. She took off her white latex gloves and rested her hands on the hips of her aqua-colored hospital pants.

Licking her full lips before biting down on the lower one she said, "Well, I'm sorry to tell you, but the fall down the well was too much for little Timmy. We lost him."

Greg cracked, "I know, Echo. You look like you just came off the set of *E.R.* or something."

She flashed a smile meant for toothpaste commercials. "I know. I know. These are my developing clothes. I'm a total grub."

I couldn't help but stare at her toned but petite frame. She might've been dressed like a "grub" but she was the most beautiful grub I had ever seen.

Say something!

"You don't use digital?" I asked.

As if we were old friends, she slapped me playfully with her gloves. "Digital? That's a swear word around these parts. Crockerman doesn't get that digital will be everywhere in a couple of years. Clearly, he also didn't tell you that we do everything old school here. I mean *everything*."

"She's right. There are junior high papers that have better technology than us, but I like it this way. Tradition. You'll understand soon enough."

"Crockerman, change is coming, and you better start to embrace it," she teased.

"Yeah, yeah. Anyway, this little firecracker is Miss Echo Landers. And this is J.T. O'Rourke."

"Pleased to meet you." I shook her hand looking for a ring. None. But I figured maybe she took it off when she developed film? I thought about commenting on her name, but from experience with my own initials, I held back.

"Well, Crockerman, it's about time you hired someone close to my age. It can get pretty boring with all these bingo players here." She thumbed at Crocker and smiled even wider. I noticed she was wearing a diamond chip nose ring that sparkled with her smile. I was already striking deals with God. Then I thought how my mom was raised racist in Southie and was probably spinning in her grave.

"Hey, I'm still a young guy here," he lightly protested as Mrs. Walsh appeared in the hall.

"Yes, Sunshine?" Crocker turned to her.

"Sorry, Greg, but Lillian Dumas is on the bat line."

"What else is new? If you two will excuse me for a minute."

"Hey, thanks for the sandwich, Sunshine." I half-waved and she smiled back.

She filled him in while walking away, leaving Echo and me alone. There was an awkward silence.

I broke it. "Bat line?"

"It's what we call the complaint line. Lillian calls at least once a week bitching about something." Echo looked around before continuing. "So, Crockerman tells me that you were a bartender at The Jar and helped him out one drunken night."

"He told you that?"

"Yeah, I'm the only one who knows. Crockerman is kind of like a father to me in a way. He doesn't have a wife and can't stomach his nephew, so I'm kind of like his little girl. He's always looking out for me. He tells me everything and vice versa. He also told me that you don't have much experience in the news-paper biz. So, why come here?"

She seemed sincerely curious, but I paused, realizing her voice had a sexy, Demi Moore smokiness to it.

"I just need a change."

"Sorry, it's none of my business."

"No. No. Don't worry about it. It's just that I'm still trying to figure it out myself. I don't know, I guess I've always loved to tell and write stories and saw my opportunity with this job. I mean, whenever it was slow at The Jar, I was writing."

"It gets slow at The Jar?"

"Day shifts. Why? You've been there?"

"Us Cape Codders do make it over the bridge now and then. I went to Emer-son, and my roommates and I went there whenever a good band was playing.

Well, at least we did. You guys had some serious talent play there, but then it stopped."

I laughed.

"What's so funny?" she asked.

"It's just that I used to book the bands, but it was such a pain in the ass after a while that I told my boss to get someone else to do it. Then he decided he was also sick of the headaches."

"Dealt with a bunch of idiots, huh?"

"For the most part they were cool with me 'cause I was the one paying them. But with the band, it was always like a VH1 'Behind the Music' episode, especially the lead singers. Talk about high maintenance. A guitarist once told me a joke. How's it go again?" I wondered out loud. "Oh yeah. What's the difference between a terrorist and a lead singer?"

"I don't know."

"You can negotiate with a terrorist."

She paused. It registered, and she let out a light laugh, and I joined in.

"Kind of a lame joke, but it sort of says it all," I admitted.

"Yeah, it is a lame joke, but y'know, I'll probably be telling it later," she giggled.

"What'd I miss?" Crocker smiled as he approached.

"Oh, nothing. J.T. and I were just getting to know one another."

I loved hearing her say my name. It kind of tripped off her tongue.

"Well, that's good you get along 'cause tomorrow, eight sharp. I want you both here. I have J.T.'s first assignment and Echo, we're going to need some good pictures."

She flipped out her cell phone. "J.T., I'm going to need your number, just in case."

"Echo is notorious for running late," Crocker explained.

"You hush," she said to him, and then her beautiful eyes stared at me, "Shoot."

"Are you a Red Sox fan?" I asked.

"Diehard. What's your point?"

"617-555-1917."

She smiled, "The year before they last won the World Series. I'll never forget that."

"Very good." I said.

"Actually, you don't have to be a diehard to know that terrible bit of New England history. Oh, damn, is it really quarter to one?"

I glanced down at my wrist. "Yep."

She hurried past me. "I promised I'd pick up David 10 minutes ago. I'll see you in the a.m. Great meeting you, J.T." She was out the door in seconds.

"Yeah, you too," I said, but I was thinking of DAVID. Of course, a woman like that always has a boyfriend. How could I be so naïve?

"So, what do you think of Echo?"

"Seems really sweet and genuine."

"Yep. She's more than just a beautiful-looking young woman. She also has it in here." He pointed to his heart. "And she's always there for David."

"How long has she been with him?"

"Been with him?" Greg looked at me quizzically and then laughed. "Oh, no. You got it wrong. David's her little brother."

"He is?"

"Yeah, Echo's mom had her when she was really young and then years later got married and had David. David is... shall we say, developmentally challenged. And Echo's almost like a second mother to him."

"Oh, I see."

"And to answer the question that is swimming around in your head, yes, she's single."

"Oh, I ah..." I paused but couldn't hide it, "Okay, you got me."

Crocker frowned. "I don't encourage office romances."

"Oh."

But then he smiled and winked. "But I don't discourage them, either. Well, enough about that for now. We have work to do. Tell me J.T., what do you know about coyotes?"

I had to force Echo Landers out of my mind and get professional.

"Nothing much at all. Why?"

Crocker patted me on the back and laughed again. "Good. Then at least we know where your starting point is.

CHAPTER 5
SEPTEMBER 19, 1970

SATURDAY

DEVLIN

Devlin drummed his thumbs against the chair's arms while he waited in Chief Gedney's office.

Maybe I should get the hell out of here while I can.

He was having second thoughts. After all, he had vowed to himself, *no waves until I'm accepted by the force.*

And now, by requesting a meeting with the Chief and Detective Prichard, the lead investigator on the Anthony Medeiros case, Devlin was dropping a boulder into that calm sea. For what? Probably nothing. But, the theory... He couldn't shake it. For the past couple of weeks, it had gnawed away at his brain like a fast-moving disease. And every time he asked about the Medeiros case, Prichard would snap, "I'm looking into your theory. Don't worry about it."

Devlin had bought that response up until the previous day. He was changing in the department's locker room when Officers Scott Gallo and Rodney Farrell entered. Gallo was a lanky wiseass that howled at his own jokes, and Farrell, behind thick, green Coke-bottle lenses, was his overweight sidekick, never adding to the joke but always grunting his approval.

59

From the corner of his eye, Devlin saw Gallo elbow Farrell.

"Hey, Devlin," Gallo said.

Devlin looked over as he slipped on his off-duty khakis. "Yeah?"

"We just saw Prichard up by the highway. He said something about having a break in some case you're interested in."

"Really?" Devlin's voice jumped.

"Yeah, said you should meet him by exit 3. You better hurry."

"Are you serious?"

"Of course, I am."

"Did he tell you what the break was?" Devlin almost zipped his fly on his shirt.

"Yeah, apparently a murder. He said it could be connected to some case you've been hounding him about."

"Holy shit! I didn't hear about this. When'd it happen? And who's the victim??" His fingers couldn't button his shirt fast enough.

"Only about a half hour ago. The DOA goes by the name of Rocky."

"Rocky?"

"Yeah, Rocky Raccoon. It's a damn shame. An eighteen-wheeler ran right over him. Hit and run."

"What?"

Gallo chuckled. "Prichard figured you could bring your tape and seal off the crime scene... wants you to take some statements from some blue jays who witnessed it from a tree nearby. Says it could be connected to that dead gull you found on the beach. Poor Rocky Raccoon, but at least you're on the case."

Farrell wheezed laughter, patting Gallo on the back. "That's a good one, Scott!"

Devlin was bullshit. Prichard had been talking to the other officers, and obviously wasn't taking his theory seriously. It was a joke to all of them. In his mind, his right fist was caving in Gallo's hooked nose.

"Yeah, you got me there, Gallo." He faked a laugh.

Devlin froze his phony smile as Gallo finished his stand-up, referring to him as "Officer Dolittle" and asked if he could talk to the animals. Five minutes later, Devlin was scheduling the 10 a.m. appointment for the following day.

But now, sitting and waiting for the Chief, a cooler head prevailed. He knew Gallo's jokes were probably more accurate than his gut feeling. He stopped his drumming and was about to rise. He had every intention of leaving — *I cancel now, no major problem.*

It was too late. Chief Gedney and Detective Prichard materialized in the doorway, chatting, and laughing with one another.

Goddamn it. What the hell was I thinking?

"Don't get up, Officer." Chief Gedney motioned for him to stay seated, and then pointed to the other chair for Prichard. Devlin nodded at Prichard, who returned the gesture with a what-the-fuck-are-you-doing stare. Like a disappointed parent, he finished the stare off with a slow shake of his head.

Doug Prichard was nondescript in appearance — medium height, medium build, brown hair, blue eyes, late thirties. His last name described him best — Prichard.

Devlin was learning quickly why some of the summer cops reversed his last name when they whispered about the detective behind his back. He definitely was a hard prick.

"Chief, can we make this quick? Like I said, I got more pressing cases to work on." Prichard was bored, his tone condescending.

"Don't forget, Detective, now that it's fall, I have half-days on Saturdays, so I'd like to get out of here, too." Gedney also sounded annoyed as he walked to his chair.

Devlin wondered briefly if he was going to receive the proper listen, but one thing Chief William R. Gedney (the third) was known for was being fair. He treated all cops equally. No favorites. He was a tall, impressive looking man with black hair that was graying slightly at the temples and intimidating blue eyes that seemed to turn a shade of black whenever he asked a question and wanted an answer.

Devlin watched the shade turn as the Chief sat down, grabbed his copy of the report, and asked, "So, Officer Devlin, Detective Prichard tells me that you are quite intrigued by the Medeiros case and the dead gull you and Officer Gordon found on the beach. So, why is that?"

Devlin was about to answer, but Prichard cut in.

"Chief, I believe I said 'harassing' not 'intrigued'." Prichard laughed expecting the Chief to join in.

The Chief shot him a look. "Detective, I'll choose my own words, if you don't mind."

"Yes, sir."

"Now, Officer Devlin, I don't have to remind you that you're not a detective, so the information gathered doesn't have to be shared with you. But you were the first one at the scene, and I can understand your interest in this case. But I'll ask again: what exactly is your concern?"

"Um," Devlin coughed into his hand, clearing his throat. "Well, sir. I really didn't want to have this meeting, but I feel this case is being brushed aside as meaningless."

"It is meaningless!" Prichard blurted, but then felt the Chief's eyes on him. "Sorry, sir."

"Detective let's understand that Officer Devlin is still a rookie, and this was the first dead body he has witnessed, and furthermore, he knew Mr. Medeiros. This has probably affected him greatly. Am I right, officer?"

"Yes, I guess so, sir." Devlin nodded, his insides screaming — I was in Nam, for Christ's sake!

"All solid reasons why he might have greater interest in this case than normal. So, Detective, why don't you go over your report this one time, and then I can go see my boy's football game?" As the Chief talked, Devlin could see what he was doing. He was handling Prichard, giving him all the power. Prichard loved it, mellowing immediately.

"Yes, sir, I'm sorry. I got a little excited. I should remember Officer Devlin has no experience in these matters. The ME confirmed that Medeiros died of a massive heart attack. I also talked to Eddie Creighton over at Phil's Pharmacy and he told me Medeiros was supposed to pick up a refill of his heart pills. He didn't. His ticker gave out. Case closed."

"Yes, but what about the gull? Did any of the Environmental Police know anything? And did you have the gull examined?

"You mean like an autopsy?" Prichard meant for the question to be absurd.

"*Yes*, an autopsy."

"Oh my God! God no. The gull has nothing to do with anything."

"But it was carved up like a Thanksgiving turkey!"

"Motorboat." Prichard one-worded Devlin.

"What about the small, bloody footprint by Mr. Medeiros's body?"

Prichard swatted the question away, "A little kid probably found the gull and stepped in blood. That print could've been there long before Medeiros had the heart-attack."

The Chief eyed the report. "You mentioned a tackle box, and a child-sized fishing pole was found. What's your conclusion on those items?"

"Well, sir, they probably belong to the kid who found the gull. I figure, when he found the gull, he got scared and took off and forgot his gear. There was no name on any of it, so I just had it stored in the lost and found. The fish are really biting these days, so I wouldn't be surprised if the kid comes forward soon to claim it."

Devlin wanted to explode with his theory, but now realized he was getting nowhere with Prichard. His best bet was to run it by the Chief after Prichard left.

"Makes sense. I guess I was getting a little excited over nothing. Sorry, Detective. It won't happen again. I guess you do have everything covered." Devlin put out his hand and Prichard shook it in victory.

"Wait, Detective," the Chief said, glancing up from the report. "What's this about finding a bucket with half a bottle of rum in it? Certainly, you don't think that was also the child's?"

"No, sir. We're pretty sure it belonged to Medeiros. We were going to finger-print it and see if it matched Medeiros's prints but Jessie... I mean Officer Gordon, had already picked up the bucket and then dropped the bottle smashing it on the jetty."

Devlin remembered how angry he was when he returned from the cruiser and Gordon's sausage fingers were all over the bucket and bottle of rum tainting what he thought was solid evidence for his theory. But he didn't remember the bottle breaking.

Gordon probably used it later that day to wash down his jelly donuts.

"Hmmm." Gedney sounded skeptical, "Well, thank you, Detective. I would like to talk to Officer Devlin alone now."

Prichard nodded, pleased, and exited quickly.

Devlin braced for the tongue lashing for wasting everybody's time, but it didn't come.

"Officer Devlin, I know you were holding back. Speak freely. What's your theory?"

"Sir?"

"You heard me, go on."

"Oh, yes...Well, first off, I don't want to use my Nam experience sounding like Audie Murphy here, but sir, a motorboat didn't kill that gull. I saw too many soldiers gutted to know that. One night when I was on patrol, I even found one of our men... His head had been cut off. Severed cleanly. That's what that gull looked like. And also, if a boat had done that what are the chances that the head would wash ashore and rest right beside the body? A million to one. You see, sir, why I want this to be investigated is the theory that keeps running in my mind, and it has bothered me. A lot. I think Mr. Medeiros was walking *to* the beach, not *from* it as Detective Prichard surmised. I mean, the man was lying, face down pointing toward the beach, so the rum bottle couldn't have been his."

"So, what's your point?" The Chief casually glanced down at his watch.

"I think Mr. Medeiros came upon someone or maybe some people butchering that gull, and that is what induced his heart attack. This man lived and breathed Cape Cod, and to witness that kind of savagery to an animal and not being able to stop it must've been a terrible way to die."

"I see."

"Do you?" Devlin wanted to ask, but instead said, "Sir, I remember right before taking the call that day, watching two gulls and thinking how much they symbolized Cape Cod. Mr. Medeiros watched that symbol get mutilated on the beach where he grew up. Isn't it our job to make it safe for an old man to enjoy a quiet night of fishing?"

"Yes, Officer Devlin, it is. If this theory of yours is correct, tell me, who would do something like that?"

"I honestly have no idea. Could be someone who's in a cult or some kid who got a book and read up on one? I really don't know. But the small footprints were only yards from Mr. Medeiros's body. Whoever it was probably went to check on him and saw he was already dead."

"I really can't imagine cult members fishing."

"True. Good point." Devlin was hopeful. At least, Gedney was analyzing it.

"And, even if we caught this person or persons, we couldn't charge them with murder or anything, so I can see why Prichard wants to concentrate on his other cases. He's a good cop and does have a lot on his plate."

"Yes, but we could get them for..."

"Look, Michael," Gedney addressing him by his first name stopped him. "You make a lot of valid points. I knew Anthony personally. I know how he loved nature. Hell, he was President of the Sandy Point Beautification Committee for many years. So, if your theory is right, it is horrible what happened. But it is just that. A *theory*. All the evidence is either gone or tainted. And even if it wasn't, there really isn't much to build any type of case. But I don't want to discourage you on this. You have a detective's mind, and if you come across something that could build this or any other cases, I want you to know you can come to me. Actually, I'd rather you come to me. I don't have to tell you that the men don't really know what the hell to make of you. Many of them think you're here just to play cops and robbers to spite your old man and sooner or later you'll get sick of it and off to Harvard or Yale you'll go. So, you have to toe a fine line, and I have to say by calling this meeting, regardless of your intentions, it's not going to win any points. In fact, you're probably in the minus category right now."

"Yes, sir."

"But know this, you don't have anything to prove to me. I served in Korea, so I know. I know you've seen shit that would make people like Prichard crap his boxers. I only said that stuff earlier to ease his insecurities. Psychology will get you far in law enforcement. Learn how to deal with these people now and you'll become a great cop, and from talking with you today, an even greater detective someday. But remember, the road will be a hell of a lot smoother if you think of the big picture next time. Alright?" He smiled.

"Yes, sir. Thank you, sir." Devlin got up and headed for the door and opened it.

"One other thing, Officer Devlin…"

"What's that, sir?"

"The bottle of rum… You were right about that."

"Huh?"

"There's no way that was Anthony's bottle." Gedney placed his hands behind his head and leaned back in his chair.

"How do you know that, sir?"

"Anthony hated hard liquor. He was strictly a beer man. God rest his soul."

———

Devlin opened the back door of his cruiser and rested the forest green, child-size fishing pole and red tackle box on the back seat. It had only taken the fifteen-second walk from Gedney's office to the lost and found for him to analyze his meeting and come to a favorable conclusion — one that suited his needs. He remembered what he wanted to remember.

And that was Gedney stating: *that is not to say if you come across something just to forget it.*

Well, he came across the fishing pole and tackle box, he rationalized as he settled into the driver's seat and turned the key. Those were pieces of evidence that still might provide answers. He also remembered how Gedney said that someday Devlin would be a great detective. Of course, as his cruiser rolled out of the parking lot, he put that little word "someday" out of his head.

He turned onto Main Street. His plan was to head to Bryden's Fish & Gear, a market that overlooked the harbor. That was where everybody purchased their supplies, and maybe, he thought, Mr. Bryden had a list of customers, or even knew who bought the equipment. He knew it was a long shot, but at least it was a shot. He hit traffic immediately and looked over at the source — the Sandy Point High School football field's parking lot, which lay directly beside the police station. Sandy Point had a one o'clock game, but the place was already buzzing with activity. Sunny and crisp. Yellows and oranges were beginning to decorate a few trees. It was a perfect day for a game. His car inched along, giving him more time to take in the game day ritual.

He had been out of high school for almost nine years, but the pre-game parking lot routine hadn't changed a bit — new names playing old roles. There was the usual group of awkward, four-eyed band members huddled together practicing the fight song, blowing away out-of-tune notes in the futile hope the cheerleaders would notice them. Of course, they didn't. Never would, 'til years later.

"Hang in there, boys, you'll grow out of it," he smiled to himself, thinking of his friend Leo Montgomery, who once held the title of head band nerd, but now was a mover and shaker on Wall Street.

There was also the typical blonde-bombshell, captain of those cheerleaders, wagging her finger angrily at a plain, nervous-looking member who was arriving late. The captain crossed her arms, tapped her foot, and berated the girl in front of her peers.

"Enjoy it now, Blondie," Devlin muttered as he had a quick vision of Linda Morrison, who thought she was God's gift to Sandy Point High School, but now was married to an alcoholic plumber and had three kids. Devlin had been reacquainted with her about a month before. He arrived at her house responding to a noise complaint. That night, he couldn't believe it. She no longer resembled the perfect cheerleader, more like the perfect offensive lineman. Of course, the cause of the noise had been her drunken husband, Silvio Clements, who had once been the star quarterback of Devlin's football team. Now, Silvio spent his nights reliving every first down with a bottle of Wild Turkey as his only mascot to cheer him on.

Devlin shook the thought away and then spotted the old-timers in their huddle clutching Styrofoam coffee cups, animatedly reliving *their* glory days and what they would do if they were the coach. The scene made Devlin thankful that he hadn't been a star in high school. Stars burn out. He had been a good-looking, strong fullback who scored a few touchdowns, but he had never let it define who he was. He hated to be stereotyped, and as he left the blaring tubas behind and continued on, he had to laugh at himself because that was exactly what he had been doing to the crowd. Stereotyping them.

When he passed Pop Tucker's store, he tapped the horn and waved at Pop who was handing Greggie Crocker a lollipop. They both smiled and waved their suckers back at him.

Good to see Greggie is feeling better.

Greggie had been sick for a few days and one of Mr. Bryden's sons had been doing his route. Devlin was in a decent mood until he passed Lareby's Market. That's when he remembered that his mom wanted him to pick up some steaks after his shift to "celebrate." Lareby's had a reputation for carrying the best choice cuts of sirloin, and normally, Devlin would gladly welcome one, medium-rare, with a baked potato covered in sour cream, and a cold Pabst Blue Ribbon to quench his end of the day thirst. The problem was he would be having the meal with his father who was "celebrating" the fact that his banker client, the family man, got off on a technicality and would be free to bludgeon more down and out girls in the future.

"I don't know how she does it," he sighed, thinking of his mother. She was a good woman, and Devlin loved her like all boys loved their moms, but it always bothered him that her sole existence in life was spent catering to Allan Devlin's needs. That realization hit him while on the troop ship heading to Nam, when a cluster of fresh-faced soldiers swapped stories about their mothers. It was an innocent scene where each soldier opened up a bit, talking about his mother's interests, whether it was painting, gardening, or teaching ballet. Like the boys they were, they talked about what they'd miss about their mothers. When they got to Devlin, he paused. Not a dramatic pause — an embarrassed one.

"Devlin, don't you know what your mom likes to do?" One of them broke the silence. He couldn't answer the question because the truth was, he had no idea what she liked to do. While he fumbled to answer, the only pictures that came to him were of his mother cooking or starching his father's shirts or listening to Allan Devlin and always nodding in agreement. Devlin's long pause was the answer.

Another soldier jumped in thrusting his hips and cracking to the group, "I know what she likes to do!"

It was meant as a light-hearted ribbing, but Devlin used the mother joke as an excuse to avoid the question and cold-cocked the comedian. He always regretted throwing that punch. He wished he'd just responded with a clever comeback especially since three months later, the comic — Private Danny Moniz, was shipped in a flag-draped casket headed for a reunion with his uncle, a grave digger at Blessed Virgin Mary Cemetery in Fall River.

And long after the grass had grown over Private Moniz's plot, the question that was asked on the troop ship had stayed with Devlin. He made a promise, *if* he returned from Nam alive, he'd make every effort to get to know his mother. That was the only reason he agreed to rent his parents' small guesthouse, which lay directly below their mansion that stood proudly on the craggy perch of Oyster Island.

"I still don't know her," he said to himself, as he pulled into Bryden's Fish & Gear's parking lot, easing the cruiser between a wood-paneled beach wagon, and a sporty, red convertible VW bug with a white roof. He hopped out of his cruiser, grabbed the pole and fishing gear, and studied the convertible.

I know that red bug from somewhere.

He moved on, walking through a maze of stacked lobster traps, scattered boat moorings and engines, and a green painted rowboat resting on blocks that had a sloppily handwritten sign attached — *Warning: Fresh Paint.*

Many of the locals complained that the front of Bryden's resembled a fisherman's junkyard, and it was an eyesore for the people who visited Sandy Point. Mr. Bryden knew better. It was the working-class fisherman appearance that always caught the attention of the carloads of tourists as they passed. They always turned around. When the city folks came to the Cape, the majority wanted to experience the fisherman's lifestyle without actually getting their toes wet. So, it was natural for them to take a trip to the entrance of Sandy Point Harbor and pop into the hut-sized fish and gear market. It might have been modest looking with parched shingles treated by the constant salty breeze, and a "fisherman's junkyard" in the front, but Bryden's Fish & Gear didn't just *sell* clams. It *made* clams. Serious clams.

The bell on the door jingled as Devlin entered, causing the handful of shoppers to glance over for a second before their eyes shifted back to what they were doing. Devlin felt one pair of eyes stay on him, so he turned to them and spotted a beautiful young woman in her early twenties. Her green eyes flamed from her tanned skin, and when she tilted her head, her long blonde hair fell to one side. It looked as if she was about to say something to him.

At that instant, it hit Devlin: the red convertible with the white top, Anna Talbot. He had pulled her over for speeding back in June and even though he tried, he still couldn't get her face out of his mind. She was an only child from an old money summer family and had only been fed by gold spoons. Devlin never wanted to give her the satisfaction of knowing that he thought she was the most beautiful woman he had ever seen. So, quite naturally, he made it a point always to ignore her. It was juvenile, but he really didn't care. It amused him. He made a quick jerking movement away from her and headed to the counter. He thought he heard an annoyed sigh escape her, and he bit his lip to avoid a smile.

"Hey, Officer Devlin, what can I do for you?" Nine-year-old Fishy Bryden's brown eyes bugged out from behind the cash register.

Fishy wore a muscle T-shirt with the store's logo on the front. Part of Devlin wanted to laugh because the little boy had pixie sticks for arms, and it really looked like the shirt was wearing him. The other part of Devlin was concerned. The little boy should've been enjoying his Saturday at the football game or fishing instead of manning a cash register. The town officials usually looked the other way when it came to enforcing the child labor laws, so he knew there really was nothing he could do about it. And he also had to admit, the boy with eyes that bulged out of his head like a flounder seemed pretty content behind that counter.

"Hey, Fishy, I was wondering if I could have a word with your dad," Devlin leaned the pole against the register and rested the tackle box on the countertop.

"Sure, thing. He's out back on the dock. He's with Captain Cardoza, though. They're arguing over lobster prices again. Wait one second." Fishy turned around and hollered to the back room, "Jeremy! Jeremy!"

"What?" Eleven-year-old Jeremy Bryden burst out from the back room with an aggravated look on his face. It changed to an "uh-oh" reaction when he spotted Devlin.

"Hey there, Jeremy." Devlin smiled.

"Hi, Officer Devlin... ah... we're not working here..." He pointed nervously at Fishy and then himself. "We're just helping Dad out today. That's all."

Obviously, the boy had been schooled.

Fishy playfully waved his hand. "Officer Devlin doesn't care. He's got some gear with him. He wants to talk 'bout fishing or something. Right, Officer Devlin?"

"Fishy's right. I was just hoping to have a quick word with your dad. That's all."

"Oh, I'll go get him." A look of relief came over Jeremy's face.

Devlin was about to say "Take your time," but Jeremy had already shot past his little brother and out the back screen door.

"So, Officer Devlin, what do you think of my boat?" Fishy leaned on the counter and Devlin noticed he was wearing a chain necklace that was also too big for him.

"What boat is that?"

"The green rowboat out front. Well, it's green now. I just painted it. It's mine and Greggie Crocker's. We found it in between some jetties in bad shape. We thought there might be a reward, but there was no name on it. Don't worry, Officer Devlin, we asked around, but nobody claimed her, so we fixed her up. Greggie thinks it will only be good for puttering around in the harbor. Great for crabbing, though, don't you think?"

"Oh, yeah. She's a beauty. I thought she was up for sale, and I was considering making an offer."

"You were? How much were you going to offer?" Fishy couldn't believe it.

This caught Devlin off guard, and he felt Anna watching him.

"Ah... fifty dollars."

"Fifty bucks! Wow! We did find a good one then. Wait till I tell Greggie!"

Then Fishy got control of himself. "Of course, it's not for sale, though, sorry."

"That's okay. What are you going to name it?"

"I don't know yet. We were thinking..." Fishy began, but Anna Talbot waved him over to the lobster tank. "Excuse me, Fishy?"

He forgot all about Devlin and hurried over to the tank.

"Yes, Miss Talbot. What can I get you?"

"Fishy, please. How many times do I have to tell you? Call me, Anna," she said pleasantly, and Devlin wondered if her charm was for his benefit.

"Oh, yes, Anna. Well, what can I get you?"

She pointed her long finger down in the tank, "Six of these poor rascals. I have some friends down from college and they're a hungry bunch. I really hate to do it to these poor fellas, but it's their own fault. If they weren't so darn tasty in melted butter."

"Yeah," Fishy laughed nervously. "That's why we don't sell skunks."

Anna's good-natured laugh traveled across the room and up Devlin's spine.

"Fishy, you're so funny." She leaned over and patted the little boy's hand.

Devlin tried to fight it. But the urge was too great. He had to check her out. His eyes quickly scanned her perfect ass that her cut off jean shorts showcased. She was also wearing a gray sweatshirt with the sleeves rolled up. The maroon blocked letters on the front spelled out that she was somebody: HARVARD.

Harvard. Maybe if I had listened to my father, I would be having lobster with a beautiful blonde like her… No, she's just another rich Radcliffe bitch.

But during his rationalization, he kept his eyes fixed, and couldn't stop watching her. And she did seem different. The way she acted with Fishy. It didn't look like an act at all. She was genuinely sweet to him.

"I *said*, Officer Devlin…" Jeremy's voice broke Devlin's spell and Anna's eyes also caught him.

He turned to Jeremy, "Oh, yes. What is it?"

"Just that my dad will be up in a minute."

"Oh, good. Thanks."

"No problem." Jeremy grabbed a Coke out of the glass cooler and hollered, "Fishy, I'll be out back shucking some clams if you need me."

"Alright," Fishy answered while he finished packaging the last of Anna's lobsters. He then pecked the register but stopped when she commented, "What an interesting necklace."

"Oh, this?" He pointed to the gold chain necklace that had slipped over his T-shirt exposing a half silver and half gold oval shaped piece of metal.

"This was given to me by Captain Blanca. This was one of his best fishing lures. He said it would flash so brightly that fish would jump to it. In an hour he could catch up to twenty keepers. Can you believe that Anna?"

"No, I can't. What's this Captain's name again?"

Fishy's eyes sank. "You mean they've never talked about Captain Blanca at Harvard? He's one of Argentina's greatest fishermen. They must've mentioned him in class. Ask Officer Devlin. I bet he knows."

Devlin had seen the necklace before and knew the story behind it from Mr. Bryden. A fisherman from New Bedford once spun a wild story and gave the necklace to Fishy. The boy was a dreamer and Devlin didn't want to burst his bubble.

Let him be a kid as long as he can.

"Yes, it's true." He snapped a quick, go-along-with-it wink to Anna who was surprised at the wink, but then put it together.

"Tell Miss Talbot why it's now a necklace."

"Oh yeah, sure," Fishy said eagerly. "One night he was fishing in his boat, and he caught a great big codfish off the coast of Nantucket. He said the codfish looked up at him from the deck and spoke to him. I mean, not out loud but in his mind. Like they could read each other's minds. The codfish told him the gods of the ocean think it's unfair to have such a beautiful lure. He said, 'If you spare my life and make that lure into a necklace someday you will thank me.' Well, Captain Blanca thought it was crazy, but he never questioned the sea, so he let the fish go and did what he asked. Do you know what happened to him, Miss Tal... I mean, Anna?"

"No, Fishy, what happened to him?"

"One night during a hurricane in the tropics years ago, Captain Blanca's fishing boat got caught in the fifty-foot waves and took on water and sank in a matter of hours. The captain treaded water for six hours and was losing strength. He knew he was going to die. But guess what happened."

"I don't know. The suspense is killing me. Go on, Fishy," she urged.

"The Coast Guard was able to spot him. They said they saw a flashing spec, miles away. That flashing spec turned out to be this necklace. He gave it to me as a good luck charm and said it would always protect me and he told me when I become a great fisherman to always respect the sea, and it will always respect me."

"Wow, what an amazing story!" Anna clapped lightly.

"Yeah... My brother says it's made-up, but I think it's true. Well, I did, but you go to Harvard, and you never heard of him, so Jeremy must be right."

"Actually, I go to Radcliffe. It's part of Harvard. Wait a second," Anna stopped and pretended she was thinking, "What was the name of Captain Blanca's boat?"

"*La Plata*. Why?"

Anna tapped her hand against her head "stupid-me" style. "That's right. *Now* I remember. We did talk about him. He's from Argentina, right?"

"Yeah! Yeah, that's him! What did they say?"

"Well, it was in my history class. We were doing a section on great explorers of the modern era, and my professor was talking about how Captain Blanca has had many adventures. But he didn't tell us that story. Wait till I tell my class. Thanks, Fishy. I'll probably get extra credit."

Fishy smiled from big ear to big ear. "No problem, Anna."

As he finished punching numbers, Anna looked over at Devlin and smiled. She had been a good sport and Devlin's bite loosened. He couldn't help but grin. She paid Fishy, got her change, grabbed her package of lobsters, and said, "Thanks, Fishy, for everything…Goodbye, Officer."

The bell jingled her exit and now she was in the forefront of Devlin's mind. She was something else. A minute later, she reentered, which caught him off guard. He felt like those green eyes were reading his thoughts while she walked back up to the counter.

"Forget something, Anna?" Fishy was still smiling.

She whispered, "Fishy, you gave me too much change. Five dollars too much." She handed the crisp President Lincoln over and he thanked her profusely.

"Thank God. My father would've killed me! Thank you! Thank you!"

This time when she left, she ignored Devlin's eyes. He was finally convinced he had been wrong about Anna Talbot. What he had just witnessed was a sweet, sensitive, honest, young woman.

Fishy lured him out of another "Anna trance."

"You know what, Officer Devlin?"

"What's that, Fishy?"

"They name boats after beautiful women. I think I'll tell Greggie that we should name our boat Anna. I know he wouldn't mind. He likes her, too."

"Anna, huh?"

"Yeah, what do you think?"

"I think the name is perfect." Devlin was really talking to himself as Mr. Bryden appeared from the back room.

"You're a jackass!" Devlin cursed himself in his rear-view mirror while pulling out of the Bryden's parking lot. There were two reasons why he felt that way. One — his attempt to play detective failed miserably. Sure, Mr. Bryden sold that brand of fishing pole that was called "Little Fisherman." But he had sold over 600 of them the previous summer. When Devlin questioned Bryden about keeping records of customers' names, Bryden had shaken his head and snickered, "Who are you, Devlin? Ephram Zimbalist? This ain't *The F.B.I.*"

It sure wasn't the hit TV show, and his remark burned Devlin because Bryden was right on target. That's exactly how he had thought it would work out. He would get a list of names of people who purchased Little Fisherman poles and maybe match it up with a list of people who bought red tackle boxes. There were no lists. Lists were only used on TV — a fact that an owner of a fish and gear shop had to point out to a rookie cop.

A minute later, Devlin coincidentally pulled up behind the second reason he was angry with himself. Anna Talbot's red bug was stopped at a red light. Why didn't he really talk to her at Bryden's? His juvenile behavior was even getting to him. He had labeled her, and what he witnessed was nothing like that label. He was beginning to see himself as a hypocrite, judging people with no evidence. And what had really sealed it, that Anna was a good person was that she returned with the extra change. A beautiful, honest woman right under his nose in Sandy Point and all he had ever done was ignore her.

What the hell is wrong with me?

The light turned green, but Anna's car didn't move. Devlin waited a second. Still her car didn't move. He tapped lightly on his horn. Their eyes met through her rearview mirror. She turned her head, and he spied a mischievous smile cross her face.

She turned back and gave a half-wave over her shoulder as if to say, *"Sorry, I wasn't paying attention."*

But, then she stepped on the gas. Devlin's brow slightly raised, but he figured she was just accelerating to the 35 M.P.H. speed limit and then she'd maintain it. He tailed closely behind and was about to turn off, but then she picked up speed heading down the private road leading to the sprawling mansions on Mackerel Beach. He checked his speedometer — 45 miles per hour. That was pretty damn fast for a residential neighborhood, but he didn't want to be a hardass after their encounter, so he beeped his horn and gave a "slow down" motion with his hand.

It drew the opposite reaction from her. He looked at his speedometer again — 50 then 55.

This chick is crazy! She knows I'm behind her.

At 60, he had had enough and flipped his toggle switch and the siren growled to life. Anna slowed down but didn't come to a complete stop until she drove up the winding entrance to the Talbot Estate. She turned off the car and got out and looked quizzically at Devlin like nothing had ever happened. There was a group of college guys and girls up above on the front lawn playing touch football. They all stopped and pointed when they heard the cruiser. Devlin turned the switch off and got out of the car. One of the kids ran down the hill yelling.

"Hey you! Why are you pulling over Anna?"

Devlin didn't even grace him with eye contact, just waved him away, "None of your business. Go back to your game."

"Hey, I'm talking to you, rent-a-cop!"

It was far from original. It would take more than that for Devlin to lose his cool. He deliberately turned around slowly to face the kid who was a wiry, good-looking guy around twenty, glaring with flared nostrils. He cradled the football under his right hand and held a pint glass that contained a half consumed Bloody Mary in his left hand. He was wearing a ripped blue sweatshirt and grass-stained khakis. Devlin noticed the glazed eyes. The kid was already well on his way.

"I'll tell you one more time. It's none of your business." Devlin sharpened.

"Don't worry about it, Jack. Officer Devlin is a friend. We were just joking around. You go back to the game, and I'll be right up."

Anna smiled at Jack, who stood there for a minute with buzzed eyes trying to intimidate Devlin before rejoining the group. Devlin waited until they were alone.

"Miss Talbot, I don't know what the hell you were doing back there, but I was not playing a game. License and registration, please." He flipped his right hand out and he knew the edge in his voice would make his point — *this is no joke, rich girl!*

He realized his first analysis could be right after all.

She didn't say anything as she went into her passenger side door and leaned over and rifled through her glove compartment. Devlin turned away, so he wouldn't be tempted to check her out again. She walked over with her registration and pulled out her license from her back pocket and handed them over.

He studied them and asked, "What is wrong with you, Miss Talbot? You acted like I wasn't even behind you. I'm a policeman, y'know?"

"Did that make you angry, Officer Devlin?" she asked calmly.

"Of course it did."

"Well, now you know how I feel when you act that way with me."

Devlin looked up, "Huh?"

"Officer Devlin, tell me, how many times do you have to pull me over for speeding before I can get your attention?" Her green eyes invaded his personal space causing him to take a step back.

Inside, the wannabe detective had put it together and was exhilarated — she really liked him! He wasn't going to blow it again. It was a game in a way, and he had to play his part.

"Miss Talbot," he began scribbling on his pad, "I'm just going to give you a warning this time."

"Oh, thanks. You're a dear," she said sarcastically.

He finished writing and handed it to her. "I suggest you read the warning carefully. Good day, Miss Talbot." He tapped the brim of his hat before jumping into his cruiser.

"Yeah, thanks again… for nothing…" Her voice trailed off.

He drove slowly looking through his rearview mirror hoping Anna would read what he had written on the warning. She did. And then she looked up, beaming from his words: — *Save me a lobster or go to jail.* — *Michael*

CHAPTER 6

JUNE 8, 2004

TUESDAY

J.T.

"No! No! No! No!" I awoke in darkness, yelling and panting, drenched in a cold sweat. It wasn't the good kind of sweat that one stretches into and savors with a yawn after a midday nap. It was the other kind of perspiration, the kind brought on by something far more sinister — *fear*.

"No," I switched on the light and got out of bed. I stared into the bureau mirror at the beads that made my face glisten like a marathoner climbing Heartbreak Hill. It was back. The nightmare. The reason I hardly ever slept. And when I did, fear often crept into my room, snuggled in my bed, and settled into my dreams. Even though I had an idea of the time from the routine, I glanced at the digital clock praying I'd be wrong. I wasn't. I caught the number flicking from 20 to 21. I peeled off my T-shirt and used it to wipe my brow and upper body dry while groaning over and over again, "I'm sick of this shit," because the first number was a three. 3:21 in the morning and good ol' J.T. was up for the day.

"Dammit!" I swore again, grabbing a yellow B.C. Superfan T-shirt, and put it on while pondering the ridiculous nightmare. I never could remember it entirely, and it came in several variations. I could only remember bits and pieces. It was those bits and pieces that really pissed me off, because they were harmless, almost comical — nothing that should cause a 34-year-old man to wake up ranting and raving, hugging his pillow in the middle of the night.

The dream always began with me wearing a blue space suit, riding in a Jetsons cartoon- style spaceship traveling to the moon. Then, suddenly I was standing on the moon yelling, "Go Red Sox!" I'd see a small figure on the other side of the moon. I never could identify the face, just the number "4" on the figure's shirt. I'd move closer, but the figure would begin floating off the moon, speaking in a language that was foreign to me. Then I'd become frantic. I'd sprint toward the figure, but the more I ran, the farther the figure would float toward space. Distorted music would play and then it would rain. I'd put my hand out to touch the drops, but it was boiling rain. It would scald my hand. Severe pain and confusion would follow. That's when the nightmare always took off, but I never could remember the rest of it — just rapid images that I couldn't decipher, leaving me with a feeling of extreme sadness. I always awoke yelling at the top of my lungs.

I went into the kitchen and pulled a carton of Minute Maid out of the fridge.

"There has to be more to it," I said to myself before pouring a glass of OJ and chugging half of it down.

"Unless I'm just really messed up." I laughed it off as always, trying to make light of my severe anxiety, but part of me was serious.

Was I messed up?

"Think of the positives," I coached myself and refilled my glass before going over to the sliding door that led to the deck. I slid it open, and the ocean breeze blanketed me, cooling my body and mind. Settling in a beach chair, I leaned back and listened to the surf rush the jetties, realizing I had a constant New Age mixtape playing outside my door always available to soothe my senses. And it was doing the job. My expression changed, moving to a grin as I recounted the positives from the previous day.

"Positive number one: other than Norman Chadwick and Paul Harrison, I *knew* I'd get along with the crew at the paper. Positive number two: Mr. Crocker has given me his cottage on the beach rent-free."

And it was *literally* on the beach! It was a tiny, two-bedroom beach hut with a wood stove, bathroom, and kitchen — everything I needed. It was also a race-dive away from the Atlantic Ocean.

The previous day, I pulled into the sandy driveway and thought I either had the wrong address or it was a cruel joke. It had to be. The hut was one of only eight cottages that stood on hurricane-prevention stilts that lined the shores of Sandy Point.

Why did Crocker give it up?

I read the note tucked behind the Domino's pizza magnet on the fridge — *J.T., this used to be my drinking hut. I don't want it to be again! Enjoy the place — Greg*

I thought briefly about my late grandfather's cabin up in New Hampton, New Hampshire, which my father had inherited and used as *his* "drinking hut" up until the day he got heaved from the force for that very reason. And because of his downward spiral, he had to sell that cabin. Where was my father now? And how was he going to afford to keep our house on K Street since I was no longer there to slide him the mortgage money? Would he end up another piss-stained bagman sleeping on the floors of the ATMs on East Broadway? And when he hit bottom, would he finally see the light and climb out of that hole? I wasn't a betting man, but even if I had been, I wouldn't have placed a dime on Billy O'Rourke to survive without me. That's why I had to forget. Forget it all.

"The positives," I reminded myself, "Positive number three: the bartending job at The Angry Fisherman."

On my way to the beach hut, I had stopped by to meet the owner and get my schedule. The owner wasn't there, but I met one of the managers, Vicki, a bleached blonde and hard looking but pleasant woman. I checked out the scene and quickly surmised it was a bar that catered to locals and tourists — the tip jar would always be full. A definite positive, but as I listened to my New Age soundtrack playing in the moonless night, that positive had another effect. It also made me feel like a hypocrite. Like Russell Crowe in *The Insider*, I was going to continue spending my nights serving the very substance that had destroyed my family.

"Hey, at least I made the break from The Jar. This is only 'til the journalism takes off," I said and then sipped my OJ. But then the nightmare reentered my head.

"Positive number four: at least you fell asleep, O'Rourke!" I raised my voice to myself. I was surprised at how easy it had been to drift off, considering I was used to leaned-on-cab horns and screaming fire engines instead of cawing gulls and a lulling ocean.

Maybe once I get settled in Sandy Point, I'll not only fall asleep, but I'll also dream, dream about people who don't fall off the moon. What did it mean?

I dismissed the nightmare before it took hold again.

"Screw it!" I smiled, got out of the chair, and gingerly made my way down the steps. I

threw my T-shirt off and sprinted across the sand, plunging into an oncoming wave.

I let the tranquility of being underwater surround me and took it in for a moment before

I resurfaced. When I did, I gasped quickly for breath.

"Wow! Oh man!" The water temperature hadn't even come close to its summer peak. God, I was such a city boy to just jump in. It reminded me of all the times I took the Polar Plunge on New Year's Day near the L Street Bathhouse.

Now I was dealing with some serious George Costanza shrinkage. I forced myself to withstand it and tread water for as long as I could. The chill cleared my mind instantly and changed my mood for the better.

"Positive number five," I said as I did the breaststroke back to shore, "I can go swimming whenever I want."

I got out of the ocean completely refreshed and dried myself while smiling, realizing what the ocean couldn't wash from my mind. Positive number six: Echo Landers.

I was going to see her in less than four hours.

CHAPTER 7

JUNE 8, 2004

TUESDAY

ECHO

3 6DD. Too big by several cup sizes... Echo Landers hated her breasts. In fact, she hated her whole body. She eyed herself critically in the bathroom mirror before toweling off.

"Too chesty. Too short. Too fat." She sighed, tossing the damp towel into the laundry basket before moving her voluptuous, 5'5" figure to her bedroom.

The men of Sandy Point would've doubled over from laughter if they heard Echo's self-analysis. Their view was quite different. And what a view it was. They'd elbow one another at bars, post offices, and town meetings, goggling and grunting about her beautiful face, big tits, and J-Lo ass. There were even stories about how her looks literally stopped traffic.

At Dan Armstrong's retirement party, the English teacher was razzed about the day he hit a FedEx truck in front of the Chamber of Commerce. He ate his "Farewell" cake, taking the abuse good-naturedly from the dowdy school secretary. But at the after party, among his male contingent and well into his eighth gin and tonic, the normally soft-spoken English teacher admitted his eyes had shifted from the road to the sidewalk, where the squatting female photographer was snapping shots of the waving symbol of freedom for Flag Day. Armstrong admitted something else was waving in his pants.

"I was mesmerized. I knew I had to focus back on the road. But that ass. That sweet juicy ass! I just couldn't..." His slur trailed off and his intent audience all nodded and patted him on the shoulder. They understood. Every man had been guilty of screeching his brakes at least once in the presence of the 33-year-old beauty.

34 in five days.

Echo wasn't completely naïve to that fact either. She had felt the eyes and heard the whispers ever since the fifth grade when she was the first girl in her school to don a bra. Now, as she rifled through her drawer in search of her hot pink, Champion tank-bra, she stopped and checked herself again in the dresser mirror. A part of her knew she wasn't too chesty, too short, or too fat, but she was definitely too insecure. There was no argument there. She sometimes feared she'd end up one of those thick-ankled, bowling-ball-breasted women. She didn't want to have a shopping cart supporting her breasts as she waited to hear her deli number called at Lareby's Market. And that was her biggest fear. Waiting. She had been waiting to grow the "balls" to leave the Point and prove to everyone that she was a real photojournalist just like all of her friends from Emerson. They worked at places like "Geographic," Time, and Life. They were making a difference, whether they were bunkered down with a cavalry in Iraq, or with a tribe wandering a desert in South Africa. They were bringing the rest of the world to America's coffee tables. Echo's world was Sandy Point, and all she was delivering to its tables were shots of newly painted crosswalks and Pinewood Derby winners every Tuesday and Friday for the local "fish wrapper."

"Why am I still here?" She asked the mirror and waited as if expecting a reply. Then, she glanced over at her alarm clock: 7:31 a.m.

I have to meet the new guy at 8.

She picked up the pace, sifting through her lacy, multicolored Victoria Secret collection in search of her favorite jogging bra. She liked it because it held everything firmly in place so she could move freely during photo shoots. She wrestled it on and then grabbed a pair of purple bikini briefs and slipped into them. Off the job, Echo wore men's boxers because they were comfortable. But for work, women's underwear was more practical. She referred to them as her "combat underwear."

Of course, I didn't wait around to ask Crockerman what kind of combat I was in today.

Echo wasn't like her best friend, Kathy Zimmerman, who, since elementary school, meticulously planned her outfit the night before. Instead, Echo dressed in accordance with the feeling of the day or the type of assignment. She walked over and peeked through the drapes at a beautiful, pre-summer Cape Cod day. Just enough heat. Just enough ocean breeze. She was a little surprised since there had been no moon the night before, and the Boston weathermen hinted at a chance of showers. Of course, they also hinted at a chance of sun, she thought and laughed, thinking how the meteorologists always seemed to cover their asses.

She went to her dresser and unscrewed a bottle of perfume that was created for her by Mrs. Kumar, an Indian woman who designed her specially blended fragrances based on the customer's personality. Mrs. Kumar felt Echo exuded the glow of the end of summer, so she mixed vanilla and tangerine oils which Echo now dabbed on her neck, her pulse points, and finished by lightly brushing the backs of her knees. She breathed in the soft, soothing smell for a second before hurrying back into the bathroom to pop in her contacts, brush her teeth, and apply mascara to her long eyelashes.

As she reentered her bedroom, she was feeling a little mischievous.

Should I wear something sexy and fun and shake up J.D. or J.T. or whatever the hell his name is?

"Nah," she decided while combing her hair. He seemed like a really nice guy, and she didn't want to give him the wrong impression. She thought about the new reporter for a moment longer. Behind his warm smile and hearty laugh, Echo detected sadness in those dark blue eyes. She had no proof. Just a feeling. What was he escaping? She was looking forward to finding out more about him. Crockerman had mentioned the new guy had been a pretty decent boxer, but she could tell that was in his past. He was handsome and probably hot at one time, but he clearly had let the late-night bar shifts go to his chin. But in their brief meeting, there was something about him she liked. His dark eyes seemed soulful and within ten minutes of meeting him, J.T., yeah that's his name, she knew he'd definitely make a good friend. Echo needed more friends in her life. The ones she had were now all married with kids or had moved off Cape.

"Yep, I think he could be a good friend," she said, picking a white, men's tailored shirt off the hanger. She put it on leaving one button undone so that there was only a hint of the pink tank bra peeking out. She slid into a pair of dark-washed jeans and squeezed into her worn brown Frye boots.

"What am I forgetting?" She asked and then answered, "Duh," when she spotted her black messenger bag that held all of her camera supplies.

She headed downstairs and smelled fresh coffee and heard morning banter between her mom and stepdad coming from the kitchen. She briefly considered ducking her head in to say, "Hi" and taking a hit of caffeine for the road, but she was running late.

Realizing she had no idea how *long* her day would be, she stopped and opened the hall closet and snagged the camel-colored leather jacket she had bought her sophomore year for a steal at Oonas, the trendy vintage clothing store in Harvard Square.

"If this jacket could talk," she said to herself, thinking back to her Emerson days, and then laughed, grateful that it couldn't. The stories. Some were good. And some she wasn't proud of at all. She lived it, though. Good and bad. No one could argue that Echo Landers hadn't had the full college experience. But those days were now long gone.

She was living at home for Christ's sake, she thought while tossing the jacket on the back seat of her black soft-top CJ-7 Renegade Jeep.

"I have got to move out of here." Echo placed her bag on the passenger seat and was about to start the engine when she heard a blaring horn that sounded like the one used for signaling the end of a period at a Bruins' game. She knew that obnoxious sound all too well.

"Drake. How'd he get by the front gate?" she muttered looking up in her rearview mirror spotting the DRAKE'S CANTEEN truck blocking her in.

Drake Underhill got out of his truck and headed toward Echo's jeep. He was a former high school stud who had dulled at the edges — balding, with a paunch rapidly becoming bigger from the hot dogs he couldn't unload on the little leaguers.

"I gotta move outta this town," she said again under her breath as he came into full view wearing black spandex umpire shorts, a Sandy Point Gold's Gym tank top, and a Jesus necklace swinging in the breeze.

"Put on a smile, Echo," she urged herself, realizing her biggest regret in life was the secret she shared with Drake. And as a result, Drake Underhill and Echo Landers would always be connected. Yep, there were things in her past that she definitely wasn't proud of.

"Yeah, I gotta get outta this town," she said one more time before turning to face him.

J.T.

I stood at the entrance of *The Sandy Point Times* and checked my watch for a third time: 8:17. As the question, *Where the hell is she?* was forming in my mind, a jet-black Jeep tore around the corner and screeched to a stop in front of me.

Echo, sporting dark Jackie O. shades, leaned over, and pushed open the passenger door, the sounds of the Dave Matthews Band escaping from within.

"I know. I know. I'm late. I'm sorry. Get in," she said as she turned the volume down.

I pointed over to the Cabriolet. "I have to drop that car off at the ferry in a couple of hours, though."

"It's not yours?"

"No, I borrowed it from a waitress I worked with. Her boyfriend is coming back from the Vineyard today and is going to pick it up."

She laughed. "That's good. I thought if it was yours, you might be a little light in the loafers. 'Not that there's anything wrong with that,' to quote *Seinfeld*. What boat is he coming on?"

Damn, she even has my sense of humor.

"His boat docks at noon."

"Oh, okay, cool, we have tons of time. Jump in and we'll come back here and then I'll follow you to the ferry. You cool with that?"

"Sounds like a plan." I hopped in, buckled up, and noticed a sweet, orange scent lingering in the air.

Where is that tropical smell coming from?

Echo nodded at the buckle. "Smart man," she said before shifting gears and we were off. She pointed at two cup holders attached to her dash, each one containing a large Styrofoam cup that read: DRAKE'S CANTEEN.

"The one on the right is yours. I guessed on the cream and two sugars?"

"That's perfect," I said, reaching for the cup, even though since 4 a.m. I'd probably had enough caffeine to fuel a Colombian village.

"Consider it a peace offering for my tardiness, Mr. O'Rourke." She grinned, turned up Dave who was singing about some ants marching, and then refocused on the road.

I took a sip and scowled, "Ugh."

"I didn't say it was good," she said.

"Yeah," I agreed and laughed, "It tastes like shit. Some peace offering."

"Sorry about that," she began, but then turned her attention back to Dave Matthews. "I love this song. It's about longing to be a kid again. I always play it in the morning. Makes me grateful that I'm not a nine-to-fiver stuck in traffic on route 28 doing the two-point-five kids lifestyle."

"Apparently, you're not an *eight*-to-fiver either."

"I know. I'm like *never* late," she paused. "Okay, I just lied there... I try not to be late." The Jeep turned down a narrow road and climbed a hill past the Sandy Point Lighthouse.

Chauffeured by a stunning woman and beautiful scenery as our backdrop. *I could definitely get used to this!*

But then Echo sang along with Dave.

My laughter made her stop.

"What? You don't like my voice?"

"Let's just say that the dogs of Sandy Point are using their paws to block their ears right now."

Echo playfully punched me as she kept one hand on the wheel, "It's not that bad. Jesus."

"You're going to need more than Jesus. Girl, you got a voice for lip-sync. And no offense, I hate Dave Matthews."

She jerked the Jeep to the side of the road and popped it into neutral. "How can you hate Dave Matthews? How can anybody hate D.M.B.?"

"Well, it's really not Dave. It just brings back bad memories. Forget about it," I answered, opening a can of worms.

"J.T., now you gotta tell me or we're not going anywhere."

"Okay. You win. We're late though. You start driving and I'll tell you."

Satisfied, she shifted gears, and pulled back onto the road.

"The truth is I used to love Dave when my sister Erin was going to grad school in the early nineties, she got into them just as they were coming onto the scene. One time I had to drive her back to Westfield and she forced me to listen to them and by the end of the ride I was hooked."

"How many kids in your family?" Echo interrupted.

I paused for a minute, "My three older sisters and me."

"Wow, no brothers? That sucks. Okay, go on. So, why the change of heart?"

"Huh? Oh…Yeah, well, I met this girl at The Jar. I think it was the summer of 2000."

"Uh, oh. It's about a girl."

"Yep. Anyway, we got to be friendly."

"How friendly?"

"Not like *that* friendly. But it looked promising. At least, that's what I thought. Anyway, I scored four tickets to a show at Foxborough. So, I went with my buddy, his wife, and this chick, Lisa. I packed an amazing tailgate — shrimp cocktail, cheese and crackers, y'know, the whole nine. Anyway, we all drank beers, had laughs, and headed into the show. So, we're not in the stadium ten minutes when this drunk asshole wearing more chains than Mr. T comes up to Lisa. He's got the chains and attitude thing going, and out of 35,000 people, he's the only one not wearing his shirt. He's got it tucked in the back of his jeans-shorts, flexing his muscles, and is hitting on Lisa. Like all in her face. You know the type I mean?"

"All too well," she sighed.

"Now I don't know what to do, 'cause we're not a couple, but I figure this guy must be annoying her. So, I say to her, 'Hey Lisa, we gotta get to our seats.' Do you know what she said?"

"What?"

"She glared at me and snapped, 'Can't you see I'm talking to someone?' Then I heard her whisper and giggle to the guy, 'No, I'm not with him.' I just stood there. I mean it blew me away. And ten minutes later, she was five rows up making out with the asshole, all sloppy and shit, as Dave Matthews is singing, "Crash.""

"No way! No way! What a bitch!" Echo shook her head. "Did you ever see her again?"

I laughed. "No, but she left a message on my cell last year 'cause she was applying for a job at a magazine in New Hampshire and it turned out I knew the publisher 'cause my parents used to own a cabin near him. Anyway, she actually wanted me to give her a recommendation. Can you believe that shit?"

"What did you do?" She sounded angry.

"I called him five minutes later and told him the story. He said he was already onto her tactics. He said she seemed really high on herself and tried flirting with him, and he knew it was an act. She didn't have a chance anyway, but he loved saying no to her."

"That's great revenge. Shows how clueless she is calling you. But what I have to know is — because of that, you don't listen to D. M. B. anymore?"

"You're damn right." I nodded as we approached a modest Cape-style house.

"So, you're going to let that bitch ruin your Dave experience?"

"Yep."

"J.T., I think it sounds like you need to give Dave another chance."

"I don't think anything could make me change that feeling I get now when I hear his music. I almost get nauseous... Hey, enough about me. Now, it's your turn to share. Boyfriends? Bad dates?"

Echo pulled into the driveway in front of the Cape and turned to me and smiled. "Geez, I wish I could tell you, but unfortunately we have a job to do."

CHAPTER 8

OCTOBER 8, 1970

THURSDAY

DEVLIN

It was getting close to 9:30 p.m. Another half hour, and Devlin's fifteen-hour workday would finally be over. Sitting in his cruiser, parked outside of the Sandy Point Federal Savings Bank, he should've been tired. But he wasn't. He was wide-awake. And it had nothing to do with the stale coffee he slurped from his Styrofoam Pilgrim's Diner cup. It was more than just caffeine causing his blood to pump like an oil well. The adrenaline rush hit every time he thought of Anna Talbot. It had been six days and he was still smiling. And it wasn't just any smile. It was a lottery-winner smile. At least, that's how Captain Tadmor had described it that morning.

Devlin had agreed that the ol' Cap was right on target. He definitely held the winning ticket. And he had no plans on giving it up. Tadmor wasn't the only one who had noticed the rookie cop's giddy mood.

At the department, Officer Scott Gallo had nudged Rodney Farrell and jokingly accused him of breaking into the evidence room and smoking all the confiscated marijuana.

Devlin responded with an over-the-top laugh.

This elicited a stage whisper behind Gallo's hand to Farrell, "He must've got laid."

Devlin laughed even more.

Yes, he was high, but it wasn't because of drugs. And it certainly wasn't because he got laid. In fact, he was high because he didn't get laid.

If I blurted that admission at The Angry Fisherman, I'd be shut off and there'd be a lot of broken glass to clean up from patrons dropping their pints in disbelief.

It was the truth. He knew he had to keep those feelings to himself, so he had only called one of his Nam buddies, Brett Beldman, who was now a shoe salesman in Iowa.

After recounting his trip up to Cambridge to visit the stunning Radcliffe student, the line was silent for a second before Beldman replied with mock concern, "Oh, shit, Mikey, this is not good."

"What do you mean, Brett?"

"You, my friend, are all done."

"No, I'm not. I just think she's a great girl. That's all I'm saying."

Beldman laughed, "Yep, sure. Hey, remember what you guys said about me when I'd always show you my Sheila's picture."

They both laughed the saying together, "You're whipped like a slave. And a slave you will be."

After a couple of chuckles, Devlin gave in, "Okay, maybe I do like her. But it wouldn't work out. She's got college, y'know… a future, and she comes from money, and she'll probably marry a politician or someone that comes from means."

"And you don't come from money? Mikey, your parents have a mansion on a private island, for Christ's sake. It's okay to want to play small-town cop, but don't deny who you are or where you came from. You're from money, too. Look, just go out with this girl and enjoy yourself. Stop analyzing everything. I have to go. Basketball season is around the corner, and we have a sale on Chuck Taylors and the store is packed. But one other thing…"

"Yeah," Devlin said.

"Call me if you decide to go to the ring store." Beldman laughed, his exit leaving Devlin with a deadline.

He took another sip of his coffee while thinking about what Beldman had said about not analyzing the moment.

Rolling down his window and emptying out what would've been his last sip, he said to the black night, "The bastard's right. I should just enjoy it."

So, he did. The memories of the last month of getting to know Anna came rushing forward. His first thought was of the day he stopped her for speeding. Three hours after their encounter, he was drinking a can of Schaeffer while taking an outdoor shower, wondering if she would call. He finished his beer slowly, massaged by the evening sun that peeked from above the enclosed shower, before turning off the showerhead. As he reached up for his towel that hung over the wooden points, it suddenly vanished.

"Mom?"

No answer.

"Mom?"

Still no answer.

"Mom, that's not funny. I'm naked."

"I know. Why do you think I took it, Michael?"

"Anna, is that you?" He asked and a second later the towel flapped over the shower door and hit him in the face. He grabbed it, dried off quickly, wrapped it around his waist, and opened the door.

"Anna sounds a lot better than 'Miss Talbot.'" She stood in front of him wearing a brown poncho and jeans and holding a large picnic basket.

"I decided to skip the phone call and the games. No more games. I think we're done with them. Don't you? So, I hopped on the ferry and … I hope you'll settle for lobster salad sandwiches. I didn't want to get involved with big boiling pots. Anyway, it's an old family recipe. I used bits of pineapple. Geez, I hope you like pineapple." Her smile was irresistible, her blond hair illuminated by the falling golden light.

"Oh… ah… yeah… I love pineapple."

Anna's smile turned to a concerned frown. She placed her left hand to her mouth to stifle a gasp and set the basket on the ground. Devlin knew why. It was a reaction he was used to. But he hadn't had his shirt off in front of a woman, especially one he wanted. He felt the sudden embarrassment run to his face. But after she digested the sight, she moved toward him. Slowly. Confidently. Deliberately. Closer and closer. Until she was only inches away — her rose fragrance choking his senses. She didn't say a word. He didn't either. He couldn't.

Her green eyes locked on his pale blue ones with an intensity that he never had felt before. Her eyes moved back to the divot-shaped scars that tattooed his chest and right shoulder. She reached out with her index finger and lightly brushed each mark as she looked up to him.

"Shrapnel," is all he could reply.

She nodded and placed her palm on his beating chest and reached up and kissed him on the cheek and whispered, "I'm sorry that happened to you, Michael. But I want you to know something now before we go any further. I want to get to know all of you. The beautiful and the scarred. Do you want to get to know me like that?"

"Yes, Anna," he whispered, "I do."

She kissed him again, this time on the lips. It was soft and slow. And he pulled her close to him. They suddenly both stopped, knowing if they kept kissing, they wouldn't stop.

Her hand felt his heart again and she smiled softly, "Feels like mine. Now, get dressed and I'll meet you down at the beach."

And the rest of that night, her wish came true. They sat by a crackling bonfire, and he opened up to her about all of his hopes and dreams. They snuggled and laughed while sipping wine and eating burnt s'mores. But he also told her about the scars — his poor relationship with his father, not really knowing his mother, and Vietnam. He confided in her about things that happened in Nam that even he hadn't been able to face. It should've been strange to share so much so quickly, but he knew it wasn't the buzz from the wine that had made it so easy for him to talk. It was a feeling that took hold of him when he first witnessed her talking to Fishy Bryden. She was a genuinely good person.

When she shared her dream of wanting to live a happy and simple life on Cape Cod with a houseful of children, Devlin couldn't help but throw another log on the fire.

A month later, he anticipated he'd take a trip over the bridge to reality, but he had been wrong. That fire was still burning. Brighter than ever. And that was why he was still smiling six days later.

Of course, it didn't start out that way... He chuckled to himself and checked his watch: 9:42. Another eighteen minutes and his shift would be over.

He started his cruiser and decided to circle the Main Street area. As he began driving, he thought of his visit to the apartment building on Irving Street that housed many of "the Cliffies."

Anna had greeted him outside, enthusiastically waving two tickets to the

Harvard-Rutgers game. She wore the same brown poncho, but this time, instead of jeans, a tweed miniskirt accentuated the lines from her thighs to her calves.

"You played football. I thought this would be fun for you," she said, grabbing his hand and skipping along in her penny loafers.

At the time, Devlin was able to feign excitement. But at the game, his light blue polyester sports coat and maroon tie with scrimshaw tack stood out in the ocean of

button down Oxford shirts and tweed jackets with suede elbow patches. He was clearly uncomfortable and had taken a belt from a passing half pint of black-berry brandy to settle his nerves. And then he had another chug when Anna's group of friends talked about an anti-Vietnam rally, they were all planning to attend.

He took an even longer gulp when the moderator of the group, Jack — whom Devlin had met when he almost arrested him on the Talbot lawn — slurred vulgarities about "baby killers" over in Nam representing the U.S.A.

Anna took the flask from Devlin, handed it back to Jack, and asked, "Did you know Michael served in Vietnam?"

Stunned, Jack answered for the group, "Uh, no."

"And did you know Michael was trained so he could kill someone with his bare hands in five seconds or less?"

Devlin tried not to laugh, lurching forward and causing the pseudo-activist to back up.

"Uh, no." He answered and nervously nursed his flask.

"And did you know, Jack, I'm pretty sure Michael wants to kill you right now. But you know why he won't?"

Jack shrugged, "Uh, no."

"He's not a baby killer." Anna then turned, grabbed Devlin's hand, and kissed him on the cheek and said, "Let's get the hell out of here, honey."

He smiled to the open jaws, "It was nice meeting all of you."

They spent the rest of the day bouncing up and down on the T, occasionally hopping off to snoop around for pre-Revolutionary War furniture in dusty antique shops and thumb through broken binder classics in musty bookstores, or to nibble on hot peanuts from greasy brown bags while dodging the desperate pigeons that scoured Haymarket Square.

It had been a great day. But an even better night, Devlin thought, as his cruiser rolled past Pop Tucker's darkened store.

He had taken Anna to The Wursthaus for a German feast with the pact that their forks had to wander to the other's plate.

"Let's not be shy," he had said. And they weren't. They attacked their dishes of Black Forest smoked ham, potato cakes with bacon, Regensburg sausages with sauerkraut, and two white beers which were served by a healthy, big-breasted waitress wearing an outfit that made her resemble the Swiss Miss on the hot chocolate box. Of course, she wasn't as innocent, leaning over in front of Devlin so her ample breasts might shake a few more, dollars out of his pocket come tip time. They did.

There was no room left for dessert, so instead they opted to take the trolley to Faneuil Hall for music and a nightcap at Lily's Piano Bar. After an hour of watching the pianist, a music major from Berklee, croon away, Anna finished her second glass of cabernet and declared herself "drunk."

Devlin crunched on ice chips from his empty Coca-Cola glass and nodded, "Let's go," and left their booth to toss a couple of crumpled bills into the oval shaped tip glass to help the Ivory Tickler pay his rent or maybe even get a haircut.

The struggling musician swayed a thank you as his fingers moved along the keys and nodded again when Devlin and Anna whisked past, out the door, leaving the eager revelers behind to finish singing the chorus of *Hey Jude*.

They may have left the bar, but the "Na na na na" chant got stuck in their heads and exited with them. They hummed it softly in the back of the cab, but they took it up a notch when they were dropped off. Arm in arm and out of key, they merrily sang it while strolling back to Anna's place.

When they got to the entrance of her building, they both stopped, each one contemplating on what would or should happen next. Neither one spoke for a while. They just stood in the star-filled, nippy autumn night staring at one another.

With his palm, Devin finally reached down and tenderly cupped Anna's face.

"For a chilly night, your face feels hot. I hope you're not coming down with something," he said.

"Oh, I think I am. But I'm also drunk, remember?" She giggled and then paused before continuing, "I hate the thought of you driving all the way back to the Cape tonight. It's such a long drive."

He laughed nervously, "I hate the thought, too."

Her eyes glanced up at the second level of the building and then back at him, "There's something you should know, Michael."

"Oh..." He had a feeling he knew what she was going to say.

"I have feelings for you, but you should know. You should know..."

"It's al—"

"That I'm against the Vietnam War. I'm going to that rally, and I'm going to speak. I really like you, Michael, but there are some things we will probably not agree on. I want to have a voice in this world. And, if you can't accept that, I don't think this will work out. I'm sorry, but I just really feel..." Her rapid-fire was halted when she realized Devlin was laughing.

"What? You think that's funny?"

"No, no, no." He waved his hand, "I thought you were going to tell me something else."

"Something else?"

"Yeah," He pointed up at the window she had been eyeing.

Anna got it, "Oh, that. No. We'll talk about that in a minute. I just wanted you to know that I am a different kind of woman. I want to have children and a husband someday, but I also want to maintain my own identity. And if you can't accept that..."

"Okay. Okay. Can I say something now?"

"Go ahead."

"First off, who says I'm for the war? If I were asked, I'd honestly say I don't know what I'm for. The only thing I'd ask of you is to remember it's fine to have a problem with the war, but the majority of soldiers over there are good men. They are doing what their country asked them to do and they don't deserve the blanket statements like the one your drunk friend made today."

"I agree."

"But, even if you didn't, I wouldn't like it, but I'd respect it. Because it's your opinion. And that's what I want you to know. This whole thing is new and refreshing for me, to be around a woman who isn't always going to nod her head because she is supposed to... Now... about the other thing." His eyes gestured up at the second level again.

She smiled. "Did you know *Hey Jude* is over seven minutes long? I figure you might have to sing it about twenty times on the ride home tonight. But get over here."

She pulled his tie and he came to her. She kissed him for a long while, the

95

nightlights suddenly spinning in the background. His body pressed into hers, Devlin's lips moved to her neck.

Anna whispered, breathing heavy, "God, I want you, Michael. But we have to stop. We have to wait. I'm sorry."

He did stop. But then he kissed her lightly on the lips, "Don't be sorry. Don't ever be sorry about that. When it's time, it will be time."

Anna placed her palm on his cheek. "I know. I just… I just… It will be worth the wait, Michael. I promise."

He kissed her again, pulled her close to him, and said, "That's one thing we both can agree on. But there was something you were wrong about earlier."

"What's that?"

"It won't be that long of a drive home tonight because you already got my engine started."

Anna had playfully punched him, and she had been right. He did sing "Hey Jude" all twenty times to the Cape. And he was still singing it as he made his loop around Main Street when he passed Spokes for Folks bike shop. But then he stopped mid-lyric. The lights were on in the back of the store.

That's strange.

Mr. Renna, the owner, was an early bird not a night owl. He spotted a sparkling baby blue '69 Chevy Camaro parked behind the shop. He knew the owner of that car and openly despised him. But, putting his personal feelings aside, seeing the car still made him curious.

What is Paul Harrison, a reporter for the Sandy Point Standard Times doing in a bike shop at ten o'clock at night?

He thought about radioing in that he was going to check out the shop for suspicious activity, but then he remembered Alice Harper just got on duty for the night as dispatcher. He didn't want to deal with her nicotine-laden sarcasm, and it was probably nothing important anyway, so he decided to park and take a look.

He walked to the back entrance of the shop and was about to knock when he heard voices coming from inside. They sounded heated. He slowly opened the screen door and headed down the dark hallway toward a light coming from the back room in the direction of the voices. He was about to announce his presence but now he was close enough to identify the voices.

Those are kids' voices.

He listened.

"Come on! Are you nuts? You want to trade me a number 173 *Dr. Strange* for my *Batman* number 117? That's not fair at all, Zach! Tell him, Chucky." The voice squeaked. Devlin recognized the boy's voice immediately: Fishy Bryden. And the Zach that he was arguing with had to be Zachary Goodrich, eldest son of the Pilgrim Diner owner and server of old coffee. Devlin had just been gypped with the mud his old man had poured him, so while listening, he figured the son was probably a swindler-in-training.

"I don't know. It doesn't sound that bad," Chucky responded, and Devlin knew it was Mr. Renna's son, Chuck, Jr.

Typical. Chucky always seems to go along with the crowd.

Another voice broke in, "No. Fishy's right. You got to add something more to the deal, Chucky. How about an *Andy Panda* number 46? You told me you don't even like those, and Fishy needs that one. So, where's the loss?"

"Alright."

"Thanks, Jared," Fishy's voice.

Jared Lareby. His father won't have a problem when he hands off the reins to his market come retirement time.

"So, we made the deal, Mr. Harrison. Was it a good one for me?" Fishy asked.

"As a lifelong collector and assessor of your comic book club deals, I pronounce that there is no clear-cut winner. You both won on that one."

All the boys cheered, and Devlin smiled to himself.

Yes, it was late, but he remembered being briefed at the station that there was no school the following morning due to the teacher in-service day. Since there was an adult to monitor the situation, Devlin was going to leave undetected, but then he heard Paul Harrison continue talking and he was curious why a man in his mid-40s was spending his night talking about Batman to a bunch of kids.

"Boys, I'm looking at our list of members and we're missing Greggie, Trafton, Davis, Jeremy, Oliver, and Murray. That's too bad, because I have a special comic for all of you tonight but maybe I shouldn't show it?"

Something made Devlin take a mental note of the names.

"No, C'mon, Mr. Harrison, show us," they all pleaded.

"Since they are going to miss the surprise, we'll keep it our secret, deal?" Harrison said, and Devlin moved closer to the door.

"Deal!" they all agreed.

"Pass this around. In this magazine is an example of comics that big boys read. And they also have beautiful pictures," Harrison said. There was no response. It was quiet for several seconds.

Something in Devlin's gut began to move, but he *didn't* move. He remained in the hallway, hoping his instincts were wrong.

Finally, Fishy Bryden broke the silence, "Mr. Harrison, what is that woman doing to that man?"

Harrison chuckled, "Having fun." And then he chuckled again.

It was the last recognizable noise he made that night. Storming into the room, Devlin spied the three other boys that hovered behind a bewildered Fishy who was holding the opened *Playboy* with the cartoon of a woman giving a man a blowjob.

"Fishy, give me that." Devlin snapped, snatching it out of his hands.

"Officer Devlin, I'm ah…" Fishy began.

Despite the rising anger, Devlin thought quickly. Decisively. They all lived within walking distance, except for Fishy who lived about four miles away.

He barked the following order, "I want all of you to go home right now. I won't tell your parents if you go home right now. Chucky, I'll lock up. I have to have a talk with Mr. Harrison. And if any of you mention any of this, you'll be in big trouble with the police."

They all hurried out the door except Fishy.

Devlin grabbed him by the collar, "Wait in my cruiser."

"But, Officer Devlin…"

He pointed at the door and released him. "Now, Fishy!"

After Fishy scampered out, Devlin grabbed his nightstick, slamming the door shut with it and turned to Harrison who was eyeing the stick. Harrison was about to speak when Devlin threw the *Playboy* at him causing Harrison to put his hands up to shield himself. Devlin bolted over and jammed the stick sideways under Harrison's throat, lifting him off the floor and at the same time pressing him against the wall.

"I didn't radio this call in, so technically I'm not here. So, whatever happens to you, people would only be able to speculate, so let's get something straight, you piece of shit! I know your kind! I've seen it. So, don't even try your bullshit excuses! I have a simple message, and I'll say it clearly and slowly." Through clenched teeth, Devlin paused, raising him higher against the wall.

Harrison's face turned a deep shade of crimson and looked seconds from passing out.

"If you go near any of those boys again, I'll kill you. You got that?"

Harrison's watering eyes moved from side to side communicating: Yes.

"I know how your kind works. You'll wait until you think you're safe and then you'll retaliate. Well, if you try that, I repeat again, I *will* kill you. I've killed for less."

Harrison's eyes, like spinning pin balls, paused long enough to answer again: Yes.

"Now, get out of here." Devlin pulled the stick back causing Harrison to collapse to the floor before rising, wheezing, coughing, and massaging his neck.

"I said get out of here!" he bellowed, and Harrison sprinted, bouncing off the walls down the hallway and out the screen door.

A moment later, the sound of the Camaro's engine roared and was quickly in the distance.

Devlin wiped his forehead clean, silently scolding himself for losing control. But what was the alternative? If he brought him in for distributing pornography to minors, he knew it wouldn't stick. It was just a *Playboy*, some would argue. But he had seen Harrison's kind in Vietnam, showing the young village boys dirty pictures and then slowly manipulating their minds to get what they really wanted. It had made him sick and seeing Harrison brought it all back. Devlin never had done anything to help the village boys. That shame would always be with him. But he was given a chance at redemption in the bike store — a chance to stop it before it started. He knew he had just made an enemy for life and would always have to keep his eyes out for the reporter in the baby blue Camaro. He picked up the magazine and shoved it in his back pocket.

"Fishy," he said to himself, took a deep breath and headed out, locking the door behind him.

He drove along and was calm but stern when he ordered Fishy to stay away from Paul Harrison. He planned on giving the same speech to all of the other boys.

Was I overreacting? Perhaps. Boys will boys…

He remembered when he was one and stumbled upon his father's *Playboys* while going through his parents' bureau to borrow a pair of clean socks to wear to church.

Of course, Devlin had *found* them. At the age of nine. He wasn't *given* the *Playboys* by a middle-aged man and instructed to study them like a geography map.

Sick piece of shit!

He was convinced even more that he hadn't overreacted when Fishy replied.

"Officer Devlin, can I tell you something and you won't tell anyone else?"

"Sure, Fishy," Devlin turned to the passenger seat urging him to continue.

"I'm kind of glad you came there tonight. I didn't feel good looking at those pictures. I just... just want to look at comic books. Does that make me different? 'Cause I probably should want to look at girls, huh? Geez, I hope I'm not queer."

At that moment, Devlin wanted to find Harrison and throttle him. In one action he had turned a happy-go-lucky boy into a confused kid. He knew he had to stop that thinking immediately.

"Of course, you're not, Fishy. When I was your age, I was just like you. I liked to fish and read comic books. I didn't like girls until I was 16."

"Oh, I like girls, Officer Devlin. Lindsey Courtland is my girlfriend. I go fishing with her when I'm not fishing with Greggie. It's just that... that... I don't like her like how Mr. Harrison was showing us. But maybe I'm supposed to? All the other boys there are older than me and they'd probably think I'm stupid if I said that, so please don't tell them."

"Listen to me, Fishy. You're not stupid... Do you have fun with Lindsey?"

"Yeah, she's pretty fun. She likes to do the stuff I do, and she's pretty good at skipping rocks. I even told her when I get old someday, I'm going to marry her and give her my lucky necklace." Fishy pulled out the half silver and half gold shaped piece of metal from under his shirt and displayed it proudly.

"I think that's great. That's the way you should be at nine, and don't listen to anyone else. Okay?"

"Okay." The boy smiled.

"Hey, so how's that boat you and Greggie found?" Devlin asked, trying to change the subject.

"Oh, it's a peach, Officer Devlin. We've taken her all around looking for treasure — and guess what?" Fishy's excited voice was back.

"What?"

"A few weeks ago, we were on our way rowing to your island to go looking for Indian arrowheads when we found a deck chair washed ashore. It's in good shape. It even has the name of the ship on the back of it. The ship's called *Island Waves*. Greggie hopes it's a treasure ship. Have you ever heard of it?"

Yeah, the booze cruise barge out of Hyannis.

He didn't want to burst the boy's bubble, especially after his innocence had already been compromised.

"Actually, I have heard of it. I heard it was a whaling ship and it only went after the really big whales and sometimes, even sea serpents. I wonder why it's in these waters."

"Oh, wow! Boy! I bet it's looking for a giant squid or something. Wait 'til I tell Greggie!"

Devlin pulled beyond Fishy's driveway and Fishy gave a thank you-nod for the gesture.

"Thanks, Officer Devlin. I don't think my dad's home, but if he was and saw the car, I think he'd get really mad at me."

"Did he know you were out alone tonight?"

"No, sir. He thought I was out with Jeremy. But Jeremy went to bed early. He worked after school for Dad and was really tired… Please don't tell my dad. I promise I won't stay out this late ever again in my whole life."

"Okay, as long as you keep the other promise we talked about."

"I will. I swear on your badge and my necklace."

"Okay, Fishy… Oh by the way, did you and Greggie ever end up naming the boat *Anna*?"

"Not exactly. We kind of did but not really," Fishy said as he opened the door.

"What do you mean?"

"Promise to keep another secret?" Fishy said.

"I promise."

"Greggie has a big crush on Miss Talbot… I mean Anna. Remember she said I could call her that?"

Devlin nodded for him to continue.

"Anyway, you can't tell anyone. I pinkie swore. Greggie would kill me."

Devlin put three fingers up, "On my badge."

"Super. Greggie likes to write poetry and he wrote a poem about Anna, and we decided to name the boat after the name of the poem."

"What's the name of the poem?"

"'*Sunshine Dream*.' He says Anna's hair is like the color of a pot of leprechaun's gold that lies behind the sunshine. And whenever we see her, he always says to me, 'There goes my dream. My sunshine. My sunshine dream.' That's all from his poem."

Devlin wanted to laugh in admiration but kept a tight lip.

Greggie Crocker was a romantic that he could take a few lessons from. The little boy couldn't have been more right in how he described Anna.

SUNSHINE.

That would be a nickname she wouldn't shake.

And as he drove off, he realized among all the ugliness he had seen in the world, he now really did have sunshine — *his* sunshine dream. It was going on seven days and his "lottery winner smile" was back.

He had every reason to believe it was permanent.

CHAPTER 9

JUNE 8, 2004

TUESDAY

J.T.

illian Dumas insisted that Echo and I relax at the picnic table in the backyard while she went into the house to "fetch us some cold drinks."

"I never even asked why we're here," Echo whispered, as Ms. Dumas hollered from the window, "Is pink lemonade okay?"

"That sounds great," we both answered and then I turned to Echo. "I guess her dog is missing."

"Are you serious? Geez, Crockerman is going a little crazy with these fluff pieces."

"There's is a little more to it. You see..." I stopped when the elderly woman with a dried-up prune face and a skeletal frame that could've been used for casket fittings appeared. She carried a tray. It held a vase that contained a daisy, a homemade carrot cake, ice-filled glasses, and a carton of NEWMAN'S OWN PINK LEMONADE.

I'm not Martha Stewart, but it seemed odd to me that we were being served from a carton considering the rest of the presentation. As Lillian poured the lemonade into our glasses, I shot a quizzical glance over at Echo. When she finished pouring, Lillian placed the carton at an angle, so Paul Newman's face was part of our circle.

Lillian took out a cigarette, lit it, and placed it in between her chalky lips. "I hope you don't mind."

"Not at all," Echo and I both said, acknowledging the lung rocket.

She choked laughter behind a plume of smoke. "No, not the cancer stick." Her yellow nails pointed at the carton, "I meant, I hope you don't mind that Mr. Newman is joining us."

"Oh... um... no!" I said, trying not to look at Echo.

Wha-ck-o!

"I mean, I know it's not the real Mr. Newman. I'm not crazy or anything. It's just that I like looking at his picture. That's all. Makes me feel young inside. Reminds me of when I was a looker. You know what I mean?" She turned to Echo.

"Oh...ah, sure..." She was caught off guard but recovered quickly. "Kind of like how I feel when I see a picture of Brad Pitt."

"Sure, I suppose. Ever sleep with Brad Pitt, though?" Laughing, she took another puff from her Marlboro Light.

"Huh?" Echo was in shock at the candid question.

"Never mind." Her eyes narrowed as she handed me an 8x10 photograph of a Jack Russell terrier. "This is Cool Hand."

The dog was wearing a blue bandana around his neck and resembled Eddie from the T.V. show *Frasier*.

How many reruns did I watch of that show at The Jar?

I studied the bandana briefly and then passed it on to Echo.

"As in *Cool Hand Luke*?" I asked, jotting down notes on my legal pad, referring to the classic Newman movie.

"Yes," She nodded.

"Wow, you *are* a Paul Newman fan, huh?" Echo added.

"Yes, I suppose I am." Lillian answered quickly and, like a magician, pulled a blue bandana out of thin air and placed it on the table in front of her. It was ripped in several places.

Her eyes watered. "I saved this. He's been gone for a week now."

"What happened to him?" Echo asked.

"What *happened* to him?" Lillian repeated the question as if to say *How can you ask that?*

"Ms. Dumas, I haven't updated Echo on what you told Mr. Crocker."

"Oh." It registered, and she took a puff and then flicked ashes angrily in the direction of the woods, "I'll tell you what happened then. Those goddamn coyotes out there had my poor Cool Hand for dinner. That's why I called Greg because something has to be done about them. They're taking over The Cape. And if you don't believe me, check it out on the net. It'll tell you. Those bastards are attacking more and more. Cats, dogs, pet rabbits. They even attacked a toddler not too long ago. The baby ended up with something like 15 stitches. Did you know that?"

I looked up from my pad. "Yes, I read that. I think it was in Sandwich."

She nodded, feeling validated, "So, you know what I'm talking about?"

"Yes, I do. But I have to ask you this question. How do you know coyotes killed Cool Hand?" I readied my pen.

"Because they've been tracking through my garden and knocking over my barrels for weeks. And I've seen them do it. So, did Cool Hand. He'd bark like crazy when he saw them."

"Did you actually see the coyotes attack Cool Hand?"

She killed her cigarette in the ashtray and then sparked up another and puffed. "No, but I found the bandana. And I just know from the circumstances."

"If it's not too painful, could you describe the night he disappeared?"

"It was last Tuesday night. He was howling. He liked to howl to music. You see, he had such good hearing and beyond the woods is the ocean. And sometimes the lobstermen play music when they retrieve their traps. And on quiet evenings, I can even hear it ever so faintly. It doesn't bother me though, 'cause it sounds like classical and, like I say, I can barely hear it. But not Cool Hand. It's a concert for him. Anyway, some fisherman must've been playing music because Cool Hand was howling away, so I let him out to enjoy it. I thought I had closed the back gate. I really did. But he took off into the woods. I called and called. Usually, he'd come back when I called. But he didn't this time. The next morning, I went looking for him, but all I found was the bandana. Nothing else. I know the coyotes got him, and it's my fault." She wiped a tear away with her free hand.

Echo said, "Don't beat yourself up. It's not your fault."

Lillian took a quick hit from her Marlboro. "You're right. It's this goddamn town's fault for being so goddamn P.C. about it. They're afraid of PETA or some other 'Coyotes Are People Too' bullshit group. These coyotes are destroying lives, and I say they should shoot those bastards. And you can quote me on that,

Mr. O'Rourke." Her nail tapped against my legal pad as I wondered what exactly in the quote could be printed.

I had the feeling that Echo was biting her lip as she snapped shots of Lillian holding the torn bandana. We thanked Lillian and told her we were going into the woods to see if we could find some coyotes so Echo could take a few shots. She muttered, "I wish those were gunshots," and cleared the table and went back into the house with Paul Newman.

It wasn't until we were in the woods that Echo spoke up, "Now that Joanne Woodward is no longer around, can you tell me what the hell I'm doing here?"

I chuckled at her joke and shrugged, "Crocker told me he wanted you to take pictures of the coyotes. Except: during my research, I found out that they're mostly nocturnal, so we're probably wasting time. But let's walk around a bit. Maybe we'll find the dog's remains."

"Oh goody." Seeming a little tense, she clapped her hands in mock joy. I ignored it.

"Hey, what's that woman's deal, anyway? You guys mentioned that she is a complainer."

"She is. About stuff like her road not being plowed or the trees on the sidewalk not being pruned. Y'know, she lives alone and wants attention, but I guess this time she might have a legitimate gripe."

"Yeah, but in defense of the coyotes, it's kind of circumstantial. Hey, why don't you sing? The high-pitch noise might draw them out?"

"Very funny." Echo raised her brow at me then stopped walking and took in the scenery.

"She seems so lonely. Is she a widow?" I asked.

"Why? You want to take her to a Dave show?" Echo laughed and continued. "My Mom told me once that she had an affair for, like, years, with a guy named Williams... I think that was his name. He lived on Oyster Island. He always promised he'd leave his wife, but never did."

"Good thing I didn't mention to her that in my research I found out that coyotes mate for life."

Echo laughed, but then sighed. "She might have a hell of a lot more to complain about than just coyotes if that bill passes."

"What bill is that?"

"The town is considering selling 50 acres or so of the woods to some big-time developer. It's an issue that's going to get heated in the coming months. But you know, a part of me wouldn't mind a bunch of condos replacing these woods."

"Really? You don't strike me at all as the type who'd want to destroy nature."

"Normally, I'm not. But these woods and I have a bad history. When I was eight years old I got lost in here. For two whole days. I mean, I thought I was going to die. In fact, I'm getting flashbacks right now. Let's get the hell out of here."

"Wow. Sure. I understand. So, how did you survive?" I said as we headed down the path back in the direction of Lillian's house.

"Well, that's why Crockerman and I are so close. The first time I met him was the second night I was lost."

"What do you mean?"

"The first night, I survived on raspberries, but the second night, when I was really giving up, Crockerman found me. He told me the whole town was looking for me. It was so late that he built a fire. I remember him giving me a Kit Kat bar and telling me about his adventures on the high seas, which I now know he made up. But, man, did those stories keep me entertained as we waited for daybreak. He kept me warm and safe that night. We've been close ever since. He's one hell of a guy."

"I guess so. But he's no Paul Newman." I laughed.

"Or Brad Pitt." She winked.

————

We picked up the Cabriolet at the paper and then dropped it off at the ferry. After I handed the keys to the parking lot attendant, I hopped into the Jeep.

"I just got off the phone with Crockerman and he asked me to help you get everything on your to-do list. Wants you to get settled so then he can really work you."

"Oh, you don't have to help."

Damn, I should've put her on the list!

"Hey, to be truthful, he said I'd be on the clock. It's either hang with you or take pictures of Girl Scout Troop 31's car wash. So, what do you gotta do?"

Thanks, Crocker!

I grabbed the piece of paper out of my pants pocket and began to read.

"One, open a bank account. Two, buy a car. Three, buy a mountain bike. Four, go food shopping."

Echo took the list in for a minute and then popped into gear, spun her wheel, and headed down a side street.

"Okay, here's the deal. I'm not only going to help you with your list, J.T., but we're also going to snag some stories for Crockerman as we do it."

"Sweet. Thanks."

She put her finger to the air. "There is a catch."

"Shoot."

"I want a purple Misty from Dairy Queen and on that shopping list, there better be a six pack of Corona, some limes, and a couple of steaks, because you're cooking us dinner when we're finished."

I bit down my grin, "How do you like your steak?"

She laughed, "Why does your tone sound like some kind of bad, sexual innuendo?"

Well...

It's not that often I have a gorgeous woman driving me around, never mind one helping me with "husband and wife" errands like opening a bank account and buying a car. So, I decided to have fun with it and pretend, in my mind of course, that we actually were a couple.

The Sandy Point Federal Savings Bank parking lot was jammed, so I jumped out of the Jeep and Echo said she'd join me after she found a spot. The first thing I noticed about my make-believe relationship is that other men would always threaten it. I filled out forms for the disinterested, red power-tie-wearing, bank president who looked to be in his desperate forties. Suddenly, his expression changed.

Mr. Trafton Brown, Jr., came to life when Echo walked through the door. I only knew his name because he literally knocked his nameplate off his desk and almost bulldozed an elderly woman as he rushed to greet Echo. The expression on his face was like a traffic light. First it was green as he chatted away, but then it flipped to red as Echo pointed over at me. Then they talked for a minute. She smiled and nodded away and must've used the buzzword — *coworkers* — because his tires squealed as his light turned green again.

Ten minutes later, he was Mr. Chatty with me, opening my account with a smile and providing a story about his passion for classical music and how his bank was funding the Sandy Point Orchestra to play for an AIDS benefit in D.C.

The power of a beautiful woman's smile!

And it was powerful. I continued to witness her control over the middle-aged men of the Point — or their points — at our next three stops.

First, we went to Murray Philbrick Junior's Dealership. Despite there being two other drooling salesmen on duty, Murray, sporting a skunk-colored crew cut and shaped like the spark plugs he sold, threw down his oily Italian sub, licked his fingers, and leapt out of his yellow, vinyl chair to deal with Echo and her "coworker." She knew just how to handle him. He was showing me a red Saab convertible that had 81,000 miles on it when Echo threw her hands up.

"C'mon, Murray, a SAAB?"

"What's wrong with that?"

"You know SAAB stands for Shitty Automobile Always Breaks down. You want him buying a car in Hyannis?"

"Jesus, Echo, keep it down," he said looking around. "Why'd you always gotta bust my balls?"

"Same reason a dog licks *his* balls. 'Cause he can." She gave a coy smile.

Murray turned to me. "She can hang with the guys. That's a problem. But the real problem is those goddamn eyes. Gets me every time. That's why she's driving that Jeep for pennies. Watch out for those eyes, man. If you know what's good for you."

The comment drew an awkward silence, but I recovered with a lie, "I won't have to worry about that. I already have a girlfriend."

I received a bewildered glance from Echo as Murray clapped his hands and laughed. "Good, 'cause my divorce is final next week. So, watch out, Echo. I plan to be hitting on you like a blackjack table."

"Except they'll be no 21 for you, Murray." She laughed.

He shook his head and said to me, "The chick is quick. You gotta love that in a woman. Now let's get you some wheels. What's your speed?"

"I wouldn't mind buying a Jeep like Echo's, y'know, something just to drive around town."

Echo smiled, "Something to drive around town for pennies is what J.T. means."

Murray rolled his eyes and then pointed to his crotch, "I know. I know. I feel the Echo Landers vise tightening again… Okay, I think I got something. Follow me… goddamn eyes…" he muttered to himself. A half hour later, I was sitting in his yellow vinyl chair about to sign papers for a 2001 red Jeep Wrangler.

I wasn't going to purchase the Jeep for pennies, but whatever power Echo's eyes cast, I knew it cost Murray some profit. He paced back and forth holding and staring at his pen for a while before finally handing it over with the painful reluctance similar to a parent giving up their newborn to an adoption agent. Murray's face tightened even more as he watched me beep good-bye and drive his baby out of the lot.

A couple of hours later, we were headed for Lareby's Market. Outside, there was a sweat-soaked construction worker guiding a jackhammer that hopped along, breaking ground for an addition. That demolition noise jockeyed for attention with the piped-in voice of Michael Bolton, who serenaded all sixteen aisles. I was rooting for the jackhammer to win, but unfortunately, there was no escaping Bolton's grating pipes. As Echo and I split up our list, I thought as long as there were supermarkets, elevators, and dentist offices, Michael Bolton would always win — long live cheesy music.

Echo strode off hunting for the steaks while I circled the store searching for the extras. In produce, I witnessed yet another example validating Crocker's *It's a Wonderful Life* pep talk on how stories were gathered for his small, seaside town paper. While I was tossing three limes into my plastic bag, a round woman's eyes zoomed in on my ring-less finger, then she flashed her pumpkin face smile and suggested that if I liked fruit and "veggies," I should check out the upcoming farmers and flea market run by the Sandy Point Hospital nurses to support the troops in Iraq.

I smiled, told her I was a reporter and took out my pen and pad and began taking notes. She frowned — her pumpkin face now resembling the day after Halloween — realizing my interest was elsewhere. But she continued to give me a great angle for a story anyway. Another nurse, Mrs. Ganet, had just received a letter from her grandson describing how he felt the military wasn't sending over enough supplies to armor the vehicles. Mrs. Ganet, "always one to take action," decided to organize a market where everything from apples to a grand piano would be sold and all proceeds would be sent to her grandson's unit.

I inked a star next to the article idea and scribbled *could be powerful,* thanked the single nurse, and headed for the "FRESH FROM THE SEA" sign to grab a couple of stuffed quahogs for appetizers. I counted in my head and was now up to three new story ideas I had acquired since talking with my assigned interview. I felt, as far as impact, the most promising idea for an article was Sandy Point's consideration of selling off 50 acres of woods to a developer.

Echo had given me that little nugget of information, which received some serious fuel when Chuck Renna, the owner at Spokes for Folks rang up my bike purchase. I thought back to how that topic came up as I studied the quahogs.

Chuck was lean and *maybe* even handsome, if ABC were to give him an "extreme makeover." He kept an overgrown, crooked goatee and a small, why-even-bother-growing-it ponytail. My first impression was that he had lived his 40-plus, mellow years running the "family business." His idea of a vacation was probably a bike tour up in Vermont to do 'shrooms and devour grilled cheese sandwiches at Phish shows. As we waited for my credit card to clear, he pointed up at the speakers, bobbing his head, informing me that "his" band was always there to put him in a joyous mood.

My guess was Chuck's serene attitude had less to do with The Grateful Dead music his ponytail snaked along to and more to do with the "legalize it" scent that the burning incense tried unsuccessfully to mask. He was a self-described "tree hugger," stapling a *Save the Rain Forest* pamphlet to my Visa receipt, but his laid-back attitude changed abruptly and became almost confrontational when I asked him if he knew of a good spot to go mountain biking.

His face darkened, and his voice sharpened, "There are no good spots. Or at least there won't be any if that friggin' bill passes."

"You mean the bill dealing with the town's woods?" I asked.

"Yeah, those friggin' bastards want to destroy Samoset's Place and..." He stopped.

"Wait, I thought you said you were new to town?"

I pointed outside to where Echo had gone back to her Jeep, "She told me."

"Well, did she also tell you that her stepfather is the lawyer for one of those asshole developers that's trying to buy it?"

"No," I said a little surprised, took out my pad, and wrote down the info while asking,

"What's the developer's name?"

"Oh, ah, Zachary Goodrich. I actually grew up with him. Used to be friends. Ironically enough, he owns Pilgrim Diner."

"Why's that ironic?"

"Samoset was the first Native American to greet the Pilgrims in Plymouth. The woods are named after him because he liked to come here to the Cape and hunt in them. That of course is true about a lot of the woods on the Cape. There's another Samoset Woods down cape as well. Anyway, the town owns the woods, but symbolically, I think it's ironic because the Pilgrims are screwing them Native Americans yet again."

"Well, when this thing goes down, Chuck, I plan on giving both sides of the story. I'll be fair. So, call me at the paper if you ever want to talk."

"Cool. Thanks, man. Giving both sides. That's a new concept. It's usually the Paul Harrison side. Man, what a ... Have you met him?"

I ignored the question, "Well, I'm a reporter, not a columnist. So if you call me, know that I'm going to cover the story without an opinion."

"Okay, thanks again, man. Oh, and don't get me wrong, I like Echo. I mean, who doesn't? But when it comes to those woods, if she sides with her stepfather, she's going to be on my shit list. She and her mom. I can't believe her mom would back that. She used to have that hippie spirit just like me."

"Hippie spirit?"

He leaned over, "You know man, likes to smoke the ganja."

"Oh."

"How about you?"

"No. I'm strictly a beer guy but I don't judge. I actually like the smell." I motioned with my hand to the store

"Cool. I like you, man. Can I tell you something off the record?"

"Sure." I said.

"You know there's another reason why I love those woods. Sometimes when I'm feeling a little tense, I'll get really high and just go walking the trails at night. There's no better way to be one with nature."

"Just pot? That sounds like an experience for something stronger."

Chuck laughed for a minute and then winked, "I learned a long time ago not to go that way."

I nodded and wheeled my mountain bike out of the store, wondering why Echo hadn't mentioned the part about her stepfather when she told me about the possible sale of the woods?

"Strange," I said to myself staring into space at Lareby's Market.

"They might look strange, but they taste amazing. But to be honest with you, they're the second best stuffed quahogs in town." A man's voice interrupted my thoughts.

"Huh?" I turned to see a built, middle-aged-looking man standing beside me, grinning with sparkling white choppers.

His teeth matched the pristine lab coat he was wearing. I noticed the name JARED.

sewn in red cursive lettering above his right pocket. I thought briefly of Carly, the waitress from the Jar, and how she'd described customers that looked like him as being "hot baldies." "You know, like Bruce Willis or Ed Harris. Those are hot baldies that you just want to jump on and do," she'd always say. If Carly were here, she probably would've been straddling him near the crab legs display. I laughed, thinking of the irony of my observation considering Carly had quite the reputation.

Jared pointed down at the quahog that I had been holding for far too long. "Trust me, you'll like them. But I do think Bryden's Fish and Gear makes the best. They have done forever. It's the secret recipe, and I've been trying to get my hands on it for years."

"Really?"

"It's probably not that smart of me to be so honest considering this is my place and all."

He laughed.

"Yeah. Will you give me directions to their store, too?" I smiled.

"Sure. But be advised that they do always charge at least a dollar more."

"Very good business move. Compliment the competition, but in the end, make the point that your product is the best value. Didn't Kris Kringle do that in *Miracle on 34th Street*?"

"Movie buff?"

"Have to be. Bartender for a million years. Lots of afternoon shifts."

"Hey J.T., you get everything?" Echo, carrying her own basket, pranced in our direction and didn't wait for my answer. "Hey, Jared, how are you?"

"I'm... great, Echo." There was a tone of shyness to him, dwarfing him immediately.

"You met J.T., huh?"

"Well, kind of." He turned, and we shook hands, "Jared Lareby."

"J.T. O'Rourke."

"J.T.'s the new reporter," Echo said.

"Oh, yeah, Greg mentioned something about that. How's it going so far?"

"Pretty good. Hey, I was wondering, has anyone done any stories on your renovations?"

"Ah... No. Not yet anyway."

"Maybe we can sit down sometime and I could do a piece for the paper."

"Yeah. Cool. Maybe when we're near completion."

"He's a natural, Jared. He's been sniffing out stories all day."

"With Echo's help. That's why I owe her dinner."

She snapped her fingers, "Oh, that's right. By the way, J.T., someone else is joining us for dinner."

"Oh, who?" I held my smile, trying not to appear disappointed.

She reached into her basket and pulled out the familiar carton, "Paul Newman."

We both burst into laughter and Jared looked at us like we had three heads.

Echo went on to tell him the lemonade story and he nodded in acknowledgement adding,

"Lillian is a character. I've had to deal with her and that damn dog of hers. What a pain in the ass he is. What's his name again? Cool Hand?"

Echo and I halted our giddiness.

"What did I say?" Jared asked.

"The reason we were there..." Echo began, but my cell chimed. I looked down at the number I had just put in and the name The Angry Fisherman flashed across the screen.

"Excuse me, I should take this."

They nodded "okay" and continued talking.

When I hung up from my call, Echo had finished telling the story about Cool Hand and Jared was feeling guilty, shaking his head slowly.

"Lillian's right. It probably was coyotes. They're everywhere these days. Geez, she loved that dog. I feel terrible about what I said."

He may've felt bad, but I felt worse as I forced a smile, "Echo that was Vicki at The Angry Fisherman, someone's sick and they need me to go in. So, I'll have to take a rain check."

I wasn't sure, but I thought I spotted the corners of her mouth drop slightly before she replied while shaking the carton, "Good, more Paul Newman for me to enjoy."

CHAPTER 10
NOVEMBER 10, 1970

TUESDAY

JUNIOR

Junior hated wearing ties. They always choked his neck, reminding him of his father's hands. Sure, two fingers were missing, but those hands had always been capable of locking a firm grip on Junior's throat, squeezing, and shaking him during drunken tirades. But today was different. He did not mind wearing a tie at all. He wore it with pride. After all, he had just found out today was a celebration.

"A 'celebration of life' is what a funeral is," Pop Tucker explained, as he gently fixed Junior's tie and then lightly rubbed his shoulder. The kind-hearted Pop had been helping the little boy and his mother throughout the ordeal.

"Can you make it tighter?" Junior pointed down at the knot. It felt loose. Comfortable. He didn't want to be comfortable. It may've been a celebration of life for the rest of town, but for Junior, his father's funeral was a celebration of death. A death he had dreamt about every waking moment of his 11-year existence. And since that dream had finally come true, he wanted that tie tied tight. Real tight. So, he could remember those menacing meat hooks and glow within, knowing that they would never wrap around his throat again.

After Pop adjusted the knot, Junior tugged on his collar. The memory was almost in his head, but he still said, "Tighter, please."

An awkward smile crossed Pop's big, fleshy lips. "It looks a little painful. You shouldn't welcome pain at your age; you never know what you'll get. But, if you ever do come across it, know that you can always come to me, kiddo."

"Thanks. I'll be all right. Tighter, please."

"Okay, then, little fella." Pop didn't hesitate, pulling harder on the navy-blue tie. This time it worked. He gasped, and Pop couldn't help but laugh. But Junior didn't mind the laughter, because with it came the thought of his father's last night alive. He planned on holding on to that precious memory and carrying it in his mind to the funeral to reflect upon. To "celebrate." God knows he had reason to celebrate. He was free. Free to celebrate.

Celebrate. What a perfect word!

But before he did that, he had to go through what his mother had referred to as the "bullshit." That was how she described the wake moments after they left the funeral home the previous night.

"That was a bunch of bullshit, but we can still make it back for the end of *Laugh In*." She had said to Junior while staring over the wheel, puffing on her Camel.

"We're going to have to go through more of that bullshit tomorrow. But then I can finally move on." A little giggle slipped from her lips. That told him everything he needed to know about the grieving widow. He really didn't blame her.

Now, settling into the second pew, he was willing to put up with his head being patted like a Christmas puppy. He'd sit and listen to the cotton ball-haired chorus's out-of-tune praising of Jesus, and the "I remember" tributes from the sullen strangers promising that his father was now in a far better place. *The bullshit.* There was a lot of it. He would put up with it, though. Even the part when his mother, wiping the black paint from her tear-stained eyes, pulled him to her as a real mother in deep mourning would.

His father would be proud of her acting skills, Junior thought, as he also got into character, pretending to gnaw on his index finger in anguish, but actually depositing spit on it and slyly dabbing his eyes to simulate tears.

Yes, I will put up with "the bullshit" because I know once the funeral is over, I can go to my Silent Place and giggle. Giggle like my mother.

But he wouldn't stop at one giggle like her. He planned on rolling around on the frostbitten grass, howling with giddy laughter that would keep him warm under the Full Beaver Moon.

Suddenly, a second thought dawned on him.

Maybe I should wait until I'm at my Silent Place to fully enjoy the memory. To really celebrate it.

But with all the talk of his father, who was now stuck in Junior's mind, he couldn't think of anyone else. And he couldn't leave. He had to sit there and listen to it. And because of that, even if he wanted to, there was no way he could erase the visions of that night. His mind floated to them. Embracing them. He could feel his soul leave his body. He was flying out of the church. Above the town. Until he was back there. In his room.

On that night.

He was lying on his bed reading about a new kind of superhero, one that couldn't be found in any of his comic books and none of the other kids could claim as their favorite. Because they never even heard of this superhero. He had found him. Or the superhero had found Junior when he tripped over a book lying on the floor in the library. He was about to put it back on the shelf because it was thick and there were only a couple of pictures. Usually, he'd never consider reading a book with so many words. And at first, he read only a couple of words but then a few more. And pretty soon all those words painted beautiful, warm pictures in his mind illustrating a colorful portrait of his new superhero — a portrait he felt only he could relate to. As he flipped furiously through the book, Junior wanted to be just like his new superhero.

But then the holler from the living room rang through his bedroom door. His father was drunk and yelling for him.

"Get in here, now!"

Junior threw the book down on his bed and hurried into the TV room.

Senior chewed on a dying cigar, holding an empty bottle of rum while stretched out on the couch.

"Yes, sir." Junior said.

Senior waved his hand at the set, "Turn that up and go get me another bottle."

Junior thought it was already too loud, but he knew better than to argue. He walked over and turned the knob and the theme from *Hawaii Five-O* thundered off the walls.

"I love this show," Senior smiled, staring at the screen transfixed, but then snapped, "Go get my rum!"

Junior figured, as long as his father had Steve McGarrett and a bottle of rum to occupy him, he would be safe. At least for an hour anyway. So he ran to the cellar door, flipped on the light that took a second to flicker awake, and then hustled down the steps. He took a bottle from one of the five cases his father had stored by the workbench and then headed back up the stairs.

But halfway up, the light dimmed again and then went out, causing him to miss a step and trip. He grabbed the handrail and caught his balance, but in the process, dropped the bottle down the stairs where it smashed against the cement floor.

He realized why the light had flickered before: the bulb had been seconds from burning out. Now in the dark, he froze, waiting to hear the booming voice attack him from the doorway. After a few seconds, there was no sound except the TV. It had been on so loud his father hadn't heard the shattering glass. Junior could still escape a beating if he acted quickly. He couldn't move too fast since it was pitch black. But all the nights of journeying into the woods on moonless nights had trained him. He surprised himself by feeling his way down the stairs and only bumping around a little before his fingers found another bottle. He held it close to him for a moment and then inched up the stairs toward the TV's glare dancing in the doorway.

"What took you so long?" Senior's voice jockeyed with the sounds of the car chase that barreled through the streets of Waikiki.

"I'm sorry, the..." Junior pointed behind him, but his father didn't wait for an answer, snatching the bottle out of his hands.

"Now get outta here!"

Relief. He would be safe, he thought, and headed back to his room, excited to learn more about his superhero. And he was safe until the television noise went silent an hour later.

"Get in here! Get in here! Get in here, now!"

Junior's mother wasn't home, so he knew the command was meant for him. Again, he dropped the book and sprinted out of his room. Senior sat up on the couch but this time his attitude was different. He was jovial. Laughing.

"Sit down, boy, and face me." He gave a drunken snarl and pointed to the throw rug on the floor.

Junior didn't say a word. He just sat down, cross-legged and stared up at his father.

"I been doing some thinkin'. I think it's time I told you about Old Heidi, and my fingers, and that violin I made you burn. Do you remember me making you throw that in the fire?"

Junior nodded.

"Do you want to know why?"

He nodded again but Senior took a swig and didn't catch the gesture.

"I asked you a question, boy!"

"Yes, sir." Junior managed.

"Good. Your old man here is going to tell you the story of how I became a miserable prick. You ready to hear it?"

The boy wasn't sure how he should answer, but then said, "Yes, sir."

"Okay, then." Senior laughed, before taking another swallow and then wiped his mouth dry on his sleeve.

For the next hour, he told Junior everything about his past. And it now made sense. Why Junior loved the violin. Why his father was the way he was. All of it. It all made complete sense. And for the first time in his life, he had a strange feeling for his father. He felt sorry for him. He didn't know what to do with the feeling. But when Senior ended the story by saying, "I wish I never made you burn that violin," Junior did something he never did before. He spoke up.

"It's okay. I never burned it."

"What?" Senior, who had drifted in thought, turned his attention back to his son.

"I still have the violin. I only burned the case." As the words came out, Junior knew he was making a mistake.

"You mean all of these years you've had it!"

"Yes, sir."

"Where?"

"I hid it in the woods. But you can have it if you want."

Senior stood up, "Get over here!"

Junior got up and moved forward slowly, "I'm sorry. I'm sorry."

"Come on. Now!"

When Junior was close enough, his father wound up and drove his fist into his stomach, causing him to slump to the floor.

"Here I was trying to include you in my life! And now I find out you lied to me! You disobeyed me! You're just like your mother. That's why you're a fuck up! You're a fuck up! You do know that?"

"Yes, sir. Yes..." Junior began but couldn't finish because his father's boot slammed into his stomach. He felt the bile rise to his throat and tried to roll around on the floor to move the pain.

Senior sucked down the last of the rum and stormed past him headed to the cellar in search of another bottle. Writhing in pain and trying to hold in the tears, he hugged his stomach while watching his father disappear through the cellar door. But then a crash was followed by an ear-splitting scream. Junior forgot about his hurting stomach and moved to the top of the cellar stairs.

He could hear his father moaning in agony in the blackness below. He pieced it together. Senior was in such a hurry he had turned on the light and begun to walk down the steps. But there was no light. He must've tripped and fallen. But what confused him was that the steps weren't that steep. Why was his father screaming in such anguish?

"Help! Help!" Senior yelled.

Junior hurried over to the kitchen drawer and fumbled through it until he found some matches. He went over and unhooked the decorative kerosene lamp that hung beside the kitchen sink. He lit it and moved down the cellar stairs, the halo of gold slowly revealing his father's figure lying face down on the floor. He placed the lamp down beside Senior and with both hands tried to turn him over, but his father squealed like a pig being slaughtered.

And then Junior understood why. The steel prongs. They were embedded in his father's chest. A garden rake had caught Senior's fall. At first, he didn't know what to do. He just stood there for a minute taking in the sight.

Senior turned his head and looked up at him, pleading with terrified eyes, "Call... police."

This broke Junior's trance. He grabbed the lamp and rushed upstairs. He went to the telephone, picked it up, and then heard his father let out another horrific scream. He paused, realizing he liked the sound. It reminded him of the gull. And the violin.

Yes, he loved the sound. And he loved that his father was making it. Senior was scared, just like Junior had been all of his life. He wanted him to have that feeling forever. He rested the phone on the receiver and listened to the sound a while longer. And that was when the plan formed.

It's perfect!

He knew he could do it. He wanted to do it. He had to do it. He went around the house and took everything that was of value to him and brought it outside, hiding it in the old shed that was 40 yards away. Then, guided by the lamp, he headed back down the cellar stairs to face his father.

"Di…d?" was the only word Senior could breathe.

"Yes. They're on their way," Junior answered and Senior nodded with a face of desperate hope. He was enjoying his father's plight. It was almost better than being in the woods in his Silent Place. He glanced over at the crates of rum and walked over and opened a bottle and took a swig.

"Wha…?" His father tried to talk.

But Junior was feeling good now. Confident.

He sauntered over to Senior. "How 'bout a drink, Dad!"

The icy delivery of the word "Dad" had the effect Junior was hoping for. His old man heaving like the gull on the beach, knew something was seriously wrong.

Junior thrived on that fear.

"Have some rum, Dad!"

Grinning, he poured, marinating his father, whose eyes now resembled the gull's eyes as he tried to move but the prongs made it impossible.

Junior focused on the eyes and that's when he decided that his father wasn't going to see God. Junior couldn't let that happen. He ran over to the workbench and retrieved the tackle box and rested it beside the lamp. He crouched down and searched through the box until he found a bait knife. He laughed uncontrollably, and Senior's brown eyes grew widest when he saw the knife.

Junior laughed even more, "Yes! Yes! Yes!"

In one quick motion, he jabbed the knife into his father's left eye. He didn't hear the scream. He felt it — a surge of energy shooting through his veins. And he felt it again when he speared the other eye. The volume of the screaming reached a level that shocked Junior. It screeched higher than any gull or violin could.

God, I love it!

Senior's hands floundered away while Junior danced a jig, clapping in celebration.

"Should I sing, Dad?" He squatted before taking off his bloody clothes and then used them to wipe the knife clean. He threw the clothes on his father's futile waving hands and placed the knife back in the box.

When he did that, he spotted the meat cleaver his father called Old Heidi and thought of using it to finish the job. It would be the perfect way to end Senior's life.

But then he came to his senses. That wasn't part of the plan. He had to stick to the plan if he wanted it to work. But before he continued the plan, he couldn't resist standing naked, looming over his father, watching, and enjoying the last sounds the man would ever make while also watching himself harden and rise before him.

Why does it always get hard when I kill things?

He didn't know, but he liked the feeling. Something inside made him think there was an even greater feeling to be achieved. He cupped his balls and laughed again and said in a voice that was much older than his years, "Dad, I don't want to sing. I'm not weak like you. I don't need to sing. Because that's why you're a fuck-up! You're a fuck-up! You *do* know that!"

He held the tackle box in one hand and the lamp in the other and walked halfway up the steps before turning around.

"You're the fuck up!" He yelled again, throwing the kerosene lamp at the cement floor where it smashed. The flames attacked the rum-soaked body and continued traveling through the cellar.

He walked at a normal pace upstairs to the bathroom and calmly washed the blood spittle off his body. He looked down at his himself. It was normal again. He wished it wasn't.

He went into his room and put on his pajamas and lay in his bed listening to the crackling fire below growing and moving. When he spotted the yellow flames in the cracks of the floorboards, he knew it was time. He jumped out of bed, gripped the box, and raced across the room, his feet pattering on the hot boards reminding him of a summer's day on the boardwalk.

When he got outside, he stored the box in the shed before pausing to watch the flames engulf the house. He thought of his new hero.

This is how he must've felt! What a feeling!

He wanted it to last longer but it wasn't part of his plan, so he jogged to the neighbors', waking them with screams of, "Help! Help! My father! My father!"

Four kids wiping the sleep from their eyes swayed out of their house. Wild looks of wonderment came to their faces, huddled behind their father as Junior also took in the scene.

Their father took charge, running back in to make the call while Junior tugged on his own pajamas hollering, "My Dad! My Dad!"

Damn! Damn! Damn! It can't be my "father" one minute and my "dad" the next. I have to act the same. Always. Always act the same!

He wasn't sure if his mistake was noticed. He hoped everyone was too busy watching the flames leaping out of the windows grasping for the brisk night. And when the fire engines and the police sirens joined as one, he knew his mistake wouldn't be remembered by anyone.

So, he picked one name. The loving name.

"Dad! Dad! Dad! Dad! Dad! Dad!"

Fire hoses desperately doused the house, but the Chief hollered above the chaos, "This is useless!"

An expression of guilt appeared on the Chief's face when he realized that Junior was within earshot. Junior knew this was his opportunity.

"No! No! No! No!" He hollered, running toward the burning house, wincing with fake grief but then ran back to the group of onlookers as the flames exploded through the living room windows.

The boy placed his hands to his head and screamed, "No, Daddy!"

And then he ran again. This time away from the house.

He heard someone yell, "Come back! Come back!"

But then he heard Officer Devlin order, "Let the boy go. Let him go."

At that moment, he was free from the burning cage. He kept running until he was in his Silent Place. He lit a fire in the discarded barrel he had found a few weeks earlier and basked in the reality of how his father would never be able to see God.

In the end, he held more power over his father than any back of the hand he'd ever received. He controlled Senior's fate for all of eternity.

What power!

He took out the violin and played it by the fire.

Yes, he felt exactly like his new hero and decided from now on, in his woods, in his world, he would be known as "Nero" as a tribute to the great Emperor whom he had read about. Nero played the fiddle as he burned down Rome in 64 A.D. in hopes of rebuilding it.

And as Junior broke from his trance and was back at his father's funeral watching the casket containing the charred remains pass by, he couldn't help but smirk, convinced that he was Nero reincarnated and he now held the same power — the power to rebuild his own life.

He stopped grinning when he felt eyes from the other side of the aisle. Those eyes belonged to Officer Devlin. The officer squinted as if he was analyzing the inappropriate expression, but Junior quickly recovered by turning the grin into a pained look, shaking his head over and over.

Inside, he scolded himself for a final time, *Nero, you can never again let them see your true feelings! Never again!*

CHAPTER 11

JUNE 9, 2004

WEDNESDAY

J.T.

It wasn't until around 4:30 the next afternoon that I could splay myself out on my chaise lounge, take in the sun, and digest the events of my first day in the Point. And man, was it eventful, especially my shift at The Angry Fisherman or, as the locals called it, "The A.F." When I arrived there, I met the owner who was as gruff as the bar's name.

He was broad shouldered with a seafaring black beard and dark eyes and looked trapped in the blue button down and floral tie he was wearing. He threw down the *Sandy Point Standard Times* he was reading, muttered, "Bunch of crap," and walked over to me, hitching up his off-white Izod pants.

"Are you the O'Rourke guy that Crocker recommended?"

"Yes, sir. J.T. O'Rourke." I put out my hand and he gripped it with a calloused lock.

"Davis Lawson. Not D.L. Not Lawson. Just plain Davis, okay?" He said, almost as an order, squeezing harder to make the point, and then released.

"O...kay... Nice to meet you, Davis."

"Yeah," he said, and I noted his extended lower lip and the Dixie cup he was holding. He was packing some chew.

"They like to talk about fishing here. Like to fish?" he asked.

"Only went once."

"Once. Not good. Well... catch anything?"

"I did but threw it back." I thought briefly about when I hooked a freshwater bass with my dad on Lake Winnipesaukee and how I released the keeper "to be with his family" while my father was retrieving the Polaroid camera from the station wagon. Man was my ol' man pissed.

Davis didn't look too happy either as he went on to his next question. "Will the Red Sox win it this year?"

"If I thought that, I wouldn't have left Kenmore Square."

"Yep. How 'bout movies? You a John Wayne fan?"

"What bartender doesn't love The Duke?" I asked, and I could see he was fighting a smile.

"Good. On slow nights I sometimes put on AMC for the old-timers. How about music? You like Jimmy Buffet?"

I wanted to say "Just hand me the Match.com profile to fill out..." but thought better of it. I knew this was his quick way of reading me.

"Honestly, I'd rather skinny dip in a pool of piranha than listen to Buffet."

He finally cracked a smile, spat into his paper cup, and said, "See that jukebox?"

"Yeah."

"I figure Buffet is played on that about 10,000 times a summer. Follow me." He walked behind the bar, and I figured I was probably not making a good first impression.

Davis pointed to a switch behind the bar and gave me a big smile, "We call that our Buffet silencer. The rule is: if you hear Buffet, or "Brown-Eyed Girl," or any of that shit the tourists love, more than three times during your shift — you're allowed to turn the switch. It overrides the jukebox. We have to cater to these assholes, but that doesn't mean we have to go insane doing it."

I laughed and in a strange way, I liked his sour attitude.

"One major rule. You get one shift drink but other than that no drinking here. My father started this business, and he never had a drop of alcohol here. At home, well that was another story. And that goes for my employees. There are plenty of other bars in the Point and I don't have a problem with you going to them. But when employees start drinking here, they start hanging out here, and the line of one free drink gets blurred into nights of free drinking. That shit adds up. But don't think I'm a cheap prick. You can pass out two comps a night. And if you've already handed those out and a chick comes in you want to work over, just write that down. Okay?"

"I understand. What kind of crowd should I expect tonight?"

"Should be very slow. This place doesn't take off for another couple of weeks when the weather gets warmer and we book some bands. Oh, which reminds me, watch out for those freaks from WHOI in Woods Hole."

"WHOI? Isn't that the place where Richard Dreyfuss worked in *Jaws*?"

"Yeah. That was so unrealistic," he said, annoyed.

"What do you mean? Dreyfuss?"

"No, Dreyfuss was a dead ringer for a marine biologist, but the scene where he brings two bottles of wine to dinner to drink with Chief Brody. Damn, is that shit hilarious? Those scientists are the cheapest bastards around. They're so cheap they stopped serving them down in the Hole one summer 'cause not one of those horseshoe crab-sniffers will ever leave a tip. That's why you gotta watch out for them. They're like a goddamn cult coming in, ordering waters and dancing around, sweating their Jerry Garcia stench, scaring away the other customers. And they bitch about every dime they spend. Anyway, we won't need a bouncer tonight, so just check IDs at the bar. Okay, I gotta go to this damn event. Vicki will fill you in on everything else."

"Sounds good. What event is it?"

"I'm a volunteer firefighter, and I helped put out a burning boat this past winter. I'm getting a plaque or some shit."

"Wow, that's great."

"Yeah.... Oh, thanks for coming in on such short notice. I'll definitely owe Greg if this works out."

"You and Greg grew up together?"

"Oh, yeah. I've known that guy since the night he pissed his sleeping bag in Boy Scouts. Did a few times here, too." He laughed and headed out the door.

Davis would've been right on target about it being a slow night, but then at eleven, a bus resembling a San Francisco trolley car pulled up carrying a wedding party of 40 bombed Macarena dancers. Similar to the way an ambulance transporting casualties does, a driver of wedding drunks should call ahead. This driver hadn't. There was no time to prepare our ER and Vicki and I got slammed with drink orders. What made it worse was they were all in their early twenties, and I couldn't let a fake ID pass by me, especially on my first night, so I checked and rechecked.

It turned out to be a tiring night of Barenaked Ladies, "Sweet Caroline," and mind erasers. But a day later, as I turned over and slapped on sunblock to protect my lily-white Irish complexion, I thought of one of the IDs and how, when I checked it, it was like one of those "WHAT IF" stories coming true.

I had seen the face trying to blend in with the crowd, but he was clearly underdressed, wearing khaki shorts and a black golf shirt with a red Polo player logo. What was even more obvious — he was not only drunk but "out of his tree," as my sister Erin used to describe my dad.

I took the ID, which was a liquor ID that he probably bought on Tremont Street in Boston. It was so fake the kid would've had problems buying scorpion bowls at a Chinese restaurant.

I stared at his Bulldog Face for a long time. He didn't recognize me.

It was busy, but I couldn't resist playing with him a bit, "Do you have back up?"

"No, man. Jesus, just give me a Bud." Bulldog Face swayed.

"Sure. One question."

"What?"

"How did the Concord-Carlisle lacrosse team do this year?"

"Well, we were... Huh?"

"You don't remember me?"

"No."

"The lacrosse ball on the highway. You remember, now, shithead?" I grabbed his collar and shook him up a little, knowing he was probably close to visiting the porcelain God.

"Aww, man," he moaned.

"Yeah, not so tough now. Are you?"

"Let me go, man!" he shouted, which in a bar is usually a feeding call for any drunk who wants to throw down. One heard the bell.

"Let the kid go!"

I turned around to find the customer Vicki had earlier referred to as "Drake" (while giving me the "don't shut him off just serve him watered down G&T's" speech) getting in my face.

"Let the kid go!"

I released my grip to face Drake and, like a wounded animal fighting for survival, Bulldog Face scurried out the door and into the night.

"That's better," Drake thought I had bowed to his threat.

"Hey," I yelled, my spit flying, "That kid had a fake ID and he screwed up my car yesterday!"

"Huh?"

"Yeah! I'm sure Davis would like to hear that you want me serving minors."

"Shit, man. I didn't know."

"Of course you didn't." I glared at him, went over to the register, grabbed a stapler, and secured Bulldog Face on the Wall of Fake IDs.

It had been a stressful night, but I started my early morning by filing a report with the police. They had been very helpful, telling me that with the picture and a few phone calls to the fancy high school west of Boston, they would be able to track down Bulldog Face's real name.

Ah, revenge... how sweet!

After I dealt with the police report, I spent the next couple of hours writing a story on a make-your-own-sundae benefit sponsored by the local Baptist church with the proceeds going to children in Africa. As I listened to the enthusiastic minister spew optimism, I couldn't help but wonder if any of the dollars would actually make it to the people who really needed help.

When I pushed him on that thought, his smile tightened briefly, before he thoughtfully answered, "If we go into it with negative thinking, no one will ever do anything for those children. But let's just say you're right. The worst-case scenario is bureaucracy, and the children will only see a fraction of the money we raise, and that money might allow only one child to live another day. But maybe that child gets help from another benefit the next day, and the day after that. And pretty soon the child is growing and who knows what greatness he or she will blossom into, and who knows how that child will change his or her country or even the world later on in life? It's called hope. We all have to have it. And when we have it, we have to pass it on. And when you buy a sundae on Saturday, you can put a cherry on top of that thought, Mr. O'Rourke."

It wasn't only a fantastic quote for the paper, but it also energized me a bit, reminding me to stay positive about my new situation. I had no problem knocking out the article in a couple of hours.

Crocker read it and smiled. "That's exactly what I'm looking for. Now go grab some beach time and don't argue. There'll be many days when you can't."

I didn't argue. I felt pretty good about myself. The afternoon sun was beating down, and I wasn't in Kenmore Square. I was about to head down the back stairs to the beach when I heard a hard, rapid knock on my door.

"Hold on! Just a second!" I grabbed my U2 Elevation Tour T-shirt, pulled it over my head, and hurried to the door. I opened it and two early-30s, beefy police officers, one black and one white, were standing in the doorway.

"Wow. You guys work quick. I was just thinking about it," I said.

They exchanged confused glances with one another before the black officer spoke, "Excuse me, are you Mr. Jameson Thomas O'Rourke?"

"Ah, yes." I didn't like the suspicious tone he took stating my full name.

The white cop flipped a picture of Bulldog Face at me, "Did you have a run in with this young man at The Angry Fisherman last night?"

"Yes. I filed a report. I have actually had two incidents with him. But you guys know that. So, you catch him?" I asked, confused, and again they exchanged glances with one another.

The Black Cop ('Jensen,' according to the name on his tag) answered, "No sir, we're not here about that report."

"Well, what report are you here about then?"

"Rutger Nelson has recently been reported as missing."

"Who the hell is that?" I blurted.

"The young man in the photograph, sir." The white cop, 'Burke,' answered.

"Oh," I said and continued speaking a thought that should've stayed in my head, "I thought it had to be 24 hours before someone could file a missing person's report."

They exchanged glances for a final time before Jensen said, "Mr. O'Rourke, if you could please come down to the station with us to answer some questions."

"Why do I have to go to the station? Why can't I answer them here?"

"Sir, could you please just come to the station? I'm sure the detective will be able to answer your questions as well."

CHAPTER 12
NOVEMBER 11, 1970

WEDNESDAY

NERO

Nero's Mom squeezed his hand, dragging him along Main Street to Pilgrim Diner for the Early Bird Special. He didn't understand why they had to go out to dinner considering earlier that day, Pop Tucker had dropped off enough groceries to keep their refrigerator full for a week.

As they jingled through the door, he thought of how kind the owner of the toy and candy store had been to them. He had given Nero's Mom the keys to one of his vacant rentals and said, "As long as you need the place. It's yours."

Nero knew Pop was married with a boy, but thinking back on his kindness, he fantasized briefly about the chance of Pop becoming his new father. He knew it was a crazy fantasy and that he shouldn't have it, so he tried to focus on something else — watching his mother.

Lingering in the entrance, she waited for a moment until she had captured all the eyes and whispers of the patrons, then she paraded confidently toward the four empty booths in the corner.

Nero followed and began to settle into the closest one, but her long nails snatched him by the collar, "No. Not that one. Go over there."

She pointed over at the booth next to one occupied by three high school kids wearing Sandy Point High School football jackets. Two of them, chubby kids, were eating cheeseburgers and sucking on milk shakes as if on a mission, while the third one, a well-built kid with dark blue eyes, was telling them a story.

He thought briefly about how pretty the boy's eyes were, but then he spied a mischievous smile cross his mother's ruby red lips — a smile that used to appear whenever his father was out of town.

When settled into the booth, he also noticed how his mother tilted her head in the direction of the kids as if she was eavesdropping. She really didn't have to.

The storyteller had a loud voice and talked as if he wanted her to hear him.

"So, I told her if she wanted to be with a football hero, she had to meet me under the goalpost in the same end zone where I scored that game winner against Dennis-Yarmouth. I told her 10 p.m. and not to tell anyone. And if she picked the wrong end zone, she wouldn't get any of this." The kid made a slurping sound wiggling his tongue and the table laughed.

"Well, did she pick the right end zone?" the chubbier of the two asked.

"She sure did. So, I gave it to her right at the one-yard line."

"Why the one-yard line?" the other boy asked with his mouth full.

"'Cause with me driving at her from behind, she eventually crawled into the end zone! You never heard of scoring a sex touchdown, Mark?" He laughed loudly, and they joined in.

Nero's Mom smiled to herself, but then she snapped her fingers at Nero who was also listening, "Look at your menu!"

He lowered his head but continued to eavesdrop on the conversation.

"Randy, I can't believe you did it with a colored girl," the first kid said.

"I had to celebrate eighteen my way. Life is quick. Cross it off my list. I plan on getting all kinds. I haven't had an older woman, yet. I could probably still learn a few things. I also figure when I go to Nam, I can get myself a Korean girl and cross that off my list, too." He leered and his companions erupted again.

Nero's Mom smiled and whispered to Nero, "Stay here. I'm going to get some cigarettes."

She stood up, turned to face the kid named Randy, and said, "Yeah, I bet you have a lot more learning to do."

The table was quiet until she was at the cigarette machine and out of earshot.

"Holy shit! She heard our whole conversation," said the kid named Jackie.

"That was my plan," Randy smiled. "Didn't her old man turn to dust in that fire the other day?"

"Keep it down, Randy, her kid is going to hear you," the kid named Mark warned.

"He can't hear me," he said to them and then turned his attention to Nero. "Hey, kid, can you hear me?"

"Huh?" Nero looked up, playing dumb but thinking how Randy's eyes looked like the color of a dark ocean, like beautiful marbles.

"Told ya." Randy turned his attention back to his buddies.

"Okay, then, so what do you mean, 'that was your plan'?" Jackie asked.

Randy rose from the table. "Excuse me, fellas, I have to pay my respects to that widow over at the cigarette machine." He walked over to Nero's mom and they started talking. Five minutes later, she called Nero over, "There's a ten-dollar bill in my purse. Go grab it."

"Why?" he asked.

"It's for you, honey. Go to Pop Tucker's and hang out there for a couple of hours. Get anything you want. I have something to do."

He was baffled by her generosity but wasn't going to ask the question twice. He tucked the bill away in his pocket. The bell on the swinging door sounded his exit.

To any eleven-year-old, having ten dollars in their hand was like having a million in the bank. But it meant even more to Nero since he never received money for treats from his parents. Maybe now that his father was gone his mother would be different, he thought hopefully as he entered Pop Tucker's store.

Maybe she'll be happier? Maybe she would even love me?

He spotted a dozen chatty girls crowded around the penny candy bins.

At first, Nero only wanted to slap them. But after five minutes of Girl Scout Troop Number 24 or whatever they called themselves, arguing about whether to fill their paper bags with fireballs or pixie sticks or both, he wished he was carrying Old Heidi. Yep, it was more than just a slap he wanted to dish out. They were so annoying with their giggles. He really wanted to chop off their pretty little heads. But now he joined in with a laugh while his mind cursed them. It was out of the ordinary for him to entertain such ideas. Well, in public at least. He had always felt as though his father could read his thoughts, so he never imagined doing bad things unless he was safe at his Silent Place. That's why he went there. To be free to unload his thoughts — good and bad. Free to think. Free to just be. But now his father had gone to hell and the bad thoughts were bubbling away in the front of his mind. And they felt good. So, good. So freeing.

I really am free!

From now on, he could think any way he wanted anytime and anywhere. And now he was thinking about the Girl Scouts and their eyes. Blues, greens, browns. They all had such pretty eyes.

God, he thought as he tried to compose himself, he loved how their eyes warmed his insides like a slow steady flame. This was a feeling he wanted to have every day. He wanted to slice the eyes out of their sockets and bottle them up. He could put them in his jar and display them back at his Silent Place — their eyes bobbing like boat buoys on a stormy harbor night.

He smirked, realizing he was pretty good at poetry. One of his teachers once told him he had "a flair for description."

Their gumball eyes dancing in their empty pigtail jars, he grinned again, thinking how he was describing the eyes as gumballs while he was in a candy store... Yes, he was really proud of his prose. That's what his teacher would've called it, he decided.

Wouldn't it be so beautiful if I were actually able to collect their eyes? I could... Stop!

"Stop! Stop! Stop!" He yelled out loud at the thought that was taking control of his mind.

The Girl Scouts all turned and gaped at him while Pop Tucker peered from behind the register.

"Something wrong?" Pop asked.

"Ah, no. Sorry." Nero shrugged while thinking — *What is going on in my head?*

Something was telling him that those were sick thoughts running in his brain. He tried to turn them off, but like a TV without a knob, the thoughts just kept playing.

"No, really. What is going on in my head?" he mumbled the question quietly to himself. It was sick. He knew it. But he couldn't help thinking bad things.

Stop thinking that way! I just want to spend my ten dollars, but the girls are taking so damn long. If I chopped their heads off, that would show the "whores" — as father would say.

A strange sensation then tingled through him as he watched.

While Pop rang up the candy orders, he realized that he missed his father. He didn't miss the verbal or physical abuse. He missed the routine. Like any routine, he was used to it. And he missed that. He knew if his father were alive, he'd know exactly how to behave. He'd be quiet. Keep his "fucking mouth shut." But Nero didn't want to be quiet, watching Pop deal with the twelve little "whores."

Whores. That's how his father would've described them on the drive home. But his father was gone. That revelation was making him feel claustrophobic — the whole situation made him antsy. He wanted to grab them all by their greasy pigtails and wrap those tails around their throats.

Strangle them!

Pop must've sensed his bizarre demeanor because he paused his pecking on the cash register to ask, "Where's your mother?"

Nero took out the ten-dollar bill and waved it in the air. "She gave me this and said I can spend it on anything I want."

Surprised at seeing the ten spot, Pop extended his index finger to the Girl Scouts and said, "One moment please, ladies."

He waddled around the end of the counter and ushered Nero over to the kite aisle for privacy.

"Did she really give you that?"

"Yes."

"Why did she give you so much money?"

"I don't know."

"Tell me." Pop's tone was sharp and out of character.

Nero recounted going to the diner and how his mother talked with the high school football player and then gave him the money and directed him to Pop's place.

Pop said, "She's at it already."

"Huh?"

"Oh, nothing..." his voice trailed, then in an upbeat tone, "It looks like you have some money to spend, young man!"

"Yep."

Pop glanced over at the Girl Scouts and then whispered to Nero, "To spend money like that right, you need your own tour of the store."

"What do you mean?"

"I mean," he smiled conspiratorially, "come back in two hours and I'll show you *all* the wonderful things you can buy with your money."

"But won't you be closed?"

"Exactly." Pop laughed, thumbed over his shoulder at the Scouts, and

135

winked, "We'll have none of them to bother us as I show you some of the new model airplanes I just got in. They're in the back room. I'll have them unpacked by the time you come back."

"Wow," the boy repeated, over and over, as he was now having good thoughts and enjoyed the foreign feeling of happiness that came with them.

Of all the feelings, this was by far the strangest one he had experienced in years. Muscles in his face were operating. Nero was actually smiling. He had no trouble smiling in the past, like when his mother slipped on ice and fractured her elbow, or when his father, trying to avoid a "fat ass" woman crossing the street, popped a tire and grazed a hydrant. He smiled then. Hell, he laughed then, too, but paid the price. This was different. His joy was odd to him. For the first time in a long time, there was nothing malicious behind his smile, and the evil feelings that had consumed him before were gone. He decided he didn't want to have those other kinds of feelings anymore. And because of it, he smiled and smiled as he skipped along Main Street, allowing his mind to enjoy his new fantasy — Pop Tucker becoming his father.

Yes, Pop was married. But, Nero rationalized, everyone thought that his mom was one of the most beautiful women in town. Why wouldn't Pop want her as his new wife? After all, Nero never saw Pop's wife. She was never at the store.

She must be ugly! Pop probably didn't want anyone to see her!

And Nero had never met Pop's son. He heard he attended private school, but he never seemed to visit even. What kid doesn't come to his father's store, a store that sells toys and candy?

He must be retarded. Or maybe Pop just doesn't like him.

A plan was buzzing around in his head and for once it was a nice plan, a happy one, one that didn't involve carving out frogs' eyes or severing rabbits' feet. He felt good about himself! He had to wait two whole hours until he could go back for his private tour, but it was worth it. He liked the feeling of looking forward to something good. But thinking about the candy store reminded him that he *was* a little hungry. He thought about going to the diner, but he was sick of eating there. And besides, he wanted to save every dime of his ten dollars for Pop Tucker's store. Then he remembered the groceries back at home. His mother told him not to come home for at least two hours, but he figured he could sneak into the apartment, make a peanut butter and fluff sandwich, and sneak out again — and she would never know the difference.

What harm would it be if I went into the apartment for ten minutes?

As he approached the small rental, he heard music coming from inside. The music was familiar to him, and when he walked in, he noticed the album cover lying on the living room floor. He picked it up and read the title: *The Doors – The Soft Parade*.

His mother treasured that album but only played it when his father was at work. His father hated The Doors. He called them "no good hippie devil worshippers."

Realizing there would be no retribution for his enjoyment, Nero felt safe to nod his head to the music. He thought that was probably why his mother was playing the album at full volume.

What freedom! We are free!

The song ended and he listened with anticipation. The needle transitioned into a big band sound and Jim Morrison's voice burst forth. He had heard kids talk about The Doors and Morrison, but this was the first time he was able to really listen, and he was enjoying himself until he spotted the Sandy Point football jacket lying on the rocking chair. The smile faded. Curiosity now took hold of him. He knew who owned it, but he still walked over to the chair, picked it up, and studied the embroidery that spelled:

RANDY "RUNAWAY TRAIN" REYNOLDS #34

He put on the jacket that was twice his size, pretending it was his, then he walked over and sniffed the empty bottle of vodka that was resting beside the record player.

Wow, that's strong!

Nero spied two empty glasses and a tipped over carton of orange juice dripping like a weak faucet onto the floor. He didn't bother picking it up. Instead, he lifted the needle off the record. He expected silence, but that was not what he heard. From down the hall, he heard the same kind of grunts and moans his parents used to make. He knew his father was dead — or had it been a dream? Was his father really alive?

He was so confused.

All the voices in his head told him to leave the house, but he had to find out if there was something wrong with his head.

Was I dreaming this whole time?

He moved slowly down the hallway toward his mother's bedroom. The door was ajar. He craned his head around the door and saw the high school kid with the beautiful eyes, hovering behind Nero's mother. It looked like they were wrestling and their clothes were falling off. His mother was yelling almost like she was speaking a foreign language. He wasn't sure if Randy was hurting her or not. Nero's mother caught his shocked expression reflecting from the mirror and that's when he knew she wasn't being hurt. She laughed as Randy also then spotted Nero.

"We have to stop! Your kid."

Nero's mother laughed even more.

"It's not like he can tell his father on me. Keep going." She urged.

He caught a glimpse of his mother's bra, so he turned his head away and closed his eyes. A memory came to him. He remembered how he had once seen two dogs in the park in the same position and when he asked an older kid what they were doing the kid replied with a laugh, "They're having a good time."

The boy went on to tell him about the birds and the bees. On that day, Nero learned about sex. What now concerned him was his mother was having a "good time," but it was not with Pop Tucker. Sex should be between a husband and wife. He didn't want Randy to be his new father, but he also still wasn't sure what he should do, so he stood frozen with his eyes closed until he heard his mother roar. When he opened his eyes, she was standing in front of him straightening her dress.

"I told you *two hours*! Get out! Now!" She slammed the door in his face.

Nero stood there in shock, then her voice through the door, "And take off Randy's jacket!"

He knew that tone. He had experienced that anger many times. It was often accompanied by the coal shovel purpling the back of his legs. Nero threw the jacket onto the floor and raced out of the house knowing where he had to go.

CHAPTER 13
JUNE 9, 2004

WEDNESDAY

J.T.

Rutger Nelson a/k/a "Bulldog Face" was missing, and Sandy Point's finest wanted to talk to me. If there was one message Officer Billy O'Rourke programmed into his four kids it was, "If a cop ever wants to ask you just a few questions, no matter what, call your lawyer. You can't trust those bastards!"

Of course, my old man was one of those bastards but "father knows best" as the old TV show always stressed. On the surface, it was solid advice, but working in the bar world, this philosophy never went over well. I learned quickly that I had to become friends with the Boston cops, or they might screw me over when it came to hammered suburbanites who had the brilliance of jumping behind the wheel instead of hopping into a cab. The few times that dilemma did wrap on the oak doors of The Jar, I solved it by calling my old man and giving him the cop's name and badge number, and reiterating the questions: Was this guy in here last night? And was he drinking? Did he cause any trouble? etc.

He'd ring back and say something like, "Frankie O'Halloran trained that cop. He's an okay kid. You can talk to him. Just let him know your connection."

Pretty soon I got to know all the cops and detectives, so I never took any heat when the drunken, dumbass yuppies guard-railed their BMWs on 128. But that was Boston. Not Cape Cod. And that was also when I was talking to my old man. Not anymore.

So, when Officers Jensen and Burke asked me to go with them to the Sandy Point Police Station, I didn't know what to do, so I numbly acquiesced. But, as my Jeep trailed their cruiser, a tape of my old man's voice played in my head, and I decided I better make a phone call just to be safe. There was no way I was calling him, but I had to call someone. I had left Crocker in a good mood, and I wanted to keep it that way, so who could I call? Then it came to me, and I grabbed my cell.

When the officers ushered me into the windowless room with the three chairs, the long table, and (of course) seated behind that table, a bloated, sloppy detective pretending to be in deep thought writing notes — I was relieved I had dialed that number.

As the detective scribbled away, I was tempted to point out that he might want to click his pen on, but I thought better of it.

He was in his mid-to-late forties and reeked of a mixture of too much Old Spice and not enough Speed Stick. A few scattered strands of red tightly-tuned-guitar-string hair clung to his bald head. I figured he probably flirted with the Atkins Diet before finding out it didn't include pizza and pasta, because there wasn't much treadmill time for that body.

He labored a bit as he pushed himself away from the table — leaving a table, probably something he wasn't used to — and then he got up, gripped my hand, and wheezed, "I'm Detective Gordon. You must be Mr. O'Rourke?"

He became all smiles, but I knew it was B.S. I didn't like his suspicious squint or the red soul patch that looked almost glued to his lower lip. I wondered briefly if the patch's purpose was to let everyone know that the good detective could still grow hair, or maybe its function was to catch dust from Cheetos on Tom Brady Sundays. Either way, it was ridiculous. But then I realized I was also treating the situation as ridiculous, playing around with my sarcastic observations. I had to be serious because something *was* serious — a kid was missing. And I knew he thought it involved me.

"Yes, J.T. O'Rourke. Detective Gordon, could I ask you why I had a police escort bring me here?"

"Yes, about that. We appreciate that. We have a lot going on considering…"

"Considering what?"

"Have a seat." He nodded to the chair across from him.

"No, thanks, I feel like standing. What's this about?"

Clearly perturbed, he sharpened. "Mr. O'Rourke, I think you'd be more comfortable sitting."

"Actually, until I know what this is about, I won't feel comfortable standing or sitting."

"How about this, buddy, you don't have a choice, sit."

It took all of a half a minute for me to break him down to his real self, and I smiled and sat, now knowing what I was dealing with — a cop who probably spent his career bullying confessions from shoplifters and Halloween egg-throwers using the Andy Sipowitz tug-on-the-belt technique.

Before he could get his first question out, I said, "So when was Rutger Nelson reported missing?"

"Excuse me?"

"When was he reported missing? Actually, here's a better question, Detective, when was he last seen?"

"Um, how do you know that this deals with Rutger Nelson?"

"Well, if I kidnapped him, I should know, right?"

"Excuse me?" He moved forward.

"I'm joking. I'm being a wise ass. And you know what, Detective? I shouldn't joke about this if this kid really is missing and not still sleeping off his hangover somewhere. It's just that there was no reason to bring me down here when I could've given the answers you need to know back at my place. I should be taking a swim right now."

"You didn't answer my question. How did you know this was about Rutger Nelson?"

"Your officers let it slip. Detective Gordon, I'm gonna tell you two things that should help you, and then I'm outta here. One, the missing boy tried using a fake ID last night to gain entrance to The Angry Fisherman. It was exactly at eleven because he tried blending in with a wedding party that had been bar hopping on a bus trolley. I confiscated the ID and was going to grab him but was distracted by another customer. He stumbled off before I could get him. He looked to be really drunk. I didn't see him after that. Now, the other thing I will tell you is that I was at the bar until two and then dropped off the night deposit at Sandy Point Federal Savings Bank with Vicki Costa, the bar manager of The A.F. That was around 2:15. Then, I went home and went to bed, and I got up at 6:30 and came here to fill out a police report about…"

"Yes, about that police report." He picked it up and scanned it. "Says here you had a problem with Rutger before all of this. Can you tell me…"

"I knew it. See, Detective, that's where I'm going to stop you. I've just given you what you need as far as a time frame that will hopefully help in finding this missing kid. But you didn't even write that down. So, I think I'm not going to talk to you about anything else without my lawyer present."

Was I paranoid? Probably. Was I being an asshole? Definitely. I didn't trust him.

I thought if I took the offensive, he'd know he couldn't screw the new guy. Who knows if that was the right tactic or not?

"If you don't have anything to hide, why do you need a lawyer?" He began rolling up his sleeves.

I laughed, "'Cause I watch TV. No more talking until my lawyer gets here."

"Well, we can arrange for you to call him in a few minutes. I know we started off on the wrong foot, but I'm worried about the boy. So, just a couple of more questions."

There was a knock on the door.

"What?" Gordon growled over his shoulder.

"Echo Landers is at the front desk." The male voice said from the hallway.

"So?"

The door cracked open and the black cop, Jensen, peeked in.

"She said her stepdad will be here in about 10 minutes or so."

"So?"

"Um…" Jensen was reluctant.

Gordon pushed, "Go ahead. C'mon. What?"

"Echo… I mean, Miss Landers… says that her stepdad, Nicholas Eldredge, is Mr. O'Rourke's lawyer, and he doesn't want you talking to his client."

"The real estate attorney?" Detective Gordon looked pissed and baffled all at the same time.

I shrugged. "That's the best I could get at such short notice, but I'm willing to bet he had a few classes that dealt with police interrogation."

Detective Gordon's face turned into a patchwork of pink blotches as he pressed his pen on and grunted, "O'Rourke, give me those timelines again."

"Sure thing, Detective. Sure thing."

CHAPTER 14

NOVEMBER 11, 1970

WEDNESDAY

NERO

Nero was beyond confused. There were several emotions swirling around in the pit of his stomach — disgust for his mother, hatred for the high school kid, and curiosity about what he just witnessed. His small frame really had trouble processing that emotion. It ached through him — a bizarre, wondrous sensation throbbed. He had the feeling all the way to Pop Tucker's store.

It had happened to him once before while lying on the couch, his eyes fixed on Raquel Welch telling jokes and batting her eyes on *The Dick Cavett Show*. But his father had suddenly stormed into the room, catching him as he desperately tried to pull his pants up.

It had been too late. His father had gripped the coal shovel and started smacking, the whole time grunting in a sour chant, "Don't make the same mistake! Don't be like me! Don't let the whores control you like that! You have to control them! Don't forget that! Always control them!"

But a revelation pulled Nero out of that memory. It was the same revelation he had been having all day — his father was dead. He wanted to unzip his jeans right there and let them fall to the sidewalk. But in the back of his mind, he knew he had to stop the forbidden excitement. If not, something would happen. He didn't know what. The thought of the unknown was so appealing, but he knew it also must be wrong. He didn't know how he knew any of this, but he did.

I will find out when I'm at my Silent Place.

All of these thoughts circled in his head, and Nero knew he was mixed-up. Beyond mixed up. Sick. Actually, he always sensed he was disturbed, but now, for the first time in his life, he felt there was hope for his problems. He could turn to somebody to help him. Someone to fix him. To fix everything — Pop Tucker. He could talk to Pop. Pop would listen. He would be like a real father. Rational. Soothing.

Nero imagined Pop rustling his hair with his gentle hand.

He would comfort him, saying things like, "It's going to be okay."

He might even tell me that it's normal and okay to have those thoughts.

Yes, I am going to be OK, Nero coached the belief as Pop's store came into view.

He was getting that good feeling back again, and it wasn't a "bad" good feeling. It was the feeling of being a normal kid. He thought of the model airplanes, and those other images began to fade from his mind.

No more of those thoughts!

He watched his new father gripping a red-handled push broom, methodically guiding the dirt off the sidewalk. Every kid in town knew that when Pop swept the walk with his special red broom — it even had bright red bristles — that was their unofficial stop sign: *Sorry kids, I'm closing. Come back tomorrow.*

Nero didn't know what to do. Should he smile? Or should he turn around and go home? But then he noticed Pop *was* smiling — at him! Not a small, polite smile but a big one, probably one of the biggest smiles ever directed at Nero in his life.

God, it feels good to be wanted!

Pop rested on the broom while he unwrapped a lollipop and said, "I still have some sweeping to do. Why don't you go into the back room and check out the airplanes I set aside for you?"

"Okay," Nero nodded.

"Oh yeah, one other thing," Pop stopped him, "There's a treat in the refrigerator for you."

Nero tapped his index finger to his chest, "For me?"

Pop laughed. "Yes," and pointed his lollipop at him, "for you."

The boy darted into the store. Within seconds, he was in the back room pulling the refrigerator door open. The dim bulb revealed what was placed on the top shelf, in between the brown paper-wrapped cold cuts from Lareby's Market and the few oranges that had rolled to life. It was a large cup with a straw. On the side of the cup, in swoopy cursive letters, was the logo that caused every kid in the Point to drool — *HAPPY FLAVORS ICE CREAM.*

"Oh, wow." Nero grabbed the frappe and took a long sip. He stopped and eyed it. It tasted a little odd. A little like medicine. But then he took another sip, and the medicine taste went away. So, he sucked on the straw again. He still hadn't had his dinner and his stomach had been growling, but with every sip, his hunger diminished, and a warm feeling rushed to his face. It almost felt like when he drank rum. After he had drunk most of the frappe, he paused and allowed himself a smile.

Pop even knows my favorite type of ice cream — coffee.

He took off the lid of the cup, tilted his head back, and downed the remaining clumps of coffee ice cream. Yes, he did have that rum feeling. He felt lightheaded. And happy.

That's why they call it Happy Flavors!

He chuckled to himself.

When he was finished, he threw the cup and straw into a trash can beside the couch and rested his hand on the rusty radiator to catch his balance. The radiator felt loose and unsteady, just like Nero, so he moved on. He made his way over to the table where three boxes of military model airplanes were placed.

"Wow," he said to himself as he studied the pictures on each box: an A-26 Douglas Invader, a P-40 Warhawk, and a P-39 Airacobra.

They have to cost more than ten dollars, and even if they don't, which one would I pick?

He then tried picturing the soldiers who flew in those planes.

What did their bodies look like when they were shot down? Did they burn and crackle to dust like my father's had? Did their screams hit a higher pitch than a quartet of violins?

"Stop!" he yelled out loud. He couldn't think that way. He had to force himself to think of something else. But then suddenly, he couldn't think at all. His mind was cloudy, and his eyelids felt heavy. He could barely make out Pop's figure approaching him.

"Go lie......... couch," were the only words Nero could make out, so he swayed and stumbled over to the couch. He was so tired. His mind was barely working.

It didn't make any sense to him. He tried to talk, but the words stalled on his tongue before his eyelids finally caved in.

For the next hour, Nero drifted in and out of consciousness.

He remembered being handcuffed behind his back and was blinded by a flashing camera. When the flashes ceased, he was able to see another man holding a Polaroid camera. The skinny man was laughing from behind a Halloween mask of a smiling, blond-haired girl.

Is that Cinderella? Nero wondered, before passing out again.

The next time his eyes opened, he saw Pop and the Cinderella man looking at pictures. Pop then moved the radiator while the masked man placed the pictures in a box and stuffed the box into a hole behind the radiator.

Pop snapped his head around and Nero closed his eyes quickly, trying not to allow the pain he was now feeling all over his body to register in his brain.

"I think he's waking up," Pop said.

Nero listened for the other man's voice, but all he could hear was a whisper. A moment later, he heard the door slam shut.

He felt his arm being tugged and took a minute, pretending he was just waking up from a long, comfortable nap. When he opened his eyes, Pop was buttoning up his shirt and hitching his red suspenders to his jeans.

"Good. You're awake. You have a nice nap?"

Nero didn't say a word. He just glared at him.

"Here's the deal, you can have all of the planes."

Nero still didn't speak. He had no memory of what just happened, but at that moment, he knew Pop Tucker could never be his father. He was now thinking of what he could do with Pop's eyes.

Pop must've felt his fury.

"Don't you ever look at me like that! Tie your damned shoes and get out of here!"

Nero looked down at both untied sneakers and quickly looped them.

"And don't think of telling nobody. No one would ever believe you, anyway."

Nero nodded.

"Good," Pop paused. "You didn't cry. They usually cry. That means you must like it."

"I don't cry."

Pop lunged, wrapping his meaty hand around Nero's neck. "But you *will* cry if you ever talk! You'll do more than cry! You got that!"

"Yes. Can I —" Nero stopped the question. Whenever he asked questions, he always got hit, and he just wanted to get out of there.

"You want to know why, huh? I'll tell you why. Why does a dog lick himself? Because he can," Pop laughed. "No one cares about you. That's why *I* can. And no one will *ever* care about you. Now get outta here! I have to get home to my family."

Nero rushed over, grabbed the boxes, and hustled out the back door.

When he was outside, the late fall wind slapped him to his senses. He stood there, taking in the chill for a minute and remembering how he never had felt like a normal boy, and now Pop Tucker had convinced him that he never would be. It was a thought he decided he would no longer fight.

It was time to fully embrace it.

CHAPTER 15

JUNE 9, 2004

WEDNESDAY

ECHO

Echo knew she should've taken a few minutes to wash her tear-stained face, but J.T. had said that he needed her help ASAP, so she used the sleeve of her silk chiffon blouse as a tissue while at the same time dialing her stepfather and then fifth gearing it to the Sandy Point Police Station. She found out quickly that she may've stifled the tears, but she couldn't hide her puffy eyes.

"Ec, you been crying, sister?" Officer Jenson, her childhood friend, had asked her just before exiting to relay her message to Detective Gordon.

She laughed and lied, "No, Jamal, my eyes are just telling me that I've got to replace these damn 30-day contacts. I'm probably on day 40."

She sat in the waiting area flipping through a back issue of People magazine. She wished it had been as simple as cloudy contacts, but it wasn't. Her past would never be that simple. She tried to get her mind off it and think of J.T. and why he was being questioned. He had said something about an underage drunk kid who tried to get into The A.F. and now was missing, but she had only been half listening at the time. And even now, as she waited for her stepdad, she was only half thinking about J. T.'s situation. Her mind was somewhere else. She was 14 years in the past with the only man she had ever loved.

Echo was a senior at Sandy Point High. They both had skipped school. They were always adventurous. They had to be. It was March. Rainy. Dreary. It was the perfect day to be under the covers, so they met at his cottage that overlooked the harbor inlet. Depeche Mode's haunting love song "Somebody" played on the stereo accompanied by the sad call of the flashing, green foghorn outside the window. He told her the light reminded him of the one in *The Great Gatsby*, and Echo had joked that he wasn't Robert Redford, and the bottle-green reflection made his place resemble a cheap hotel on some desolate desert strip. But there was nothing cheap about how they felt for one another. Nervously giggling, they sipped wine coolers, speculating where the mist-covered fishing boats were headed. And then he kissed her softly, but with a power that no boy — and now no man — had ever been able to replicate. He told her that he loved her and asked if she felt the same. She remembered she hadn't answered his question with words, but with wanting eyes.

Yes.

It was time.

On that gloomy, beautiful day Echo gave her virginity away and even now, after all the pain he had put her through, she didn't regret it. She never would.

She then thought about when he first left town. On rainy days, as if the Jeep drove itself, she always ended up at the harbor parking lot, drinking coffee and welcoming the moaning foghorn. It always made her remember. It got to the point where she began to look forward to the rain. But one stormy day she forced her Jeep to turn away from the harbor entrance. And on the next storm, she drank her coffee in the donut shop's parking lot. It took several years, but now whenever that foghorn sounded, she only thought about the bad weather. She was moving on. Finally.

Shortly after returning from a photo shoot at a luncheon for a 50th anniversary, and moments before J.T.'s phone call, Echo had gone into her room to check the email on her photography website. She had scanned the subject headings for the usual possible jobs — a senior picture, a fall wedding, a 70th birthday party, etc. But one subject title stood out: HEY, MATTIE!

She froze. It was the secret nickname he had given her after she admitted to being so obsessed with *Ethan Frome* that she had read it eighteen times. Her mind began rereading the email.

Hey Mattie,

It's probably a little strange hearing from me. I was at my computer and thought to Google your name and up came your website. Great to see that you stuck with the photography! It's amazing because I've thought a lot about you lately. I know it's been years. But I'm coming to Boston in the fall and was just wondering...

"Damn, him!" Echo yelled out, turning off her memory of the email she had read earlier that morning.

"Huh?" asked a voice a few seats down.

"Oh, sorry, nothing," she replied before even seeing the lanky, malnourished-looking kid in his early twenties staring at her. He was wearing a stained yellow FREE TIBET T-shirt, dirty Levis, and a worn-out pair of Birkenstocks. She then noticed his shoulder length — blonde — dreadlocks.

A white kid with dreads... You don't see that every day.

"If you mean that cop," Dreads gestured to an officer who was chatting on the phone behind the front desk, "you're right."

He then walked over, riding on a wave of patchouli that almost knocked Echo out, and settled in the chair next to her.

Dreads continued, "All I came here for was to help them out. And now I've been waiting for like a half hour. Just another example of how messed up this country is."

After Echo's nostrils got accustomed to the pungent smell of earth, she actually welcomed the distraction.

Anything to get my mind off the email...

"Oh, really," she said. "So, what are you here to help with?"

He scratched the early beginnings of a beard. "Are you *really* interested or are you just being polite?"

"I work for the *Sandy Point Times,* so I'm always interested."

"You a reporter?"

"No. A photographer. I'm actually waiting for the reporter. He's in the back with one of the detectives."

"Was the reporter the guy you were talking about when you said, 'Damn him'?"

"No, that was someone else. The reporter's a nice guy. Anyway, whenever I hear about a story, I pass it on. So, you got anything good?" She smiled.

151

A mischievous grin crossed his lips revealing teeth that matched his yellow T-shirt.

"You know then, I might have something for you, but..." He let the word hang.

"But, what?"

"But, if you decide to pass on my information to your paper, you'll also have to put some things about me and my cause in your article."

"Only the reporter can make that promise. I will say, if it's relevant to his story, I know he'll put it in. That is, if your story is newsworthy."

Dreads thought for a minute and nodded, "Oh, it is. And so is my cause."

"Okay, well shoot then," she nodded.

"Well, last night I was urban foraging and I..."

"Urban foraging?"

"You know, dumpster diving."

"Oh."

"And I found something."

"O...kay..." Echo hesitated. "Before we go any further — dumpster diving? Does that mean you're homeless?"

He laughed. "Do I look homeless?"

Echo almost answered, "Yes," but then realized he was being rhetorical.

"I'm a freegan. So anyway, I was dumpster diving outside of Dave's Bakery, you wouldn't believe all the donuts those waste mongers throw away. I go strictly for the fruit though. Anyway, as I was sifting through the dumpster..."

"Sorry to interrupt, but what's a 'freegan'?"

"I thought you might ask that, and that's why I'd want that mentioned in the article. *People* should be educated about us and our cause. You know what a vegan is, right?"

Echo nodded, "Yeah, I think. Aren't they like vegetarians because they don't believe that animals should be our source of food? That it's cruel or something like that?"

"Or something like that? It is cruel. But don't get me going. I'll tell your reporter all about it. Anyway, being a freegan, we take it one step further. We live in such a throwaway society that we freegans believe in waste reclamation."

"Meaning?"

"Meaning, we forage in the dumpsters for food and other products that we can use."

152

"So," Echo paused, "you eat food from the trash?"

"I can see the disgust on your face, but if you don't have the knowledge, why should I condemn your ignorance?"

"My *ignorance*?" Echo didn't like that.

Dreads softened, "What I mean is, do you know the old saying 'someone's trash is another person's treasure?' That really is the freegan lifestyle. We recycle almost everything, and you'd be surprised how much good food gets dumped."

"Okay, I got it. So, what does this have to do with why you're here?" she asked while glancing out the window and spotting her stepdad's black Infiniti S.U.V. pull into the parking lot.

Dreads did his job and killed time, but now I have to get going.

"So, last night, well actually it was at around 1:00 this morning, I was at the dumpster behind Dave's Bakery and Spokes for Folks and found this." He reached into his pocket and pulled out a cell phone.

"Oh, so you're returning a cell phone. That's good of you." Echo began to rise.

"It's not just *any* cell phone." He stopped her.

"Huh?"

"This afternoon I was back foraging at the dumpster behind Pilgrim Diner and heard two of the cooks talking as they threw away some absolutely succulent cantaloupes and blueberries. Anyway, they were talking about how the cops were looking for some kid who went missing last night."

Echo turned from the window and her attention was back on Dreads. "Oh, yeah? Go on."

He squinted, "I was going on."

"Oh, yeah, sorry."

"Yeah, well, anyway, guess whose cell phone this is?"

"The missing kid's?"

"Yep."

"How do you know that?"

"I heard them say his name: Rutger Nelson. Check this out." He turned the phone on and it lit up and the screen's greeting read: What up, Rutger Dog!

Rutger, I know that kid! His father is Commodore Nelson, the head of the Sandy Point Yacht Club. Commodore Nelson has a lot of pull in town. No wonder the cruisers were already looking for him.

She went through her bag, taking out a pad and pen.

"Did you tell the cops?"

"I told them I had information and before I could get the word 'cell phone' out they told me to wait over here for some detective named Gordon. So, here I am."

She wrote it down. "When did you find the phone again?"

"Around one." Dreads turned off the cell and put it back into his pocket.

Echo knew J.T. probably didn't get out of The A.F. till around 2. So, Detective Gordon was really wasting his time, especially when a huge lead was literally waiting. She also realized if the cell phone was found in a dumpster, Rutger Nelson really was missing and not on some drunken binge on a boat to the Vineyard or sleeping it off on the beach.

"See that guy?" She pointed outside at her stepdad who was grabbing his briefcase out of the passenger seat of the Infiniti.

"Yeah, the guy driving that absolutely disgusting environmental assassin-mobile?"

"Ah, yeah, I guess. That's my stepdad. He's a lawyer. Can you tell him everything you just told me?"

Dreads scratched his wanna-be beard again, "I don't know. I have a real problem with people who drive SUVs."

"Me too. But if you do, I guarantee my reporter friend will do a whole article on your freegan lifestyle."

"How can you guarantee that?"

"Because he owes you."

"Owes me?" Dreads thumbed his chest.

"Yeah, you just backed up his alibi."

CHAPTER 16

JUNE 10, 2004

THURSDAY

NERO

After he entered the woods, Nero checked his watch – 1:54 A.M. It was now a full day later and he wondered if the kid was still alive.

God, I hope so!

A young, fear-glistening naked body is what he needed more than anything else right now. He had to enjoy the moment because he knew things might soon be changing for him. He tried not to think about it — getting caught. Not now. Not in his woods.

"I can think about that later," he whispered to himself.

The back of his mind was ringing a warning bell because for the first time in a very long time, he had fucked up. And boy did he fuck up!

Everyone in town was now looking for Rutger Nelson, and because of it, he had to be extra careful as he made his way to his Silent Place. That voice in his head tolled a different bell the night before — the dinner bell. Why did he listen to it? It was so unlike him to be sloppy. He always planned his "dates," as he called his abductions, down to the most minute detail, but when he spotted the

155

kid incoherently mumbling and stumbling along the sidewalk, the urges lit up his insides with the fury of a Molotov cocktail thrown into a hay field.

And the voice in his head then followed: *Nero, it will be so easy.*

He was going to resist it, but then the kid had to tempt him further — by being in a drunken tantrum, throwing something into the dumpster, and then passing out seconds later.

He had pulled his car up, leaned toward the passenger window, and asked, "Hey kid, you, alright?"

The kid was already snoring.

His adrenaline shifted into high gear. He had looked around. No people. No headlights. Nothing.

Nero, just a little taste. No one will ever know. — the inner voice had seduced.

That was all it took. It was never just a little taste. There was no turning back. He didn't even look at the kid's face as he stuffed him into the back seat of his car.

If I had recognized the drunk's face, Rutger Nelson would've awakened with just a bad hangover.

He had figured it was some out-of-town college summer kid drunk and lost, not a summer resident! Not Commodore Ethan Nelson's wise-ass son. But by the time he realized who it was, it was too late. He had already pulled the golf shirt over the kid's shoulders, and his sticky-tongue was licking the side of the boy's face. But then it had hit him. The eyes. He knew the eyes. He had seen those eyes every summer for the last ten years. It had made him stop for a minute. But, when it registered that it was indeed Rutger Nelson, the panic of knowing that they might finally start looking for Nero actually gave him one of the stiffest erections ever. It reminded him of another time. So long ago.

His teeth then locked onto the back flesh like a junkyard dog gnawing on steak gristle, marking his territory and waking the kid so he could bathe in his own horror. And he did. Rutger Nelson had one of the highest pitched screams he had ever heard.

After Nero's sweaty body finished bucking away and released, he took out his violin and played back the sound of the scream to Rutger. The kid didn't disappoint. He countered with his own screams.

Yes, Nero enjoyed their time together, so much so that he decided to let the kid live one more day. That is, if the kid had the will to live. It was a test. Did he pass it? If he did, the sex and pain would be taken to another level. And the screams...

God, the screams.

Nero had made it. He was finally at his Silent Place, and in a few moments, he would find out what kind of will Rutger Nelson really had.

Reaching down for the twine handle, he pulled open the hidden door. It was in the mid-'70s when Nero first sculpted and cut out the sod-covered camouflaged door and dug a three-foot hole to hide his jars of trophies. But the older he got, the bigger the trophies got, and it seemed every year he tunneled a little deeper until one day he realized he would have to create a complete underground home, so he could actually stay with all of his trophies and study them and remember. The other obvious reason for tunneling underground was that no man or animal would ever be able to detect the smells when his trophies aged. And some were very old.

But it wasn't until the early '80s when Nero really made his underground hideaway into a home. He was up in Laconia for Motorcycle Weekend searching for sexually confused bikers and wayward sluts. There were plenty of both, but he couldn't find any loners. He needed a loner — someone with no ties. Someone, who wouldn't be missed. Not that hunting ground. They all traveled in packs. It was too risky.

On his way out of town, he thought his trip had been a waste of time, but then he pulled over to check out a yard sale and that's when he found them. He felt they were literally sent from God because they were resting on the table beside a Bible. The Bible was a buck fifty. The HOW TO BUILD A BOMB SHELTER plans were only twenty-five cents. It really was a revelation.

Nero scooped up the plans and had flipped the coin into the air like he was tipping a shoeshine boy.

Snatching the quarter with his oil-stained palm, a slight smile appeared from the elderly man. "So, you want to build a shelter, eh?"

He replied, "Maybe."

The man smiled broader showing he had only three teeth. His fingers that had been pulling on the cotton growing out of his right ear then reached into the pocket flap of his heavy lumberjack shirt. He pulled out an unopened Budweiser, tossed it to Nero, and said, "Follow me, then."

After six more warm cans, Nero had been given a tour of the man's bomb shelter and heard all the old codger's thoughts on what and what not to do. It had been valuable advice that he kept in the front of his mind during the long hours of construction. It had taken him five years of sneaking through the black woods with bricks, steel plates, shovels, and everything else. But now, as he flipped on the flashlight and directed the beam on the rope ladder, he could hear the frantic whimpering below. Nero now realized it was the best twenty-five cents he ever spent.

He undid the ladder, and it swooshed down into thin air until it hit the floor. He turned off the light and climbed down into the darkness. This was one of his favorite parts. It was so dark that the boy couldn't see him. Only hear him. So, he stood only inches away and let Rutger wonder where he was. The boy's hands were in the always reliable handcuffs, and his legs were bound with silver duct tape. Nero stood in silence listening to Rutger scream and wheeze behind the oxygen mask he had attached to the boy the night before.

After fifteen minutes of Nero remaining silent, breathing in the boy's piss and shit soaked figure, the boy finally settled down. He was probably thinking that his captor had fallen asleep.

Yes, Rutger Nelson did have will! This should be fun!

In one quick motion, he flipped on the light, throwing the yellow beam at the boy blinding him.

"Hell–ooooh," Nero's cheery tone mimicked the waking a lover on a Sunday morning.

Rutger jerked back to life and flapped around as if that might be the key to breaking free.

It never would be.

"Good to see you're okay, Rutger. I was worried. I've never been completely satisfied with my ventilation system," he said as he walked over and flashed the light on one of his old jars that read: CHRISTMAS SEASON OF 1972.

He studied what was in the jar, and almost forgot about Rutger.

Maybe I'll use that tonight?

"Wow, I haven't thought about that in a long time. I'll think about that later tonight. Outside on the grass," he said to himself, at first ignoring Rutger's muffled yells but then stabbing his light back over at him.

"Shut up!"

The boy didn't.

"Shut up or else!"

That did the trick.

Nero unwrapped a red lollipop and swung it around like a magic wand before licking and then asking, "Rutger, I have one simple question for you. Do you want to see God tonight?"

He heard the noisy response but went over anyway and pushed the mask off his face and up to the boy's wet forehead.

"I didn't understand you, Rutger. Do you w—"

"NO! God, no! Please!" He spat furiously.

"I didn't finish the question. Do you want to see God?"

"I said no! Please! You know my father! He's rich! He'll pay you."

"Pay me? Hmmmm… So, you think it's about money? Well, if that's the case, the answer you should give me is a very simple one. Please say, 'No, I don't want to see God.'"

"No, I don't want to see God." The boy said it all in one breath.

"I was hoping you'd say that."

Nero headed over to the trusty old tackle box, unbuckled it, and lowered his flashlight. The reflection off the sharp silver blade shined up at him. It was the meat cleaver his father had named "Old Heidi."

I'll use that later.

Then he pulled out the thin bladed knife — the one he used for eye removal.

"Don't worry," he said over his shoulder, "I'll make sure you won't see God tonight or tomorrow night or any other night for that matter."

CHAPTER 17
CHRISTMAS EVE

1972

DEVLIN

Officer Devlin sat in his cruiser parked on the dock. He was waiting for Captain Tadmor's ferry to arrive. It was only 4:30 in the afternoon, but his body was dragging. He was no different from everyone else in Sandy Point — the whole town was sleepless ever since the news broke. The holiday spirit had been wrenched from the stomachs of the people of The Point and almost no one was thinking about Christmas. Those who did shop were doing it in quiet, zombie-like trances.

How can you shop for your own son when you know there is a little boy missing?

The Sandy Point Standard Times had run that quote a few days earlier, attributing it to Audrey Renna, the owner of Spokes for Folks bike store, and the single mother of Chuck, Jr.

Any other time, Devlin would've laughed his ass off considering the source: Mrs. Renna, a woman who had a taste for screwdrivers as well as being screw-driven by bad boys. She would never be nominated for "mother of the year."

But this was no laughing matter. When Devlin first heard the news, he thought immediately of the night he caught Paul Harrison showing the boys the

Playboy. He called Detective Prichard, who admitted it was a solid tip. But then he phoned Devlin back moments later stating, "Paul Harrison left two weeks ago for a vacation in the Caribbean. That's a week before this happened, and he's with people who can verify that."

After Devlin had hung up the phone, he first had a feeling of relief — that his not reporting that night hadn't come back to haunt him. But then the guilt smacked him.

Maybe if I had been in town, I would've noticed someone or something, and this wouldn't have happened.

So, he cut his trip with Anna short and drove back moments after speaking with Prichard. And since coming back to town, the first few days he had put in about 22 hours searching, but whenever he got home, he still couldn't sleep. How could anyone? He eventually stopped going home for the catnaps.

He vowed: *no more sleep until there is at least a lead.*

But there were no leads. Clues. Ransom demands. Nothing. So, during his most recent sleepless string, he had racked up 38 hours straight without a wink. The auditory hallucinations had crept into his system and started controlling him the previous night.

He was driving along, shining the cruiser's white floodlight onto Samoset Place when he thought he heard the sound of a violin in the distance. He knew it was crazy, but he stopped the car anyway. After he flipped on his flashlight and walked around the woods, it grew silent again. He realized that without sleep, he was like a man without water in the desert, and the mirage he was witnessing was of his trip from the week before: Anna wrapped in a bed sheet, sitting on the window seat and staring out at the falling snow.

He shook the memory away and headed back to the station. But then he found out that he could not will the hallucinations away and that they were actually getting dangerous when he almost rammed Chief Gedney's car while driving into the station's lot that afternoon.

Chief Gedney jumped out, slapped Devlin's hood, pointed through the windshield, and ordered, "You're no good to no one if you're not alert! You need at least six hours of sleep, Devlin. Go home, Officer."

But would he really sleep?

The dying, pink sun was now a movie backdrop for Captain Tadmor's ferry that sliced through the angry winter surf toward The Point. Devlin knew he had at least ten more minutes to wait. But instead of closing his eyes, he opened the glove box, pulled out the black ring box, and stared down at it.

A week ago, life was good. No, life was great.

One of those great things was his professional life. He had been a patrolman for the Sandy Point Police Department for almost three years, and after a long and rocky start he was finally considered one of the boys. He hadn't gained acceptance by jumping in front of an exploding grenade to shield anyone like he had in Nam. He had been subtle in his approach. Simply, when he had seen an opportunity, he had taken it.

He conquered Officer Smart Ass, Rodney Farrell, by finding Farrell's gun moments after the officer had left it on the counter of the Pilgrim Diner.

Devlin spotted Farrell in the Sea Glass Beach parking lot, in a desperate search, ripping apart his cruiser.

He handed Farrell the gun and said, "I don't think I have to report this to the Chief. Right, Rodney?"

There were no more wise cracks after that.

Patrolman Jessie "Jelly Donut" Gordon was won over the day he brought his young son into the station. Gordon paraded his boy around telling everyone that the kid was going to be a detective when he grew up.

When Devlin was introduced to the red-headed ball of baby fat, he had pointed back at Jessie and said, "Your dad's one of the best lawmen I know."

Of course, it was a lie, but Devlin felt that it might motivate Jessie to work harder, and he also felt that it wasn't his responsibility to tell the kid, "There is no Santa Claus."

You eventually find that out on your own, he had thought, a glimpse of Allan Devlin defending an Irish mobster hit man appeared in his mind.

Jessie shrugged and beamed at Devlin's comment that day. A few nights later, while Devlin was manning a speed trap on the outskirts of town, Jessie showed up with an extra cup of coffee for Devlin. The cheap bastard never bought anyone coffee, including himself.

The final holdout was Detective Prichard. But then one fall night, Devlin caught one of the local kids with a can of gasoline trying to torch Prichard's 40-foot sailboat.

When the news got to Prichard, he actually thanked Devlin and asked him how he caught the kid.

Devlin had responded, "Lately, the kid had been acting different. I saw him with the gas can, and I felt like he was up to no good."

Prichard was now in his corner, "Great instincts, Officer, if you ever consider trying to become a detective, don't hesitate to ask me any questions."

He seemed *genuine*, Devlin thought, as he flipped open the ring box and stared at the diamond.

Anna.

The other reason life had been so good, the only reason. They had been dating for over two years. She had not only become his lover, but also his best friend. It was *almost* perfect… if it weren't for the families. Anna and Devlin had come to a fork in the road in their relationship where a decision had to be made about their future. She had spent her first year out of Radcliffe working as a receptionist at the *Sandy Point Standard Times*, and her family accepted the low-paying job as a diversion for her. A lark. Play time on the Cape for a year. But now her father feared the reality of having a small-town cop sit at his holiday table every year. He was pushing Anna on the idea of finding someone who could provide her the lavish lifestyle she deserved, and if that wasn't the immediate solution, then he begged for her to travel to Europe. Play a little longer. And then maybe in France or Spain, she would drink and dance the cop out of her system.

The irony was that Carson Talbot's attitude had delighted Devlin's father to no end. Allan Devlin saw it as his opportunity to push his own dream.

"It's still not too late to further your education, Michael. I bet if you showed Mr. Talbot that kind of initiative, he might let you marry Anna," he said at more than one Sunday dinner while cutting through his bloody sirloin from Lareby's Market.

Anna had taught Devlin restraint, so he would only reply, "Yeah, maybe."

Not arguing with the defense attorney turned out to be Devlin's best retaliation. It drove the man crazy.

Allan Devlin would almost choke on his steak while mimicking, "Yeah, maybe! That's all you can say!"

"Yep."

But Devlin also knew he had to decide soon. Anna did have opportunities, and he should either marry her or let her go for someone or something better. He analyzed the situation during many long shifts and finally came to one conclusion: no one would ever love Anna Talbot as much as he did. It was that simple.

His mission was set. He found out Mr. Talbot had lunch every Tuesday at Anthony's Pier Four which overlooked Boston Harbor. Devlin switched his shift and drove up in an early December snow duster to make his case for her hand.

When he finished his plea, Carson Talbot tossed his napkin at him and said, "Wipe your eyes, you're crying. No wonder we're losing in Nam."

In shock, Devlin dabbed his eyes dry. "I can't believe I'm crying. I never cry."

"Son-of-a-bitch!" Talbot exclaimed, almost shaking the oil lamps off the tables.

"What?" Devlin asked.

"You really do love my little girl," he said as the maître d' approached, nervously rubbing his hands.

"Yes, Mr. Talbot, I do love her, and I always will."

"Okay, then. But it will stay Mr. Talbot. You got that?"

"Huh?"

"None of that 'Dad' shit. I'm not your dad and I never will be. I hate when they do that. Anyway, if you don't usually cry and you're going to cry for my girl, then I know you must love her. And I also know if you love her then you will protect her. In the end, that's all a father wants. Well, at least, that's what my wife keeps bitching in my ear every night. So, let's hope for your sake Anna says yes. Now let's drink."

"I have a shift that I..."

"Well, then one drink for you, but I'm going to celebrate."

Mr. Talbot turned to the maître d', "Renaldo, a bottle of Mr. Jack Daniels, please, and an extra glass for my soon to be son-in-law."

And it did look to be soon. A week later, Devlin called his Army buddy Brett Beldman and confessed that he went to the "ring store" and for Brett to put his tux on standby. Then his next call was to make reservations at the Maple Tree Inn up in the Berkshires.

It was the natural setting for him to propose. In July, Devlin and Anna had stayed in the suite that contained the only fireplace at the inn. At the time, they both speculated on what it must be like in the winter. Back then, it was 80 degrees, there was no need to build a fire, especially when there was one already lit. Anna was burning up with virginal desire, and her flames were scorching Devlin's insides. They somehow managed to contain the feeling and spent the early evening across the lawns at the Tanglewood Performing Arts Center listening to the Boston Symphony Orchestra playing under the silver stars.

But then she grabbed his hand and cooed, "I bet we can hear this from our room. I'm finally ready, Michael. And what beautiful background music this will be."

She was right. The string melodies rode softly across the balmy summer breeze, faintly playing through the bedroom window for the two shy, naked lovers that found one another — shy no longer, finally joining as one.

That was why he decided it was the perfect setting for him to propose. Devlin had it all planned. They would arrive at the inn Friday night, have a romantic supper in the dining room, and then go back to their room and make love under a quilt by the fire. The next morning, he would suggest they go snowshoeing.

As they tracked along, laughing and throwing snowballs at one another, they would suddenly hear the sound of violins playing from Tanglewood.

Anna would say something like, "Who would be playing music outside in the cold?"

Devlin would suggest that they check it out.

They'd arrive and see the quartet he hired, bundled up strumming away, acting like it was a bright summer's day.

Anna would watch in awe and then finally turn back to Devlin, "Michael, can you believe this?"

By that time, he would be on one knee with the ring box open. He would say something like, "Miss Anna Talbot, since I've met you, every moment is like a warm summer's day. As little Greggie likes to say, you are a sunshine dream. Will you be my sunshine dream forever?"

Anna would then kiss him, and their life would begin.

But it didn't work out that way. During the early morning before the proposal, Devlin was lying in bed watching Anna wrapped in a sheet sitting on the window seat. She was staring out the window. He hadn't seen her face, but he sensed something.

"What's wrong?" He had asked.

She turned around and had tears in her eyes. "I don't know, Michael. I just woke up with this horrible feeling. I don't know why I'm so sad. Something's wrong."

"With us?"

"No. I don't think so. I just feel it. I have such dread. But I don't know why."

Ten minutes later, Detective Prichard rang, and they both realized what Anna's premonition might have been about — a sweet little boy was missing.

Devlin broke from the memory by shutting the ring box and opening the glove compartment. He was about to put the box away when something beyond the ferry caught his eye. It was a flock of birds circling the tree line on the other side of the harbor.

It didn't look like gulls.

A strange foreboding feeling began to brew in his gut. He didn't know why he felt this way, but something was off. He had sat in his cruiser waiting for the ferry thousands of times before, and not once had he seen so many birds fly in that area. They were only about three hundred yards away, but the sun was slipping into night, so he couldn't quite make out what exactly they were doing, but he knew something wasn't right.

Probably more hallucinations.

He placed the ring box into the compartment, shut it, hurried out of his car, and opened the trunk. He grabbed the binoculars and scanned the area realizing it wasn't a flock of just any birds. It was what poets and filmmakers always liked to describe as a murder — a murder of crows. He knew the meaning behind that name all too well. He sucked in a short breath and put the binoculars to his side for a second as the morbid thought ran to him.

"No, I just need some sleep. That's all," he reminded himself, eyeing Captain Tadmor's ferry that was about to dock.

But the sounds of the crows' screeches then traveled across the harbor and pulled on that ominous chord inside him. He raised the binoculars again to check.

It looked to be at least eight of them.

They were all taking turns dive-bombing into the wooded area right beside Mackerel Beach.

"Please, God, no..." The words were barely audible as they left his lips.

"Aren't you going to catch the rope?" Captain Tadmor hollered, but Devlin wasn't listening.

He was already in his cruiser racing out of the harbor parking lot. He thought for an instant about radioing it in but knew better. If the Chief found out he was still searching for the little boy and not on that ferry, he would be in hot water. Plus, the fact, a part of him knew the Chief was right about his hallucinations, and the circling crows might actually turn out to be another one of his mirages.

And, even if they weren't, that still didn't mean anything was wrong. But he still felt...

He fought the urge to turn on the siren, but that didn't stop the needle from wavering quickly to the right and fluttering a bit until it steadied on the number 65. The increased speed caused the cruiser's tires to squeal as he turned left onto Harbor Way that led up to Mackerel Street, the road which ran parallel to the other side of the harbor. Devlin's knuckles whitened as he spun the steering wheel to the left again, swinging around the next corner to the straightaway where he accelerated before finally easing on the gas when he came to the foot of the woods next to Mackerel Beach.

At that point, the cruiser came to a slow crawl as he popped his head out and looked up at the trees. It was only about five minutes to sundown, but he was able to make out a couple of crows flying and calling to one another. He slammed on the brakes, and then turned off the ignition. He grabbed his light and hopped out of the car.

Before he entered the woods, he stopped to throw the flashlight's beam on a large construction sign. It read: FUTURE SITE OF THE SANDY POINT BIKE PATH. GROUNDBREAKING: SPRING 1973.

Devlin suddenly reverted to his old survival behavior. He was back on patrol in Nam. His mind ordered his heart to slow down, and the rate lowered immediately. He was calm and calculated and was taking in all the sights and sounds around him. One of the sounds was the shrieking crows in the distance. They didn't sound normal.

"Take everything in. Always be aware of things that seem out of place. And always be careful, or pieces of you will be going home in a body bag." His commanding officer, Lieutenant Ellis, used to bark the same speech over and over at his platoon before they would go out.

The asshole probably saved a lot of lives by drilling it into their heads that one misstep and a Viet Cong booby trap would assure a closed casket service. He brought that extreme Zen-like concentration back home with him, but being a cop, now the reason for caution wasn't just for his own safety, but also necessary when it came to looking for evidence. And just as he remembered that reasoning, his flashlight illuminated a piece of ripped red elastic fabric caught on a branch. It looked as if someone had been running and the branch had snagged it. He got as close as he could to the elastic fabric without touching it, and that concentration he had prided himself on suddenly vanished. He knew where the red elastic fabric could've come from.

"No, it couldn't be..." he said, but he had to push it out of his mind and continue on to the crows' calls.

Deeper into the woods he ventured, the more he needed the flashlight, and the more his heart rate rose. His personal thoughts and feelings were now getting in the way. He had to shut them out. He had to stay in control, but then he saw it and his heart rate rocketed.

A dozen black birds were digging their blood-covered beaks into and picking away at a small body strewn motionless on the ground. One of the birds was perched on what looked to be a stick coming out of the ground at an angle. He couldn't decipher that part of the scene, but he did know one thing. He smelled it. Tasted it. Death was lying in front of him. Devlin couldn't fool himself into thinking otherwise; he had witnessed death too many times.

"Goddamn!" He drew his gun and aimed at one of the crows, but at the last second fired up into the sky. The birds took wild flight. Then, he ran over but stopped in mid-stride falling to his knees when he came to the realization of what the stick really was and why it was at that strange angle. The bile burned his throat and he almost gagged as the rage and sadness met in the middle of his chest. The stick was a red push broom, bristles and all, and it was sticking out of the bare bottom of the little boy who had been missing for over a week.

"No! No!" Devlin yelled as memories blanketed him before he finally pushed them away and made it to his feet. Like a wild man, he zigzagged out of the woods, still panting and yelling.

He opened the cruiser door and was about to grab the radio when his mind went blank.

"What's the code numbers? What's the fucking code numbers?" He cursed himself. He could only think of the set of numbers he had memorized due to the events of the past week.

He clicked on, "Oscar 9, over?"

Alice Harper responded, "Yes? Go ahead, Oscar 9."

"The 10-70.... the 10-70..." That's all he could remember.

It meant "missing person."

"Yes, what are you saying? Oh my God! Did you find him?" Alice's voice sounded hopeful.

He tried to regain his composure. Stay calm, he thought, "Yes. Yes, I found him. I need backup. I'm at the foot of the woods by Mackerel Beach. Over."

"Oh my God. So, should I send an ambulance?"

Devlin clicked back, "No need."

"Devlin found him, and he doesn't need an ambulance..." Alice was saying to someone else, and Devlin thought he heard people in the background erupt in joy.

She continued, "Officer Devlin, should I send an ambulance anyway, so he can be checked out by a doctor for precautionary reasons? Over."

Oh my God, Devlin then realized — *I didn't use the code numbers for homicide. I just made it sound like I had found him and now they think he's alive! What are the code numbers?*

"No ambulance. I need the ME. We're dealing with a DOA here! I repeat..." He paused trying to lock down his emotions, "We're dealing with a DOA here... Send Prichard now! All signs indicate it's a homicide! Oscar 9, over."

After a stunned second, the radio crackled to life followed by Alice screaming orders to "all units" and then came awakening sirens in the distance flying toward the scene. After Devlin re-hooked his radio, he sat in shock trying to fathom how anyone could not only commit such a horrific act, but how they could also do it to one of the best little boys in town? One tear was able to escape before he thumbed it out. He knew the red elastic fabric came from suspenders. Only one person in town wore red suspenders. He also knew that same person owned a red push broom and lived in a mansion on the other side of the woods overlooking Mackerel Beach. The evidence pointed to Pop Tucker.

Devlin made his hand into a fist and banged the steering wheel several times before biting on his lower lip, "As Christ is my witness, I swear to you, Fishy, I'll make that bastard pay."

But after what had just happened to little Fishy Bryden, Devlin couldn't help but wonder if Christ even existed.

CHAPTER 18

JUNE 11, 2004

FRIDAY

J.T.

There was a quick clap of hands that rang in my ears. I had been lost in thought. Not after the loud clap.

"J.T., wake up, you ready to go or what?"

"Jesus Christ, Davis. Yeah, I'm ready."

"Ice those bitches down." Davis Lawson, the owner of The Angry Fisherman, pointed to a dozen pint glasses.

"Yeah, yeah. Jesus Christ," I mumbled to myself.

The Catholic guy said "Jesus Christ" and didn't bow his head. Believe me, if I didn't have other things on my mind, I'd be bracing for that eight-carrot whack Helen O'Rourke used to deliver whenever one of her children took the Lord's name in vain. I actually had a permanent divot in my Irish melon from when I was 12 and blurted it after I had pissed the bed for the fifth time in four days. I know. Not good — certainly not an O'Rourke family Kodak moment. I probably could count those moments on one hand. Or maybe a finger. A middle one.

Anyway, after I said "Jesus Christ," I have to admit that I did scan the bar briefly, out of habit. But then it dawned on me that Mom really was gone. Dead and buried. God rest her soul. Never should've suffered like that.

I felt a breeze wafting through the windows that cooled my thoughts. It was an ocean breeze. I wasn't used to that kind of relief. The only breeze at Tilt the Jar came from Fat Pete when he'd burp his drink order in my face.

I know Fat Pete sounds like a *Sopranos* character, but no, he had no mafia connections. At least, I don't think so. He did grease down his hair and wear chains, but that's where the similarities ended. I always kind of wished he had been affiliated with the mob. That would've at least been worth the spray. No, Fat Pete had no character. His only real claim to fame was being known as the worst scalper around, always huffing and puffing while circling Fenway Park in an outdated T-shirt that read something like "Mo Vaughn for President" and squeezed into his black bicycle shorts that must've been made out of old bus tires. The pathetic bastard was never able to unload the majority of his tickets until the second or third inning. Meaning below face value. Giving him that dishonorable distinction of worst scalper in Kenmore Square. Then he'd spend the rest of the night sucking down our cheap pint piss, bragging about how he had been a Little League hero back in the day in Woonsocket, Rhode Island.

The cool breeze was a gentle reminder that not only was my family album of bullshit tucked away up in Boston, but so were the Fat Petes of the world. I wanted to keep them there. I was looking for a fresh start. A new community. A new life. One much saner. But then the revelation rolled over me. I had been in town for less than a week, and I had already been questioned in a Missing Persons case.

Yep, the Southie guy was a suspect.

Maybe not quite a suspect. I did get cleared as quickly as a Kennedy, but I was still a stranger to The Point. Word got out that I had been questioned and people were whispering about me.

So much for anonymity and trying to ease into the scene.

I knew the town would continue to whisper as long as Rutger Nelson was missing. And the longer he was missing, the louder the whispers would get, even if I did have a solid alibi. I knew that. It's human nature to speculate without the facts or to simply disregard them. Gets in the way of a good story. Whenever there was a big murder in the news, I had done the same thing by entertaining the patrons at The Jar with my theories of whodunit.

In this case, there was no proof of murder, but it didn't look good for Rutger

Nelson, The *Boston Globe* all-scholastic lacrosse player and loving son of Commodore Ethan Nelson. Or simply as I knew the kid — Bulldog Face. It had been three days and there hadn't been a call. Or one use of his credit card. Or one sighting. Still, not one clue. The kid had vanished. There had been speculation that he took a late-night swim and the worst had happened, so family and friends and volunteers scoured the beaches. Everyone's telephone was decorated with Rutger Nelson MISSING posters and maroon and gold ribbons signifying his school's colors. The news trucks had flocked to the town and the bright TV lights were now lighting up reporters on every street corner. The town was realizing that this was real.

The more I thought about it, as I finished the glasses and checked the supply of Bloody Mary mix, the more I began to have a steady feeling of emptiness. Almost like I wanted to puke. I really felt sick about the kid. It wasn't a feeling of guilt, like I could've done something like stopping him as he left that night.

No. I knew that wasn't my fault. I came to that conclusion the moment Drake Underhill spilled his G&T on me as I tried grabbing the kid before he scurried away. No, it wasn't guilt.

And to be honest, as I began looking into the story for the paper, I was quickly learning that Rutger was what my buddies and I — and really any decent guy who breathes — would describe as a "dick." When I was able to track down one of his lacrosse teammates and get him on the phone, Rutger hit the immortal "dickhead" status. And the kid went on to describe Rutger as, "a towel snapper always picking on the underclassmen."

Obviously, Crocker didn't let me run with that quote. Actually, everything I was collecting, Crocker asked me to "save for later." I didn't understand the method behind his madness until he explained that he wanted Harrison to write all of the early pieces until my involvement in the case blew over.

"J.T., I have a feeling this case is going to hang around this town like a New England ice storm. So, keep your ears open. Keep your notes. I don't think this thing is going to end with a smile and a reunion hug. And, if I'm right, I want you to be the one to knock out the big feature on what happened to this kid. Of course, that's our secret. I haven't told Harrison that. He thinks he's number one on this tragedy."

It was a tragedy. There was no proof yet. But I felt it. It was like having a deep cold in my chest, knowing it's only going to surface and get worse. A lot of people felt that way, too. To be honest, despite the whispers about me, I don't think anyone really thought the kid had been murdered or kidnapped. If they were asked to put their hand on a Bible, many believed Rutger weaved himself along the beach or dock and fell into the ocean and in a day or two a fishing trawler would drag his poor skinny ass up just in time for the six o'clock news.

"I heard one patron say he'd "wash up on a dune covered in seaweed like the naked swimmer chick in Jaws."

Of course, I keep saying there were no clues. That's not entirely correct. There was one: the cell phone. Why was it in the dumpster? It wasn't like it was broken. It worked fine.

I was thinking about that when I heard a male's voice.

"Excuse me?"

"Oh, sorry," I looked up from the full bottle of Bloody Mary mix and instinctively brushed my fingers along the taps, "What can I get you?"

"No beer for me."

"Oh, sure. Yeah. I know. You look like a whiskey man. Am I right?" The truth was, he looked like a '70s porn star straight down to the black, floppy mustache.

Damn, he looks familiar!

I wondered if maybe I was having flashbacks from eighth grade when I learned about sex by watching Cinemax sometimes waver in on our TV from the neighbor's cable by mistake. He definitely had the cheesy guy vibe going. He was wearing a blue shirt, a tie, and khakis.

I thought: they don't wear ties here in the summer.

"No booze. Water with a lime," he said.

"Sure thing. Need a menu?"

In my opinion, The Angry Fisherman didn't do a full menu. It was basically fried appetizers with the occasional fish special depending how lucky Davis got that morning.

I figured the Porn Star probably just needed some cheese sticks.

"No food."

"Okay," I was trying to piece it together. Other than the mustache, he certainly didn't resemble one of the "WHOI freaks" that Davis had warned me about. But he did order just water. Then he stared at me for a while as I handed it to him.

"Do I know you?" I asked.

He took a sip before answering. "I don't know. You might. Is your father Billy O'Rourke? The Boston cop?"

The mention of my father's name floored me. My bartender's smile vanished. "Ahh… yeah… How do you know my father?"

"Is it true that he got thrown off the force for being an alcoholic and having serious anger problems?"

The rush of customers hadn't begun and there was no music playing, so the question echoed throughout the bar. There were four landscapers shooting the shit, banging shots, and savoring their post-work pints. They heard it. They stopped and glanced over.

I shrugged off their looks and leaned over and got into Porn Star's face.

"Who are you? And what do you want?"

I thought I had whispered it, but apparently, I was wrong.

Davis, who was talking to a stout guy who had just walked in, stopped mid-conversation and yelled over, "J.T., everything alright?"

I looked at the Porn Star and yelled back, "I'm not sure, Davis."

The Porn Star seemed unfazed by my anger.

"I'm only asking you that because I heard you were questioned in the disappearance of Rutger Nelson. You see, Mr. O'Rourke, I already have that angle of the story. It's a damn good one, too. That… you know… you were raised in a hostile environment… your old man and the booze problem, how he got thrown off the force… Your mom… the clinical depression and, well, I'll just say 'etcetera, etcetera,' for now. I think we can run with some of that background at 11, but it would be great to get your side of your two run-ins with this Nelson kid, so maybe you can clear things up and people will stop spreading rumors that you got some of your Southie boys to jump him."

"What? That's absolute bullshit!"

He thumbed behind him, "I have my camera guy outside. It would only take a couple of minutes to clear things up for our viewers."

I finally put it together. I could hear the voice in my head, "Reporting live, Vic Hauser, Channel 14 News."

Channel 14 was the Boston station that, every night, specialized in pain and death. Stories about puppies rescued from storm drains were banned from their airwaves unless, of course, the puppies had drowned. They thrived on controversy, and Vic Hauser was their ace when it came to that, always stirring the pot with his microphone.

I was blindsided. I couldn't put two words together. I was too busy trying to control that O'Rourke anger he had been talking about.

Davis came to my rescue, "Is that your news truck outside?"

Hauser turned to him. "Yes, I just need to talk to your bartend—"

"Did he buy anything, J.T.?"

I took a breath. "Ah, no. Just got water."

"Good," Davis said to me and turned to Hauser, "You're loitering. Time to go."

"If you want me to buy something," he turned and looked at the tap, "I'll have a…"

"Too late, asshole." Davis grabbed him by the shirt.

"Hey, get your hands off me. Or…"

Davis laughed, "Or what?"

"Well, by 11:30 tonight I could ruin this bar," Hauser protested with a smile.

Davis let go. "You're right. I shouldn't put my hands on you."

Hauser wiped the wrinkles away from his shirt. "That's better."

Davis snapped his fingers and the stout guy who had been standing at the door hurried over.

"Gonzo, this is J.T."

"Hey, J.T." Gonzo smiled. He wasn't big in height, but he looked strong. Not bodybuilder strong. More like a barrel-chested strongman you'd see on ESPN late night pulling cars with his teeth. I noticed he was wearing a black golf shirt with the emblem stitched in white — The Angry Fisherman.

"Hey, Gonzo. Good to meet you," I said as Hauser looked on, wondering why he suddenly wasn't the main attraction.

"J.T., Gonzo's our bouncer. Been here forever. Part of the decor really. Anyway, I told you I felt summer is finally here, so tonight he begins another year. He usually starts carding at 10, but let's get him back into the swing of things." He turned from me to Gonzo. "Can you escort this piece of shit out of here?"

"Sure thing, Davis." Gonzo grabbed Hauser with one hand, "Let's go, buddy."

"If he throws me out… I'm telling you… It will be all over tonight's late edition!"

Davis good-naturedly hollered, "Good. That will be before last call! I'm sure it will help business. Thanks, asshole!"

The landscapers at the end of the bar chuckled sentiments of, "Good for you, Davis." and "That Hauser douchebag is a prick."

175

After Hauser was out the door, I said, "Thanks, Davis. I'm really sorry if this is going to give you a bad name. Maybe I shouldn't bartend for a—"

"Did you serve the Nelson kid that night?"

"No. You know I didn't."

"Exactly. All you did was your job. Screw that guy and everyone else. And no need for that 'Thanks' shit. We take care of our own here. Now, back to work."

Gonzo walked back in, laughing. "That was friggin' hilarious! I had his camera guy laughing his ass off. You can tell he hates him, too. Yep, Davis, another summer really has begun!"

There was more laughter, but I couldn't enjoy it. I was too busy wondering if Vic "Acehole" Hauser was going to expose my family secrets for all of New England to chew on. Not that anyone in Southie didn't already know them. The majority of my neighborhood could relate. They lived their own secrets. But Hauser's clinical depression crack told me he had made his way along the alphabet alleys, and someone actually *had* talked. The new Southie. Whitey's gone. No more code of silence, I guess.

I tried to get it out of my mind, and I did. Thanks to the Sox. Once their game with the Rangers began, the bar swelled with patrons. I was in full swing, running my ass off using up those chilled glasses Davis had been so adamant about icing. He had been right. Summer was here.

I should've iced more of them down, I began to realize, but then a White Russian order was screamed at me by an unfortunate-looking woman. She may've been ugly, but I didn't feel sorry for her. I knew by closing time she would be considered a MILF — Mother I'd Like to Fuck — to some equally unfortunate and unfocused soul.

Our first bottle of Kahlua was already dead, so I crouched down and went for the relief one. The strangest thing then happened. I smelled something — something very familiar to me. It smelled like vanilla and tangerine. It was pleasing. Gave me a feeling of comfort. Made me stop to take it in. I was enjoying the scent but didn't know why. I searched for it by dipping my nose into a couple of the surrounding bottles. Not as pleasing. The scent really had my mind wandering. I felt like I had experienced it before. I squatted for a minute longer and strained my nostrils. I didn't place where it came from, but I finally realized why the orange scent made me feel so at ease.

It brought me back to one of the few happy memories of my childhood. I was ten, hanging with my buddies on Broadway on those brutally hot July days.

Always needing relief. Then, I'd see it. I'd spot Ralphie's ice cream truck coming toward us. But just as he'd approach, he'd step on the gas and accelerate past my crew in search of the shiny quarters down at Castle Island.

We'd chase after him, yelling, while clutching our dirty coins we had collected from broken payphones or thrown-out couches. One by one, the gang would give up, flipping him the bird as he chugged on. But not me. I'd pump my arms and legs and race after him even though my green and white Adidas sneakers were practically sticking to the molten pavement. I wouldn't stop though, because I knew if I caught Ralphie's truck, an orange creamsicle would be my reward. Sometimes it took me three to five blocks, but I always caught him.

And Ralphie was always pissed off saying, "Here's your goddamn creamsicle, you little rug rat bastard."

Years later, Ralphie admitted that it was his favorite part of the day because he knew I really worked for my ice cream.

"I was trying to teach you kids a lesson about life. Nothing is handed to you. You were the only one in your gang who got it, though," he had said solemnly, referring to four of my buddies who discovered heroin in the late '80s and, one by one, ended up dead or jailed.

But I was back in the early eighties. Funny how a smell can transport you to a place. I really didn't want to leave that place either. And because of it, I must've been crouched below the bar for longer than I had thought.

"You gonna be down there all night, barkeep?"

It was too raspy to be the last call MILF, I thought, and said as I was rising, "Oh, sorry about that."

"What's up?" Echo smiled.

"Oh, hey there. Just making some drinks," I managed, realizing that tangerine scent was Echo Landers. A hell of a lot better than orange creamsicles.

I quickly made the MILF her White Russian. As I leaned over to hand her the drink, it struck me that I had been generous with the MILF comment earlier and by the end of the night she'd be lucky if the worst of lushes even considered her a GILF — Grandmother I'd... Yep, not pretty. But, full of confidence in herself, she cackled, "Thank you!" and sauntered off to try and bag the last remaining landscaper.

I turned my attention back to Echo by giving a light clap. "Okay, what will it be?"

"Hmmm," She placed her index finger on her full, brown lips. "I'm tempted to order something exotic just to see if you have any of the Brian Flanagan moves."

"Brian Flanagan?"

"*Cocktails and Dreams…*" she led me with a raised eyebrow.

"Oh, yeah," I laughed. "Tom Cruise's character."

"Yep."

"Well, miss, I can't twirl glasses like him, but I've been known to spout some pretty bad poetry now and then."

She slapped the bar. "Let's hear some."

"'Nother time, if you're lucky. And, as for his other moves in that movie, you'll just have to wonder."

"Poor me," she pretended to sulk.

There was an uncomfortable silence that I broke.

"Woman, I got a bar to run, so what will it be?"

"Well, barkeep, as you see from my attire, I am dressed to watch my beloved Sox, so screw Flanagan and his umbrella drinks. I'm here to sling down a few cold ones. How about a Miller Lite?"

"Draft or bottle?"

"Draft. I get a little more bang for my buck that way."

"A Miller Lite draft it is then."

I really hadn't noticed her "attire" because I had been trapped in her deep, dark eyes. But as I tilted her glass and pulled the tap, I casually checked her out. When I first met her, I felt she might be the most perfect girl I had ever seen and now I was sure of it. At least, she was for any guy from New England. She was wearing a Red Sox hat for starters. But not just any Sox hat. Not the girlie pink kind that the Johnny Damon cult members wore, but the ol' school, red and blue 1975 style. I had visions of Fred Lynn, Dwight Evans, Jim Rice, and obviously Carlton Fisk hitting his walk-off homer in game six of the World Series. But then I heard the voice of my old man always grumbling, "Carbo never got his due credit for hitting his homer to tie that game. No, just that goddamn Indian waving his arms like he was sending smoke signals."

He had been referring to Fisk.

Yep, I thought as I leveled the pint, racism begins at home. My Dad would've had a shit fit if he knew that I thought a Cape Verdean woman — or "colored" in his politically incorrect world — was beautiful. Actually, 99 percent of my buddies would, too. They would've called her a "porch monkey," "yard ape," or "moon cricket."

When I was a kid, I was guilty of using most of those slurs to get laughs, but as I got older, I stopped drinking the ignorant Kool-Aid that had been served to generation after generation of Southie kids. I also knew something else. Beauty. Echo was beautiful. I took a free peek at her as her attention was on the TV screen above me.

She was wearing a mens tailored white shirt that was unbuttoned halfway, exposing the white wife-beater tank top that subtly accented her voluptuous figure. I wondered if the shirts were from the rack or from the back. And if they were from some guy's back, who was the lucky bastard?

"Here you go." I handed it to her. She grabbed it with one hand and with the other reached into the back pocket of her faded Levi's and handed me a five.

"Keep the change." She settled into her barstool.

I took it. "Two-dollar tip. Not much bang for your buck when you do that, though."

"The key is to tip big early, so the bartender remembers you. Then you begin to give less and less when you move up to the expensive drinks."

"Oh, I'll remember you. But also remember, as the night gets longer, the drinks don't always get stronger. It all depends on the tip. But women don't ever have to buy drinks if they smile after 10. There's always some sucker. But you know that."

Echo gave a guilty laugh before sipping.

"Is it true that creepy reporter from Channel 14 was here?"

"Wow, word travels fast."

"You'll learn that in this town. Gonzo spilled it when I walked in."

"Oh... Gonzo a good guy?"

"Yeah, he's the best. He'll have your back if you ever get in any shit. Just make him his Captain and Cokes every night around 11 or so. Make them strong, and he's loyal to the end. So, what did the reporter want?"

"Davis told me no free drinks to the help."

"Gonzo doesn't count. He's family. He married Davis's cousin a few years back. So, tell me about the reporter."

"Nothing to tell. Just wanted to make a story out of nothing. By the way, I left the paper around 3:30; anything new about the kid come in?" I asked while grabbing a Corona, liming it, and handing it to the landscaper whose eyes were getting glassy. I made a mental note.

"Well, there may be something. I was at the gas station and—" Echo began.

She was interrupted by a pretty woman in her early 30s shaking her brown bob calling Echo's name. The woman wore a green Izod sweater over a pink golf shirt and matching pink shorts. She looked like she had just popped out of the old *Preppy Handbook*.

"Echo, sweetie, I'm so sorry I'm late." She kissed a greeting on Echo's cheek. "Paul had to show a house to a couple from Jersey. And bitch, bitch, bitch about the price. And blah, blah, blah. And, you know, I don't think they're even going to buy it. Then he comes home, and now little Neil decides tonight that he doesn't *like* hot dogs anymore, when that was all I could get him to eat two days ago. So, he's crying and crying. So anyway, honey — I'm so sorry I'm late." She paused for a breath before snapping, "Bartender. Appletini."

"Sure thing."

She didn't even make eye contact. I began to turn, but Echo grabbed my hand.

I could feel my face flush a bit like I was at a roller rink date in the fifth grade or something. I prayed that Echo hadn't noticed.

"J.T., I want you to meet my friend, Kathy Zimmerman. Kathy, this is J.T. O'Rourke, he's the new reporter I was telling you about."

"Oh, yes." Her eyes now acknowledged I was actually human.

"Nice to meet you." I shook her limp fish, but then my glance shifted because I was following Echo's eyes. They had left me and were at the entrance where a tall black stud laughed with Gonzo and then walked in. He looked familiar, but I couldn't place him. Where had I seen him?

Echo smiled. Maybe a little too much.

"If you two will excuse me? Kathy, unwind with J.T. I'll be back in a few minutes."

"Girlfriend, you take as long as you want." Kathy snapped her fingers like she was Sista Prep Dog from the hood.

The black stud brightened and waved Echo over.

"Yeah, I might be a while. You can give my spot away. I'll stand when I come back." She took her pint, rose, and walked over to him.

A moment later, Murray Philbrick, the sparkplug who had sold me the Jeep, swooped in taking her stool.

"J.T., when you're done with her drink, a rum and Coke please. And I got Kathy's."

I nodded to him from the bar mirror as I moved the shaker.

He palmed the bar and leaned over to her, "This must be my lucky night to grab a spot right next to Kathy Zimmerman."

"Murray, you know I'm married." She yawned.

"So was my wife, but that didn't stop her getting her oil checked by anyone with a dipstick!" Murray laughed, looking for someone to join in, but my back was turned to him, and the lone landscaper was too busy wrapping his arm around the GILF, preparing to make a mistake he'd regret tomorrow morning. And every morning after that.

Time to shut him off and save him.

I looked for his tab and caught Echo in the mirror's reflection. She was still smiling.

Definitely, way too much...

ECHO

Echo was smiling. After touching J.T.'s hand, she noted that he actually blushed.

How cute, she had thought, and then she couldn't help but enjoy the admittedly vain thought that ran through her mind — she had the "it" factor working for her. She could still make grown men blush like schoolboys. She took a sip of beer to cool her reaction, but then the smile spread again, this time for a different reason. She spotted her childhood friend, Officer Jamal Jensen, sharing a laugh with Gonzo and then walking into The A.F.

Echo excused herself and headed for Jamal. She caught J.T. watching her in the mirror. The bartender was transfixed. And now she beamed. She liked being watched by him. Maybe because it was someone new watching her.

Deep down, I think I'm a bit of a tease. Yep, of course I am. And J.T. does seem so sweet. Fun, even. Maybe too sweet. And there's no way I'd ever hook up with him. I have to be careful. I can't lead him on. Wow, I'm thinking like a bitch.

"Hey bitch," Jamal playfully whispered.

His muscular arms swallowed her small frame causing a wave of beer to splash over the rim of her glass, but she regained balance of the pint, kissed him on the cheek, and said, "You know, you just read my mind. I think I *am* a bitch."

"What do you mean?"

"Oh, nothing, honey. You want one? I'm buying." She pointed down to her pint that had swished back to safety.

"Nah, I really can only stay for a couple of minutes. With the Nelson kid missing and all, been burning the midnight oil. It's amazing I'm finally getting the night off considering what's going on. Might get called back. If not, going over the bridge to the North End tonight."

"Hot romantic date?"

"We'll see." Jamal shifted his eyes before whispering, "Got set up by one of the C crew."

It was short for "Closet Crew." That's how he referred to his four friends who were still too afraid to tell the world that they were gay. He was, too. He was basically president of the group. Echo was one of the few people who knew. She found out long before, back in junior high after they played spin the bottle. The kiss had been passionless. Dead lips even. Out of nothing, Echo sensed something. When they were alone, she called him on it. And in between painful sobs, he told her about the "strange feelings" he had for boys. She had hugged him and said they were "different feelings, but not strange," and then vowed never to tell anyone. And she hadn't. No one knew. Not even her best friend, Kathy Zimmerman, who first thought Jamal was a catch when she saw him wearing a tux at the freshman semi-formal. A million years later, Kathy was still giving the thumbs up from her barstool. Echo thumbed back. She was good at keeping secrets. Beyond good.

Jamal had been petrified that his father would disown him if he knew the truth. Not to mention being a cop. But now it was 2004. Everyone was jumping out of the closet, and after all, his father had died in a car accident the summer before. So, what was there to fear? But Jamal still wanted to keep that closet door shut. Echo, true to her word, would hold onto that key as long as he wanted. She knew she was no one to judge. She had her own secrets. She also had another reason for staying silent, one that she didn't want to think about.

She followed his example and also scanned the bar before whispering, "Well, who's the lucky you-know-what?"

"An architect. Lives in Salem."

"Keep me posted. So, what couldn't you tell me earlier?"

"Let's move over by the jukebox." He didn't wait for her reply. He headed over and pretended to scan the selections.

"Hold this," She handed him her pint, grabbed a dollar bill and slid it into the machine.

This will get J.T. going.

"Jamal, watch this." She pressed some numbers and smirked.

A second later, "Two Step" by the Dave Matthews Band played. Echo nudged him and they both looked over at J.T. who was handing Murray a drink. When J.T. heard the song, he turned toward them and gave her the finger. Echo burst into laughter. J.T. then cracked a quick grin before turning his attention back to the bar crowd.

"That wasn't for me, was it?" Jamal asked.

"No. Not at all. Long story." She giggled.

"It's funny 'cause the O'Rourke guy is really the reason I'm here."

"Really? Why?"

"Well, you know how I had to bring him in for questioning the other day. I knew people would start speculating so I felt kind of bad for him."

"Oh, they have been talking. The Channel 14 guy was just here trying to cause all sorts of problems."

"Wow, I'm surprised that Hauser guy doesn't know yet, but they're trying to keep it hush hush. You see, when I saw you at the gas station, I didn't know everything. But I just got a call from Burkey who gave me some major stuff. Anyway, word is going to get out. That's why I thought I might give you and the O'Rourke guy a jumpstart for the paper. 'Cause in a few hours no one will be thinking your friend did anything wrong."

"Why is that? What's the deal?"

"Obviously..." Jamal paused.

"I didn't hear it from you," she finished for him.

"Well, some evidence was found only a couple of hours ago."

"Where?"

"Along the bike path."

"Wait. Was it around five or so?" Echo asked.

"Yep."

"Damn, I thought something was strange. I was coming from a photo shoot and saw cruisers as I passed one of the entrances. Burkey was directing traffic.

183

Said there was a downed power line along the route. I knew something was up. He's not a good liar."

"Yeah, I know. Worst poker player ever. Anyway, they're trying to keep it on the D.L. as long as possible."

"Keep what?"

"At one of the memorial benches he found Rutger Nelson's license."

"No shit. Wait, who is 'he'?"

"Chuck Renna. You know how he likes to close his bike shop and take a ride along the path and watch the sunset."

"Among other things... Yeah, I see him out there when I go rollerblading. He does it like clockwork every night."

"Well, apparently, every night he also stops at the same bench and sits on it for a while and feeds the squirrels. And that's where he found the license."

"So where was the license? Under the bench? Do they think the kid passed out there? He *was* drunk..." Her mind was racing.

"No. It was fastened to the bench. Someone super-glued it. Burkey said it kind of looked like a tribute to Rutger Nelson, like it was his own memorial bench. But that's just it. It's already someone else's memorial bench and that's why by tomorrow, I don't think people will be talking about him." Jamal pointed over at J.T.

"Why is that?"

"'Cause O'Rourke just moved here. He's got no clue about Sandy Point history. But whoever did this *does* know. *Big time.*"

"What do you mean, Jamal?"

"The license was fastened to Fishy Bryden's memorial bench," he whispered.

Echo didn't need any more explanation. Everyone in town knew about the murder of the little boy whose body was found one Christmas Eve. Like a ghost story at a campfire, it was handed down from generation to generation.

"Holy shit," she managed.

"Yeah, another missing kid's evidence ends up on a murdered kid's memorial bench. That can't be just a coincidence, Ec."

"Well, they got the guy who killed Fishy years ago, right?"

"Yeah, I know. But maybe someone in this town has been inspired by the story."

"Or wants Fishy Bryden's story to be remembered, for some messed up reason," Echo added.

"That's exactly my point. We both know what that reason could be. Could be a copycat. I hate to say this, but I'm pretty sure they won't find Rutger Nelson alive. That's the sign of a killer who taunts. Not a kidnapper who wants money or anything. But who knows, I could be wrong."

They both fell silent knowing Jamal wasn't wrong. Then their gaze caught Vic Hauser outside The A.F. He clicked his cell phone off, bolted toward the news truck, and jumped into the passenger side. The truck roared to life and hauled off. Whoever Hauser's informant was had just come through for him. He had his story. The camera lights would soon be shining brightly on his floppy porn star mustache.

CHAPTER 19
CHRISTMAS EVE 1972

DEVLIN

Officer Devlin may've been able to secure the crime scene, but when it came to his own feelings, that was another matter. Nothing. Not even Nam had trained him for this kind of pain; this kind of seething rage that swam through his veins like toxins polluting harbor waters. It definitely poisoned him. He was no longer thinking like a cop. More like a madman. He was thinking beyond the moment, to when he could leave the crime scene and do what had to be done — what must be done. He had one job now, and that was to make sure Fishy hadn't died without justice. Not that plea bargain bullshit justice that Allan Devlin was so famous for getting by winking, handshaking, and drinking. No free drinks and deals made during this tee time. He wanted real justice. And when he was through with Pop Tucker, the sick piece of shit would be pissing blood out of his filthy dick the rest of his days — as few as there would be.

If any, Devlin nodded in resolution.

Obviously, he should've concealed his intentions, but when Detective Prichard first arrived Devlin clenched his fist and spat out Pop's name, referring to him as "that gaddamned spineless killer."

Prichard reacted by chiding and reminding the officer, "Don't jump to conclusions."

This forced Devlin to bite his tongue. Prichard was the detective. The solver. Not Devlin. No detective ever wants to be told who did it. They want to solve.

So, let him solve.

It didn't matter, anyway, considering what he had planned for Pop.

And the evidence certainly was there. Any asshole could figure that out. But as desperate as he tried to hide his emotions and stay in control, his body language told the true story. His hand shook uncontrollably when he pointed at the red elastic fabric caught on the tree branch. He snapped his head over for the detective's response. Prichard remained calm, but his eyebrows arched slightly before holding a longer glance on Devlin's shaking hand.

They were both silent for a minute — an unspoken dialogue going on between them.

Finally, Prichard said it, "It does look like it could come from red suspenders, but that certainly doesn't mean—"

"There's more." Devlin jumped in before continuing through the woods, Prichard following closely behind until they were both standing over Fishy's body.

Prichard gnawed hard on his right index knuckle taking in the sight for several seconds.

Finally, he whispered, "Jesus, Mary, and Joseph."

Devlin nodded, gritted his teeth, and then wrapped his shaky hand around his gun belt.

There was no need for pointing now. At least, that's what he thought. But then he saw it.

Prichard's eyes also found it: a lollipop stick.

It was sticking to Fishy Bryden's right buttock.

———

After Chief Gedny arrived and inspected the scene, he ordered Devlin — for the second time that day — to go home.

"I don't normally do this, but I want you to write your notes at your house and get a couple of hours of sleep. Then you can come back to the station and write up your report. It might be a little against procedure, but you don't look good, and I want you to be fresh. In the next few days, we'll definitely need everyone on this. This town is about to face one of its biggest tragedies. A firestorm has just hit us. And to think it's Christmas Eve..." his voice had trailed off.

Devlin left the scene intending to head for the harbor, but at the last second, he spun the wheel in the other direction and before he knew it, he was parked in front of Pop's Treats & Eats, the toy and candy store that had been his sanctuary as a child. Not anymore. His emotionally worn eyes now had a different view — a clearer view.

Bits and pieces of a memory from his youth came back to him and now made sense. He remembered a time when Pop was closing for the night and he, little Mikey Devlin, was the last customer in the shop, thumbing through a comic book. Pop had sidled up to him and, with his big hands, rubbed his shoulders. The shop owner then invited him to go into the back room to see the latest toys. Devlin had felt uneasy, and something seemed wrong about the situation, so he had refused. At the time, he hadn't understood why he had that odd — almost frightened — sensation and why he had turned down such a fun opportunity... But now, years later, he realized that there had been a sixth sense lurking in his stomach, and it was that feeling in his gut that had saved him.

Fishy Bryden hadn't been blessed with that caution. He was too kind. Too innocent. Too trusting.

Fishy had been the perfect prey for Pop, Devlin thought, as he watched the final last-minute Christmas shopper duck out the front door. A moment later, the lights went out and the store was in darkness.

No turning back.

Devlin unhooked the latch on his gun belt, pulled out his revolver, and then opened the glove compartment. He paused. For a minute, his eyes moved back and forth from the gun to the black ring box. The consequences of what he was about to do and what they might mean for his future with Anna began to seep into his psyche. He remained still for another minute gripping the revolver but then in one quick motion, he pushed those thoughts away by placing the revolver into the glove box and slamming it shut.

No guns.

Guns were too easy. He wanted Pop to feel it. To suffer.

He slipped out of the cruiser and momentarily thought about entering the store through the front, but then realized that if Pop opened that door, it would probably attract more last-minute shoppers. The last thing he wanted were witnesses, so he made his way around the corner to the back of the building. He jiggled the service entrance doorknob. It was locked.

"Smile, Devlin. You can't let him see it," he whispered to himself, referring to the rage and hatred that had burrowed into his light blue eyes turning them black.

He wrapped on the door and hollered, "Pop!"

Several seconds passed. Nothing.

He knocked again, this time slapping his palm against the tin door, "Hey, Pop. I need your help!"

A few more seconds passed and just as he was going to knock the reply came, "Who is it?"

"It's Michael Devlin."

Pop didn't answer for almost a half-minute.

He finally responded, "What do you want, Michael?"

Devlin put on the best fake laugh he could before saying, "I want to get out of the doghouse."

"Doghouse?"

"Well, I will be in the doghouse with my girlfriend. You see, Anna asked me to pick up one of those model airplanes for her little cousin and I just remembered. So, can you let me in?"

"Um… yeah. How 'bout you go to the front door?"

Why does he want me to go to front?

"I don't know if that's a good idea. I saw a few last-minute shoppers out front, and I bet if you open that door you'll be here till New Year's." Devlin forced a laugh.

"Okay. Okay. Just give me a minute." Pop was clearly annoyed.

Five minutes passed before the service door opened and a frazzled Pop, avoiding eye contact, greeted Devlin, "Sorry, I had to clean up. The place is a mess."

Pop walked quickly out of the back room. Too quickly. Devlin had never seen him move that fast and decided this was where it would happen.

"Hold up a second, Pop."

Pop turned, "What?"

Devlin pointed and said, "Look," and then walked over to a table that had a few boxes of model airplanes on it.

"Michael, there are better models out front. Let's go out there."

"No, I like it in here."

"Huh?"

"Yeah, it looks so comfortable, like home. You know, I used to think of this place as home, but I never got back here. I should've. I mean you've got boxes of toys and a nice cozy looking couch. Is that new or do you get a new one every few years?"

"I don't know. I guess it's a few years old. Why do you care about my couch? You're making no sense, Michael."

Devlin picked up one of the boxes and walked up to Pop and stared him straight in the eye and handed it to him.

"I'll take this one. I'm sorry I haven't had much sleep since Fishy Bryden went missing. I'm kind of losing my mind."

"Oh, yes, the Bryden boy. That was terrible."

"*Was* terrible? You make it sound like it's over. He's still missing. We might find him alive and well. But you said it 'was terrible,' like it's too late or something."

"Well, no, I mean it *is* terrible. Michael, I have to say, you seem a little strange. You really probably should go home and get some sleep."

Devlin pointed over at the couch, "Maybe I could sleep over there? Or is that couch only for little boys?"

A part of him hoped Pop would reply with a clueless expression and it would turn out there had just been a bunch of bizarre coincidences pointing the finger of guilt. But the expression on Tucker's face said it all.

He reddened immediately, completely flustered, feigning surprise but tripping over his response, "Wha... ah... are... ah... you talking about? Don't believe... ah..."

"Don't believe who?"

"Ah... I mean is... ah... what are... you talking about?"

Devlin didn't need to ask a follow-up question. He knew. And then Pop knew Devlin knew because he didn't wait for the officer's answer. Pop turned and lunged for the door, but Devlin took his nightstick, reached out and swung it in between Pop's legs causing the store owner to fall face first to the floor. Devin then threw the stick aside. He was going to make him pay with fists. He grabbed Pop's shoulder with his left hand and turned him over.

"No! Please don't..." Tucker tried to raise his hands to shield the impending blow but was too late. Devlin unloaded a right fist into the toy store owner's face, breaking the nose instantly, blood rivering out. It was just the beginning.

"You fucking pervert!" He then wound up and punched Tucker, pounding over and over, tattooing his roast beef jowls.

When he finally paused for breath, Pop surprised him by kicking his boot into Devlin's groin and knocking him down. The officer doubled over and clutched his lower body while trying to regain his wind. Meanwhile, Pop stumbled to his feet like a desperate prizefighter.

Devlin was low to the floor, an easy target for Pop, who wound up and kicked his face like a soccer ball, snapping Devlin's head back and sending him crashing to the floor. With the pain bulleting to his brain, he didn't know what happened, but then Devlin realized that his nose too was fractured. There was no time to dwell on the stinging sensation. He wiped the blood away, and the only red he was seeing was the fiery rage that gave him enough will to jump to his feet. When he did, he was eye to eye with Pop. It was a second of a locked look that seemed to last forever, but then he fired a left jab that slammed into Pop's right eye and then followed with an uppercut that caught the bottom of Tucker's triple chins, sending him backward, twisting and turning in the air looking for something to break his fall. Pop found it. The radiator. He tried to hug it for support, but instead of breaking his fall, he pulled it to the floor with him. The radiator rested on top of his barely conscious body. The sight puzzled Devlin, who was breathing heavy, his anger finally tapering to an end. He knew if he continued to beat him, he'd kill him. He focused on the radiator again.

How did it topple so easily?

He ignored Pop's moaning and walked over and studied the wall and floor. There were no marks in the wall or the floor. The radiator had never been attached.

That's odd? Why would it be here then?

He spotted what the radiator had been hiding: a hole about a foot wide. He crouched down to inspect the hole and found a shoebox.

"What the...?" he began while opening the box. And then all words and senses left him as he fell to his knees. He had never seen anything so disturbing — hundreds and hundreds of photos of naked little boys sleeping. Clearly passed out, the boys had been posed in every obscene position possible. As grotesque as the positions were, that was not what made Devlin sick to his stomach. It was the boys' faces. There were several recent photos of young boys from

Sandy Point. He looked at a couple of the pictures and it dawned on him: these boys had been crying out for help in their own way to me, but I hadn't heard them.

And, as he continued to leaf through more of the photos, they went all the way back to when Devlin was a kid. There were the faces of kids he had played little league with and the faces of kids he was in Cub Scouts with and — the most devastating realization — the faces of his friends.

He stared in a trance at the face of his friend Leo Montgomery, who had been a shy band member in high school and was now a big name on Wall Street.

This sicko raped Leo!

He was struggling to grasp the thought and didn't hear the shouting at first.

"Devlin! Devlin! What did you do?"

Dazed, he turned to look at Jessie Gordon standing in the doorway. Jessie rushed over, pulled the radiator off Pop, and pushed it away.

"Devlin?"

He didn't answer. He couldn't. Instead, he pointed to the shoebox. Jessie went over and looked into the box and randomly grabbed a couple of the pictures.

"Holy shit!" Jessie said, shaking his head before glaring over at Tucker who was moaning louder and coming to life.

"I can't believe all the boys…" Devlin's voice trailed off.

"Any pictures of Fishy Bryden?"

"Ah… no… I didn't find one." Devlin answered.

Thinking Devlin was in mild shock, Jessie ordered loudly, "Look, don't move. I'll be right back, Okay?"

"Okay," he responded and watched Jessie run out the door toward the front of the store.

When Jessie left the room, Devlin looked at Leo's picture again. Leo was doing so well in life now.

He thought of the time they had met up in the Big Apple and Leo had said, "I'll never go back to Sandy Point. I hate that place." He never understood why there was such venom in his normally gentle voice. He now knew.

He put Leo's picture into his pocket.

"You won't ever have to come back, Leo," Devlin was about to get on his feet when Jessie appeared again, this time carrying a shotgun.

"Don't move!" Jessie pointed the gun at Devlin who put his hands up.

"What are you doing?"

"Is Mrs. Dorf home?"

"Huh?"

"The lady who lives above this place. She goes away, right?"

"Oh. Yeah. Mrs. Dorf. Yeah, she's at her daughter's place in Vermont for Christmas. Why? What are you doing, Jessie?"

Jessie grinned slightly, "That's what I thought. Just shut up and move your hands. Put them on your ears."

"Huh?"

"Just do it! Do it now!"

Devlin covered his ears and then Jessie aimed the shotgun above and blasted it into the ceiling causing a storm of sheet rock to rain to the floor.

Jessie walked over to Pop while laughing over at Devlin, "Did you think I was going to shoot you or something?"

"I didn't know what to think."

"Hey, I figured if I'm going to put my ass on the line and cover for you, I had to have a little fun," Jessie laughed again before continuing, "Tucker keeps this shotgun behind the register." He knelt down, placing the shotgun beside Pop.

"Now, before we get our stories down on what happened here," Jessie paused, "I have one more thing to do."

"What's that?" Devlin steadied to his feet and picked up his hat.

"This." Jessie wound up and kicked Pop in the ribs three times cracking them like dry wood.

Then he leaned over and spat on Tucker's swollen face, "You like that? You fucking ankle grabber!"

Jessie wiped his brow and turned to Devlin, "We really should kill the sick bastard, but in the end, I guess we are still cops."

"Yeah, I guess, we are." Devlin nodded, staring at the blood trickling off the badge that was attached to his hat.

CHAPTER 20
JUNE 12, 2004

SATURDAY

NERO

Nero moved busily around in his shelter. He thought about his past as he worked — when he first began to kill. Back then he viewed himself as a messenger from God. His job was simple — decide who would see God and who would see the eternal blackness of hell. That's why he stabbed through his father's eyes and that's also why he had left Fishy's eyes intact.

His father deserved to die, but Fishy was a means to an end. Fishy unknowingly had helped him set up Pop Tucker and, because of it, Nero had graciously let his childhood friend fly to heaven to see God. As the years went on and Nero's killings continued, there was a set of judgment eyes that haunted his dreams, but they didn't belong to Fishy. And no matter what he did, those eyes sometimes still appeared during his deepest of sleeps.

I should've taken them!

He turned on the small propane tank. The blue and yellow flame danced. He placed the pot on the grill. He continued his reflections as he warmed the liter of Rutger's blood while realizing the judgment eyes weren't the only reason his killing style had changed. Shortly after that killing where he had let another soul fly to heaven, a desire got stronger, but it wasn't one of destruction. Strangely enough, it was a feeling of preservation that controlled him. He wanted to preserve the beautiful marbles. After the judgment eyes were set free, he decided from that point on that no matter if his victims were good or evil — he would cut out their eyes. So, two nights earlier when he asked the boy if he wanted to see God, Nero had been making an inside joke. Remembering the past. None of his victims had seen God in a long time, and future victims never would. He always made sure of that.

And now, 48 hours later, the decapitation and eye removal had already been performed. But Nero wanted to relive the scene, so he stripped naked and then began heating the blood he had collected. The sperm filled condoms he had used on the boy he also threw into the pot. He fondled himself with his left hand as he used a wooden spoon in the other to stir his creation. This part of the recipe always excited him.

Symbolism at its best!

He smiled — his life force meeting the victim's death force. Two worlds colliding.

YES!

When it was warm enough, he poured himself a jar and sealed it before splashing the rest of the blood over his naked body, rubbing it in as if he were applying sunscreen. Then, he grabbed the jar, his violin and bow, and another jar, and made his way up the ladder. He lay on his back on the lush green grass and played his violin while looking at the other jar he had placed on a tree stump.

Rutger's lifeless eyes floated up and down in the jar like some sort of macabre snow globe.

What a beautiful sight!

He became erect. But it wasn't just the eyes or the screeching sound that reminded him of the boy's screams that hardened him. It was something new — what he had just done to the town.

He had always known that something might happen in town that would expose him, but meeting Rutger had been fate and that fate had sped up the timeline for Nero's ultimate unveiling. He didn't have long in this world, and he wanted them to learn his brilliance before it was too late. So, he decided to run with fate and that was why he left Rutger Nelson's license at the perfect spot — Fishy Bryden's memorial bench.

His mind drifted into the past for a moment.

Would Rutger get the same beautiful send-off that Fishy got? Probably not.

They'd never find Rutger's body, so they'd keep searching with endless hope. *Maybe years from now they'll have a memorial mass with an empty casket?*

He laughed again before he turned his focus back on his violin and played it for several minutes. Until his foreplay was finished. He was throbbing. He desperately needed to release. Nero put down the violin and unsealed the jar. He drank, gurgling and savoring the boy's salty blood before swallowing and accepting him into his soul. He let his mind think back on the days of Fishy Bryden, his present situation with Rutger Nelson, and what the future would bring him.

"Oh… the… fut…ure…" he let out.

"Yes, the future." He smiled and palmed the sweat off his forehead.

The game he had been secretly playing for years with the people of Sandy Point was finally ready for the whole town to join in — men, women, and children.

Nero would make sure everyone was going to play.

CHAPTER 21

JANUARY 6, 1973

SATURDAY

DEVLIN

Michael Devlin opened his closet and instinctively reached for his blues before remembering what the Chief had said the day before, "Michael, I've made some phone calls and Officer Gordon's report of what happened in Tucker's store will stick. Even though we…" there had been a long pause, "Look, you didn't follow orders. I told you to go home and you did just the opposite… I, at least, have to suspend you for a month without pay. But don't think this is about me trying to save face. See, Internal Affairs is telling me if I suspend you without pay for a month this whole thing goes away. If I don't, they're going to have to get into it and this thing could get bigger. Even I.A. wants to look the other way on this one. That hardly ever happens, but it's either look the other way or — because you decided to play vigilante — investigate. And if they do that, it could possibly result in letting a child molester go free. So, I don't want to see you in that uniform until February fifth."

"Yes, sir. Thank you, sir."

"Don't thank me, officer. I'm beyond disappointed. I really thought you had the fortitude and dignity to do this job right. I'm not so sure anymore. Over the next month, you might want to think about what it means to be a police officer, and if you can live up to those demands, because you have just demonstrated to me that you can't."

"I understand, sir." He barely answered, crushed that he had let Chief Gedney down.

And a day later, Devlin wasn't so sure if he could or even wanted to live up to those demands. He moved his hand along the racks and settled on a somber black sports coat. As he laid it on his bed, he noticed the black ring box on his dresser. Anna had forgiven him for what he had done to Pop Tucker. She admitted she wished she could've done the same thing, but there was now a distance between them since that night. It would take some time to rebuild their happy, little world. The ring box would stay shut.

"Hopefully, today may be a step closer."

To where it was.

A week and a half had passed since Fishy Bryden's funeral, but Sandy Point was still numb. The innocence had been ripped from its core. He knew it would take an even longer time before the town would not only recover from Fishy's murder, but also from the whispers swarming around.

Who were Pop's other victims? Who were the boys in those pictures?

These were questions everyone was asking. Detective Prichard was building his case, and he instructed Devlin and Jessie Gordon to keep their mouths shut. Not one word. That wasn't hard. Neither one of them wanted to remember what they found behind that radiator, let alone talk about it.

But, after Devlin dressed and headed out to pick up Anna, he knew he was about to see a few of Pop's victims again. He had already seen some of them hours after Fishy's funeral.

A group of a dozen boys came over on the ferry and knocked on his door. When he answered with swollen red eyes, he scanned the group and recognized at least five faces from the pictures. He couldn't let those faces know what he knew, so he desperately strained a smile and came outside. The boys vented to him about how they thought the funeral Mass was "rubbish" — how it had been cold and distant.

"Geez, the priest didn't even call him Fishy. It could've been a funeral for a dog, and no one would've known the difference." Davis Lawson shook his head in disgust.

"Yeah, Officer Devlin, it was not the proper way to send Fishy off to heaven." Trafton Brown kicked a stone in front of him.

"Well, what do you guys think would be a good way?" Devlin asked.

"Greggie came up with a great idea. Tell him, Greggie." Jared Lareby urged Greggie Crocker to come forward.

The once bright-eyed happy adventurer, now avoiding eye contact, quietly told Devlin his plan. The group solemnly nodded along.

"So, what do you think, Officer Devlin?" Chuck Renna asked with red eyes.

Devlin didn't answer.

"We came to you because of what you did to... *him*. You were looking out for my brother. You cared about my brother like we do. So, I'd like to know, do you think that is a good way to send Fishy off?" Jeremy Bryden tried to sound strong but failed as his voice quivered and his eyes filled up.

Devlin felt his pain, thinking *If I really had looked out for Fishy, he'd still be alive.*

He stared beyond all of them down at the incoming winter whitecaps for a minute. Then he smiled. "Yes, Jeremy, Greggie has come up with the best way to say goodbye to Fishy. I'll call Captain Blanca. I know he'll come down from New Bedford to help us. I think you guys should do this on a Saturday afternoon so everyone in town can be there."

Devlin was back in the moment, pulling into the entrance of the Talbot Estate. He hoped that supporting the boys' ritual was the right thing to do. That it would give them some comfort.

He then gave a sarcastic snort, "Comfort."

Would any of them really ever have comfort again?

Their childhoods had been snatched away never to return. He was about to get out of the car when he noticed Anna sitting on the bench by the driveway. Lethargically, she rose, slowly walked over, and got in.

He leaned over and gave her a quick kiss on the cheek.

"Honey, you're freezing. Why were you waiting outside?"

"Just wanted to. I didn't feel the cold. Really can't feel anything lately."

Devlin placed his hand on her left gloved hand. "I know. But we'll get through this. Together."

For several days, Anna had sobbed uncontrollably, but Devlin now noticed a change in her demeanor. It was as if she had cried herself out of all feelings. Gave up. And all that was left was an empty shell. That shell sat next to him giving him one-word answers all the way to Sea Glass Beach.

He almost missed the tears, he thought, as he spun the wheel and parked behind the long line of cars that made the beach resemble a bustling summer day. Devlin got out of the car, opened Anna's door, and took her hand.

"The boys did a good job getting the word out," he said, referring to the large crowd that had gathered at the shoreline around the rowboat. Men and women turned around and gave Devlin looks that spoke to him: We support you. Then they moved aside as if he and Anna were royalty, allowing a path for them to get closer. They nodded thank-yous and stopped at the boat. Devlin stared at the child-cursive writing painted on the back.

Sunshine Dream
Sandy Point, Cape Cod

He was lost in the memory of the day Fishy came up with the name.

Anna broke his trance, "Your parents."

She pointed over at Mr. and Mrs. Allan Devlin who were standing to their left at the foot of a jetty talking with some mourners.

"Oh, yeah."

"I suppose we should go stand with them," she said.

Greggie Crocker broke from the crowd and went over to the other side of the rowboat and palmed it with his right hand. He stood there, his eyes filling up.

"Yeah. I'll be over there in a minute. I just want to talk to Greggie."

Anna looked at Greggie and nodded to Devlin. She joined Mrs. Devlin, who greeted her with a hug.

The crowd whispered to one another while Devlin walked over to Greggie who was now massaging the boat with his right hand.

"How are you doing, buddy?"

Greggie kept his eyes focused down on the rowboat staring at its cargo. The boat that used to carry two laughing boys now contained a mound of kerosene-soaked kindling.

"He was my best friend, Officer Devlin. We were going to sail all over the world someday... I'll never have a friend like him. Ever."

Devlin wanted to muster up words of solace but knew he couldn't and shouldn't.

Greggie no longer deserved to be treated like a child.

"I know, Greg," he answered, watching Captain Blanca approach, holding an unlit torch.

The captain was in his sixties, but his long, white beard and small hunched over five-foot frame made Devlin think of Rip Van Winkle. He was wearing a tattered suit jacket, a faded blue tie, and his best jeans that only had one hole in the left thigh. From his appearance, no one would ever guess that he owned a fleet of fishing boats and serviced several five-star restaurants across New England.

Devlin leaned down so the captain could whisper in his ear, "Michael, we have to get started. The Chief has another commitment later." He motioned over to the Fire Chief who was there to make sure the ceremony was safe.

Devlin nodded, "Okay" and turned to Greggie, "You might never find another friend like Fishy, but remember you were lucky to have him. Not many people have friends like that in their life — ever. And now, we have to say goodbye to him the best way we can. And you came up with that way. So, let's go stand over with everyone else and let Captain Blanca start." Devlin placed his hands on the boy's shoulders and like a frightened animal, Greggie flinched at the touch.

Then he realized what Devlin was doing, wiped his eyes, and followed him over to the crowd of mourners — *boys who shouldn't know the feeling of wearing ties.*

"Um, ah..." Captain Blanca cleared his throat, "Could I please have every-one's attention?"

The murmurs turned to silence.

"I see a lot of faces I know before me, but for those of you who don't know me, my name is Captain George Blanca and... and I want to tell you about my friend Fishy Bryden." He pulled on his beard for a minute to get his bearings.

"I'm sorry. I'm a little nervous. Some of you might not believe it possible. I've been told I'm a bit of a storyteller and I never shut up."

He paused again, allowing the polite laughter.

He chuckled, "But I'm not used to such a big audience for one of my stories, so I hope you'll stay with me. My story about Fishy begins with me. I was born in Argentina and moved to this great country when I was four years old. My father was a businessman and did very well, but early on in life I knew that wasn't for me. My life was the sea. By the time I was 10, I was stowing away on the tuna boats out of New Bedford. I told my Papi that I probably wouldn't be a businessman."

Again, light laughter.

"Especially the time I actually made it to George's Bank undetected. After that trip, my Papi greeted me at the dock. He was not happy, and I didn't know what was going to happen to me. I knew it wasn't going to be good, but the captain of the boat came to my rescue by handing me my share and telling my father that I was a natural fisherman. Papi then decided if I was going to fish, I had to learn from the best. So, every summer he sent me to be with my Abuelo... Um, my granddaddy, and learn the ways of the sea. My Abuelo told me I was a child of the sea and that he never met someone who loved and respected the ocean as much as me. We look out at that ocean today, and I can tell you that I have fished for more than 55 years, and I always agreed with my Abuelo. No one loved the sea more. I always felt that way, that is, until I met little Jimmy Bryden. I know. I know. No one here knows him as Jimmy. He was Fishy to us. He will always be Fishy to us. I met him when he was six years old. I remember I was gassing up at the dock by Bryden's when I saw this little boy with big flounder-like eyes. I asked him what he was fishing for. He said he was going to catch a bass for his mom to cook for dinner that night. I told him it was very unlikely he'd catch any bass that time of day and in the harbor. But he was determined, and sure enough 20 minutes later he did. He was so excited that he was going to bring a fish home to his mother. But then he measured it. The fish was a quarter inch from being a keeper. At age six, most kids would probably keep the fish, but little Fishy didn't even hesitate. He threw it back in and said, "I'll just tell Mom we'll have a bigger meal next year when I catch it again.""

There was a sob that cracked through the cold breeze. Captain Blanca stopped as Mr. Bryden put his arms around Mrs. Bryden who cried, "No. No. Not my boy! Why? *Why?*" and then collapsed into his chest.

"Please. Please continue," Mr. Bryden managed to say to the captain before escorting his wife off the beach to their car.

When it was quiet again, he resumed, "I have been fortunate to share count-less stories with Fishy, some true, some we like to call 'fishing tales.' I will miss that. You see, Fishy's heart flowed with kindness as steady as those waves over there greet the shore. He is not just a symbol of the beauty of the ocean. He is the symbol of what is beautiful about this town. We see it today. His family and friends have come together to send this child off to sea. I once told Fishy about how the Vikings would burn the ship of a lost captain to send him off to the other world. Fishy asked me, 'In the other world, is there an ocean where you can fish every day?' I told him there was."

"He said, 'Then I want to go there someday.' I told him that I... ah... that I... would already be there. I remember him saying, 'I will meet you there, Captain Blanca, and we'll fish." Blanca, who had made it this far through the tribute, was suddenly losing control. The tears rolled down his cheeks as the realization that it was no longer just a story. It was the real thing.

The Fire Chief came over with a lighter and lit the captain's torch. The group of boys then assembled on each side of the rowboat and, disregarding their clothing or the cold, pulled the boat and waded with it into the water.

Captain Blanca turned to the beach and held the torch high and tried to bellow away his pain.

"It's time that Fishy Bryden, the child of the sea, goes home. I know we will all be with you someday to fish again, my little friend. I promise." He waved the flame onto the kindling and nodded to the boys who pushed the boat away from shore. It rose over an incoming wave and then settled into a burning and crackling display of orange and red flames. The mourners stood in silence until the *Sunshine Dream* was nothing and all that remained were sea and smoke.

———

Twenty minutes after the service, the lone vehicle parked at Sea Glass Beach belonged to Michael Devlin.

"I don't know what the big deal is. Your own mother gave them to me. They're just meant to calm the nerves."

"They're goddamn Valium, Anna! How long have you been taking them?"

"I don't know... about a week? Really, take it easy, Michael. Your mom says some ladies even call them 'mother's helpers.' So, with a name like that, I'd hardly think they're anything that bad. It's just to get me beyond this sadness I have for Fishy."

"Jesus, Anna, did you ever think that maybe that's why my mother walks around like a goddamn zombie half the time! She pops that stuff like they're Certs!" Devlin banged his hand on the steering wheel.

"God, Michael, you know, sometimes you can be so self-righteous it makes me sick!" Anna shot back.

Devlin's eyes widened. Anna never criticized his character so harshly, and she never swore like that. It hurt. Bad.

What was going on with them?

He didn't say anything. He let his silence answer. It was the first time since he'd known her that he didn't even want to look at her, so he stared beyond, through the window down to the shoreline.

He spotted a little girl around 11 or 12 bundled up in a snowsuit skipping rocks. He kept watching the girl who was full of energy bounding about, searching the sand for rocks, sizing them up and side-arming them toward the ocean. Snowflakes that resembled the size a second grader would craft suddenly began to fall. He wondered two things. Why was the little girl by herself especially in view of the recent events? And how was Anna going to break the silence? It wasn't in that particular order that he pondered those questions. He prayed Anna's next words would be an apology.

They weren't.

"Can you just start the car and go?"

"No." He pulled the keys out of the ignition, jumped out, and slammed the door. He hurried down to the beach wall. Instead of taking the stairs, he hopped off the wall, and headed toward the girl.

"Excuse me," he shouted through cupped hands from 40 feet away, so he wouldn't startle her.

She turned around, "Yes?"

"What are you doing?" He asked, softer, as he continued to approach.

"Skipping rocks, Officer Devlin." She smiled and then turned and threw one that only skipped twice. She knew his name, but he didn't think he had ever seen her before.

"Aw, man. I'm no good with these mittens. But it's getting cold now. I gotta wear them. Earlier though, I skipped one eight times."

"Wow, that's good. It is getting cold, though." He rubbed his hands and blew on them.

"Shouldn't you be getting home?"

"Just a little while longer, Officer Devlin. My papa doesn't mind." She pointed over to a dune where a man was standing below it, smoking a cigar. The dune had blocked the man from Devlin's view from his car.

Oh, good, she's not alone.

The man waved a hello with his cigar and Devlin waved back.

"Is that Mr. Silvia from the post office?"

"Yep. Papa said I could skip stones if he could smoke his cigar and I promise not to tell Nana he's smoking. So, do you want to skip some with me, Officer Devlin?" She began searching again.

"Sure. But how do you know my name?" he asked, scanning the sand.

"Everyone knows you. But I know you mostly 'cause Fishy talked about you all the time. I think God sent these big snowflakes as confetti for his goodbye party. He's a little late, but maybe Fishy's with him and he sent them just for me. What do you think?"

"Huh?" Devlin asked.

"Lindsey?" A voice came from behind them, and they both looked up. Anna was walking toward them.

"Anna!" The little girl sprinted over to Anna, and they hugged. Anna took the girl's hand and walked over to Devlin.

"So, Michael, you've met Lindsey?" Anna threw him a look that only two people who were deeply in love would know: *I'm sorry. Real sorry.*

His pale blue eyes answered: *It's okay. I love you.*

With an extra lilt in his voice, he gave his attention back to the girl. "Well, I kind of met her. So, your name is Lindsey Silvia?"

"No. I'm Lindsey Courtland. My Papa is a Silvia."

"Oh."

"I baby-sat Lindsey from when she was about five to eight. But she's getting so old on me. And beautiful!" Anna smiled and patted her hat.

"Not as beautiful as you, Anna," the girl said, "but look!"

She took off her hat and her blond hair fell to her shoulders.

"Your hair is so long and lovely!" Anna beamed. Devlin noticed the glow was back.

"Yeah, but not as lovely as yours. Can I tell you a secret?"

"What's that?" Anna leaned down.

"I don't have to whisper. Officer Devlin knows the secret."

"He does?" Anna raised her brow.

"*I* do?" Devlin asked.

"Yeah, Fishy told me he told you," Lindsey said to Devlin and then turned to Anna, "Greggie Crocker writes poetry about your hair. He and Fishy actually named their boat after you — *Sunshine Dream* — after Greggie's poem. It was

205

more Greggie's idea 'cause Fishy was my boyfriend. He liked you, but you know, not like that."

LINDSEY COURTLAND — the name had sounded so familiar and now Devlin got it. She was the girl Fishy had talked about the night Devlin drove him home from the bike store. Fishy had referred to her as his girlfriend and talked about how they loved skipping stones together.

"So?" Anna asked.

"Huh?" Devlin had missed the question — his mind had wandered back to that night. He could see Fishy saying that he would someday give his lucky fishing lure necklace to Lindsey Courtland and marry her. He was so innocent.

Does Detective Prichard still need the necklace as evidence?

"I was saying I thought I gave me the nickname 'Sunshine.'" Her mouth curled.

"No," he laughed, back in the moment. "I said one of the boys called you that. I just didn't tell you it was Greggie. It was a secret, remember?"

"He's right. So, don't tell Greggie I told you. He'd kill me. He told Fishy once that he prays that you never cut your hair short like women do when they get married. Will you ever cut it? I hope not. Promise me you won't," Lindsey pleaded.

Anna looked at Devlin who smiled.

"Yes, promise us," he joined in.

"I promise you both I'll never cut my hair short." She held Devlin's gaze and then asked, "Now what's the stone skipping all about?"

"Fishy and I used to do it all the time. We'd do that and just tell stupid jokes. He made me laugh all the time." She said and then tears appeared as quickly as the snowflakes had.

"It's okay to cry, Lindsey." Anna hugged her, and the girl let it all out.

After a couple of minutes, Lindsey caught her breath and said, "Oh, I know it's okay to cry, Anna. My Nana tells me I should let the tears come whenever I feel them. She said showing my sadness is a tribute to all the happiness that Fishy gave me. Oh, and Officer Devlin, Nana knows my Papa is smoking his cigars. But don't tell him. He thinks he's being really sneaky. It was her idea I skip some stones and think of Fishy by myself, so I think I might finish up now. I mean alone. If that's okay?"

"Of course," Anna and Devlin nodded and walked arm in arm back to the car.

When Devlin opened the passenger door, he stopped Anna, "You did promise you'll never cut that hair? That means never. Even when you're 80 and gray."

"So, I'll know you when I'm 80?"

"And beyond. I promise. I know what a promise is. Do you?" He cupped her face.

"Yes. I know what a promise is." She welled up a bit before they kissed tenderly.

"Now, before I take you home, I have to go somewhere," he said.

"Where?"

"To see if we can get Lindsey her wedding gift."

"Huh? Lindsey is only 11. I don't get it?"

"I think true love has nothing to do with age and it can exist beyond this world. I will explain in the car."

"Where did you come up with that philosophy?"

He smiled. "I don't know. Maybe I picked up some of Nana Silvia's wisdom?"

Anna smiled and kissed him. "She's a wise woman, that Nana Silvia."

CHAPTER 22

JUNE 12, 2004

SATURDAY

J.T.

I checked my cell phone for the time. 9:17 a.m. The oddest thought popped into my head as I climbed into my Jeep: *cell phones have probably put more than a few watchmakers out of business.*

I laughed. I had more important things to contemplate especially after the night I just had. Echo received a major scoop from her cop *"friend"* about the Rutger Nelson case, but I didn't want to think about any of that until I got to the paper.

What was the sense anyway? I had left countless messages for "Crockerman," as Echo called him, and he hadn't returned one. Why get my hopes up since he might end up handing my information over to Harrison to cover the story?

So, I decided I just wanted to be mindless for the ten-minute drive while my headlights waved through the early morning mist. And, speaking of mindless... I pecked the radio dial to the sports station to hear all the experts dissect the Sox win over the Rangers. I chuckled in anticipation. Even after a win, it was always the same song and dance. From "Bobby in Revere" to "Matty in Marblehead," all the callers seemed to know just a little bit more than the Sox skipper, in this case,

Terry Francona. Their brilliance made me laugh my ass off. It also kind of comforted me in some strange way. It was like listening to a group of buddies hanging out at The Jar. I often talked back to the radio because, let's face it, I knew what I was talking about. Power of talk radio.

Unfortunately, this time when I flipped it on, the two acidic hosts were not mulling over pitch counts or lack of sacrifice bunts. They were now experts on the war in Iraq, berating a caller who offered an opposite viewpoint. God, forbid. The schoolyard bullies gave verbal wedgies to "Steve from Cambridge" calling him a "wussy-ass latte drinking liberal."

I kept my finger on the dial for a minute to see if Steve would hand over his milk money. When he did, I turned off the radio and headed onto Main Street. I wanted to get my mind off it, but then I remembered how I had met the woman at Lareby's who had told me about the nurses' flea market to support the troops. It was today from 11 to 6 at the Village Green in the center of town.

Note to self: if Crocker says "no" to my covering the Rutger Nelson case, then definitely stop by there, especially after what I had just heard. The proceeds were going to be used to armor one of the nurse's grandson's tanks in Iraq.

I came to the crosswalk in front of the post office. I eased on the brakes for a sullen skateboarder who was about to enter the walk. Legally, I could've kept going, but I decided to stop and wait for him. He threw his board down to the pavement and glided across. Of course, he didn't give me a "thank you" wave. Today's kids. I held my sarcastic tongue and noticed that, instead of sneakers, he was wearing black combat boots. The irony didn't escape me.

My eyes wandered to my right to a half dozen people carrying signs picketing in front of the post office.

At first, I thought they were disgruntled employees but then I read one of the signs. It was set up like the acronym signs from Monday Night Football that cleverly spells out something using ABC.

These were different initials painted in red block letters:

We people
Must
Do
Something now for peace!

The middle-aged woman holding the sign had long, blond hair. She looked familiar. A smile spread across her face, and she threw me a peace sign — Mrs. Walsh from the paper.

With her hair down, she looked damn good. At least ten years younger.

I pulled over into a spot by the mailboxes, jumped out, and walked over to her.

"Hey, Sunshine. I almost didn't recognize you with your ah…" I wiggled my index finger.

She patted her head with her free hand, "Oh, I know, J.T., my hairpin fell out when I was arguing with a George W. sympathizer and now I can't find it! I must really look like an old hippie, huh?"

"A hippie chick is more like it."

Laughing, she playfully hit me with the sign. "The blarney boy strikes again."

"You do this a lot?"

"More than I'd like to."

Just then an idea struck.

"Hey, I was thinking of covering the nurses' flea market today. You know 'bout it?"

"Yep."

"Well, it would be interesting to combine it with an article about you and your crew. What do you think?"

"I think you should run that by Mr. Crocker first."

"Why?"

Before she could answer, the sound of what I thought was a boat horn went off. I turned around in time to see it was actually the horn from DRAKE'S CANTEEN followed by a stubby, middle digit stretched over through the passenger window.

"Move to Iraq, you Commies!" Drake's eyes caught mine.

He didn't expect to see me. He hesitated for a second before driving off like he'd just been caught hitting his neighbor's mailbox with a baseball bat. He could retreat, but in the end, he'd have to face me.

Shut off time on his G&Ts will be a lot earlier.

"Oh, poor Drake. He's one pathetic soul. I don't know what Echo ever saw…" she stopped.

"What do you mean? Did she use to go out with him?"

"Just in high school. Anyway, it's because of people like Drake that Mr.

Crocker will want you to stay away from the whole Iraq thing. He wants to keep the town idyllic."

"That's no way to run a paper. This is the news in the town."

"I know. He might be in his forties but a part of him really is still a boy. It's all going to catch up with him if he doesn't start facing reality."

"God," I shook my head and laughed in jest. "If he doesn't let me cover that story there's no way in hell, he'll let me cover what I found out last night."

"What's that?"

"Actually, Sunshine, if you could keep this on the D.L. you might be able to help me."

"D.L.?"

"Oh, sorry. The down low." I made a "sssh" sign with my index finger.

"D.L.," she laughed, "I like that. Sure. It'll be our secret. What do you need to know?"

"Do you remember a kid named Fishy Bryden? He was murdered, I think, in…"

I didn't have to go any further. The cloud of anguish that covered her face told me she knew him. Her sign fell to her side, and she looked off for a minute.

"They found his body Christmas Eve 1972." Her voice was barely audible, "Why do you want to know?"

"I have a source who tells me the police found evidence that may in some way connect the Fishy Bryden murder to the Rutger Nelson missing persons case. I know they haven't found Rutger yet, but from what I found out, it could be a copycat killing situation."

"Oh my God." She put her hand over her mouth, and she now looked every bit her age. She then turned quickly to me, "Did you tell Greggie— Greg?"

"No, not yet. I left him messages to call me last night. Nothing."

"Yeah, he would've found out from the police," she said almost to herself.

"Well, I'm going to the paper to see what I should do with what I found out."

"He won't be there."

"Where is he?"

"He'll be on his boat. You better go over there now."

"Why?"

"'Cause Fishy Bryden was Greg's best friend. He thinks he's responsible for Fishy's murder."

"Why?"

"Because the day Fishy disappeared they were supposed to go Christmas shopping. They were going to meet in the woods near where the bike path is now. That's where they always met. Greg never showed. He can't forgive himself for leaving Fishy alone. I know that guilt is the reason he drinks."

"Oh my God." I knew all too well what that could mean, but I had to ask one more question. "Why didn't he show up that day?"

"That's a question he's never answered."

A car horn beeped lightly, this time accompanied by a peace sign.

———

While I headed to Sandy Point harbor to find Crocker's yacht, I pondered half a second on Echo's past love life with Drake Underhill. She'd probably been the hottest girl in school, and no doubt Drake had been captain of something. I didn't judge her. When it comes to high school, beauty and popularity are the only ingredients used in the relationship mixing bowl. The real ingredients are found on the higher shelves much later in life.

Hopefully.

My bigger concern was Crocker. I prayed he wasn't drinking.

Sunshine had told me that he was on his yacht but looking at the several boats docked, I realized I should've asked her the name of the boat.

I parked in a spot that overlooked the harbor next to a white truck with blue lettering on its side: NSTAR, the electric company. Then I looked to my right at an empty, pristine, silver BMW convertible.

Small Penis car.

I focused back on the harbor and took a deep breath to collect my thoughts and noticed the fog lifting and like a magician's curtain, the day would soon unveil a summer gem.

But how foggy was Crocker? Was the veil still over him? Maybe Sunshine was over-reacting and he just lost his cell phone or something.

"No use stalling," I said to myself.

I got out, glancing at the two guys in the truck slurping their coffee and wolfing down their Egg McMuffins. I thought about asking them if they knew which one was Crocker's boat, but then changed my mind. They seemed too engrossed in their conversation about wishing they could be having "Legs and eggs at The Foxy Lady instead of 'eating this shit'."

Then I spotted a bent over figure straighten and hop off the biggest yacht docked. The figure walked toward the BMW but then saw me and flashed a sly smile.

I knew that smile. And I hated it.

"You looking for your boss?" Paul Harrison pushed his glasses up to the bridge of his nose.

"Ah, yeah. *Our* boss," I stressed.

"Our boss. True enough. What he says goes, then."

"Huh?"

Harrison thumbed behind him at the boat he had just exited and laughed, "Never mind. Seems Greggie had a rough night… and morning."

Goddamn it, I thought, trying to think of a snappy retort. Nothing.

"Anyway, I think Greggie could use you. You should go to him now." Harrison almost sounded sincere as he walked around me, got into his Beemer, and keyed it to life.

"What do you mean?"

"Well, you *are* a bartender, right? I bet he could use a Mimosa."

He broke into laughter, pulled out, and took off.

"Asshole," I spit it under my breath and headed over to Crocker's boat. It reminded me of one of those racing yachts that Ted Turner sailed in the America's Cup.

I checked the name painted on the stern —

Sunshine Dream 2
Sandy Point, Cape Cod

Mrs. Walsh's nickname is Sunshine. Do they have more of a past than I had thought?

"Mr. Crocker, you round?" I half yelled as I walked onto the boat.

No answer.

I leaned down to the hatch below. "Mr. Crocker, you there?"

Nothing.

"Mr. Crocker, it's J.T."

Still nothing.

"I'm coming down," I hollered and turned to climb down the ladder.

"Who is it?" A voice came from below.

"It's me, J.T."

"J.T.? 'J.T.' who?"

Aw, shit, he's worse than I thought.

"J.T. O'Rourke from the paper."

"Oh, yeah. Come on down, J.T., and have a drink."

I descended the ladder into darkness, except for a beam of light shooting through the porthole that was like a spotlight illuminating Crocker, lying on a small couch drinking out of a bottle.

I could smell the stench of sour rum and vomit. The beam revealed orange puke spittle on the front of Crocker's white button down shirt. His eyes were fighting to stay open as he focused on me.

"So, why are we celebrating?" I asked.

"You want some?"

"Little early for me."

"Suit your... Did you know — up until last night, I hadn't had a drop of booze on this boat for three years?"

"Really?"

"Well, I had booze on the boat, but never drank it, actually, a case of Goslings that I picked up a few years back in Bermuda. God, I remember drinking half that case right smack in the middle of the Triangle. I planned on ending it right then and there. Just jump off. Go with the sea. But, like a jackass I passed out. Couldn't even kill myself right. Woke up in a raging storm and my boat had sailed unmanned about 30 miles off course. I decided to fight the storm. Let Mother Nature decide... Never more alive than sailing in that storm. And so, Mother Nature decided. So, I put the rest of the rum away. Never touched the stuff here. Never wanted to. I even forgot about it until last night."

"So why last night?"

"Remember your first day I told you I had more slips than a Provincetown drag queen. That's a pretty funny line, huh?"

"It was funny then. Not so much now."

He squinted, not liking the truth.

"Yeah, well... Sometimes it's easier to drink."

"Why? So, you don't have to think about Fishy Bryden?"

"Fishy? How...? Did Sunshine tell you?"

"Yep. Told me you were supposed to go Christmas shopping with him the day he went missing. And it doesn't take a rocket scientist to figure out that you heard they found Rutger Nelson's license last night attached to Fishy's bench."

"When does it take a rocket scientist?" he took a swig. "But more to it than just that."

"Like what?"

"Nothing... I told Harrison to cover the story."

"But I left it on your voicemail that I had a lead."

"And then I got that lead and I found out Harrison also has it. It's better he covers it. He'll be sensitive."

"And *I* wouldn't be?"

"No, it's just that..."

"You *are* running a newspaper business. It should be about reporting the truth. But to play on your philosophy... sensitive. He doesn't strike me the type." I said remembering what Harrison had told me at my Jeep: "What he says goes then."

"Harrison was around back then. He knows how to handle this story. It's the only time I'd ever trust him. Look, let me tell you something, J.T."

"What's that?"

"Something few people know. I've been seeing a shrink like, what's her name on *The Sopranos*. What's her name? Goddamn it... What is it?"

"Lorraine Bracco." I answered, to keep him talking.

"Yeah, that's it. Lorraine Bracco. Nice legs, just like Sunshine's. Anyway, been going to my shrink on and off for years to keep me away from this," he raised his almost empty bottle.

I nodded.

"My shrink wouldn't believe I'm drinking on this boat. You know why?"

"Why?"

"'Cause she thinks that I love my boat 'cause I feel safe. Like it's a mother's womb 'cause it's really the only place I get a good night's sleep. Can you believe that bullshit? Eighty bucks an hour and she doesn't even have nice legs." Crocker laughed for a good minute.

I didn't do anything.

"Still not so funny, J.T.?"

"It won't be when you sober up."

"That's a hell-of-a thing..."

"Look, Mr. Crocker, I'm worried about you, but I refuse to nurse another stray dog. Clearly you drink for a reason. You gotta figure it out and deal with it."

"Who's the other stray dog?"

"Huh?"

"The other stray you took on?"

"Oh… Umm… my father."

"What's the reason your dad drinks, J.T.?"

"I don't know. He just likes to."

"No, there's got to be a reason. It can't be that he just likes to drink. What do you think it is?" Crocker suddenly sounded like the sober one.

I was getting annoyed, "I don't know."

"Never thought about it?"

"No. Didn't have time. I was too busy picking his drunken ass up off the floor to do an Oprah on him. Anyway, I'm here about you. But maybe I'm wrong. Maybe you drink 'cause you just like the taste of it."

"And the feeling I get?" Crocker pointed to the orange spittle stains on his shirt, "No, J.T., I have a reason why I drink. I want to forget. That's why most people drink. I bet your dad wants to forget something, too. You should ask him."

"Let's talk about you. What do you want to forget? Fishy's murder? Why didn't you show up that day? And maybe if you did, he'd still be alive?"

After I said it, I realized I had been too quick and unfeeling. But at first, I didn't think it affected him. I thought Crocker was coughing but then I realized he was crying. I went over and tried to put my hand on his shoulder and comfort him, but he shielded himself with his hand.

"I want to forget… I want to forget… being… ah, Jesus… I was… ah… raped."

The word reverberated through the room. It was like he was saying the word for the first time. I was guessing that might be the case.

He continued in a haze, "And I want to forget the… forget the fact that… that I let him get Fishy. If I had just said something… Anything."

I stood there in shocked silence.

After a minute, I managed, "The candy store owner?"

His tears turned into sarcastic snorts, "It was also a toy store. Sounds like another bad joke. Pop Tucker, the toy and candy store owner. What a cliché! That's worse than having a priest saying Mass at the Neverland Ranch."

Any other time, I might have laughed at the joke. I couldn't.

Crocker laughed for a minute but then was quiet again.

"I've never had a proper relationship because of him. I can't… even be… intimate with a woman… I'll always fear him. He won't leave my goddamn head, for Christ's sake!" Crocker punched his head hard twice. And then again.

"Don't do that!"

He stopped.

Desperate to say anything I continued, "Well, maybe if you got more treatment. This guy is in jail. He's never going to hurt you again."

"Jail? Who told you that?" He glared at me.

"Well, I just figured."

"That son of a bitch is not in jail. Tucker was never even convicted for what he did to us. He got off too easy."

"What do you mean?"

Crocker savored his last sip and then gazed through me as if he were looking at something else. I knew he was. The past. When he was a boy. A time in his life he was desperately trying to escape. And then for one day he did.

Seconds later, he passed out, comforted by the waves from the outgoing ferry softly rocking him back and forth like a newborn in a crib.

CHAPTER 23
JANUARY 7, 1973

SUNDAY

DEVLIN

I t was the day after Fishy Bryden's send off and Michael Devlin was still trying to track down Detective Prichard to ask him about Fishy's necklace.

Anna and he had stopped by the station the night before but were informed by Officer Scott Gallo, who was manning the front desk, that Prichard was out on "police business" and he didn't know when he'd be back.

"Could you radio him? It's kind of important," Devlin asked.

Gallo hesitated but then realized he had power over Devlin again.

He tried holding a poker face but broke, "Sorry. We can't radio our officers for just anyone who wants to shoot the bull. And also, Devlin, I heard Chief Gedney say something about not wanting you coming around here until your suspension is over. As a friendly suggestion, I think you and Miss Talbot should leave before you do even more damage to your career. If you still even have one."

Officer Rodney Farrell, who was at the vending machine, whistled a laugh.

The next morning, as Devlin parked in front of Prichard's house, he felt the molar groove inside his cheek from biting on his anger.

"If there was a dark alley in this town, I'd…" he grunted before getting out of Anna's car and heading up the brick walkway to Prichard's door.

On the other side of the door, he heard Prichard's voice, "The tickle monster is going to get you," and then he heard a little girl's laughter followed by giggling, "Daddy, please stop. You're making me laugh too much."

Prichard. The Hard Prick away from the job was "father of the year." Devlin never would've guessed that. He paused, staring at the yellow doorbell. It was Sunday morning. He really should wait till Monday to approach Prichard, but he couldn't help himself. He pressed it.

Ding-dong.

"Daddy, now you have to stop. Someone's at the door."

"Coming!" he yelled to the door and then said to his daughter, "You got away this time, princess. Now go brush your teeth or the tickle monster will strike again."

The little girl gave an exaggerated shriek and Devlin heard her take off.

Prichard opened the door. He was still wearing his pajamas and bathrobe. He patted down his messy hair with his left hand, but his laughter and smile quickly changed to a frown. "Officer Devlin?"

"Good morning, Detective."

He looked behind him and then back at Devlin, "Well, it was a good morning. You know it's Sunday."

"I know. I'm sorry."

"And because of the Bryden boy's murder I have very limited time with my family, two hours tops."

"I know. Again, I'm sorry. But this is about Fishy. May I ask you how old your daughter is?"

"Six. Why?"

"Imagine if she were 11 or 12 and her first love was murdered and…"

Prichard looked behind him and then turned back to Devlin, "What the hell is wrong with you? I don't even want to go there in my head."

"You're absolutely right. That was the wrong approach. It's just that I…" Devlin paused.

"Is this about the Courtland girl?" Prichard softened a little.

"Yes. Lindsey Courtland. Fishy's little friend. How did you know?"

"I am the lead investigator. So, what about her?"

219

"I think there is a way to at least give her some sort of solace. And I think you could help me with that. Could I just have a minute of your time?"

Prichard studied Devlin for a minute.

"Come on in. My wife just put some coffee on. We can talk in my study."

Mrs. Prichard, humming to herself greeted Devlin with a surprised expression. Devlin nodded and followed the detective to the study in the back of the house.

The room was decorated like any other officer's study: family pictures, a mounted bass, framed commendations, diplomas from Northeastern University and the Massachusetts Criminal Justice Training Council. But there was something else — a chalkboard on wheels.

Devlin studied it quickly.

On the left side of the board, it read: FISHY BRYDEN MURDER CASE

There was a list of facts — time, place, cause of death, etc.

On the right, it read: POP TUCKER'S POSSIBLE RAPE VICTIMS

Devlin scanned beyond the names to the last number: 26.

"Holy sh..." Devlin began but Prichard swung around, saw what he was looking at and flipped the board over to the other side that was blank.

"You shouldn't see that."

"Yes. I understand. I just didn't think we found that many pictures."

"All I'll say about that is we found more pictures at his house. And I'm sure there are even more victims than that."

"I can't believe none of these boys talked."

Prichard went around his desk, sat down, and folded his bathrobe over his legs. "I can. At that age, or at any age for that matter, who would want to admit to such a thing? Would you?"

The tone in which Prichard asked the question felt strange to Devlin, almost like Prichard was interrogating him.

"Now that I think about it, probably not," Devlin sat in the chair facing Prichard.

"Plus the fact, some of the victims might not even know they're victims."

"Huh?"

"Tucker drugged them. I bet half these kids just woke up in the back of his store not knowing what happened to them. And, because of it, they may've even gone back there over and over not knowing they were being molested."

"Jesus."

"Yep. Jesus is right. I'm finding the common denominator with the victims is Tucker picked boys that had no father or came from unstable homes, kids who couldn't go to an adult. Easy prey. Okay, now what's this about the little Courtland girl?"

"Well, one time I was giving Fishy a ride home and he..."

Prichard put his hand up. "You say 'one time.' Are you saying you gave him rides on more than one occasion?"

"Ah, no. I only gave him a ride once."

"And that was after your run-in with Paul Harrison at the bike shop when he showed the boys the *Playboy*?"

Now Devlin definitely felt like he was being interrogated.

"Yeah, why?"

Prichard motioned with his hand, "No reason. Go on."

"Anyway, when I was dropping Fishy off, he mentioned that someday he was going to marry Lindsey Courtland and he was going to give her his lucky necklace."

"Lucky necklace?" Prichard leaned forward in his chair.

"Yeah, you know, the one Captain Blanca had given him."

Prichard's look urged Devlin to continue.

"You know the one. It's an oval fishing lure. Half silver, half gold. The one he always wore. Anyway, I wasn't sure of two things. Was it buried with him? And if not, is it still evidence or could you make sure Lindsey Courtland gets it when the case is closed?"

Prichard jumped out of his chair and rifled through his file cabinet.

"Devlin, you say Fishy wore this necklace all of the time. When you say 'all the time,' what do you mean?"

"Just what I said. It was his lucky necklace. Why?"

Prichard didn't say anything for a minute as he went through the cabinet.

"Here it is," he said to himself, grabbing a manila folder. Prichard pulled out some papers and read through them for a couple of minutes before turning his attention back to Devlin.

"Just what I thought. There was no necklace found on Fishy Bryden. I'm guessing Pop Tucker probably snatched it from him."

"Why would he do that?" Devlin asked.

"Sometimes killers do that to remember their victim. This is good, Devlin."

"Why?"

"Because if we can find that necklace at Tucker's house or store it will strengthen our murder case and we can put the sick asshole away. Right now, everything is just too damn circumstantial."

"Yeah, but don't you have enough to put him away already? You got his broom, a lollipop stick, ripped material from red suspenders." Devlin gestured; palms open.

"That's what's bothering me the most," Prichard said.

This time Devlin didn't ask why. He just waited for him to continue.

"For a guy to rape at least 26 kids in this town without anyone noticing and now to be so sloppy doesn't make sense. And suspenders are made out of elastic. I can't picture them ripping on a tree. They shouldn't rip unless they were cut."

"Are you saying someone else may've done this?" Devlin asked.

"I would never voice a thought like that. But I will say: if we can find that lucky necklace, it will sure make it a hell of a lot easier to prosecute the sicko. Good work, Devlin."

Devlin nodded, thinking *I really underestimated this guy.*

The shrill of the phone ringing came from the kitchen and a moment later Mrs. Prichard called for the detective.

"I'll be right back," Prichard excused himself, and Devlin thought he actually got a smile from the Hard Prick.

Devlin was tempted to go to the chalkboard and turn it back over but before his curiosity took him to that point, Mrs. Prichard walked in carrying a tray with coffee and donuts.

"Here you go, Officer Devlin." She handed him a cup.

"Oh, thank you." It was the first donut he had had in a long time.

Mrs. Prichard smiled and was about to exit but then turned around.

"Officer Devlin?"

"Yes."

"My husband is a by-the-book officer, and he would never tell you this, but he doesn't blame you for what you did to that animal."

He knew the animal she was referring to was Pop Tucker.

"My husband told me he wished he could've had the opportunity to… y'know… make that animal suffer for what he did."

"Well, ma'am, all I can say is, your husband is a by-the-book officer, and I can learn a lot from him. He's a good man." Devlin never thought he'd ever say that about Prichard but now he understood him. He was all business on the job, but he didn't bring it home.

Well, at least he didn't bring it into his living room. He kept it locked away in his study.

"Yes, he is." Mrs. Prichard agreed before leaving.

He was almost done with his coffee when Prichard, fuming, stormed into the study.

"Something wrong?" Devlin, startled, almost dropped his cup.

"You tell me, Devlin. Why exactly are you here?"

"Huh? I told you, the necklace." He put his cup down on the desk.

"You sure it's not to find out what holes we have in the case?"

"Holes? Why would I want to know about holes? Detective, what the hell are you talking about?

"Maybe to help your father." Prichard snarled.

"Help my father?"

"Yeah, I just got off the phone with my buddy, the warden at Brickford Penitentiary. He keeps me updated on who's been visiting Pop Tucker. Which hasn't been hard to follow. The list has been zero. That is, until ten minutes ago, when the number one defense attorney in the state, Allan Devlin, strolled in to have a chat with the sickest fuck around. Does your old man have any morals at all?"

Devlin didn't hear the question. He was already out the door.

CHAPTER 24

JANUARY 7, 1973

SUNDAY

DEFENSE ATTORNEY ALLAN DEVLIN

During the week, Allan Devlin wore Italian crafted shoes to complement his custom-tailored Brooks Brothers suits, charging a hundred and fifty dollars an hour for his skills at finding "reasonable doubt," but on Sunday mornings he dressed and acted quite differently.

He wanted to appear to the town as a regular Joe — he was one of them. It was good for business. So, he'd wear modest ties under V-neck sweaters and stand at attention in his worn, black loafers waiting for his cue from Father McCarthy. Then, instead of clutching his briefcase, he'd walk down the main aisle carrying a collection basket attached to a long stick. He'd humbly nod "thank you" to the coin and dollar droppers while he moved from pew to pew guiding the basket like a metal detector on a sandy beach.

Due to his demanding job and other personal obligations over the years, Allan had missed wedding anniversaries, birthdays, Little League, and high school football games, but he prided himself on never missing a Sunday morning as head usher at St. Michael's Church.

But this Sunday was different from all of the others.

This Sunday he received a phone call. One he couldn't ignore.

And because of it, he hadn't had time to change. Now waiting and sitting in his church clothes in the Brickford Penitentiary visitor's room, he felt like Superman without his cape.

After all, Pop Tucker's words had the effect of kryptonite: "I have a secret that could hurt your family. Everyone will know if you don't come now."

The barrel-chested guard, Stanley, whom Allan had slid many Cuban cigars to over the years, escorted the shackled Pop Tucker into the room.

Usually, Stanley greeted the defense attorney with a smile followed by a corny lawyer joke. Not this time. No smiles. No jokes. Not for people who represent child molesting murderers.

Stanley was all business, "Stay seated, Counselor. Sit there, Tucker." He pointed to the chair behind the metal table across from Allan Devlin.

Pop Tucker chuckled before plopping down. That chuckle told Allan everything. Despite facing life in prison, the man wasn't scared. He was dealing with one sick bastard. But it wasn't the first time.

The lawyer almost didn't even recognize Tucker, not because of his behavior or the bruises covering his face that were still purple and yellow, but because of the gray prison jumpsuit he was wearing. It was the first time he remembered seeing Tucker in anything other than his white shirt, red suspenders, and blue jeans.

"Can you uncuff me, Stan? I'm going to be doing some writing for my lawyer," Tucker asked.

"Call me 'Guard,' asshole, or don't talk at all!" Stanley barked into his face.

Allan had never seen Stanley act like that to an inmate. He was always firm but respectful.

"Sometimes it's hard, but it sets a calm tone," he had once told Allan. But even Stanley couldn't fake his feelings for Tucker.

"And by the way, Tucker," teeth gritted, Allan leaned menacingly toward Pop, "I'm not your lawyer." Now it was Stanley who was surprised — the defense attorney never lost his cool. There was a tension of forced restraint in the air that, at any moment, Devlin or the guard would snap. It was a feeling unfamiliar to both men.

But not to Tucker.

He grinned, "Well, you might not be my lawyer yet, but trust me, you will be."

Silence invaded the room. The defense attorney and guard tried to comprehend the statement.

Stanley finally took out his keys.

"What hand do you write with, Tucker?"

"I write with my right hand, Guard."

Stanley unlocked the right cuff and then relocked it to the steel bar attached to the left side of the table.

Tucker looked down at the table, "I see paper, Guard, but I need a writing utensil, please."

Stanley shrugged, unperturbed.

"I have one." Allan reached into his pocket and tossed a pen across, clanging it off the table where Tucker's free hand snatched it on the bounce.

"You like that grab? I'm a regular Rico Petrocelli. Don't you think? Although, come to think of it, he had 13 errors this year. I wonder how I knew that. I don't even like baseball." Tucker smiled and began writing.

Allan had a quick flash of once picking up stuffed quahogs at Bryden's and Fishy spouting off facts about various species of fish and different Red Sox players. He wanted to jump across the table but held in his hate resulting in a thin bead of sweat that formed on his forehead, glistening under the white lights.

Allan loosened his tie, his mind urging him to stay professional.

Stanley's eyes bore down on Tucker for a minute before turning to Devlin.

"You know the routine, Counselor. I'll be right outside."

"Thank you," Allan nodded.

When the door shut, he didn't hesitate.

"Tucker, what the hell was that phone call all about?"

Tucker looked up, "Gee, I'm no longer 'Pop' to you? I'm also disappointed you dressed down for the occasion. I have a lot of money to keep you in your fancy suits."

"I don't have time for this."

"On this paper I'm about to hand you is a list of names of boys whose pictures weren't found."

"I'd suggest you don't hand me that. I'm not going to rep…"

"I don't care what you decide. Just take a look." Tucker pushed the paper across the table.

Allan put on his reading glasses and looked at the four names. He knew three of them. He had quick memories of seeing them around town. They were good kids who were a little mixed up. The type of kids who might grow up to be defendants or defense attorneys, depending how they handled what life threw their way. And now he knew that life threw them something that nobody should ever have to experience.

"I have their pictures hidden. They won't be found. Unless..." Tucker trailed off.

Allan tried desperately to remain cool by flicking the paper back to him, "I don't know why you're in such a good mood. There's no way you'll ever beat this."

"Beat this? Nice pun." Tucker looked down at his pants and laughed for a minute, "I've been doing a little too much of that, don't you think?"

"Look as a lawyer — not *your* lawyer — you don't have a snowball's chance in hell and that's where you're going. And I couldn't be happier."

"I don't think so. I have a couple of wild cards to play."

"Wild cards?"

"I will tell you all about them at our next meeting."

"Next meeting? You're crazy, you know that?"

"Those boys' pictures... You know I could sell them. Believe me, there is a profitable market out there. That would be very embarrassing to their families. Don't you think?"

"Speaking of families, you sick asshole, you only got me here by mentioning my family. So, get to it."

"Oh, that's right, I forgot to write something," Tucker looked down at a new piece of paper and began writing again while he talked.

"I suppose right now it's useless to say I was set-up. I think it was probably by one of the boys. Some are pretty old now. I do have a few ideas of who might have done this to me."

"You know, Allan," Pop continued, wistfully, "I was just thinking about when Michael wasn't Michael, but when he was just little Mikey."

Allan felt his blood race through his system.

"Mikey was a good kid and boy; did he love coming to my store. I really felt bad for him. He'd always complain how his daddy never had time for him, how he was always up in Boston working..."

"What are you telling me?" Allan heard himself shouting.

Stanley peeked through the glass window.

Tucker glanced up from the paper, smiled, went back to writing, and picked up where he left off, "Yep, his daddy was always up in Boston working on a case. Of course, I knew you didn't have just cases up there in Boston. I've always kept an eye out for you, just in case this moment ever was to arrive. I know all about the young female clerks you'd dine with at the Union Oyster House and then bed up in your Back Bay brownstone."

Allan exhaled a deep breath and laughed for the first time.

"Nice alliteration, I'll give you that. Is that why you dragged me down here? You think you're going to blackmail me into taking your case? And if I don't, you'll tell my son I was having a few meaningless affairs?"

"Yep." Tucker looked up from the paper.

"First off, Michael would never believe a sick piece of shit like you. Secondly, even if he did, my son knows I'm not perfect. I'm sure he figured that out on his own long ago. I don't really see Michael hating me much more than he already does. As for my wife, we have what one would call 'an arrangement,' so I'd say you're shit out of luck. I'm not a perfect man, but there is one thing I've never done and never will do and that's represent child molesting murderers." Allan rose from the table and yelled to the door, "Guard, I'm done here!"

Stanley opened the door and rushed in.

"Whoa, hold on," Tucker waved with his free hand and wrote some more, "I'm not done."

"I think you are." Allan was back to his old confident self.

"If the Counselor says you are done, then you are done," Stanley was now Allan's teammate, unlocking the cuff from the bar and relocking both of Tucker's hands.

"But…" Tucker began while Stanley pushed him out the door.

"No time for buts," Stanley said.

"There is time for one," Tucker said and then hollered over his shoulder, gesturing to the paper on the table.

"There is another reason your son might hate you, Counselor!"

The door slammed shut.

Allan picked up the paper, his eyes blinked twice:

#5 Michael Devlin

While you were fucking around so was your son. With me!

Only I know where the pictures are so don't try getting some warrant to try looking for them.

You'll get them back when you clear me. I have ideas on how we can cut a deal!

See you tomorrow.

P.S. Could you bring me a lollipop? Preferably, cherry...

His face flushed, he almost fainted, crumbling into the chair. There were no tears. Just shock. He sat there staring into nothing for several minutes. He then tried to discount it, arguing it away in his lawyer's mind, but he couldn't argue away the memories. He saw himself dropping his son off at Pop Tucker's, practically shoving the boy through the door so he could head off to Boston.

No wonder Michael was so out-of-control after he found Fishy!

He took out a handkerchief to catch the bile that filled his mouth.

The tears followed.

Allan knew he had done this to his son. He never had been there for him and because of it...

His son wouldn't be a victim again. Not this time. This time he would do whatever he had to do to protect his boy. He wiped his eyes dry with the sleeve of his sweater and then studied the letter again and realized one line that stood out.

Only I know where the pictures are so don't try getting some warrant to find them.

If only Pop Tucker knew where the pictures were and there was suddenly no Pop Tucker, then there would be no pictures to be found.

The attorney found his answer.

Only two weeks before, he called in a favor and was able to get one of his clients transferred to Brickford, so the inmate could be closer to his home on Cape Cod.

The inmate was serving time for manslaughter. Killing someone with a knife during a fight. But he was now doing easy time. He even got the inmate a job in the mailroom.

The inmate owed him. Big.

Stanley opened the door, his manner was much quieter, "Mr. Devlin, you need something else?"

Allan acted casual, "Yes, I'd like to visit one of my clients. I just want to check on him. His name is Larry Tadmor."

"Yes, new guy. I know him, just finished visiting with his father only an hour ago. Nice man, his father. Said he was a captain of the ferry that goes over to your island. Said great things about you. That he's known your family for years."

"Probably knows my family better than I do," Allan mumbled.

"What's that?"

"Nothing."

Allan Devlin nodded, putting his crumpled, stained handkerchief back into his pocket.

CHAPTER 25
JUNE 13, 2004

SUNDAY

J.T.

8:39 a.m.

Since I rolled into town, it was my first real day off from the paper, The A.F., and police interrogations. I was looking forward to *hopefully* having a normal and relaxing day. It sure wasn't starting off that way.

My head was ringing for two reasons. The first was no sleep. The nightmare had jarred me awake again. I thought about it for a minute.

Me, riding in a Jetsons' cartoon-style spaceship traveling to the moon. Then suddenly standing on the moon yelling, "Go Red Sox!" Seeing a small figure on the other side of the moon speaking in a foreign language to me. Then me, chasing the small figure but it falls off the moon. Then came the distorted music and boiling rain scalding my hand.

God, during the waking hours, it made me laugh because it reminded me of a bad MTV video from the early eighties that Duran Duran or The Cars would've made — when they still showed videos.

But the truth was it scared the shit out of me. Every night waking up and screaming for help was not cool at all for the psyche.

8:41 a.m.

I had been up for five hours lying in my bed pondering the nightmare. I glanced over at my box of several unpacked books. In the box with my Cobens and Lehanes, I had all of my psychology books from B.C. I knew I could've sold them back to the bookstore for beer and ramen noodles money, but I always prayed that someday I'd get the balls to face my problem and read up on the real meaning of dreams. I avoided that chapter at college.

Maybe that's why I could only pull a B- in Abnormal Psych.

No question about it. I was abnormal. Anyway, no sleep was one reason my head was ringing. The other reason was my cell phone.

It was 8:42 a.m. and I had already received three phone calls.

1. Lillian Dumas: the woman I had interviewed about the coyotes possibly killing her dog, Cool Hand.

"I thought Friday they were going to publish the article about Cool Hand missing."

"Actually, Ms. Dumas, the article is more about the overpopulation of coyotes."

"But you *do* mention Cool Hand."

"Of course, Ms. Dumas. Ahm, by-the-way, who gave you my number?"

"Norman Chadwick."

Figures!

I briefly wondered if Crocker was able to keep his latest slip secret from his nephew.

"Well, Norm could've told you that it was pushed back til Tuesday considering what's going on and all."

And it might not even get in the paper at all.

"What do you mean, what's going on?"

"The missing boy. Rutger Nelson."

"Oh, yeah. Well, I hope it will be in on Tuesday. The sooner it's in, the more dogs we might be able to help survive this epidemic. Thank you and bye."

2. Trafton Brown, Jr.: President of Sandy Point Federal Savings Bank.

"Hi, Mr. O'Rourke?"

"Yes."

"Trafton Brown. I met you a few days back at the bank."

"Yes, Mr. Brown, I remember."

You almost stepped on your tongue when you greeted Echo.

"Well, I'm calling because I need to pass on a message."

I know I have bad credit. But who doesn't?

"It's Sunday, Mr. Brown. I didn't think you guys worked on Sundays."

"We don't. This is about your boss, Greg Crocker. I'm his A.A. sponsor and he wanted me to call and tell you he just went to a meeting and if you could keep it quiet about his drinking and everything else yesterday you were witness to. He'd really appreciate it."

"Sure, but you calling, isn't that what they call co-dependency? I think that's a no-no in your club?"

"I see. You're familiar with the program?"

"I'm a bartender and my father's a drunk. I'd say *familiar's* an understatement."

"An *alcoholic*."

"Huh?"

"Your father's an *alcoholic*."

Don't preach to me, buddy!

"I call it the way I see it. And my old man's a drunk. And you're a co-dependent. Believe me, I know, Mr. Brown, I've been a co-dependent for years."

"Well, you're right. I am bending the rules a bit. I guess in the end, we're all trying to do the best we can. Have a good day, Mr. O'Rourke."

Like clockwork.

3. Denny: Owner of Gilligan's Pub on K Street in Southie. Across the street from where I was raised. Many nights growing up, I'd watch from my bedroom window as my father rubbed his hands together and entered the pub with the anticipation and glee of a boy walking into a circus tent.

"J.T., I heard you moved to the Cape, so I hate to call you but..."

"Let me guess, my old man's waiting for your place to open?"

"Yep. He's first at bat. Too early for anyone to be on deck since we don't even open for another few hours."

"Jesus, Denny, c'mon, we both know you've probably got five people at the bar right now."

"Hey, wait! I don't need you using the Lord's name on me. I was just calling you because you asked me if he ever showed up again to do the right thing. And I'm doing the right thing."

"I'm sorry, Denny, you're right. You are doing the right thing and I appreciate it."

About 30 years too late but you're doing it, Denny, God bless you.

"So, should I serve him?"

"From now on, you don't even have to call me. I'm all done. He's on his own. But if I were you, make sure he has money before you start pouring. Take care, Denny." I hung up.

Avoid thinking about it, my mind told me, and I lay back on my pillow. My cell chimed two seconds later. I almost didn't answer it but then I looked at the caller ID: Echo Landers.

"Hello?" I tried to sound casual.

"Did I wake you?"

"No. I've been up for a while."

"You're not ah…" She paused.

"Ah, what?"

"With your girlfriend. You know since it's your day off and all."

"Girlfriend? I don't have a girlfriend."

"But you tol… never mind. Anyway, the reason I'm calling is kind of cheesy. You ready?" Echo asked.

"Sure, shoot."

"My family is throwing a party for me tonight for my birthday."

"It's your birthday? Well, happy birthday, Echo."

"Yeah. Yeah. Thanks. Anyway, it's going to be a traditional Cape Cod clambake at the beach around 6:30."

"Sea Glass Beach?"

"No, a private one. Wow, that's pretentious, huh? Anyway, I wasn't sure if the city guy would be up for some cake and lobster. Not in that order of course."

"So, being a city guy I gotta know. How's that work? Do you eat that together?"

She laughed, "You'll have to come and find out. You in, O'Rourke?"

"I'm in, Landers."

"Cool. It's easier to email you the directions. I'll do that in a little while."

"Cool. May I ask how old?"

"You just did ask. 34."

"Wow! But I'm 34." I always thought she was in her late twenties or very early thirties at the most. Not my age.

234

"So?"

"Well, *I'm* an old bastard."

"Well, I guess then today that officially makes me an old bitch," she laughed, "see you tonight."

8:51 a.m.

What had I learned? Being afraid to even analyze the nightmare proved I was still a psycho. I was writing meaningless, unpublished articles about coyotes, and my boss and father were both drunks. But Echo not only invited me to her birthday party, but she also slipped in the girlfriend question. My first real day off was looking pretty damn promising after all.

I checked the TV and Channel 14 was replaying a montage of Vic Hauser's reports from the entire week. In them, he didn't mention me, but he did mention a license being found (which was the talk of the town) on the Sandy Point Bike Path but not once did he mention the license being attached to Fishy Bryden's bench.

I was really surprised. Apparently, Hauser's informant on the Sandy Point Police Department didn't give him everything. If they had, it would prove that this case might have a little more sizzle to it than just a missing boy — a copycat killer trying to link the present to the past. Of course, a body had still not been found, only Rutger Nelson's license. But even that theory alone would send producers and big time TV lights like *Dateline* or *48 Hours* down to the Cape. Those lights normally would be on Mr. Porn Stache, but he didn't break that vital information on his report.

That meant Paul Harrison now had the upper hand in the story. When the paper came out on Tuesday with that information, I knew Harrison, via satellite, might soon be rubbing elbows with the creepy Keith Morrison types that invade small towns in trouble.

I had better things to do.

Yeah, right.

For the next couple of hours, I typed up a story on "Pointers" (I found out that's what they call the Sandy Point locals) who have turned to bicycles as alternative transportation to commute to work.

Something I should think about, I thought, as I typed away and then looked over at my brand new bike. It reminded me of a dog waiting at the door to go for a walk. My guilt for not exercising tugged at me. I thought about it for a minute.

Not today.

After I pressed SAVE, I checked my email from "the Ol' bitch," as Echo had signed it, and then printed up the directions to Mackerel Beach. I remembered hearing someone mention that Mackerel Beach was the richest section in town.

"She *so* doesn't strike me as a rich girl," I said to myself, mimicking how one of my sisters, Casey, always talked.

I probably should catch up with all three sisters, I thought briefly. The one good thing that had resulted from the bad O'Rourke parenting, the kids were extremely close. We had to be. We grew up having to look out for one another.

"I'll send the girls emails tomorrow," I said, glancing out my window at the waves rolling onto the beach. I picked through my box of books and almost settled on one of the psychology ones, but then went for some fictional psychology instead, grabbing my worn copy of *The Alienist* by Caleb Carr.

I went outside, smoothed out my towel, lay down, and escaped to the late 1800s in New York with Dr. Laszlo Kreizler as he searched for a serial killer. When I had no customers at the dark, dingy Jar, I had gone on this hunt with Dr. Kreizler many times before and it never got old. I always found something I had missed. But what was new this time was I was reading the book on the beach, soaking in the pages and unknowingly also soaking in the sun. I paid no attention to the time or the power of the rays beating down on my Irish skin. After about two hours of flipping pages, I felt really hot. No problem. A cool swim was my short-term cure.

It wasn't until around 5:30 or so that I realized exactly what I had done to myself. It was the owner of Lareby's Market who put the whole thing into perspective.

"You're screwed."

"Huh?" I looked up.

I was in the wine section trying to pick out a bottle for Echo as he approached wearing his white coat and a concerned grimace on his face.

"It's J.T., right?" He pointed.

"Yeah, and you're..." I spotted the cursive-stitched name on his coat, "Jared, right?"

"Yep." He scratched his bald forehead with his right knuckle, "Aisle seven is where we keep the aloe gel."

"Oh, thanks but I'm just here for wine."

He laughed, "Well, you better drink a lot of it because tonight you're going to be in a ton of pain."

"What do you mean?"

"You *do* know you have a bad sunburn?"

"Really?" I felt my face. Feverish.

"If you're red now, wait til later tonight."

"Bad?"

"Haven't you been sunburned before?"

"Just garbage man tans because, come to think of it, I haven't really been outside for an extended period of time for years. I'm always working in the bar."

"Here's what you do. Get the aloe and refrigerate it for a little while before you put it on. Then it'll be nice and cool when you put it on your skin. Should help a bit."

"Hey thanks, Jared."

"No problem. It's my job."

"Then can I ask your expertise on something else?"

"Sure. Go ahead."

"I'm going to a clambake with lobster and all that on the beach tonight. So, I was wondering what wine should I bring? My bartending skills have only prepared me for what goes well with beer nuts." I smiled.

Jared returned the smile, "Echo's birthday, right?"

"Yeah. How did…"

"It's my job, remember? Echo loves Pinot Grigio. But what woman doesn't?"

He was right about that. I had poured rivers-full over the years. That would've been my guess, but he took it a step further.

"Santa Margarita is your best bet. She buys that a lot." He pointed to the bottle, and I grabbed it.

"Cool. Thanks."

"Anything else?" He laughed, "Like what to give her for a gift?"

"Oh, man. What *do* I get her? I hardly know her."

"J.T., when it comes to women, do we really *ever* know them?"

I gave one of those *I hear you, man laughs* that show camaraderie while he went on his way through the swinging doors into the back of the store.

A moment later, I called Sunshine for advice on what gift to buy. First we talked about Crocker, whom she had communicated with and, she informed me, was having the day-after drinking regrets. She went on to ask me not to tell anyone, especially his nephew, who was waiting for this day to come. That wasn't a problem with me. I knew Crocker's future of running the paper was at stake, and I certainly didn't want Norman "Napoleon" taking over. I also knew I held a much bigger secret than just Crocker's drinking. I knew why he drank. He had been molested. What I didn't know was how I was going to handle that knowledge. He had been so blitzed, he might not even remember his confession to me.

I probably should see how it plays out, I thought, and then I told Sunshine about my dilemma of what to buy Echo. She didn't even pause, directing me to a little store on Main Street owned by Mrs. Kumar from India, who made custom designed fragrances for her clients' personalities.

Mrs. Kumar, a sweet woman with a cute Indian accent that one couldn't help but impersonate, gave me a bottle of what she referred to as "Echo's Whisper." She wrapped it, promising me that Echo would love it. I really didn't need her promise. I had already experienced the power of Echo's Whisper and was pretty sure I bought the ideal gift, not just for Echo but also for me.

When I arrived at the gated community of the Mackerel Beach Estates, I was stopped by what looked to be a former grade-school hall monitor who had made it up the ranks and now, in his golden years, was manning a guardhouse. He was wearing a blue wannabe police officer's shirt and white Bermuda shorts with matching white nylon socks stretched to his kneecaps. When I pulled up, he instantly took a bite out of crime by throwing down his copy of *Soldier of Fortune*, jumping to his feet, and waving his toy walkie-talkie at me to stop.

The expression on his face — "there is no way in hell you're driving by me without getting questioned."

He skipped any sort of civil greeting and demanded to know why I was there. I responded with a "Jesus, calm down," before answering the question causing him to give me a double take before checking the guest list.

"Your name isn't on it," he sounded excited before eying his radio. "Are you sure you really were invited?"

His tone — "uh-oh, possible security breach!"

I laughed, putting my hands up, "Damn, Jack, you caught me! Are you gonna call Chloe for backup?"

"Jack? Chloe? What are you talking about?" He pointed to his nameplate, "My name is Scott not Jack."

"Jack Bauer. You know from the TV show *24*."

Not amused at my sarcasm, he just squinted.

I got serious and handed him Echo's email, "Anyway, of course I'm sure I was invited. She emailed me."

He scrutinized the email looking for the secret code before handing it back. "Just keep driving straight for about a mile and a half and you'll see the beach. Park behind the line of cars."

No shit.

"Thank you, Scott." I saluted and squealed off.

I might as well have been driving a tour bus in Beverly Hills, driving by all the mansions set on their million-dollar landscapes. The road finally ended at the beach.

I took in the view of the red gumdrop sun about to be swallowed up by the horizon before parking behind the last Lexus in line.

That's one expensive view, I thought, but like the Mastercard commercial boasts, I had to admit it was priceless. I grabbed the wine and gift, jumped out, and walked toward the couple of dozen partygoers drinking their beers or mixed drinks milling around four campfires. Somewhere in the background a radio was playing James Taylor setting a real welcoming and mellow mood.

But then a loud voice broke that vibe. "Holy shit, J.T, you got fried! And you kept your sunglasses on, too!"

I nodded "yes" to my boss from The A.F., Davis Lawson.

Davis turned to the guy next to him who was sporting a toupee from the old Marv Albert collection.

"Zach, he looks like a Goddamn raccoon. Don't you think?"

"Not funny, Davis. The poor guy looks uncomfortable." The man seemed genuinely concerned, shaking his head from side to side. I wondered briefly what kind of glue was under that rug.

"Thank you," I said to him. "I can tell you have more class than your friend Davis over there. The sunburn chills are starting to hit, so I appreciate your sympathy, Mr…" I put my hand out.

"Goodrich. Zachary Goodrich."

"J.T. O'Rourke. Why do I know that name?"

Davis piped in, "Hey, I have a shitload of class, and maybe you know Zach 'cause he owns Pilgrim Diner?"

"Oh yes, that must be it," I said but thought, *You're the guy who wants to develop Samoset Place.*

"Best omelets in town," Goodrich advertised.

"Yes, but still the worst coffee," Echo's stepfather added as he approached.

"Gotta keep my old man's tradition alive," Goodrich smiled and then blessed himself.

"You know what they say about the sins of the father... J.T., good to see you again." Mr. Eldredge threw me a warm smile followed by a firm handshake.

"You too, Mr. Eldredge, especially considering the last time I saw you I was in jail."

"Jail?" Goodrich was confused.

Mr. Eldredge's voice shifted to serious, "J.T. was the last person to see Ethan's son before he disappeared. When he's not reporting, J.T.'s a part-time bartender for Davis. Rutger was trying to sneak a drink at Davis's place. They brought J.T. in for some questions, and so Echo called me and I got to play defense attorney for the afternoon. I shouldn't admit this, in light of the circumstances, but it was a little exciting. Reminded me of my Yale days when I was considering criminal law."

"Ah," Goodrich nodded.

"And, for the record, J.T. didn't serve that kid," Davis added.

I wanted to say, "Yeah, but the bigger issue is the kid is still missing," but I remained silent.

"Not like when we were kids, eh, Davis?" Goodrich laughed. "I think you and I were drinking there when we were around 17 or 18."

"Hey, O'Rourke, you made it." Echo waved from down the beach interrupting our conversation. I waved back.

I noticed she had dressed down for the occasion, wearing a pink hoody over a lime green tank top, jeans, and flip-flops. Echo turned to a black woman beside her who looked to be in her early 50s, said something, and they both headed over.

I figured the woman had to be her mom because she had the same good looks. She also had Echo's free-spirited fashion style. She had on a big, dark blue sweater, jeans, Birkenstocks and wore her hair under a white and blue polka-dot scarf. The one difference was her skin color was much darker than her daughter's but even from far away, she exuded the same natural beauty which causes sunburns to rise in temperature.

"Here are my two girls." Mr. Eldredge gave a light kiss on his wife's cheek.

"What are all of you men talking about?" Echo's mom smiled at the group and her dark eyes lingered on me a little longer.

"How your husband almost got into criminal law at Yale," Goodrich said.

"Oh, yes. I think our lives would've been absolutely miserable. Honey, you should tell them a better college story, the story of how you fell for me when you were an undergrad at Amherst."

"That's okay, honey."

"Maybe I should tell them." She threatened, good-naturedly.

"Oh, yes?" Goodrich egged her on.

"Well," Mrs. Eldredge took the bait, "I was visiting a friend at UMASS and…"

"Please, Mom, not tonight. It's my birthday. And that story is so sappy," Echo interrupted and turned to me. "Anyway, I want you to meet … Wow… damn, you got burnt, O'Rourke. You've been on the Cape a week and already you're trying to become Cape Verdean?" She flashed her hands to display her skin color, and everyone laughed.

"Yeah, yeah, yeah. I've already heard it from everyone else."

"I'll cut you a break, then. The last thing I want to be is unoriginal. Anyway, Mom, this is J.T. O'Rourke." Echo showcased me with her hand.

"It's a real pleasure, J.T. I'm June Eldredge, proud mother of this little fireball, who apparently doesn't believe in romantic stories anymore." Her smile was perfect with the whitest teeth I'd ever seen.

"Let's not go there," Echo pouted and pointed at the bottle. "J.T., can I get you a drink or do you already have one?"

I looked at the wine and handed it to her, "Oh, no, this is for you."

Then I handed her the wrapped box. "Oh, and this, too. Happy birthday."

"Oh, thanks! My favorite wine. And the wrapping paper tells me this could be from my favorite store also, perhaps? Thanks, J.T. You're a…" She didn't finish her sentence because her best friend, Kathy Zimmerman, came frantically running along the beach.

"Neil! Little Neil! Where are you? Neil!" She hollered and turned to us, "Have you seen Neil? He wandered off."

"Is he around five years old?" I asked, spotting a little boy at the shoreline pushing a red cooler over.

"Yes."

"He's right behind you," I pointed, and she turned around.

"Neil, what are you doing?"

"Oh, no," Davis yelled. "The lobsters are in that cooler."

The group hustled down to the overturned cooler where Neil was standing. I

241

couldn't help but burst into laughter with Echo when we realized what he was doing. About 30 or so banded lobsters were hightailing it toward the ocean while the little boy looked at us and excitedly waved them on, yelling, "You're free, guys! Go! Go! Uh, oh! Hurry, guys, hurry! They're coming to get you!"

Davis hollered to the beach, "The lobsters are loose! Everyone grab the lobsters!"

There must've been a lot of hungry people, because in a matter of seconds, half the party was at the shoreline running around retrieving the lobsters while little Neil, head buried, was crying on Kathy's shoulder.

When the last one was caught, Mrs. Eldredge wiped the sand off her hands and commented, "Little Neil is a lot like you, Echo."

"How's that?"

"The summer you were 12 and refused to eat lobster and called us all murderers."

"Really?" I said.

"Yeah, she was trying to save everything back then."

"Well, I do have some hippie blood running in these veins, don't forget." Echo said.

"You were a hippie, Mrs. Eldredge?"

"A bit. Echo is actually referring to her biological father."

"Oh, does he live in town?" I asked, thinking I had probably served him at The A.F.

Echo laughed, "No, I have no clue where he lives or what he looks like. He could be Jerry Garcia for all I know."

Her mom glared at her and turned to me, "If you will excuse me, J.T."

Mrs. Eldredge walked over to little Neil and comforted him.

"Oops. She gets a little pissed now and then because I'm so casual about it. She thinks my joking is covering my pain or something. But truthfully, I don't let my mystery father define who I am."

"What do you mean, 'mystery father?' You must at least know his name."

"Oh, yeah," she laughed. "Well, you see, J.T, Mom says she fell in love with my hippie dad when she was only 16. They hung out for a couple of weeks. He left and bang, nine months later, I came into the world."

"Have you ever tried tracking him down?"

"It's pretty hard when..." she laughed again, "You're trying to find a guy named 'Rainbow'."

"Rainbow?" I tried not to laugh.

"Yeah, that's what he called himself during those two weeks. I'm sure he changed his hippie name at every new place he went."

"Well, why do you say that?"

"A couple of years ago, I was bored and tried tracking him down on the web, you know, writing to old hippie message boards, etcetera, but no one ever heard of him. I figure he made up the name for his trip to Cape Cod, so he could persuade some naïve girl and wham, he found my mom."

I wanted to ask her more questions but her mother, holding little Neil's hand, had just walked over and was gesturing for everyone to gather around.

"I have just talked to Neil and told him that everyone gets a lobster. So... Neil wants to release his lobster into the ocean, so the lobster can have many baby lobsters."

"June, c'mon, I got these at Bryden's. They weren't cheap."

"Davis." Mrs. Eldredge shot him a look.

"I'm just saying." He shrugged, and everyone laughed.

"Neil needs a volunteer to take the bands off his lobster. I was thinking our new resident of Sandy Point would be the perfect choice. J.T., could you come forward, please?" She waved me on, and Echo pushed me out front.

"Everyone, this is J.T. O'Rourke. Please give him a warm welcome."

The group clapped, and I waved a hello before saying, "Mrs. Eldredge, this is not my forte."

"Please call me June and all you have to do is hold on to the lobster's body and I'll pull off the bands."

I held the squirmy lottery winner and raised my voice for the crowd, "Neil, what's your lobster's name?"

Neil placed his finger on his lips for a minute, "Larry."

"Larry the Lobster." I smiled down at him.

"Larry the Lobster. That's real original," Davis heckled, and the crowd berated him in unison, "Davis!"

June pulled off the bands and I quickly put Larry the Lobster on the sand, and everyone watched as he raced to freedom. Everyone, that is except for Davis, who was grabbing another beer.

I leaned down, "Your lobster's going to be just fine, Neil."

"Thanks, mister. Mom, can I have a hot dog, I'm hungry?" Neil tugged on Kathy's blue capri pants.

"So, you like hot dogs again?" Kathy arched her brow.

"That's a good idea. Let's all eat." Nicholas Eldredge waved his arms for everyone to go back to the campfires. I was feeling great, with that sense of community I had been searching for.

Had I found it?

Zachary Goodrich came over and handed me a Miller Lite.

"So, are you covering Rutger's case for the paper?"

"No. It's kind of a conflict of interest or at least it was, considering for a brief moment I was a suspect. Mr. Crocker has Paul Harrison covering the case." I popped open my beer and took a swig.

"Oh, that guy. So, what are you writing about?"

"Nothing that special yet. I figure I should get my feet wet with a few fluff pieces and get everyone to like me before I expose the dirt in this town like that guy on Channel 14." I laughed.

Goodrich pointed to his lip, "You mean the guy with the mustache?"

"Yep. Vic Hauser."

"God, I hope you don't end up like him, but if you ever do need any dirt, feel free to ask me. I've been living here all my life, so I know a lot. Plus, wouldn't mind getting on your good side in case you ever cover me for a story." He patted me on the shoulder and was about to leave.

"You mean, like the one about the Samoset place you're trying to buy?"

"Wow, J.T., you're good."

"Yep. I'll be all over that one when the time comes. Both sides, though. Already had a pow-wow, excuse the pun, with Chuck Renna at the bike store. Not a fan."

"I know. Too bad. Chuck and I used to trade comic books when we were kids. He's a little weird, but I liked him. Now all we trade is insults. Things change. I think years back, June over there would've been dead against it, but I want to build quality condos for middle income families on that land. Actually, I still don't know if she is for it, but at least I have her husband representing me… Well, J.T., I hope when the time comes, we can talk about this further. I'm going to go help them cook the lobsters now."

An idea came to me, but I knew I had to tread lightly, so I decided to lie. "Before you go, Zach, quick question about that dirt you're willing to give me."

"Yeah, shoot."

"I was looking up old articles and I came across the murder of a boy named Fishy Bryden." I said the lie casually while thinking, *Why didn't I look it up?*

I didn't have to look too hard to see Goodrich's reaction. I realized then that the expression about someone "turning white as a sheet" can actually happen.

"Ah, yeah. What about Fishy?"

"Did you know him?"

"Yep. He also traded comic books with me, except he was a couple years younger."

I thumbed over my shoulder, "Earlier, Davis was talking about buying the lobsters at Brydens. Any relation?"

Goodrich took his eyes from me and began fidgeting with the tab on the beer can.

"Yeah, that was his father's place. I should really..."

"One other thing."

"What?"

"I was reading up on his killer Pop Tucker, but then I got called on an assignment. I never found out what happened to him. Did he do some serious jail time?"

Goodrich squeezed the can, looked beyond me to the ocean, and gritted his teeth, "Nope. That fat asshole went like Fishy."

"He was murdered?"

"Yeah, in prison. They never caught who did it. I think the guards just looked the other way. Who wouldn't? But that's not what I mean by him going like Fishy." He stopped as if he had said too much.

"Well, what do you mean?"

"They found Tucker stabbed to death with a broom sticking out of his fat ass," he paused and took his eyes off the ocean and smiled at me.

"Definite payback, 'cause, you see, when they found Fishy, the broom Pop always used at his store was in his... you know... Yep. Whoever did that to Tucker is a hero to this town. Now let's get some of that lobster before Neil frees them again. I'm starving." Goodrich laughed.

"Sure thing," I said, even though my appetite was long gone.

CHAPTER 26

MAY 13, 1977

FRIDAY

NERO

t's been over five years since I sent Fishy flying to heaven. I wonder if he's flying with the gull.

Nero allowed himself a moment of reflection while he sat in the orange Volkswagen bus parked across from the Sand Dollar Boarding House. He waited. The night before, he knocked out the streetlight he was now parked under for one simple reason. Tonight he was going to kill.

The VW bus was completely camouflaged by the dark of the midnight, moonless night, but he was still taking a major risk — *one police officer driving by and running the bus's plates...*

Like fate had read his mind, four minutes later, his eyes widened when headlights entered the rearview mirror. It was heading his way. When it got a little closer, he could make out the outline of the model of the car and the siren attached to it.

A fucking cop!

He ducked down into the passenger seat, craning his neck to see above him while also demanding silence from his heart.

Stay in control! Even if he ran the plate, the VW wouldn't come up stolen, yet. But how am I going to explain why I'm in it and why I'm here?

Slow movement of the spotlight passed through the VW but then stopped and targeted the open, passenger window. Nero lay out of the beam's reach and listened.

"Anyone in there?" hollered the officer from his cruiser.

What the am I going to do?

Nero didn't have to ask himself the question twice because the cruiser's radio barked to life interrupting the officer's inspection. He strained his ears but couldn't hear what the dispatcher said, but he did hear the officer's response. It was loud. Clipped.

"Oscar 9, responding. I'm on my way. Over!"

The floodlight clicked off followed by the sound of the cruiser's engine accelerating. He lifted his head in time to watch the cruiser speeding down the road, bending around the corner, and hauling toward Main Street.

He smiled. It was a sign. Not a sign to abandon his plan, but just the opposite: fate was telling him he was going to be safe. He was meant to kill the fiddler.

He had first seen the fiddler at The Angry Fisherman a month back. He watched passively as the fiddler entertained the crowd. Inwardly, he yearned to play his violin with the same skill. He had passion; it was skill he lacked. So that night, Nero waited outside The A.F. for the fiddler who went by the stage name Johnny the Bull.

Nero stopped the short, handsome man with dark Spanish eyes.

"I have a violin. It was given to me. I would like to play like you. Can you teach me?"

"How much training have you had?"

"Well, none."

Johnny the Bull howled for a minute and Nero's fists tightened into a ball. He instantly hated him and wanted him dead.

He got the hint that Nero wasn't amused, "I'm sorry, I didn't mean to laugh. But, Jesus man, I've been playing since I was practically in diapers. There's no way I could teach you."

"Okay..." Nero said and began walking away while thinking: *how will I kill him?*

"Wait a second. Maybe I can give you a couple of lessons. But you'd have to do something for me?"

"Sure. What's that?"

"Do you know where I can get some good grass?"

Nero brightened, retracting his previous thought, "Sure do."

"Cool, man. Why don't you bring some by tomorrow night? I'm staying at the Sand Dollar. Room 11. Come by around six o'clock. Bring your violin, we'll drink some beers, smoke some grass, and I'll show you a few tricks of the trade."

Nero broke away from the memory of that night for a moment as The Fiddler — that's what he'd call him — emerged from the boarding house and packed his blue station wagon.

12:09 in the morning and this fucker really is leaving town! No chance for him now!

Other than the police officer almost putting a wrench into everything, Nero felt confident that he had a foolproof plan.

Note to self: find out what pig is Oscar 9.

It was the little details that made him so good at what he did. He had gotten so much better at his craft since killing his father and Fishy.

He thought back on his father and Fishy again. He had been extremely lucky then. He was just a kid. On the job training and, fortunately, a lot of things went his way. With his father, the fire was so powerful there was barely anything to put into the coffin.

Also, the Fire Chief bought the story of Nero's father tripping down the cellar stairs and having the lantern touch off cans of paint, gasoline for the lawn mower, and bottles of rum — something that the Chief admitted to a colleague, "There were cases of rum down there. Looks like he was a closet drunk. Who would've known?"

As for Fishy, any seasoned detective would've looked at all the incriminating evidence Nero had left behind — fabric from red suspenders, the lollipop, the broom — and surmise it was a little too perfect. That would cause an inquiry into the theory that Pop had been set-up. And that theory would take on even more steam after Pop was interviewed. Pop would offer possible suspects capable of setting him up and Nero would be on that list. Maybe at the top.

But Pop screwed himself over because he refused to talk to anyone until he hired a lawyer, but someone got to Pop before that happened. And when he was found murdered, the town literally wanted to use Pop's push broom to sweep those memories under the rug. The only person who would've caused a problem for Nero was Detective Prichard, but he too wanted to escape the black cloud that now covered Sandy Point, which he did when he moved his family out of town shortly after the Chief closed the case.

What luck! Or was it really fate?

Either way, it was time for everyone to move on. A fresh start.

But for Nero, he had gone too far to turn back. He had tasted and felt the power of taking the lives of people who had hurt him. After Pop's death, there was no one to hurt him anymore.

Of course, there was still his mother. The slut. But he knew he could never touch her, or someone might put together all the "coincidences." So, there really was no one else to fuel his steady flame, but that didn't mean it had burned out. There was still that insatiable desire to kill. Plenty of desire consuming his thoughts, and it was happening during the times he shouldn't be thinking about it — the times when he wasn't at his Silent Place. He wore that desire under his shirt every day until he decided he'd take the lives of another kind of prey — the innocent.

Sure, it wasn't a completely new feeling, and Fishy had been innocent... But he was the means to Pop's end. At the time, Nero *had to* kill him. Now he *wanted* to kill the Fishy types.

This new feeling was as constant as the waves meeting the shoreline he drove past every day while searching for the perfect victim. The stranger. "I'm new to town."

The stranger also had to be a loner. He met his first loner two years before.

Hans Henckel, a sixteen-year-old kid originally from Germany. When Hans was fourteen, his father landed a job in America as a scientist at the Space and Rocket Center in Huntsville, Alabama.

Hans, an only child, had lost his mother in a car accident two months before the job offer, and naturally, absolutely despised his father for moving him away from all his friends in Borbetomagus to a foreign country that served grits as a side dish instead of sauerkraut.

When Hans had saved enough money from working at a carwash, he took off with his thumb extended for his adventure across the country.

When Nero met him, Hans told him he spoke very little English and had no one. After they shared their second six-pack, Hans went on to tell Nero that he had called his father several months before, when he was working as a dish-washer in a small town in a place called Pennsylvania.

The secretary at the space center informed him that Dr. Henckel had moved back to Germany. Hans asked when his father had moved and found out it was only two days after he had run away. Hans now had no money and no one who cared about him.

But after the third six-pack, the one that only the German drank, Hans was told he did have one person. His new friend was Nero.

What a thrill it was to actually give out my true identity!

And after he finished the fourth six-pack, Hans Henkel indeed had Nero. He had Nero inside of him, thrusting away while a fishing line wrapped around his neck stole his breath from his body.

When Hans awoke it wasn't just with a pounding hangover but also with the terrorizing thin-bladed knife just before it pierced the outer edges of his eye-socket.

As he cut his victim that night, the screams comforted him like a down blanket on a snowy day. Nero had laughed, thinking of how Hans had sealed his fate when he confessed that the modern name of his hometown of Borbetomagus was actually "Worms."

It was a sign.

Hans Henckel, soon after that admission, was back with those worms.

It was a near perfect kill, but there were two problems that night that made him realize he needed to work on his craft. After killing Hans, he lit a torch and casually walked down to the beach to exhale, reflect, and take in the full moon. A party boat appeared out of nowhere, but Nero threw his torch, extinguishing it immediately.

Stupid! If they saw me, they might follow.

He sprinted back up the dunes to his Silent Place. No one followed. He was lucky — or again, was it fate? He was still angry at his own arrogance and began to remove Hans's eyeballs. Nero quickly realized he still couldn't remove an eyeball with surgical precision as he sliced through the cornea he so desperately wanted to preserve. But, after some cursing, he decided, like everything else: in the future, he would learn from his mistakes. He would teach himself until he could operate like a master surgeon.

A few days later, while the worms played with what was left of Hans Henckel, Nero took a trip up to Boston and bought several medical books at the Tufts University Bookstore.

After another misstep with another loner, a seventeen-year-old named Graham Murray from Louisiana, Nero got so good that he was able to laugh while still keeping a steady hand as he removed the beautiful marbles from those now vacant spirits — good and bad.

Ever since he perfected his surgical style, he decided he'd send the good ones to heaven and the bad ones to hell, never to see God. He would take their eyes.

Nero leaned forward as he trained his thoughts back to tonight's mission. He watched intently as The Fiddler carefully placed something in the back of his station wagon. Nero knew exactly what it was. His violin. The fiddler had lied to him and was leaving town with Nero's violin.

Three nights before, Nero had arrived at apartment eleven with a dime bag of Maui's finest in one hand and the battered violin case he had picked up at a flea market in the other hand.

The fiddler's eyes sparkled as he watched Nero roll a fatty, light it up, take a hit, and pass it to him. But his eyes really blazed to another color — the color of money — when he opened the violin case and pulled out Nero's violin.

"Where the hell did you get this?"

"I told you it was given to me."

"Given to you? But you don't play, man."

"That's why I'm here."

"Yeah, but who gave it to you?"

"It doesn't matter. Why?"

The fiddler, who had been turning the violin over and over, inspecting every inch, exclaimed, "Holy, shit, man! Do you know what you've got here? Do you, man?"

"What do you mean?" Nero asked.

"What do I mean? I mean you got—" he stopped abruptly, falling silent and changing the mood by faking a laugh, "a violin that needs to be restrung."

"Wait? Why were you so impressed a minute before? Is this violin valuable?"

"Valuable? Huh?" The fiddler laughed, "No, way. Oh, I don't know what I'm talking about, man. Sorry, I'm all over the place probably making no sense. I must be high. Give me another hit, man, will you? Actually, no, check that. I gotta drain the main vein, if you know what I mean. I'll be right back."

He walked out of the room, supposedly headed for the community bathroom, but Nero knew a liar when he heard one. He had been mesmerized by Nero's violin and then a second later acted like it was a piece of shit.

The night Nero killed his father, moments before Senior fell down the stairs, he had told his son a story about the history of the violin. He always thought it was another drunken make-believe story.

Had it been true?

Nero opened the door a crack, just enough to pop his head out and look down the hallway to where The Fiddler stood with his back to him. He was talking a mile a minute on the phone. He certainly didn't sound like someone high and mellow, Nero thought, as he watched The Fiddler cradling the phone to his ear.

"I'm telling you, man… I'm telling you…" He paused to hear the person on the other line.

"Yes, I've been drinking. And yes, I've been smoking a bit but, Whitford, I'm telling you, as Christ is my witness, the guy has a Strad, man. I got to hold a Strad in my hands. And, I might add, the guy has absolutely no clue."

He listened and then went on. "No, I don't think it's stolen, at least not by him. The kid has no clue… Yeah… Okay… I did show interest, shit, it's hard to hide that kind of excitement, but I played it off pretty well… Yeah, I'll take off after my last gig… You move it and we both win. Jesus, we'll talk about your cut later. He's still in my place. I gotta go. Bye."

Shortly after that phone call, Nero got drunk with him and watched with amusement as The Fiddler said, "You really need new strings. Leave your violin with me, and I'll order some and restring it for you. And then we'll begin lessons. I like you and want to teach you. Of course, you gotta also get me some more grass."

Nero handed the violin over. He was already hatching his own plan, and now three days later the script was set in motion.

The plan was simple. Follow The Fiddler until he went onto the road that led to the highway. Then he'd ram the back of The Fiddler's car just before the road opened up into the highway. He would do it right before the dirt side road that led to a new development that was being built. As the victim of a fender bender, The Fiddler would have no choice but to pull over onto that road.

It would be quiet. Vacant. Nero had learned that the crew building the new lots had actually suspended work there until they finished another development down Cape. The whole area would be vacant, and the only noise would come from the accelerating cars as they climbed the outer road for the highway.

Perfect.

The fiddler, fuming, would get out of his car, check the orange dent on his back bumper, and storm over to the VW bus.

As he approached, Nero would flash the high beams briefly blinding him. He'd then jump out of the VW, sprint over, and wrap the braided green and white fishing line around his neck.

Then he would begin to strangle The Fiddler with the fishing line he had purchased at Bryden's — a morbid irony that always amused Nero. He'd strangle The Fiddler but only to the point of making him pass out. This was another skill he had learned from trial and error. Now he was quite good at it.

Yes, that is what he would do to The Fiddler. And when he awoke, that would be when the real fun would begin.

Yes, it's a perfect plan.

But as Nero followed with the headlights off, he thought about what he was going to do after this kill. This kill would be different from all the others.

This might be the best one yet! Yes, years from now, long after I am dead, this kill will immortalize me. Nero will live forever. I will make it so they will never forget me!

"Here we go," he said to no one before putting in the 8-track tape of The Doors and hummed along briefly, thinking of the night he watched his mother with the football player.

I'll have to start making women like my mother pay soon. I can't think about that now. Get it out of my head.

He picked up speed and was closing in on his next victim, Johnny the Bull. But, again, that was not how Nero thought of him. Labeled on an empty jar he was 'The Fiddler.'

Nero rammed into the car and smiled knowing that the jar wouldn't be empty for long.

CHAPTER 27

JUNE 15, 2004

TUESDAY

J.T.

I t was just a little after 7 a.m. when I arrived at Sea Glass Beach to meet up with Mr. Crocker. The meeting was my idea; the location was his. He'd been ducking me ever since his drunken confession about being molested when he was a kid. It was time to clear the air. So, the night before, I fired off an email and two minutes later the yellow envelope appeared in my inbox.

He responded with a question: *J.T., you a morning person?*

I answered his email by typing with instant message speed: *Yep. Any time after 7.*

He wasn't as quick. A few minutes later I received: *7:15 Sea Glass Beach. I'll bring the coffee. Goodnight – Crocker*

I was concerned about Crocker's well-being, but I also wanted to meet with him for another reason. He hadn't kept his end of the bargain. I was a little pissed off, considering even the lame assigned stories I was writing weren't even making it into the "fish wrapper." The day before, my frustration boiled over when Norman Chadwick gave me a new duty: "I want you to write the copy for the *On This Date* column."

Crocker was out sailing so there was no one to have my back.

"Doesn't one of the high school interns do the *On This Date* section?" I asked Norman.

"Yes, but I think it would be good experience for you, considering..." He smirked, leaving the last word hanging in the air.

I headed off to the morgue — that's what they call the room where all the archives are filed — but not before uttering under my breath that Mr. Second-in-Command should go screw himself.

Norman pretended not to hear me but the shade of red his face turned told another story.

A part of me was mad at myself for letting a bit of the O'Rourke temper escape. I knew that wasn't the way to win over the asshole, but I also knew it would take time to deprogram the way I had been raised. I had grown up in a cocoon of constant tension that was made up of yelling and silence — the perfect balance to foster a dysfunctional family.

The result: hurt them before they hurt me. I had been working on changing this attitude for years, and as I looked around the beach, I knew mornings like the one I was witnessing might be the first step to getting me onto that path to serenity. Shit, I was thinking like an A.A. book, but I didn't care. That's how I felt.

A seagull squawked in the distance while I stared at the bright sun reflecting off the incoming waves, making them resemble silver ribbons wrapping up the shoreline. My eyes scanned for Crocker but the only person around was a dark-skinned teenager driving a tractor. I watched as the tractor moved slowly back and forth along the beach smoothing out the sand, so the tourists could have a picturesque first impression of Sea Glass Beach.

I laughed before making my way toward a bench that overlooked the entire beach. I had barely dipped my toes into the Sandy Point waters, and I was already thinking of other people as tourists. Who the hell was I?

I was about to sit down when the engraved plate attached to the bench stopped me.

IN MEMORY OF ANTHONY MEDEIROS
IN MY HEART, WE'LL ALWAYS BE FISHING
LOVE,
Anthony Jr.

"Anthony Junior, whoever you are, you don't know how lucky you had it," I said to the bench, thinking of the one time when I was a kid and went fishing with my ol' man.

What a nice memory — being on a dock on Lake Winnipesaukee, throwing my fish back into the water and then having him bitch me out as a group of kids in sailboats passed by. I remembered locking eyes with one of the kids who turned away, visibly embarrassed for me.

"Ah, the memories," I said sarcastically to myself and sat down.

"Memories of what?" Crocker asked from behind me as he approached with a tray of Dunkin Donuts coffees in one hand and the orange, purple, and white bag in the other.

"Oh, nothing," I said while Crocker handed me a coffee and sat beside me.

"Bagel and cream cheese?" He offered the bag.

"No, thanks. Coffee's fine," I answered after taking a sip.

"Hey, David!" Crocker waved to the kid in the tractor, and he waved back.

"That's Echo's brother." He turned to me, and I straightened immediately looking at the kid who threw a wave our way.

"No, shit. I didn't meet him at Echo's party."

"Probably collecting shopping carts. He works three jobs. Part of his condition is that he loves to work. He loves Echo, but he keeps a strict schedule." Crocker sipped.

He savored his coffee and the sight of the day in front of him for a minute.

Finally: "Well, J.T., I've got some good news."

"Yeah, what's that?"

"Last night I went back to the paper and moved a few things around. We're running two of your stories today."

"Really?"

"Yep."

"The one I did about the nurses raising money for the war?"

"Nope. I still feel that's too partisan."

"Well, I already told you that's a bunch of bullshit but anyway... Which ones?"

"The one on the freegan lifestyle and the one about the overpopulation of coyotes."

"Okay. Well, that's good news for Ms. Dumas, and I've bumped into the freegan kid a couple of times having breakfast out of the Pilgrim Diner dumpster. He should be happy."

"Yeah, they'll both be happy. We're even running the photo Echo took of Lillian Dumas holding a framed picture of her dog, Cool Hand. It's actually very touching."

"Of course, we don't know if coyotes really killed Cool Hand," I pointed out.

"Yeah, but it will get Lillian off our asses."

"True enough."

"I also heard that, while I was out sailing, Norman put you in charge of the On This Date column. And you weren't too pleased."

"'Pissed off' I think is the correct description. 'Cause first of all, you told me *you'd* be giving me the assignments." I stopped and watched him nod in agreement.

"Second of all, all I'm doing is writing a paragraph rehashing whatever happened 10, 15, and 20 years ago. Where's the journalistic challenge there? It would be one thing if I could do a follow-up story like the kind you see sometimes on *60 Minutes*."

"What do you mean?" Crocker seemed intrigued.

"I'll give you an example from what's running today. Did you know that 15 years ago today there was a fire in the bottom floor of the old Sandy Point Police Department? So, why not do more than write a paragraph stating that. Did they ever figure out how it got started? Were there witnesses? Where are they now? I'd like to do those kinds of stories with the On This Date section. Maybe not a story about that fire, but I'm just using that as an example of what I'd like to do if I have to cover that section now."

Crocker laughed, "Geez, was that fire really fifteen years ago?"

"Yeah, what's so funny?"

"You know Chuck Renna, the bike store owner?"

"Yeah, the guy who found Rutger Nelson's license attached to the Bryden boy's bench."

"Oh, yeah, that's right. That's him..." Crocker paused for a moment before resuming, "Anyway, on the basement floor of that dusty old firetrap was the evidence room, and one week earlier, Chuck had been picked up by the cops with six dime bags in his car."

"Was he a dealer?"

"Dealt a little back then but was more of a user. Still is. So, when the place went up in flames, not only did it destroy a lot of old evidence from past cases, but the whole place smelled like a damn reggae festival. A bunch of us watched the place burn, and I swear to you, half the firefighters got high trying to put it out. We all realized that because of the fire there was no way they could prosecute Chuck, so it kind of became a big party. Folks were passing the flask around and celebrating. Everyone was happy except for Chuck."

"Why wasn't he happy to get off the hook?"

"He told all of us that they also had confiscated his favorite bong," Crocker laughed, "He said watching the fire was like watching his best friend go up in flames."

I couldn't help joining in on Crocker's laughter.

"I suppose that's one story I couldn't write."

"No. Sorry, J.T. I know you think I'm probably pretty strict about the content in the paper, but I do like this idea maybe for future On This Date stories. Just keep presenting them to me."

"Fair enough."

"There's something else you should know," Crocker paused.

Here it comes. He's going to talk about the day on the boat.

I waited.

"You know that information you acquired about Rutger's license being fastened to Fishy's bench?"

"Yeah."

"I'm not going to let Harrison run with it."

"What? But he's supposed to come out with that in today's paper."

"That's why I changed things around."

"I don't understand how you could disregard it."

"Other than you and Harrison finding out, the police have been able to keep it out of the news."

"I know, and it's your job to put it in the news."

"Not necessarily."

"What do you mean?"

"I mean it's my job to run a paper that serves the community."

"Exactly. And by not reporting that this could be linked somehow to the Fishy Bryden case, you're not serving anyone except yourself."

"Myself?"

"Well, let's face it, once it comes out people are going to look into that case and it won't be long until they find out what happened to you as a kid. And clearly that seems to be something that you don't want people to know."

"I see. You think that's why I wouldn't run it? To protect myself?"

"What other reason could there be?"

"The Chief of Police and Detective Gordon asked me if I could hold on to it for a while. They feel it will aid their investigation if that information isn't known at this time. I told them I'd give them a few more days but then I'll have to report it."

"Oh… And Harrison was cool with that?"

"Surprisingly enough, he was."

That seemed odd considering a story like that could splash his face everywhere.

"J.T., I just need to know if you're on board?"

"I'll keep my mouth shut, but I'm going to predict something. You had a major scoop handed to you on a platter, and I bet now that you have killed the story, it's only a matter of time before someone tells the *Cape Cod Times*, or the Boston papers, or worse, Vic Hauser from Channel 14, and he becomes a media star."

"I know. You might be right. This could all backfire on me, but the Chief thinks if we can keep that information out of the paper, they still might have a chance of finding Rutger."

"He didn't say *alive*, though, did he?"

"No, he didn't. But he thinks whoever did this could be very angry at not seeing his message in print — because it had to be a message of some kind."

"Yeah, no question about that," I agreed.

"Anyway, the Chief thinks it might trip that person up. So, if that costs us a scoop, then so be it."

"You're a better man than me, Mr. Crocker."

"I'm just trying to get by, J.T., which leads me to the next thing I know we should talk about — that day on my boat. I thought I had confessed to you but until you just said that stuff about me trying to protect myself, I really wasn't sure. I thought maybe I had dreamt it."

"Well, that's understandable. You were pretty gone."

"I guess I just want you to know a couple of things now that I'm sober. I've fought those memories and nightmares for a very long time, and I decided I'm finally going to face them. I'm doing more than just A.A. I've gone back to my shrink and..."

"The one who doesn't have nice legs," I interrupted.

"I said that?"

I nodded.

"Jesus, I'm an animal when I drink. Dr. Courtland's a nice woman. Anyway, I've gone back to her and I'm starting to face things. Face the fact that I've been afraid to pursue any relationships."

"And how's that going?"

"Well, it's going to take me a while, but at least I'm talking about it. She asked if I had a guy friend, someone I felt I could talk to. I told her all of my friends I've known since I was a little kid. I don't want to tell them certain things so we both decided you might be a good confidant for me."

"Me?"

"Well, yeah, I feel I can trust you."

"But you don't even know me that well."

"I know you well enough. You're a good person, J.T. You are also brutally honest, which you just displayed a minute ago."

"No other way to be."

"Dr. Courtland thinks that if I share my thoughts with someone, I might then be able to act on them. But maybe I shouldn't burden you..." He began to get up.

"No, it's fine. I guess. What're your thoughts?"

"Well, I've already told you about the biggest secret in my life."

I nodded.

"Well, I have another secret."

"You're not gay, are you?"

He laughed for a long time, "No, I'm not gay."

"Not that there's anything wrong with that," I laughed and then got serious, "really, there is nothing wrong with it."

"Well, thank you. But no, I'm not gay but my other secret does have to do with sex."

"Look, you don't have to tell me anything."

"I know I don't, but I need someone to talk to."

"Well, you can tell me. Remember, bartender's seal of confession."

"Oh, yeah, that's how we met. Well, my other secret is that I haven't been with many women in my life."

I was going to tell him that he already confessed that and actually he had told me "none," but I decided, what's the sense of kicking him when he was already down?

I waited.

"My problem is I am in love with a woman and it's tearing me up inside. I don't know what to do."

"I'm hardly a lady killer myself but maybe I can help. Anyone I know?"

"Anna Walsh."

"Sunshine!"

"Yep."

"You're in love with Sunshine," I repeated.

"How do you think she got her nickname?"

"She's a little older than you."

"When you get to my age, it doesn't matter. And you've seen her."

"Geez. Wow. Well, I can't say I blame you. So, how long have you had these feelings for her?"

Crocker laughed lightly and looked me dead in the eye. "Probably since I was eleven."

CHAPTER 28

MAY 18, 1977

WEDNESDAY

DEVLIN

Officer Michael Devlin breathed on his hand and smelled it to see if the whiskey from the night before was still there. It was. He popped some mints.

"I've got to stop doing this shit," he said to himself while putting on his white dress gloves for his morning detail.

Directing traffic at a funeral service was never an enjoyable experience, but he knew today would be ten times worse. He looked from his cruiser's window at the sky that was as black and as somber as the hearse that waited for its unlucky passenger in front of St. Michael's. The rain hadn't started yet, but the distant thunder grumbled a warning that it was coming. He had an even louder grumbling noise in his head.

Earlier that morning while dressing, he had been tempted to hide a flask in his raincoat, so he could chase away that hairy, hangover dog that barked in his brain, but then he decided to tough it out. Be strong.

I might be drinking a lot these days, but I will not drink on the job.

"I will not drink on the job," he voiced his thought and then spat, "Jesus, Devlin, ain't that noble of you!"

But don't I have reasons to drink?

He thought about his wife, Anna — a month before she had had her third miscarriage. The devastation finally broke her carefree spirit, and she was now being treated for depression at the Metropolitan State Hospital up in Waltham.

Devlin tried staying positive, holding her hand and reassuring her, "Honey, we can adopt. We'll be fine, you'll see!" but Anna cried until there were no more tears. And then the doctor urged, "Mr. Devlin, your wife is close to a catatonic state and needs to be admitted for further observation."

After agreeing and returning to the Cape, Devlin was a battered man but still had hope. He was not beaten, yet. He needed to regroup. He needed a drink. He was not much of a drinker but decided to go to The Angry Fisherman for one pint — think up a plan for how he could help them through their latest miscarriage. Their love had been tested before, and Anna had been there for him. He was not going to give up on her. He was convinced it was that love that would get them through their most recent tragedy, but then came the fatal shot that now had Devlin losing himself and thinking about bringing flasks to work. The shot came in the form of Bushmills Irish whiskey. Actually, it hadn't been the whiskey that had been fatal but the person who sent it over to him — Larry Tadmor.

Devlin's father had defended Captain Tadmor's son, Larry, years back for stabbing a college kid to death because he didn't pay off a measly $50 bet. But when the shot was placed in front of Devlin, he looked over and hadn't recognized Tadmor. Thinking it was a concerned patron sending a condolence shot, he raised his glass to Larry, downed it, and chased it with his beer.

Larry, who was short and chubby and had a two-day beard, wore a brand new Bruins T-shirt and also a new Celtics hat over his long, greasy black hair. He walked over and leaned against the bar next to Devlin.

Devlin smiled, trying to come up with his name, "Thanks for the drink... ah..."

Larry laughed. "You have no idea who I am, do you?"

The snorting laugh gave Devlin a bad vibe. A cop vibe. Plus, the guy's clothing made Devlin think that he was probably an ex-con trying to blend in. An old ploy. Instantly, he wondered if the greaseball was someone he had arrested.

"No. Sorry. I don't remember you."

"My old man is Captain Tadmor."

"Larry?" Devlin straightened, his chest tightening with rising anger.

"Yep."

"I thought you were..."

"Just got out last week. Good behavior and all that shit."

"Oh."

There was a long, uncomfortable silence. Devlin hated himself for taking the shot. And hated Larry even more for what he represented. "Good behavior." Another victory for his late father, defense attorney Allan Devlin — a man who had represented every kind of scum, even child molesters.

"Well, I'll be working on my old man's ferry taking his late shifts. He's getting up there, you know. Just thought I'd send you a drink, so we'd be cool, you know what I mean?"

"Can you do that?" Devlin asked. He didn't want to "be cool" with a murderer.

"Do what?"

"Pilot the ferry?"

"That small piece of shit? Shit, I could point out 10 guys in this bar who could. Easy as riding a hooker in the combat zone. My old man had me piloting that thing when I was, like, eight."

"That's not what I meant. I meant can you do that *legally* since you're an ex-con and all that shit." Devlin mimicked Larry. It wasn't much in the way of sand kicking, but it was enough.

Now Larry straightened, "Oh... Oh, I see how it is. You're gonna bust my balls, Devlin, huh?"

"Yep."

"I see how it is, the old hot-shot, Army hero that's now a shit-for-nothing cop and not so special anymore. But you gotta try to keep that upper hand somehow. I know your kind. You'll probably go around town, tell everybody how they should act to the ex-con. Ignore him and shit. Make my life miserable. That will make you feel like a real big man. Is that it?"

Devlin hadn't dealt with the miscarriage and was thirsting for an outlet for his pain and anger and Larry had just poured him the glass.

"Yeah, that's it. That's me. So, don't forget it, you pathetic piece of shit. You know, I think I'll start making your life miserable by talking with the selectmen because I just don't know how safe it is for a murdering, ex-con piece of shit like you to be piloting…"

Larry almost pushed Devlin off his barstool. "Why don't you shut up?"

"Why don't you make me?" Devlin heard his voice answer.

Inside, a part of him was embarrassed at the juvenile remark, now he really was kicking sand, but he still rose and loomed over Larry.

Clearly overmatched, Larry looked up at Devlin and his mood shifted to laughter. "You know what, Devlin? I think I *might* be able to shut you up. Yeah, in fact, I know I can. Let's go outside. We need to talk. I'm gonna bring you down a notch or two and then maybe you won't think you're so much better than me. Shit, how many years did I have to hear that shit from my old man? 'You should be more like Michael Devlin.' That shit made me sick, considering the things I know."

"Larry, you felt sick because your father is nothing like you. He's a good man. I don't think we need to talk about anything. Out of respect for your dad, I won't kick your ass tonight. But stay away from me. I got nothing to say to your kind."

Larry, unfazed, looked around to make sure no one was listening and pointed over to a guy in the corner of the bar opening up a violin case, "That guy's been playing here ever since I got home. He gets a good crowd. In ten minutes, this place will be pretty loud. I think you'll want to be somewhere where you can really hear from "my kind," and you're not going to want no one else hearing it, Devlin. You might know my father better than me but I sure as hell know something about your old man that you don't. And it will all come out if you decide to make a shitstorm for me. I just want to start over, so let's go outside and clear the air before you do anything stupid. We wouldn't want to ruin you or your father's reputation. Don't you agree?"

"My father? You want to talk about my *father*?" Devlin hadn't uttered the word "father" since they buried the bastard back in '73.

Larry smiled, "Yep," and walked out of the bar.

Ever since Devlin followed him through those swinging doors, he couldn't shake the story Larry had told him. The few fleeting times it had left his mind there was always someone or something to bring him right back. On this morning, it was his detail in front of St. Michael's Church, the one place other than a courtroom that Allan Devlin had been faithful to. It was also the same place Michael Devlin had refused to enter on the day of his father's funeral because he held the belief that the powerful defense attorney had planned to represent Pop Tucker.

Now, as Officer Devlin stared out of his window at the pure-white church doors, Larry Tadmor's voice echoed in his brain.

"Your old man was in bad shape when he came to me... I mean, mentally. But he was still clear on what he wanted done. He wanted Tucker dead, and he wanted me to be the one to do it. I asked him why he wanted him killed and he told me it was personal. Now normally I wouldn't have considered it, but since your old man saved my ass and it was a child molester he wanted offed, I figured killing Tucker might make things right with God and me, so I told him I was in. Your old man arranged it with a guard to get me into Tucker's cell when he was sleeping, and well, you know the rest."

"I... I... I..."

"Cat got your tongue, Devlin? By the way, the broomstick was my personal touch. 'Poetic justice' I heard that's what they call it. After all, I knew some of the kids in town who that bastard played with. Thought the town would get a kick outta it. I'm sure you did."

"I can't believe this."

"Believe it, Devlin. And think about this, the day after your old man arranged it, he goes up and dies. What the papers write? Oh, yeah... he fell asleep at the wheel. What time was it? Like 4:30 in the afternoon. I heard he was doing about 90 when he drove off the road. Couldn't take it. The guilt got him. Your old man wasn't the killing type. Yep, the guilt bit him, man."

"I don't believe you."

"I don't care if you believe me. But tell me this, why would I tell you this shit if it weren't true? I'm not exactly innocent here. You could turn my ass in, but then I'd have to bring your old man's memory down with me. I don't want that. You don't want that. I was actually going to keep quiet about it with you, but I figured after your attitude in there, you and I should put everything on the table. You won't believe it, but I *have* changed. Shit, I know I messed up. And now I just want to work, have a few beers, and get laid now and then. I'm not out to bother nobody, and I don't need nobody bothering me. So, I'd appreciate it if you'd just let things be about me taking some shifts on my old man's ferry. I know the selectmen will look the other way 'cause they all like my old man and all. But if you bring up my past it could cause..."

Devlin wasn't listening. "No, none of this can be true."

266

"Huh?"

"My father. I heard my father went to see Tucker because he was going to take his case."

"Wow, shit man, you thought that?"

"Well, yeah, he was a defense attorney. What other reason would he see him?"

Larry snorted more laughter. "You are so off on that one. You must've thought a lot of shit about your old man over the years when the truth is he really was just trying to get payback for your ass. Literally."

"What do you mean 'payback'?"

"What other reason would he see him? Come on, Devlin, you don't have to play games with me. I know."

"Know what?"

"I found out what your old man meant by 'personal.' The guard who will remain nameless, a good guy who actually helped me get my shit straight, told me what he heard when Tucker met with your old man. Tucker tried to blackmail him into taking his case."

"Blackmail him? How?"

"You don't know?"

"Why would I?"

"That's cool. Play it that way if you want. I gotta go. I need to relieve my old man."

Devlin grabbed his arm. "Really, I don't. Tell me."

Larry looked down at Devlin's grip clenched onto his forearm, and then back up at Devlin who slowly removed his hand.

"Please, Larry."

"Alright, man. I wouldn't think you'd want to hear me say it, but it's your party. Tucker said he had pictures of him playing with you when you were a little kid."

"*What?*"

"Yeah, Tucker told your old man that only he knew where the pictures were and that he'd give them to him only after your old man defended him. So, your old man was screwed. Either he represents a child molester, or, you know..." he let Devlin figure the rest out, "I gotta go." Larry left Devlin standing there.

That night he wanted to yell at him and protest that Pop had been lying, that he had never been touched by the molester. But, in shock, he couldn't form the words, and it really hadn't mattered what Larry thought. It was Devlin's father who needed to be told. But he was dead as a result of everything, and the realization of that fact chipped away at Devlin's mental stability a little more every day. He began to drink to quiet the thoughts that shifted from guilt at having hated his father over the years to anger that his father never came to him with the information about Pop.

Did my father kill himself?

That thought alone could send a man spiraling, but there was also something else that put an exclamation point on his instability.

Don't think about it!

He got out of the cruiser, took his post, and signaled to a station wagon to turn into the church parking lot. Of course, being in the middle of the street and alone with his thoughts, he couldn't help but think about it. It was something Prichard had told him in the Detective's study four years earlier.

"Some of the victims might not even know they are victims because he drugged them. I bet half these kids woke up in the back of the store not knowing what happened to them."

He shook his head and looked up at the sky and then the rain came. He thought about what Larry had said about "poetic justice." This moment was more like poetic irony or maybe it was justice since he was staring at the church he had refused to enter — a decision that crushed his mother who died a year later from a stroke. He wondered if after the service, he should go in and light a candle for his father, but then the thoughts came again.

Did Pop Tucker rape me? Are there pictures of me out there somewhere? Was that the reason I was so quick to go looking for him that day?

When the caravan of mourners left the parking lot, the rain steadied, and he decided there was no reason to light any candles when clearly God only enjoyed blowing them out. He got into his cruiser and was about to point it toward Gary's Liquors. He'd sneak into the package store, grab a half pint, and quiet his brain, just for a little while.

Until I get myself together.

It had a back entrance designed for customers with his dilemma. He'd be in and out and no one would take much notice. If they did question him, he still lived on Oyster Island. No stores over there. He could say it was for after work. He could taste the relief coming... but he was interrupted by the dispatcher who informed him of a report of a stolen vehicle from the Sandy Point Bus Terminal.

There was no need for urgency, but, what the hell? He flipped the toggle switch and gunned it down Main Street anyway.

The rain let up and the black clouds moved on, freeing the mid-morning sun to finally get to work. He eased on the brakes and entered the bus terminal. He expected the person who had reported the stolen car would still be standing under the roof of the ticket office by the payphone. He was wrong.

No one.

Then he spotted two kids in their late teens to early twenties in the back of the lot waving him down. They were standing beside an orange Volkswagen bus. He continued driving toward them and realized the VW looked familiar.

That bus looks like the one I saw the other night parked in front of the Sand Dollar.

When he parked beside it, he was sure it was the bus. A few nights before, he had a policeman's intuition about the vehicle, but before he could run a check on its plate, he got a call that a vandal had thrown a brick through the window of Spokes for Folks bike store.

Now his interest piqued, and for a moment he was able to set aside his personal life. He parked beside the VW, got out of the cruiser, and walked over to the two kids who wore matching Levi's jean jackets and jeans. They were medium height with longish brown hair and brown eyes. They weren't twins but they didn't seem to have any characteristic that set them apart. They looked like a million other kids he had encountered, and he wondered briefly if it was just his age catching up with him.

All kids look alike these days…

"Are you the ones who reported the stolen car?" he asked, taking out his pad.

"Yes, sir." The boys answered respectfully.

"I'm going to need your names and the make of the stolen vehicle."

They exchanged confused glances unsure of how to answer.

"What?" Devlin asked.

"Well, this actually is the stolen vehicle." Jean Jacket #1 answered.

"Huh? If it's stolen, why am I looking at it right now? Is this some sort of joke?"

"No, sir." Jean Jacket #1.

"It's kind of hard to explain, Officer," Jean Jacket #2 offered tentatively.

The kids had been polite, which told Devlin they were probably just nervous about interacting with an officer, something that happened to him often, so he decided to tone it down.

"I understand. I'm listening. Take your time. Why don't you tell me why you called?"

He pointed his pen at Jean Jacket #2 and then buried his head in his pad.

"You see, Officer, our friend Ross parked his VW here last week."

Devlin looked up, "His full name?"

"Oh, Ross Greenberg."

He knew Greenberg and liked the kid. He and Anna had seen him shine as Don Quixote in the Sandy Point High production of *Man of La Mancha* a couple of years back. Last he heard, the boy was now attending NYU and doing quite well.

"And your name?"

"I'm Andy Kelly, and that's Brian Lansky."

I don't know those names.

"Where are you from?"

"Down Cape. I'm from Chatham, Brian's from Truro. We bummed a ride to get here."

"Go on."

"Well, Ross took the bus to Logan and then flew to California for a couple of weeks. He left his keys under his visor because the plan is, we're going to drive to New York and stay there at another buddy's place. Then, Ross is going to fly back to New York and the three of us are going to drive his VW on to Canada where we're going to work at an acting camp for the summer."

"Okay..."

Do you want to give me your acting resume, too? Get to the point!

"So, today when Brian and I came to get the VW, we noticed that the keys were in the ignition and there was only half a tank of gas. That didn't seem right because I talked to Ross last night and he told me that he had filled the tank, and he left the keys above the visor. And then, Brian noticed this..." He walked around to the front of the VW and Devlin followed. The kid named Andy then pointed at the bumper that was severely dented.

Devlin crouched down and inspected it and noticed lime-green paint marks that indicated that the VW had locked horns with another car.

"When did Ross leave for California?"

"It was a Thursday, May 12th," the kid named Brian answered.

Devlin wrote it down.

"When I talked with Ross last night, he didn't mention getting in any accidents lately. I say lately because I rode in the van just last week, and it was in perfect condition."

Devlin counted the days in his head and figured it was five days ago, the 13th to be exact, when he saw the VW bus, and there was no evidence of an accident then.

"When was that?" he asked Andy.

"It was last Wednesday, the 10th. We finished finals that morning, and I drove home to the Cape with Ross."

"That's a long ride," Devlin said.

"Yeah, it is, but we were running lines."

"Excuse me?" Devlin looked up sharply.

"Oh, I mean... well... we're actors. It's a term. 'Running lines.' Like going over lines in a script. Ross has a couple of auditions in L.A. So, he drove and I quizzed him. It went by pretty quick."

"Oh. And where were you, Brian?"

"I was already done with finals and home, so I borrowed my dad's car and came to the Point to pick up Andy. You know, so Ross wouldn't have to go all the way to Chatham and back."

"So, neither one of you was driving this vehicle on the 13th?"

They shook their heads, no.

"Why did you pick that date, Officer?"

Because that's when I saw the VW parked outside the Sand Dollar.

"You know how on TV they always have the officer say, 'I can't divulge that information.'"

"Yeah?" they both said while taking mental notes for future auditions.

"They're not making that stuff up. I can't divulge that information. Now I'm going to take a look inside if that's all right with you guys."

They shrugged, "Sure."

He opened the side door and looked around. It was pretty clean except for a couple of empty Coke bottles under the driver's seat and a large spool of heavy, green, and white fishing line.

"Does Ross fish?"

They both laughed.

"What's so funny?"

"It's just that, that night we ended up staying in Sandy Point and we went to The Angry Fisherman, and over a few beers, Ross told us this funny story about

271

how he went deep sea fishing as a kid. Puked his guts out all over his uncle. He said he's probably the only kid on the Cape who hates to fish!" Andy was still chuckling, "Why do you ask?"

He moved to the side and pointed at the spool.

"That's strange."

"Yeah, it is." Devlin agreed before asking more questions.

"Did you talk about your trip at the bar?"

They looked at one another again.

"Yeah, that's about all we talked about," Andy answered.

Devlin glanced up from the pad. "That Ross was going to leave the keys above the visor?"

"Yep."

"Did you notice anyone listening in?"

"No. The place was packed with people, but I don't see how anyone could hear us because there was a guy playing the fiddle and the place was pretty loud."

"You'd be surprised how many people listen in on conversations." He kept writing.

After he sent them off on their trip, Devlin experienced that police intuition again, and he didn't like what he was feeling. He spent the rest of the day thinking about the stolen VW while directing traffic as a road riddled with potholes got repaired.

The night that I saw the VW, wasn't there a blue car parked on the other side of the street? Why would someone steal a car to go fishing? Or maybe that fishing line was used for something else? Damn, it really felt like someone was hiding in the VW when I pulled up.

The good thing about the stolen car was it kept his mind off his father and on his job, but then he changed out of his uniform and put that cloak of guilt back on. And it was heavy.

A couple of drinks wouldn't hurt.

Then he justified the thought.

And, I could ask some questions at The A.F. about the stolen VW. Probably some kids just took it joyriding... But what if it's something more than that?

He really thought that if he went to The A.F., those drinks might get his mind straight. They didn't, initially, so he had a couple more.

God, it tastes good.

He thought about the word "initially."

Initially. My life is about that word. Initially, everything in my life was good. Maybe a couple more drinks. Hey, wait, I know those boys over there. They're really young men now. They must be 18 or 19. Shit, that tells me something. I need another drink and I know they need more. I'll send them a round.

He sent the drinks to the table of teenagers — boys who, when sober, he couldn't even look in the eye. He always fell asleep with the feeling that he had failed them. But not tonight — shit, he was drunk and was out to forget about it all.

Fuck it, I'm gonna get shitfaced. I'm gonna drink with them.

He sent them a couple more pitchers of beer and they sent him a shot in return.

Bang. He threw it down. Then another. Bang. Then it was bang. Bang. Bang. Bang.

God, I feel so good.

"Come on, Officer Devlin, drink with us." Hands waved from the table.

He tried to focus but, drunk or sober, he hadn't seen clearly in a very long time. He strained his eyes but all he saw were the teenagers' faces — except they were their faces as children, coming to his house, asking him to make things right for Fishy.

He couldn't then. He never could. He found himself sitting at their table.

God, I hurt…

Now the same boys had another request, one that seemed so small… meaningless, really… but it chanted… echoed with the suds sloshing around in his glass.

Fuck it! Fuck all of it!

"Okay, Jesus." He put the pint to his lips and drank to the boys egging him on with, "Drink! Drink! Drink!"

Devlin heard himself laugh after slamming his empty pint to the table. Their laughter howled in the background and showered over him. He could see himself stumbling toward the bathroom and yelling and pointing to the bartender —

what's-his-name-again, "Anything those assholes want, it's on me."

"Okay," the bartender replied. "Are you okay?"

"Yeah… I think…" Devlin then saw himself pausing, looking over at the table, and then back at what's-his-name and yelling, "Yeah, I think I am. At least, I was okay with your wife last night!"

The young men, who Devlin still saw as little boys, roared with laughter, banging the table. It was that laughter that warmed him as he bounced from table to table, lurched through the bathroom door, and hugged the urinal in front of him.

They laughed. Maybe they came out of it undamaged? Maybe I didn't fail them?

He straightened and unzipped, watching his piss attack the ice chips, melting them before his eyes. He looked to his right at one of the boys who now was standing beside him taking a leak. The kid talked to him, but his friendly words suddenly became jumbled and foreign.

I'm losing it. I better get out of here before I can't drive. If the Chief finds out I am out in the cruiser and drinking, that could be more than just a suspension this time. It could mean my job.

He nodded to the kid, zipped up, and turned to leave but stumbled. The kid caught Devlin in his arms.

"Are you okay?"

"Huh?"

"Are you okay?"

"Oh, yeah, sanks. I'ves had a too little… little too much." He slurred and was about to push away from the kid when he noticed something. The kid's necklace had swung out from under his shirt.

Devlin strained his eyes at the necklace. It was an oval — half silver and half gold.

Why does that look familiar?

He strained again, but the kid saw what he was looking at and hastily slipped the necklace back under his shirt.

Wait a second. That looks like Fishy's necklace!

"Hey! Hey! Where'd jyous…" He grabbed for the kid at the same moment the bartender walked into the bathroom followed by the bouncer.

"Get your hands off him," the bouncer pulled Devlin away from the young man and then said to the kid, "Go back to your friends. We'll handle it."

"He's really drunk. He's making no sense," the kid said before taking off.

Devlin pointed, "Why'd yous let em go? He's got Fishy's thing… You know… I think it's Fishy's thing… Jyous know…" he motioned to his own chest.

274

The bartender spoke up, "*Jews know?* I suppose they do. But I'm not a Jew. So, I don't know what you're talking about."

"Not Jews. Jyous. *Yous.*"

"Yeah, anyway, he's right. You're making no sense. Look, Officer Devlin, you're extremely drunk and you're acting like an ass. And I know you're not an ass, so I also know you're not going to like yourself in the morning. I didn't want to embarrass you out there, so we came in to tell you that you gotta go now."

"Alright, alright, but just let me go out and talk to..."

"No. You go now. Or we call the Chief." The bartender was firm.

The Chief! But I'm drunk, and I have the cruiser — I have to sober up. Did I just see Fishy's necklace? Or did I imagine that? Why would he be wearing it? Did Fishy give it to him? I have to get out of here. I have to sober up and figure this out.

"I'm going." He headed for the door to the bar, but the bartender pointed to the side door that read "Staff."

"If you follow me, Officer Devlin, we can get you out through the back door and no one will notice." The bouncer gingerly moved him along.

"I don't sees what's the big... deal... is."

"I know you don't. In fact, you don't see much of anything. You didn't see yourself knock over a pitcher of beer on that woman in the corner," the bartender added.

"I... sss... did?"

"Yeah, you just kept going, stumbling in here."

"Oh, no. I sh... ould goes and apolog..."

"That's okay," they both said.

"But I... sss... don't... want.... to go out these..."

"Enough of this shit." The bartender pointed to the bouncer.

"Let's go, Officer," the bouncer ushered him along with speed and force, out the Staff door, down the hallway, and out the service entrance.

"Go home and sleep it off," the bouncer ordered and then slammed the door shut.

Michael Devlin stood in the rain trying to make sense of it all.

CHAPTER 29
JUNE 24, 2004

SATURDAY

ECHO

Echo worked the stick, downshifting so her Jeep could climb the winding road up to the Sandy Point Lighthouse. The mental schedule she had set earlier put her at least two hours behind for her assignment: snapping shots of the lighthouse being moved back from the eroded, endangered cliff.

Her two addictions were the reason she was now hauling ass. The first one was her former boyfriend from her high school days — Tobias Russell. He was a drug she thought she had flushed from her system long ago, but a few days after she received his email, she replied with one of her own. She typed it in a mad dash of suppressed emotions, hit "send," and instantly regretted her honesty.

But an hour later, he had written back with the same intensity, and since then, the emails had been as constant as a grade-school couple trading notes in class. Even after everything he had put her through, Echo knew a part of her still loved and wanted to forgive him. She hated herself for being the desperate woman who pined away for her man — the kind of woman she always mocked — but 16 years later she still couldn't resist Tobias. And the early morning email had announced the possibility that maybe the stars had finally aligned and their time had come.

Last night my wife and I decided that it's not right to raise our little girl in a loveless marriage. We've decided to separate. Say you'll visit me when I come to Boston in the fall!

Echo had responded with one word: *Yes.*

She spent the rest of the morning like the weather outside — in a fog — a happy one. And then the sun broke through and, while she finally dressed for her assignment, Echo wondered if the break in the weather was a metaphor for her life.

"There's going to be a lot of workers. I better go with something out of the Kathy Zimmerman collection," she laughed to herself, thinking of her best friend while slipping on a pink polo and wiggling into a khaki skirt. But she couldn't be completely conservative, so she laced up a pair of black, low-top Converse sneakers and grabbed her Red Sox hat.

The Red Sox, her other addiction, were the other reason she was late. They were playing the Yankees. Echo had stopped by The A.F. to watch a few innings, but the rain in Boston delayed the start. After nursing a Miller Lite and trading John Hughes movie one-liners with J.T., she realized it was time to do her job.

But as she was leaving, Commodore Ethan Nelson stormed in and caused a scene by yelling at J.T., "If you hadn't kicked my kid out of this place, he wouldn't be missing!"

Echo watched J.T. restrain himself, squeezing the life out of an empty V-8 can with his left hand while Davis escorted Nelson out. It was the second time the Commodore had verbally attacked J.T., and Echo could tell it was wearing on him.

The only positive for J.T. about the situation was that, ever since the license was found, the police had moved on from "the new guy did it" theory and were now focused on people who knew the tragic history of that bench. They had publicly cleared J.T. as a suspect without revealing why.

Echo hoped J.T. hadn't been serious when he said to her, "Maybe I should just go back to Boston."

Back in the moment, Echo turned on the radio and was greeted by the voices of Joe Castiglione and Jerry Trupiano analyzing the game that had finally begun.

"There's my men," she said to the radio, but continued thinking about her new friend J.T. She loved hanging out with him and trying to counter his quick-witted, Irish sarcasm that she inwardly admitted was a bit of a turn-on. He may've been a little overweight, but he was handsome, and his charisma made up for any extra pounds. She wondered what he must've looked like when he was in shape during his boxing days. But it was more than looks that intrigued her... They were getting to know one another, slowly sharing more personal aspects of their lives, and it was a welcome change for her to have fresh stories to dissect.

On a slow night at The A.F., he had opened up, telling her about his lousy upbringing and watching the heroin boom in the late '80s steal most of his Southie friends. In return, she offered her collection of "facing racism" stories and how she sometimes felt like a bit of a failure for not leaving the Point.

Their conversations always seemed open. Honest. She viewed J.T. as someone who was becoming a good friend but only a friend. But she also purposely hadn't mentioned her long-lost love coming back into the picture... Then again, Tobias Russell was still the biggest secret in Echo's life.

Maybe not for long...

She was smiling as she pulled into the parking lot behind the lighthouse. She saw cranes and backhoes parked near the lighthouse, but no one around them. It was a ghost town.

That's odd.

She gazed over at the clearing where the lighthouse was eventually going to be placed. There were a few workers huddled between a maroon Department of Public Works truck and the silver-sided Drake's Canteen.

"Oh, Drake. Lucky me," she muttered to herself and decided she was in no rush to deal with him. She stayed in her Jeep, turned the volume down to five and stared out at the panoramic, ocean view.

She then heard an airplane in the distance but couldn't see it, but what she could make out was Crockerman's sailboat. She wasn't surprised. It was anchored about a hundred yards offshore hovering over his favorite snorkeling spot. She waited a couple of minutes for the canteen to leave, but no luck. With a defeated sigh, she began turning off the radio but stopped when Jerry Trupiano's voice exploded across the airwaves describing a bench-clearing brawl. She spun the knob to eight and leaned in to get closer to the action.

"Holy shit! Get 'em, Tek! Kick his ass!" She yelled to the picture the sportscaster painted of Red Sox catcher Jason Varitek slamming Yankees third baseman Alex Rodriguez to the ground.

"What's going on? Something wrong?" A dirt covered DPW worker in his early fifties appeared out of nowhere.

Echo knew the guy from around town and silenced him with her hand, "Sshh, listen, Jackie! Major brawl. Tek just slammed A-Rod."

"No shit!" His sweaty elbows smudged the driver's side window. She thought she smelled beer on his breath but realized, despite her peppermint Altoid, it might be her own.

They remained quiet, speaking only with wide-eyed glances as "Trupe" and Joe recounted the melee at least three times before things settled down.

Finally, she clapped her hands, "That'll get the guys going!"

"I doubt it, Echo. And, even if it did, you know in October they'll break our hearts again."

"Jackie, that's blasphemy. This is the year."

"Like I told my kid in '86, 'If you still want to believe in the tooth fairy, too, I'm sure as shit not going to stop you. But don't come crying to me when there's no money under your pillow.' Echo, you remember what happened in '86. How'd it go again? Oh yeah, 'Ground ball to Buckn—'"

"Don't say it!" she jumped in, waving her arms.

"Anyway, you gave me a freakin' heart attack. I thought someone was attacking you or something." Jackie laughed and stepped away from the door so she could get out. She hopped down and felt his eyes undressing her.

"A heart attack, huh? Well, it's good to know if I ever had a problem, you'd be my knight in shining armor."

"Anytime, me lady," he replied gamely, not picking up on her sarcasm.

"Speaking of ladies, how's the wife doing?"

His face transformed from teenage fantasy back to middle age reality.

"Oh, she's good, working at the flea market for the summer. So, Echo, what the hell are you doing up here?"

"I guess I'm here to take some pics of you and the crew over there," she motioned to the trucks, realizing the workers and Drake were no longer in sight, "Wherever they went."

"Huh?"

"Where'd they go? Are they behind the trucks?" she asked.

"Yep. They're camouflaged. So why do you want to take their picture?"

"Well, aren't you guys moving the lighthouse?"

"Shit, no. The town hired a private company for that."

She looked around. "Oh. Well, where are those workers then?"

"They just unloaded all their supplies yesterday. They start Monday."

"So, I could still be watching the game at The A.F.?"

"Afraid so."

"Damn, I must've got my signals crossed with Crockerman. So, what is your crew doing up here?"

"We're just doing small shit. Took down the fence around the lighthouse, moved a memorial plaque, and now we're digging up a time capsule."

"A time capsule?"

Echo walked toward the area and Jackie followed behind trying to keep pace.

"Yeah, one of the Sandy Point senior classes buried it in the exact place where the lighthouse is going, so we gotta move it. The guys are behind the trucks digging it up."

"Sweet!"

"Huh?"

"Sweet, meaning 'cool.' Meaning: that will make a great shot. You know, you guys removing the capsule?"

"Ah, yeah. Ahm…" he stalled, looking over his shoulder, then added, "I don't think that's a good idea." A man's voice cracked through the mellow breeze.

"Jackie, finish your piss and grab us another round! Robbie's gonna open this shit up!"

Now sure of who owned the beer breath, Echo glanced down, pointed to his zipper, and said, "Your fly *is* down."

Jackie checked and zipped up while Echo pulled her camera out of her bag.

"I'll just take a pic of your boys and be on my way."

"My boys?" he asked, looking back down at his zipper.

"No, Jesus, not those boys, your boys over there opening the time capsule. I'll get a couple of shots of that, and my day won't be wasted."

"Aw, shit. Aw, no."

"Whoa, whoa. What's wrong?"

"Well, the thing… the thing is… Well, it's a couple of things. You see, it's a Saturday and no one's around."

"So?" Echo said as she took the lens cap off and massaged it while smiling at him.

"Well, look… Ah, shit… I'm gonna be truthful with you."

"Truthful is good."

"Yeah…Well…"

"Hey, Jackie! You're missing this shit! Get over here! Drake needs another beer, too!" The voice from behind the trucks yelled again.

"Yep! Almost there!" he hollered back and then turned to Echo, "Okay, look, you don't want to go over there, 'cause ah… Fuckin' A!"

She put her hand on his shoulder. "Jackie, I think I've got it. Let me break it down for you. You guys have had a few beers and you don't want anyone to know. It's cool with me. No biggie. Am I right? You're paranoid cause you guys don't want to get caught drinking on the job?"

"Well, yeah."

"I won't tell anyone. Hell, I was just at The A.F., so technically I've been drinking on the job, too. So chill, will you?" She motioned for him to lead the way.

"Yeah, but the other thing is we're not supposed to open the time capsule, but…"

"Are you taking a dump or something? Hurry up, man. Silvio's got it open!"

"Oh, cool," she took a step toward the trucks, but then Jackie moved his sweat-drenched body in front of her, "Jesus, Echo, we could get in some major shit if you take pictures."

She learned a long time ago how to deal with guys who have only a four-letter word vocabulary. Use it back.

"Jackie, what do you think I am? A fucking asshole?"

"Huh?"

"Do you think I'm a fucking asshole?"

"No, I heard you. But what the hell do you mean?"

"'Cause only a fucking asshole would sell out anyone who wanted to have a few pops on a hot day and check out something cool from the past. That would be a fucking asshole. Am I right?"

"Yeah, I suppose."

"We'll just say the lock broke or something if we have to." Echo didn't wait any longer. She rushed ahead and spotted two barrel-guts, both in their early sixties, wearing DPW uniforms and standing in a five-foot trench. She stopped behind Drake who was looking down into the trench and scarfing down one of his infamous hot dogs. One of the barrel-guts looked familiar.

He was holding bolt cutters with one hand and high-fiving his coworker with the other. She noticed an engraved plaque lying near the scattered beer cans and dirt mound beside the trench. The plaque read:

Below is a Time Capsule that was buried here on May 1, 1977, by the Sandy Point High School Senior Class. It is to be opened on May 1, 2077.

"Help me with this, Robbie," said Gut #1 after he threw the bolt cutters aside and crouched down to pick up the capsule. Gut #2 nodded, squatted, and helped lift the long, metal coffin-shaped capsule out of the hole. They struggled out of the trench, still unaware that Echo was watching them.

"What do you think they put in it?" Drake asked.

"We flip up the lock hinge and we'll find out," said Gut #1, who was about to open it but stopped when he saw Echo. "Who the hell are you?"

"It's cool," she responded.

"I don't think so. We're doing town work."

"Hey, Echo," Drake interrupted.

"What's up?" she nodded in his direction.

"You know her, Drake?" Gut #1 asked.

"Yeah, she was my girlfriend back in high school."

Drake said that so often she wondered if he'd have it etched on his gravestone someday.

"She's cool, Silvio, she promised she won't get us in trouble," Jackie added.

"Trouble?" The guy named Silvio squinted, "What do you mean, trouble?"

"The beers and stuff. She just wants to take a few pictures for the paper," Jackie said.

"The beers and stuff. Jesus H. Christ, Jackie! What the hell did you tell her?"

Echo snapped her fingers. "Wait, Silvio? You're Silvio Clements, right?"

"Yeah. Why?"

She wanted to say, *I heard you like to beat your ex-wife Linda now and then*, but instead she went with, "I took your picture a year or so ago when you were elected to the Sandy Point High Hall of Fame. That was one hell-of-a speech you gave."

"Oh... ah... thanks."

"Those were some funny stories, Silvio... Look, I told Jackie that if the paper decides to run any of the pictures, we can just say the lock was busted and stuff was falling out and that's the reason you guys opened it. That cool with you?"

"It's not a complete lie," the guy named Robbie said.

"What do you mean?" Echo asked.

"Well, we did find another broken lock next to the capsule when we were digging it up. So, we're covered."

"Really? That's kind of weird," Echo hesitated.

Robbie reached into his pocket, pulled out the lock, and showed it to her.

"Not really. Probably had two locks and one broke or something." Silvio shrugged.

"Maybe..." She nodded, but then she began fidgeting with her lens.

Silvio now seemed content with her answer.

"Alright, let's see what the class of 1977 was into." He flipped the hinge and opened the capsule.

Echo moved closer, adjusted her lens again, and peered down on the findings. She snapped away, listening to the workers' reverie about the popularity of Pet Rocks and their comments on a pair of Earth Shoes, a *Rocky* movie poster, and a 45 record of "Southern Nights," a song by — as Robbie described him — "the immortal" Glen Campbell. The workers kept sharing their time capsule memories but stopped when Robbie hit the jackpot by finding the Class of 1976 yearbook.

"I don't get it," he said as he flipped through it. "If the capsule was put in by the class of '77 why is there a class of '76 yearbook?"

Silvio took the book from him and thumbed through it. "'Cause the yearbooks always came out the following Thanksgiving and they put this thing in the ground in May."

"Oh, yeah." Robbie said.

"What the hell is this?" Silvio said, looking at the inside back cover.

"What?" Drake asked.

"It looks like someone painted it in brown paint."

Echo looked over his shoulder. "I don't think that's brown paint."

"Yeah, you're right," Silvio said after inspecting it longer, "I think it's dried blood. I don't have my glasses. What's that say?"

Silvio handed the yearbook to Echo. She looked at the blocked, brown brushed words.

"Nero was here... Who the hell is Nero?" She asked.

"Beats the shit out of me," Silvio shrugged.

"Ah, guys..." Jackie interrupted them.

"What?" Silvio and Echo turned around.

"Can any of you tell me what this is?" Jackie held up a mason jar with masking tape attached to it.

"Is it a science project or something?" Drake asked.

The jar was filled with cloudy gray liquid. In it, bobbing like lava in a lamp, were two lifeless eyes staring back at them.

"Holy shit!" Silvio shouted what was in Echo's mind.

"Jackie, put that shit down!" Silvio ordered. Jackie placed it on the ground and they all huddled around the jar. Drake peered at the writing on the masking tape and read it aloud to the group. It was in the same brown blocked letters.

"The Fiddler Will Never See God."

CHAPTER 30

MAY 18, 1977

WEDNESDAY

DEVLIN

The rain from the morning had returned. It was softer now but steady, and Devlin stood for a moment, hoping it would wash away his drunkenness. It didn't. His head was spinning, reminiscent of the feeling he'd get after clambering off the teacup ride at the county fair.

I always rode those rides alone. My father never took me to the fair. He was always too busy working. Why am I thinking of him? Did Pop rape me? Did my father kill himself? Wait, why was he wearing Fishy's necklace? I probably just imagined it. I'm losing my mind. I have to get out of here now.

He began to walk and realized the bartender and bouncer hadn't been overreacting. His eyelids felt like they had fish-weights attached to them and it wouldn't be long before the lids were pulled down. He had parked up the street near Sea Glass Beach and forced himself to pick up his pace.

There's the cruiser. It's only a five-minute drive to the ferry. But can I drive? All I have to do is make it to the ferry. Then I can sleep in my cruiser.

The key somehow found the ignition. He started driving and saw two yellow lines.

Uh, oh. How do I fix this?

He then did what a drunk once had confessed to him. With one eye shut and the other cocked, he followed the two yellow lines that then became one.

It works!

He drove with the slow deliberate care of a retiree with no place to go, maneuvering the ocean road at 15 miles per hour until he finally arrived at the ferry landing.

Slanting rain was falling on Larry Tadmor, who was silhouetted by a white neon light. Larry flicked the cigarette, toed it out, and waved the cruiser up the ramp. Devlin snailed forward and parked. He turned off the car and let out a sigh of relief. A five-minute ride had felt like five days.

Never again.

Larry tapped on his window and Devlin rolled it down.

"What?"

"You got your commuter pass? I need to punch it."

In his right hand, Tadmor clicked away on the silver puncher like it was a nutcracker, while taking quick drags from a fresh cigarette in the other hand.

Devlin felt around, looked in his glove compartment, picked up his handcuffs that were for some drunken reason lying in the passenger seat, and finally turned back to Larry. "Iss don'ts seems toos knows wheres is it is."

"You've been drinking, boss man?"

"Yeah, a little."

Larry held a smile and nodded, "I don't blame you. Don't worry about it."

"Sanks."

Larry looked behind him at headlights approaching, "Well, it looks like we might actually have another passenger tonight."

"Oh... Could you dos me a favor?"

"What's that, Devlin?"

"Wakes me up when's ah... we dock."

"No, problem. That sounds like a good idea. A 15-minute nap might do the trick." Larry tapped his exit on the driver's door before heading toward the headlights.

Larry's not a bad guy.

He lay down, resting his head on the passenger seat. He felt the rain coming in through the open driver's-side window, but he didn't have the energy to sit up and close it because those weights on his lids finally dropped. He was out cold.

He heard the screams and figured they were in his head. He was probably just having another nightmare about Vietnam, but the difference was he didn't see the faces behind the screams. He thought he heard the car door open. The door and the screams caused him to stir but then it was silent, and his eyes remained shut.

I'll sleep a little longer. Maybe I'll dream about Anna.

His mind coached his slumber and he suddenly saw her that early fall day so long ago... wearing her Harvard sweatshirt and cut-off jeans shorts.

"What's wrong with you, Miss Talbot? It's like you acted like I wasn't even behind you. I'm a policeman, y'know?"

"Did that make you mad, Officer Devlin?"

"Of course, it did."

"Well, now you know how I feel when you act that way with me."

He could see himself smiling in his sleep. He then felt her taking off his shirt and pants the first night they made love. He could feel her pulling him toward her. He reveled in the dream.

But it all stopped. A sharp pain came from his stomach. He felt it again, and this time his eyes flew open. He was sitting upright in the driver's seat. He looked down at where the pain was coming from and saw blood — a pool of it flowing from his body.

No! No! No! No! Did I drive? Did I get in an accident? No! No! No!

He realized he was naked and felt the searing pain again, and this time he saw the cause.

A knife. The blade was going in and out of his stomach.

The hand! I have to stop the hand!

But he couldn't move. Devlin felt blood rising to his throat and he began to choke on it desperately gasping for breath. He was able to turn his head to his right side toward the passenger seat. He had no strength to react. All he could do was wonder.

Is this a nightmare? It has to be!!

The sight of empty eye sockets staring back. They belonged to Larry Tadmor whose naked corpse was strapped in beside him.

"Larry will not see God," Devlin heard a voice from his left say softly, "I will not let him."

He turned his head toward the voice and could hear himself screaming, almost as if he were watching the horrific scene at a grindhouse, not living it.

But it was real, and the cloud of death approached him quickly. His vision was fading. He couldn't see the face of the voice, but he could see the necklace — Fishy's necklace — against the voice's bare chest. Devlin didn't need vision. He knew who it was.

Why is he doing this? I need to get Fishy's necklace.

He tried to speak as he reached out, "W...h..."

"Do you want to see God, Officer Devlin? Do you?"

He couldn't answer, blood completely filled his throat and poured out of his mouth.

"That's alright. I know you do. And tonight I will be the one who will let you see God."

Devlin stared at the voice and reached again for the only thing he could see — the shimmering half silver, half gold necklace that flashed even brighter.

Suddenly, the darkness brightened.

It was a sunny day and the seagulls with their friendly shrieks were flying above Devlin as he walked along the dunes. He smiled. It was the dream he always had in Vietnam.

Thank God! This is a dream!

Officer Michael Devlin held on to that belief as long as he could until the final breath of life escaped, freeing him forever.

CHAPTER 31

JUNE 26, 2004

MONDAY

NERO

Nero thought it was more than just a little bit ironic to be driving off Cape, away from the media lights and horrific news that now pulsated The Point. It was a glimpse of what he wanted his future to be. His endgame. Ride off into the sunset and make them all wonder. Not yet. He had much more work to do, and he had to do it while he was still able.

Under normal circumstances, he would've been pissed that the DPW workers messed up his plan of revealing Nero to the world. He may've even felt a little fear at getting caught. Back in '77, he came very close to using The Fiddler's blood to write his own birth name in the yearbook, but at the last minute, he chose his new moniker.

After all, it was Nero who committed the act. Not him. And it would be fun. *Make them look for Nero in a hundred years.*

That is how he thought back then, but now he was driving toward the reason that today he had no fear even though the truth may now come out.

"It is my belief that serial killers are incapable of feeling fear. In fact, most are probably incapable of truly feeling anything." He mimicked the squeaky voice of

Dr. Joy White, a criminal profiler he had seen speak at a bookstore in Vermont a few winters back. The good ol' Doc had all the answers of the how and why serial killers do what they do.

"Yeah, a real expert," Nero spat as he accelerated along the highway, "The only thing she ever cut was her finger while preparing salad for her anorexic frame."

Dr. White had been correct on what Nero liked to call, "the fun facts of a serial killer" — terrible upbringing, killing animals, starting fires, sexual abuse, blah, blah, blah.

You didn't need a PhD to know that shit!

A&E, Dateline, 48 Hours, and all the others made millions serving that up on weekend nights to bored housewives and stay-at-home losers.

He had learned those facts several years before when he read a book on abnormal psychology. He read it a few days after the night on the ferry. He wanted to know why he kept seeing those eyes. He never got the answer. But his new knowledge of how he had come to be hadn't been the cause for his depression. He hadn't felt depressed that society had turned him into what he was.

No, his sadness came from the fact that he found out that he wasn't that special from the average serial killer.

Dr. Joy White, you see, I do feel! You dumb smelly twat!

Back in the moment, Nero passed I-195 and laughed. That was the exit to New Bedford. "New Beige." Land of the Crack Hoes. Several times, he had thought about killing women, but it was only after reading the book that he realized there was a greater reason to kill both sexes. He could never show them a pattern. Some of his kills would be for pleasure. Others had been and would continue to be out of necessity for survival. And the best ones would be for both reasons. He had to keep the Dr. Joy Whites of the world guessing.

His first kill of a woman came after he picked up a whore in "New Beige" one night in the early eighties. She had been, alone smoking crack on a dark side street. He pulled up. She crouched into the driver's side, saw him smile, and flash her some green. She scampered around and jumped into the passenger's seat.

A half second after she asked, "Suck or fuck?" he slammed her head against the glove compartment.

When she awoke, he knocked her out again — this time with the point of his elbow, and then he drove back to the Cape. He threw her frail, battered body over his shoulder and brought her back to his Silent Place. After waking her with smelling salts, he pulled her by her mountain of moussed up hair eventually pushing her to the ground. He ordered her to stay on all fours in front of the long mirror leaning against the wall of thorns.

"I have lots of money and I pay. You do what I say, you live and get the money. You don't do what I say you die. It's that simple."

She nodded into the mirror.

He instructed her to play with herself and moan while he shined his flashlight on the mirror with the other.

"Smile into the mirror!"

She did as she was told. And her smile actually crinkled to a genuine one when he threw a wad of hundreds beside her. This was the biggest thrill for him. She thought she was safe, and this was just some sort of sick and twisted sex game she'd rehash to the working girls in the morning over coffee and cigarettes. She grabbed the bills off the grass while he gently patted her backside.

"Please stay on all fours just a minute longer so I can enjoy the view. I won't hurt you and I'll give you two hundred dollars more. Please." His voice was gentle.

She nodded, stayed on all fours, and looked into the mirror.

He snapped the flashlight off, took out the old tie that he wore at his father's funeral, wrapped it around her neck, and strangled her.

Ah, bitches do have the highest pitch screams… Good ol' New Beige!

He ventured to that hunting ground one more time before moving on to other places with other hookers and other lonely screamers. Since his departure, another killer had fed on prostitutes from there and if he were ever caught, Nero knew his two kills or "missing women" in their files would be just lumped in and pinned on that hunter. Not him. It had been a very fortunate coincidence.

For someone born into shit, he did have luck when it came to his kills especially in the beginning. When he drove long distances, he always liked to contemplate on just how lucky he had been. After he grabbed a cup of coffee at the Burger King on 24, he continued on and did just that.

He thought of his first lucky break — the intense flames that devoured his father and the time period he grew up in.

Holy shit, nowadays, they would've looked directly at him as a prime suspect. Never mind planning endgames, his games never would've even begun.

Then came Fishy's murder. It had been extremely easy to set Pop Tucker up for Fishy's murder. He had just slipped into the store and stole a push broom, some red suspenders hanging in the back, and of course, the pictures of his naked sodomized body. He also stole pictures of other victimized children. At the time, he didn't know why he took them but now those pictures were insurance to him.

Setting Tucker up was the easy part. He played on the town's rage, and on the knowledge that the victims wanted to keep all of it secret. They all wanted to forget.

Now with age, he knew if Tucker hadn't been murdered in prison, "they" would've taken a longer look at the case and Nero would've been exposed. To this day, he could kiss or blow, whatever the wish, the inmate who offed Tucker.

That unknown inmate did a wonderful service for him. Now they would never be able to connect Fishy's murder to him, especially after Nero torched the evidence room fifteen years earlier.

He had seen a program about three little initials that were about to change criminal investigations forever: DNA. And as always, he was one step ahead of everyone.

After a month of planning, the lollipop-stick with his saliva went up in flames with the other pictures and every other type of evidence for every type of case collected over the years in The Point including fifty pounds of confiscated marijuana. Arson took a back seat to the comical story around town of how all the firefighters got high trying to put the fire out. He had planned it that way. It was sheer brilliance.

But everything I do is brilliant. They'll all see that someday.

He braked on his trip down memory lane when he thought of the night on the ferry. He could only think about that night at his Silent Place, because anywhere else the eyes would invade his head. So, for the next forty-five minutes he kept his thoughts on where he was going and what he was probably about to hear.

Why suddenly the meeting? Why couldn't he tell him on the phone? It must be really bad news.

He laughed, thinking that if it were bad news, it would really make his day. When he got there, he grabbed the ticket from the attendant, parked, and took the elevator. He walked past colorful murals painted by children and briefly thought of the drawing he made of the ax slicing through his mother's head.

I wonder if they would have hung that up, too? It was colorful. A deep red.

He tried to suppress his grin when he entered the office, signed in, and waited a half hour before being called.

He went into the next room and jumped on the table contemplating if he should be taking off his clothes.

Ah, screw it.

He was unbuttoning his shirt when the door opened and two men wearing white lab coats and holding clipboards walked in. The one he had dealt with for over a year waved for him to keep his clothes on.

There are two of them. This must be worse than I thought. Good.

After they exchanged pleasantries, the one he knew talked.

"The reason my colleague is here today is because he is working on a book."

"And?" Nero said.

"And..." he cleared his throat. "I diagnosed you with terminal cancer thirteen months ago. And you stopped all of the treatment..." he glanced down at his clipboard, "four months ago."

"Is this going to be another lecture, Dr. Lyons? Because we already went through this before..."

"No, no, no," Dr. Lyons halted him with his hand. "Let me finish."

Nero nodded for him to continue.

"The book Dr. Katz is working on is about people who have defied all odds and have beaten cancer. Let me rephrase, because we never know if you can completely beat cancer. There's always the chance it could come back. Anyway, Dr. Katz was hoping you would be willing to participate in it?" Dr. Lyons and Dr. Katz glanced at one another and then smiled at him.

"I don't understand. I'm dying. I mean why would I..."

Dr. Lyons laughed, "Ah, sorry — this is my way of telling you that your latest test results revealed that you are in complete remission."

"What? I don't understand." Nero felt his blood quicken.

"I know you're probably in shock, but it should be a good shock, right?" Dr. Lyons patted him on the shoulder.

Nero was processing it and felt a wave of nausea hit him.

"So, you mean I'm not going to die?" He asked hoping it was just some cruel practical joke.

"Nope. Not yet at least."

"I can't believe..." He felt the white lights bear down on him.

"I know. I know. It's a miracle really, especially after stopping treatment.

Quite frankly, you're bad for how we do business around here." Dr. Lyons let out a guttural laugh.

"So, as someone who just found out that he is going to live, how do you feel?" Dr. Katz readied his pen for his answer.

"I don't feel anything," was all he could manage.

Nero was going to live. This changed everything. Now that they were looking for him, they may actually finally find him. And if they found him, they would throw him in a cage to rot with those animals for the rest of his life. That was not how he planned to be remembered. He was smarter than them. He was smarter than all of them.

It had turned out to be the worst day he'd had in a very long time. Nero's endgame had just been destroyed.

CHAPTER 32

JUNE 27, 2004

TUESDAY

J.T.

4:56 a.m, and Ambulance Chaser-at-Law, Marvin T. Miller, asked if I had been injured on the job. If so, Marvin promised to get me the compensation I truly deserved. Before turning off my TV I wondered if his definition of injured at work could extend to stolen bylines?

Of course, nothing really had been stolen from me, I thought as I tied my gray Asics. Like a good soldier, I followed Crocker's lead when he helped the police by keeping the discovery of Rutger Nelson's license a secret. Since no other reporter had broken the story, I still hoped to eventually get the go-ahead.

Then came the second major story.

I scored the inside track for that one, too. Echo handed it to me on a silver platter Saturday afternoon, frantically calling me at the bar. She said she had been taking pictures of the Sandy Point High School class of 1977's time capsule which was being moved to make room for the lighthouse. The workers had found a jar with a masking-tape label in block letters that read "The Fiddler Will Never See God." The jar contained two human eyeballs floating in some gray liquid. Next to the jar was the yearbook from the previous class. In that book —

in what looked to be dried blood — someone had written "Nero Was Here" in the same block lettering.

Echo sounded totally freaked out, but I chalked that up to good acting. I figured she was playing with me, feeding me some serious Hannibal Lecter bullshit, so I laughed, hung up on her, and got back to pouring pints.

But seconds later, she called again shouting, "This is no joke! Get over here!"

Ditching on my shift at the bar, which had been busy since the Sox mounted a serious comeback on the Yanks, hadn't pleased the co-manager, Vicki. Any other time, that kind of move would've got my ass booted, except for one reason. At the scene, I overheard the ME confirm to Detective Gordon that the eyeballs were "indeed human and in quite good shape."

Vicki would later find out it hadn't been some lame excuse for me to bail on my shift to drink beers and go fishing or some shit. I had probably stumbled onto the biggest story in Sandy Point history. I spent the rest of the day filling my pad with notes and quotes. The only problem was my story wouldn't run until Tuesday. That was a lifetime away. So, I may've had the inside track but my competition at the daily *Cape Cod Times* or Vic Hauser could catch up easy if any of them found out. I knew my chances of keeping it quiet until Tuesday was less than zero. When the Channel 14 truck pulled up forty minutes later, I realized it was less than that. There was no competition. I had lost to Hauser.

By the time dinner rolled around, Hauser had turned Detective Gordon, the DPW workers, and even canteen boy, Drake Underhill, into media darlings. And by Sunday morning, "The Search for Nero and The Fiddler" story had gone national and Pornstache Hauser was now the face of it, even being interviewed by his idol, Geraldo Rivera, "Live via satellite."

Geraldo, as always, stumbled along and awkwardly joked at the end of the interview, "Vic, remember reporters with mustaches are sexy. Maybe ah... you and I ah... can sometime look for Al Capone's safe together... you see, guys in the control room, I ah... can laugh at myself."

Really, Geraldo?

My piece was coming out later in the day, but what was the point? Everyone already knew everything. I was pissed. It should've been me breaking the story and joking on cable TV about growing facial hair.

I needed an early morning run to blow off some steam. But I wasn't just pissed about my life as a bi-weekly newspaper reporter.

The night before I went into The A.F. to make sure I was cool with Davis —

which I was — and I bumped into my ol' man's former partner, Paddy Magill. I never liked Magill. He always acted like he was better than everyone else in Southie, especially the O'Rourke family.

With a good glow going, he told me, "Well, ain't that the shit. My brother-in-law just bought a house here. So, Jameson Thomas, you'll be seeing a lot of me." He always loved stressing the fact he knew my full name.

I couldn't believe it. Out of the fifteen towns on the Cape, his brother-in-law had to settle in Sandy Point. God, I was so pissed. Magill represented the types of people I was trying to escape from — my past. I didn't want my past coming over the bridge and ruining my future.

I opened the door, hopped down the steps, and put on my iPod. My blood was already pumping but I figured some AC/DC would get my legs to follow. I blasted "Hells Bells," directing my jog toward the bike path, a quarter of mile stretch down the beach road. The bells tolled through my ear buds, and I picked up pace to the ascending guitar riff, and thought of the reason I finally said no to cheese sticks and buffalo wings and yes to getting my ass into gear: Echo Landers.

Recently, I had joked with her that I hadn't always been such a fat slob. She replied with all of the politically correct stuff like, "Don't put yourself down. You look great. You're handsome," etc. I wanted to believe her, but I look in the mirror every morning. I had blown up like a goddamn wood tick on a skin binge.

Two of my reasons for moving to the Cape were to mentally fix my life and also to get back in the fighting shape that helped me knock out Jose "Machine Gun" Gutierrez.

Of course, that had been a decade before. And in fairness to Machine Gun, after his 17-hour drive from Alabama to fight me in a dingy hall in Worcester, well, let's just say that night his chamber was pretty much out of bullets.

He also wasn't ready for a southpaw. I laughed, replaying my second-round uppercut that caught his glass chin sending his 'Bama tide rolling to the canvas.

"But that was then. This is now," already with heavy legs, I grunted to myself and continued past the ocean that lay in a dim darkness on my left. It'd be another forty minutes before the sun would reveal the shoreline and everything else to the world, making my run a bit tricky as I entered the Sandy Point Bike Path.

I wanted to get lost in thoughts of my slim chances with Echo but forced my brain to focus back on the crazy events that had everyone in town now playing whodunit. A simple point then dawned on me. Instead of crying "poor boy" about losing past bylines, I should be thinking about trying to break the biggest story on the East Coast. The real identities of Nero and The Fiddler were still mysteries. If I could uncover that story, forget Geraldo, I'd be doing *Nightline*, morning shows, and even book tours.

"Journalism is never about the personal fame. It's always about the story. If you make it about yourself, you'll never get the story. Focus on the facts and they'll lead you to the right questions to ask." The words of my journalism teacher, Professor Maurice Kazarian, preached in my head.

"Okay, okay," I said to no one while Fuel's "Shimmer" pumped away in my ears.

So, what are the facts?

Fact #1: Someone in 1977 buried a jar with two human eyeballs in the senior class's time capsule.

"Wrong," I breathed. I couldn't assume just because it was in the '77 time capsule that the jar was actually put there back then. There's a good chance it was, but I couldn't assume anything.

I laughed, thinking that in listing the first basic fact I had already screwed up. I continued down the bike path.

Fact #2: The names and where they were written. It appeared that The Fiddler was probably the victim since his name (and the other little fact that he would never see God) was written across the jar that stored the eyes, and Nero's name was written in the yearbook. Again, the old adage about assuming sounded off in my brain.

But the question that arose from that fact was: Did Nero attend Sandy Point High School? If so, it would narrow down the list of suspects considerably and possibly narrow down the connection with the victim.

That was a real positive. I had two avenues to go down. Search for the suspect that could take me to the victim or vice versa.

I had struggled for about three miles and daylight was finally breaking through, revealing trees on both sides of me. It would be another two miles or so before the woods opened to the trail along Mackerel Beach. I could use that ocean breeze. I just couldn't get there. I was tired and knew there were a couple of benches about a half-mile ahead. Fishy Bryden's Memorial Bench was one of them. I kicked on feeling a bit guilty that I wasn't thinking about the Rutger Nelson story, but my rationale was until I got the go ahead from Crocker, I wasn't going to let my mind wander there, especially since Paul Harrison was technically the lead reporter.

Okay, Fact #3: What is the significance of the names? From a quick Google search, I had been reminded that Nero was the Roman Emperor who was known for playing the fiddle while Rome burned. Wikipedia explained, in so many words, that Nero was a complete whacko, so that made sense. Nero would be the perfect name to choose for yourself if you were into storing human eyeballs in a jar.

Interesting, I thought, Nero was known to play the fiddle and the possible victim was dubbed The Fiddler. What the hell was the connection there? Was there any?

My analysis stopped abruptly, followed by my feet, when the burgeoning morning light illuminated two figures up ahead sitting on Fishy Bryden's bench. I turned off my iPod, slowed my pace to a walk, and bobbed along pretending I was still listening to my music as I approached them. It was a favorite hobby of mine, and this time I hit gold.

"Jesus here comes someone. Didn't I tell you this was a bad idea," a man sitting on the bench stabbed his finger in my direction.

"Calm down, Jeremy. He'll pass and then we can continue," a short woman, round like a Weeble toy, replied.

Like hell I will!

I was intrigued especially since the gaunt and balding "Jeremy" was wearing a green T-shirt with big white lettering: BRYDEN'S FISH & GEAR. Wearing that shirt and sitting on Fishy Bryden's bench couldn't be just a coincidence.

What the hell is this all about?

I walked directly across from them to the bench on the other side of the path. I noticed the blank brass nameplate attached to it.

No memorial here.

My bench was still waiting for a victim.

I wonder who the poor bastard will be who gets the honors for this one? Man, these Cape Codders sure love their memorial benches.

I pulled out one earbud and waved over at the couple.

"Hi. Good morning," I grinned.

"Good morning," Weeble wobbled by returning a pained smile at me while Jeremy completely avoided eye contact.

"Wow. I'm out of shape…" I paused, feeling awkward that it was obvious I was not the only one. "Need to catch my breath for a minute."

There was no reply.

"Okay, well gotta get back to my music. Have a good one!"

I popped my earbud back in and softly sang a few lyrics from the '80s metal anthem "Cum on Feel the Noise" accompanied by no soundtrack while I strained my ears to eavesdrop. I have no idea why I picked Quiet Riot as the fake band playing on my iPod, but I almost laughed from the instant memory that followed.

In the eighth grade, I asked my teacher, Mrs. Lawless, why Quiet Riot spelled "come" with a U instead of an O. That got me a detention for my "wise behavior" even though, being Irish Catholic, I had no clue what my question broadcasted to the rest of the class.

The couple's voices lowered and Weeble eyed me for a minute. I kept bobbing my head and my act worked.

"See, Jeremy, he's just resting for a minute and he can't even hear you. So, before we continue, why don't you take a deep breath the way I taught you and relax."

"No. No. This was a bad idea. I know you mean well, but I can't do this. I'm sorry, Lindsey. I don't like this. I have to go." Jeremy hopped up and walked off.

Her eyes followed him until he was gone and then she shifted her gaze to me. I continued bobbing my head and humming pretending I didn't feel her stare, but her eyes were fixed on me. I finally looked her way.

"Thanks a lot, Mr. O'Rourke," she sighed.

I should've been surprised that she knew my name, but it was getting to the point that everyone in town knew me before I knew them. I almost replied to her, but remembered I wasn't supposed to be able to hear anything other than my music.

"Did Greg change his mind? Is that why you're here?"

I froze. I couldn't believe it. And I also couldn't understand it.

"Excuse me," I motioned to my ear buds. "Did you say something?"

"You can cut the act. 'Cause you're a lousy actor." She pushed off the bench, hoisting herself up with the agility of a child in a snowsuit rising from the ground. She smoothed out her pink "Breast Cancer Awareness" T-shirt, crossed the path, and sat beside me.

"Do I know you?" I asked.

"You know of me. I'm Dr. Courtland, Greg Crocker's therapist. You can call me Lindsey. And you're J.T., right?" She squinted and put her hand out.

Her oval face had a youthful shine to it, and I guessed she was between her late 30s to early 40s.

I shook her hand. "Oh, yes. Nice to meet you."

"I'm hoping it's nice to meet you too, J.T."

"Huh?"

"Well, I'm wondering why you're here. Was it also to track down Jeremy for an interview? I thought Greg agreed to keep things quiet?"

"Look, I have no clue what you're talking about. And who the hell is Jeremy?"

"The man who was just here. Fishy's brother. Really, stop playing dumb with me."

"I'll say it one more time. I have no friggin' idea what you're talking about. I'm just out for a run."

Lindsey studied my expression and smiled slightly.

"J.T., I just told you that you're not a good actor, so this time I actually believe you're telling the truth."

"Good. I guess. So, could you tell me what you're talking about?"

"I might as well since you're going to find out by the end of the day anyway, once Vic Hauser tracks down Jeremy."

"Vic Hauser?"

"Yep. He called Jeremy last night asking for an interview to get his reaction to the fact that the police found Rutger Nelson's license attached to Fishy's bench."

"Ah, shit!"

It made sense. I knew the Chief didn't leak it, but my guess was Gordon did. He was becoming a minor celebrity and probably couldn't keep his mouth shut. But that also went for Officer Jensen. He had been pretty quick to fill in Echo.

"I know! Shit is right! It's bad enough for this town with what's going on with the time capsule story and bringing Fishy's murder to light again. The painful memories for Pop Tucker's victims will now resurface and it could be devastating for some of them."

I just nodded. I couldn't tell her that wasn't what my "Ah, shit" response was all about.

"And J.T., you know one of those victims." Lindsey said.

I nodded again, thinking of the day on Crocker's boat and how he admitted he had been molested by Tucker when he was a kid. Suddenly, the thought of getting a scoop before Vic Hauser now made me feel dirty, but I still pushed on.

"Are you also Jeremy Bryden's therapist?"

"Nope, I'm just an old friend trying to help him through a bad time. I fear it's going to get worse for him and, as I said, for the other victims."

"Do you think any of those victims are capable of kidnapping Rutger Nelson?"

"There were dozens and dozens of victims, and the names have never been made public. It's an old wound that no one ever wants to talk about. But to answer your question, it's been my experience that some victims will grow up and repeat the pattern of abuse. The victim becomes the molester. So, yes, I would not be surprised if there is a connection."

We were both quiet for a minute.

"J.T., you actually know another victim from back then."

"Who?"

"I'm only going to tell you this because, at this point, Greg might need a matchmaker not a therapist. I think he could use a man in his life to be his friend and advise him. A confidant."

"Yes, he mentioned that. But what does that have to do with another victim?"

"Well…" she sighed and paused, "It's Anna Walsh."

"What? Sunshine? Oh my god. But I thought all the victims were boys."

"She wasn't a direct victim of the molestation. It would be inappropriate of me to say what happened to Anna was worse, but I will say it was horrific. There's no doubt it has scarred her for life."

"What has?"

"Look, it's clear Greg loves Anna and I think Anna has grown to love Greg, but something still keeps getting in their way. And it's not just what he confessed to you on his boat. There is something in Anna's past that she can't shake."

"What's that?"

"She's still in love with her first husband, Michael Devlin."

"Her *first* husband?"

Lindsey frowned and nodded, yes.

"Well, where is he?"

She inhaled before continuing. "Funny you phrase it that way. I don't mean good funny. I mean strange. You see, J.T., that was the question people in Sandy Point asked for almost twelve years until that fateful summer day in August."

CHAPTER 33

AUGUST 16, 1989

MILTON, MASS.

FRIDAY

ANNA

Anna Walsh loved her Fridays in the summer. Her breakfast consisted of a buttered English muffin and a Valium chased with a Mimosa. She never counted the Mimosa as her first drink of the day. It was "fun, refreshing, and harmless" — certainly not a *drink* drink. She'd then mix a Bloody Mary, tune into *Good Morning America,* and pack for the weekend. She always packed while she was still sober, so she wouldn't forget anything like Jack's bathing suit. He had quite a temper when she forgot things... like the night he was at a Town Meeting and Anna neglected to blow out a candle. She had "fallen" asleep on the couch listening to a Beatles tape and awoke to see flames consuming the coffee table like a pile of campfire kindling. Trying to retrieve her secret photo album from the burning table, she singed her hand. It was too late. Every picture of Michael Devlin was destroyed. Later, she had thought, it was good that it happened. Seeing his pictures only started a film playing in her head of happy memories of her previous life.

Her Friday routine continued with a second Bloody — always extra spicy and extra potent — while she vacuumed to the noon news before her day of soaps. Come soap time, her drink of choice became vodka and OJ. Very light on the OJ.

Fridays were also the best day for the soaps. After four days of regurgitated story lines, there was always at least one plot twist. Being pretty buzzed by that time, she'd shout to no one, "Oh my God! I can't believe that happened! He came back to her!"

After her soaps, Anna's husband, Jack Walsh, city councilman for the town of Milton and public defender — to anyone who had a dime in their pocket — would pull into their driveway. He'd lean on the horn, and a few minutes later, they'd be off to drive an hour and fifteen minutes to Cape Cod for their weekend binge.

She had met Jack while attending Harvard. They had partied together back in college. But honestly, she could barely stand him, never mind entertain the notion that someday she'd marry him. He had just been someone to hold the tap for her at the keg parties. But Jack became much more than that when he reappeared in her life a couple of years after Michael Devlin went missing — or took off — depending on her mood.

Jack had bumped into her at a Harvard reunion. Several drinks and laughs followed, and before she knew it, she was back at his place straddling him. The next morning, she smoothed out her short, blond hair and did the walk of shame back to her car. She had never been like that in her younger days, but she stopped being herself the day the police informed her that Michael had vanished. Since then, she was hollow inside, and when Jack took her home that night, she knew she needed to feel something even if it wasn't love. Lust might get her to the next day. And it did.

Shortly after that night, they met up again. There were unspoken similarities that drew them to one another. They were both in pain from being rejected by their spouses. Jack's wife, Donna, left him for the chiropractor that massaged Donna's tennis elbow — and apparently everything else.

Anna's story was a little more difficult to explain or comprehend. She didn't know the exact reason Michael Devlin left her. Her friends tried to convince her that he didn't leave her, but her mind played those soap opera scenarios out too often. She sometimes guessed the reason was all the miscarriages that led to her depression and pills. He had warned her if things didn't change, he would do something drastic. She often imagined that he took off and was living on a farm in Nebraska or maybe even on a tropical island somewhere with a beautiful wife, one who *could* give him children...

Some days, she believed what everybody else in The Point believed: that Larry Tadmor had murdered Michael. It was a more logical explanation... when she wanted to be logical. Tadmor disappeared the same night. He was a convicted felon, and a murderer no less. And Michael couldn't stand him. Witnesses said Michael had been drinking that night. Michael and Tadmor probably got into a heated argument on the ferry, and it escalated... But it really didn't matter anymore.

Dwelling on either scenario only brought her more pain that she found ways to dull. The only fact that mattered: the love of her life was gone, and he was never coming back.

What really brought them together was how they shared their pain. They loved to drink and do drugs, and what really made their relationship work was never judging each other for using. In fact, they encouraged one another. She taught him to pop them, and he taught her to snort them. In their blissful drug highs, their ghosts never appeared, and that's where they both tried to stay.

Surface friends ignored their self-destructive behavior, but the ones that were honest secretly whispered at the wedding that, "It was a love born in the aisles of Phil's Pharmacy and Gary's Liquors."

One of those friends was Greg Crocker, but being a recovering alcoholic himself, he never whispered. He'd always tell Anna exactly what he thought. She was going down the same path he had.

And that's why she began her Friday morning ritual by erasing his message from the previous night. He sounded so frantic.

"Sunshine, it's Greg. Please call me. I really need to talk with you. It's urgent."

She knew why. Greg had cornered her at Phil's the week before and was in one of his sober phases preaching Bill W. to whoever would listen. She didn't want any part of his bullshit that day, and she certainly didn't want it now, on her favorite day of the week. She decided to turn off the machine and ringer so she wouldn't be interrupted.

Anna made her Mimosa, took her pill, and watched a segment on *GMA* about Woodstock twenty years later.

"Twenty years," she blurted at the TV.

It seems like yesterday I was driving around listening to Charles Laquidara — or was it Peter Wolf, she wondered — on 'BCN, raving about what Woodstock meant for the future of music and also for the politics of our country.

Back then, she cared about calling out injustice, preaching peace, and believing in hope for the future. Now her future consisted of waiting for another plot twist on *General Hospital*.

When *GMA* ended, she noticed the red light blinking on her answering machine and a glowing 6 indicating the number of messages.

"Goddamn telemarketers!"

She headed to the living room closet to grab the vacuum but stopped when she spotted a blue Camry wrap around the circular driveway and park.

"Shit," she said, knowing it was Greg Crocker.

He's a persistent S.O.B. I can't believe he drove this far.

She hurried back into the kitchen with the goal of turning off the TV and pretending she wasn't home. But just as she put her hand on the knob it froze.

"Coming up at noon. A recreational diver off Sandy Point, Cape Cod, yesterday afternoon found the police cruiser of Officer Michael Devlin. Many will remember that Officer Devlin went missing back on May 18, 1977."

A grainy black and white news photo of Michael Devlin smiled from the screen at Anna just moments before she fainted, collapsing to the floor.

CHAPTER 34

JULY 6, 2004

TUESDAY

J.T.

It had been a week since I talked with Dr. Courtland on the bike path, and I concluded: screw trying to get investigations going on two of the biggest cases in New England. At least, screw investigating them for the paper. It was obvious that all Crocker was concerned with was protecting Sandy Point's image and depicting it as an East Coast Disneyland. I knew I was being a little harsh because, after talking with Dr. Courtland (who wanted to be called Lindsey), I could tell there was so much more going on with Crocker than just protecting the town's image. There was the pain of the past that still haunted him. I liked the guy and I did feel bad, so I decided I'd give him what he wanted — upbeat stories about "puppy dogs and ice cream" (as Vince Vaughn said in *Swingers*). But on the side, it was time for me to take notes for something much bigger. I decided I was going to write a book.

I almost talked myself out of it, but then I confided in Echo, and she thought it was a great idea. She wanted in as my researcher and photographer. I took her up on it, and the previous night I had given her an assignment: track down the lead detective for the Fishy Bryden murder case.

But now I sat on my deck, cracking open a fresh three-ring notebook while the early morning sun rose, wondering one thing: *Where do I begin?*

I didn't even know if my book would be fiction or nonfiction.

What I did know: I was learning some truly crazy details about The Point, stories that hadn't seen the light of day in a very long time. Of course, some were now seeing the light of TV cameras. Moments after I talked with Lindsey, Hauser reported the news about Rutger Nelson's license being attached to Fishy Bryden's bench and then all hell broke loose.

Commodore Nelson was furious that he hadn't been given any of that information about his missing son and was threatening to sue the police department. I couldn't blame the guy. In his mind, he was still holding out hope that Rutger had run away, but now the situation looked far more sinister. All of this occurred a couple of days prior to the Fourth of July celebration, just adding to the fireworks from the time capsule story and sending more TV trucks to town.

After staring at a blank page for ten minutes, I figured I'd write everything down and sort it all out later. I scribbled – NO ORDER – and, since the conversation was fresh in my mind, I decided to write about what I had learned the night before at the bar.

Selectman Oliver Kempton, a forty-something-year-old Bart Simpson double, joked with Chief Noah Harding (also in his forties but looking a decade younger) that during the Fourth, he had felt like the Mayor of Amity trying to keep the beaches open, "And," he pointed at Harding, "you're Chief Brody."

Harding didn't laugh. He grabbed his pint, that looked more like a shot glass in his massive hand, and sucked down his beer in silence.

I wondered if I could take him. Probably in the ring, I figured, but someone at the bar had mentioned Harding was a former "bad ass" Marine. I had an uneasy vibe that in his day he snapped a few necks during covert desert missions.

Finally, he spoke. "Everyone on the Cape loves talking about that movie. The difference between Jaws, which came out in the seventies, and the two cases we now have open is simple. Back then, people ran away from a town if they thought there was any kind of danger. Now those assholes flock to dangerous towns because this world has become a bunch of voyeurs that love watching tragedies and making a buck from them. Even my own men."

"True dat." Kempton slightly buzzed, appropriated some old hip hop slang, which caused Harding to visibly cringe. I wanted to join him, but bit the inside of my cheek, wiping down the bar and trying not to get caught listening in.

There was another long pause from Harding.

Then: "And that's why I'm here. I just want you and the other selectmen to know that I gave Detective Gordon a thirty-day unpaid suspension."

"Wow. Little harsh, don't you think?" Kempton asked.

"He's lucky I didn't fire his ass for talking with Hauser. His family police tree spared him, even though I hear his ol' man wasn't much of a cop. Just so you know, I still might let him go."

"Well, you know the selectmen will back you on any decision. You're the boss," Kempton assured.

"As you'd like to say, true dat," Harding cracked his first smile, threw a fiver on the counter, and left.

After I jotted that down I thought back on my conversation with Dr. Courtland. Lindsey had been extremely candid with her information, making me wonder if her clients could trust her. She had also read my mind.

"Anything I am revealing to you is either public knowledge or client approved."

She told me a fascinating story about Anna "Sunshine" Walsh who had once been married to a Sandy Point cop named Michael Devlin. Devlin and a local ex-con named Larry Tadmor went missing in May of 1977. Many believed that Devlin and Tadmor had a "beef," and that one of them had killed the other and then went on the run.

Twelve years later, in August of 1989, a recreational scuba diver discovered Devlin's police cruiser. If there had been any remains, the ocean took them away long before that. So, now the belief is that Tadmor killed Devlin, and he was the one who went underground.

I asked her why that was the theory.

"Larry Tadmor sometimes ran the ferry that Devlin took back and forth from his home on Oyster Island. He was running it the night Devlin disappeared. So..."

"So, that doesn't prove anything. Couldn't it have been the other way around? Devlin could've killed him, dumped his cruiser, and took off," I countered.

"True. But the ferry was found docked that night, and unlike the majority of Pointers, Devlin wasn't much of a boater and wouldn't have been able to navigate the ferry."

"Okay, that makes sense. But let's backtrack. You said Anna was, in a way, also a victim of Pop Tucker's molestation."

"Well, having her husband disappear and then presumed murdered was the straw that broke her back. But to backtrack: as you say, she was an indirect victim because after Fishy was murdered, Anna began taking Valium and eventually got hooked. Later, she added alcohol to the mix. You see, she shopped at Bryden's all the time and was very fond of Fishy. It was doubly painful because Officer Devlin was the one who found Fishy's body."

"Wow, poor Sunshine," I paused, "You're not her therapist, too, are you?" I asked, thinking she sounded like the town gossip.

"No. Again, I guard all of my patients' secrets unless they advise me otherwise. That sometimes makes it difficult for me because I could probably…"

"Probably what?"

"Well… Help their situations. Most of my clients' difficulties are a result of keeping it all bottled up… Anyway, now that she's in recovery, Anna is quite open about her past and, as a result, is thriving in life. It's ironic, since it was Greg who was the one who brought her to her first A.A. meeting and then, after she cleaned up, gave her a job. It's funny how the world works… And yet, she still remains a victim of the past."

"How's that?"

"Greg loves her, and she loves Greg. But because of his inability to put the past behind him, they can't move forward. That is why I ask you to be there for him. He needs someone from outside this town, hell, even outside of me, to talk to. Everyone in Sandy Point is connected to these tragedies, even me."

"How are you?"

"Jimmy was my first boyfriend. If you can call it a boyfriend at that age."

"Jimmy?"

"Oh, I mean Fishy. He was the kindest boy you'd ever meet. And again, in a strange way, I think that's how I got into the therapy business. I saw what that murder did to this town, and I wanted to help people. Now I do, or at least I try. I try to help them find a healthy way to cope with tragedy." Lindsey smiled, and I knew she meant it.

I put my pen down and cracked my knuckles and thought of Sunshine. Could I write a book and capitalize off her tragedy? Maybe whatever I did come up with I'd turn into fiction instead?

"Research it first and decide later," I counseled myself.

310

My cell phone chirped, and Echo's name appeared on the screen.

I clicked on. "What's up?"

"Douglas Prichard."

"Huh?"

"He was the lead investigator on the Fishy Bryden case."

"That was quick."

"That was the easy part. It was in the first article about the Bryden case. The hard part is, or was, that Prichard moved out of town not too long after the case was closed and no one at the police station would tell me where he went."

"Damn."

"Hold on. I do have a source at the police station."

"Your cop boyfriend Jamal?" I interrupted.

"Hardly a boyfriend," she laughed. "Yes, it's Jamal, but doesn't it sound so much cooler to say 'source'? Anyway, he was able to access the files of former employees, and I got Prichard's current number and address. He lives up in Boston in the Back Bay."

"Wow. Sounds like he's done well for himself. Can you throw me his number?" I readied my pen.

"You won't get him if you call now. He won't be home until nine tonight."

"How do you know that?"

"I called and got his wife. I asked her if I could talk with him since I was doing a criminology paper for grad school on the history of the Sandy Point Police Department. She said she'd leave him a message because he was working at his daughter's boutique on Newbury Street."

"Perfect! Today's my day off, so I might take a ride up there. Can I grab the name?"

"A Touch of Sass."

"I like the sound of that," I chuckled, "Hey, you want to come with me?"

"I would, except I planned on spending the day with my brother."

"Oh... Okay, well good job. I'll call you when I get back. Later, Ec."

"No prob. Bye."

After I hung up, I went inside to grab some OJ from the fridge and noticed my Red Sox schedule magnet. I smiled and then called the scalper, Fat Pete, and a few minutes later dialed Echo.

"What's up?" she asked.

"Does David like baseball?"

"Yes, he loves baseball. Why?"

"Good. I just scored three tickets to tonight's game against the A's. I thought the three of us could hit Newbury Street and I could talk with Prichard while you two walked around. Then we could go to the game. You know, make a day of it. What do you say?"

"I say great! But I have to talk with him. We had planned on going fishing. When David has something planned sometimes it's very hard to change his mind. But the Sox... Can I call you back in ten minutes?"

"Sure." I hung up and realized I shouldn't have committed to all four tickets — like all scalpers, Fat Pete refused to sell in odd numbers. It seemed like I was waiting forever.

My cell sounded twenty minutes later.

"He wants to know if the seats are any good?"

"Wow. Really?"

"That's part of who David is. He tells you exactly what's on his mind. He doesn't sugar coat anything."

"They're in right field before the foul pole. I think that's pretty good for last minute."

"Hang on a sec," she said to me and then hollered, "David, they're right in front of the Pesky Pole."

A moment later, I got the answer I was hoping for and after putting the top on my Jeep, the three of us headed over the bridge. Since Echo never told me what her seventeen-year-old brother's "challenges" were, during the ride I used my B+ knowledge from my developmental psych class to form my own diagnosis: a high functioning form of Asperger Syndrome.

I could've been wrong, but when I glanced in the rearview mirror at the back seat after asking a question, he avoided eye contact. Also, Echo had warned he was extremely blunt with his observations.

One of those observations was somewhat embarrassing: "Did you buy a Jeep like my sister's Jeep because you like her, and since she likes Jeeps, she might like you?"

"Umm..."

"Because if that's why you bought it, it won't work."

I tried to laugh but it was obvious by my hesitation and the quick burn to my checks I was faking it.

Echo stepped in. "David! You know it's wrong to say things like that. And anyway, don't worry about J.T., he already has a girlfriend."

I almost asked, "I do?" but then remembered I'd told Echo that lie one night.

"Then why isn't J.T. taking his girlfriend to the game?" David prodded.

I looked over at Echo who broke into a smile in the passenger seat.

"He asks a good question," she pointed out innocently.

"I'll put it this way. The distance thing killed us, and just a couple of days ago, we decided to take a break," I lied and then hollered over my shoulder "Never mind me, David, do you have any girlfriends?"

For the rest of the ride David reeled off around twenty or so names.

I struck parking gold and found a meter right on Newbury Street.

I pumped it with quarters and whispered to Echo, "Sounds like your brother is the Wilt Chamberlain of Sandy Point."

She didn't laugh. She made sure that David was out of earshot — which he was, trying to pet a flock of pigeons — and turned to me.

"Obviously, those girls are ones he remembers saying 'hi' to him over the years. I know you were just joking, but it saddens me that he'll never know the rush of excitement of finding true love."

"Geez... I'm, ah... sorry."

She acknowledged my apology with a nod before leading us down the street. We continued until we spotted a burgundy awning with white lettering spelling out "A Touch of Sass" projecting above a small walk-down boutique.

Before either one of us could do anything, David bounded down the steps and ran into the store.

"Pretty excited to go into a boutique," I remarked.

Echo pointed to a hand-painted sign in the window: 20% OFF ALL HAND-MADE WALLETS AND HANDBAGS.

"That's probably the reason," she said before following him down the steps.

"I don't get it."

"You will." She opened the jingling door, and I followed her in. I didn't really see anything that would be considered "sass" and realized it was a name that was chosen so men would follow their wives. It had multicolored racks of everything. I pictured women poring over every item on every rack while their men became antsy handbag holders. I scanned for an elderly man behind the counter or walking the floor, but there were only two female customers carrying more hangers than Mommy Dearest.

David was over by a display case talking to a woman who pointed at various wallets.

"Yes, I designed almost everything in here. Are there any particular wallets you're interested in?" the woman asked politely.

"I don't want to buy one. I make wallets like you do, too. Look." David pulled out of his back pocket a shiny red one and handed it to her.

"Wow, you used duct tape. You made this yourself?"

"Yes. I've made 112. I'm a duct tape artist. That's what my dad calls me."

"That is so cool!" The woman sounded genuinely enthusiastic. She inspected the wallet, and as we approached, glanced up and smiled. I liked her smile. It was playful. She was probably a couple of years older than me but had the healthy attractiveness of Kate Winslet in *Titanic*. My mind couldn't help but wander to the scene when Leonardo painted Kate sans clothes, and I briefly wondered why I never took art lessons back in the day.

"Hi," Echo said to her. "You have quite a store."

"Thank you. We've been open six months and overall, it's gone well. Today is slow but we'll pick up once the sun goes down," Kate Winslet said.

Echo jumped right in. "So, Douglas Prichard is your father?"

"Um, yes." She looked surprised.

"I'm Echo Landers, this is my brother David, and this is J.T. O'Rourke."

"Nice to meet you. I'm Charlotte Prichard." It felt like she was smiling at me. At least, I hoped so since she still carried her maiden name, and I didn't see a ring.

"My dad just went out back to grab some water. Let me get him," she began opening a curtain to the back room but stopped. "Actually, I can't leave the store unattended. Can you wait for a moment?"

"Sure thing," I answered for us.

"So, how do you know my dad?" she inquired, but David interrupted and pointed at me.

"He just broke up with his girlfriend. If you like him, you should be his girlfriend. Then he can take you to the Red Sox game with us."

"David!" Echo scolded.

Charlotte laughed. "That's okay… I mean… Not about breaking up with your girlfriend."

"Thanks. I'll survive." I laughed.

"So, how do you know my dad again?"

"How does *who* know me?" The curtains parted, and Douglas Prichard, a fit man for his late seventies with silver hair and tanned skin peered out.

"Hi, Mr. Prichard." I motioned with my hand, "This is Echo Landers, her brother David, and I'm J.T. O'Rourke."

"Landers. Is your mother June Landers?" he studied her face as he walked over.

"Yes, sir. You know her?"

"I can see the resemblance. I knew her when she was a teenager. A wild child, that one. Is she doing well?" Prichard asked, but I could see he was trying to put it all together.

"Yes, she's doing great. Still lives in Sandy Point. And still a little wild."

"Okay, good. So, what's this about?"

I cleared my throat. "I'm a reporter for the *Sandy Point Standard Times* and I wanted to ask you a few questions about the Fishy Bryden case."

The tan drained instantly from his face. He paused, then took a sip from his bottle of Poland Springs and looked over at his daughter.

"Dad, are you okay?" the concern evident in her voice.

"Yep. Charlotte, give me a few minutes?" he patted her arm and turned back to me, "Let's go in the back."

I nodded and, while he turned, I casually put my hand in the pocket of my cargo shorts and pressed the record button on my mini tape recorder. I noticed a slight smile from Echo as I walked by her. I also realized from Charlotte's glare that the party was over and I wouldn't be painting her lying naked on a couch anytime soon.

I followed Prichard into the cramped back room that held a table, a couple of chairs, a mini fridge, and a coffee maker.

"Coffee?" he offered.

I've had a theory that if you share a drink with someone, the conversation tends to be more open and casual. I don't know if that was from being a bartender or watching too many *Magnum P.I.* episodes as a kid. Magnum always had his theories.

"Sure."

"How do you like it?"

"Like my women. Black." I pointed beyond the curtain.

The tension in the room lifted as he let out a hearty laugh. He poured the cup and handed it to me and sat down with his Poland Spring.

315

"I don't blame you. She's just as pretty as her mother. Girlfriend, eh?"

"Nope. Just my photographer and researcher, that's how we found you."

"Ah. Well, I shouldn't be surprised you're here. Once I saw it on the news about that kid's license on Fishy's bench, I knew someone would be calling. I expected it would be that greasy prick from Channel 14, but a part of me hoped maybe no one would show."

"Why is that?"

"When I left Sandy Point, I left the memories of that case with it. I wanted to start fresh."

"So, you stopped being a cop altogether?"

"Yep. I started working for my brother-in-law in his real estate office, and I became good at it. I've had a nice life since I left that place."

"So, it was the Bryden case that made you leave?"

"Let's hold up a bit, Mr. O'Rourke." He placed his bottle on the table.

"J.T." I smiled.

"J.T., O'Rourke, whatever. Let's get something straight. You're not going to get me on the record for anything." He leaned over and his hot breath struck me.

"I don't get why you're so defensive." I said, my curiosity piquing.

"You want the answer to that?"

"Yeah."

"Off the record?" he cocked his brow.

"Sure."

"Because I was a detective."

"I don't follow."

He didn't say anything for a full minute. Finally: "Where are you from? It can't be The Point."

"Nope. Southie. Why?"

"You go to Catholic school?"

"Nope."

"But raised a Catholic?"

"Yes. Mr. Prichard, what does this have to do with my question?"

"It has everything to do with it. O'Rourke, you were raised knowing the sacred vow of the seal of confession." Whether he did it intentionally or not, I noticed him steeple his hands.

"Yes."

"Then you understand it's similar to a reporter's vow of keeping a name off the record if they are told something."

Now I got it and nodded, "Yes."

He sighed. "Okay, I'll give you my opinion, off the record, if that helps you look into it, but then I'm done. Deal?"

"Sure, one thing though." I pulled the tape recorder out of my pocket, pressed stop, and placed it on the table in front of us.

"You were recording me?" his agitation was back, and then some.

"I was. Past tense. You might be pissed, but think about it. I'm showing you can trust me. So, go ahead, erase that first part and now let's go off the record."

I didn't have to ask Prichard twice. He pushed the erase button, then took another sip from his bottle and began.

"My point earlier was that I was a detective. I think I was a pretty damn good one, too. Anyway, it never made sense that Pop Tucker killed Fishy Bryden."

"Why? Didn't he molest a lot of kids?"

"At least twenty-six," he blurted.

"Wow. How do you remember that number from so long ago?"

"I'll never forget that number," he looked off.

"Okay, but wouldn't that be more of a reason to murder Fishy? Maybe he was going to talk."

"Possibly. But if Tucker did it, he'd just murder him, dump his body, and be done with it and on to molesting the next kid."

"But isn't that what happened? The old articles I read said they found Fishy's body where the bike path was being built, and not far from Tucker's house on Mackerel Beach, I might add."

"My point exactly. Doesn't that sound a little too convenient? Why would he leave the body so close to his home? This guy was able to rape twenty-six boys and get away with it. He was a master at what he did. He wouldn't be so damn sloppy. And there are a few other things that you won't find in those old articles."

I waited as he mustered up the courage to tell me.

"Tucker wore red suspenders. Ripped suspenders were found on a tree branch. How could suspenders rip? They're made from elastic. And the handle of Tucker's push broom was found..." he hesitated, "inside Fishy's backside."

"Oh my God." I closed my eyes.

"You see, as I was putting the pieces together, it was really shaping up to

317

resemble an amateur murder. Someone was trying to set up Tucker. The problem is the day I went over my progress with Chief Gedney, Tucker was found murdered. That news satisfied the town. Against all of my objections, the case was immediately closed."

"Is that why you quit and moved out of town? You were frustrated?"

"I left because of what we found in Tucker's house."

"What was that?"

"Multiple copies of pictures of boys being raped."

"And that obviously sickened you?"

"Well, shit yeah, but that's not it. Think about that word 'multiple.' It was bad enough that there was one sicko raping boys in our town, but Tucker would only need one picture of each crime to relive it in his head. So why did he have 'multiple' pictures? I'll tell you why. He was either selling or trading them with other sickos. My guess is there had to be more than one of those diddlers living in The Point. And my other guess is Devlin may've found something out about one of them. That case gnawed at him every day. He was a good cop. Not a good detective, but a good cop."

"Wait. I thought the theory was that Larry Tadmor killed Devlin and then went on the run."

"There is no way in hell Tadmor could stay hidden all of these years. He was a low-level loser who liked to drink and fight. I'm not saying he wasn't capable of murder because he had done time for that, but his ass would've shown up dead or in a cell by now. He wasn't the brightest bulb on the tree. And it's because of all of that, and something else, that I moved." He shuffled in his seat.

I waited.

"There was also a lockbox found in Tucker's house. I have no proof, but I think it held his sick recap journal of everything. And if not that, it held something important. Maybe even the names he sold or traded pictures with? We didn't have the key, but the plan was to have it opened, but coincidentally enough, that was the same day the case was closed. But that's not all."

I waited longer this time.

"I convinced the Chief to just have the box opened and if there was nothing that kept the case going then he could close the case. He hemmed and hawed but eventually agreed. So, I went to the evidence room to retrieve it, but it was gone. I looked everywhere. The box was missing."

"Missing?"

"Yep. And that's why I moved. I knew that one of those sick fucks that liked to look at pictures was on the force, and I knew too much. At that moment, I also knew my family would never be safe if we stayed in town. You might think of me as a coward for running, but until you are faced with the need to protect the lives of your family, you'll never know that feeling. That is why I'm off the record. But I take back one thing that I said earlier."

"What's that?"

"That I'm done. The guilt has been eating me up for years, and my detective's gut tells me that somehow this Nero character is involved in the Fishy case. Maybe if I had stayed, I would've figured it all out. What I'm saying is: keep me off the record, J.T., but call me anytime with questions. I want to help."

"Well, here's a question, could you give me a list of the twenty-six victims or as many as you remember?"

"I remember them all, but that's one question I will never answer."

"You just said…"

"I know what I said, and I know there's a good chance that one of them may be Fishy's killer, but those boys are victims. They deserve their privacy."

"Are you serious?" My frustration showed in my voice.

"You never saw the pictures. I vowed to protect their identities, so they could go on to live normal lives — or as normal as one can. I don't want innocent men brought back into this thing."

"Yeah, but as you just said, one of them may not be so innocent."

"Look, I will help you, but no names of victims. Those are my terms. Now I have to get back to my little girl."

Prichard got up from the table and, like a magician, vanished behind the curtains, leaving me completely stunned.

CHAPTER 35

JULY 31, 2004

SATURDAY

DRAKE

Business wasn't just good for Drake's Canteen, it had been "through the roof." The increase of green in Drake Underhill's pocket was due to his newest product — homemade lobster rolls. They were literally selling hotter than hotcakes. Part of the reason was his recipe: mayonnaise-based with chunks of meat packed in a buttered sweet Portuguese roll grilled to perfection.

The other part was price. Drake sold his "World Famous Lobster Rolls" for a few dollars less than every other fish market and restaurant on the Upper Cape. Word got out, and not just to customers.

A few weeks earlier, the canteen had been parked at Lareby's Market renovation site and Jeremy Bryden showed up accusing Drake of "cutting the legs out from everyone else."

He brushed Bryden away with a "Fuck off" while doling out lobster rolls to six more hungry hardhats. Moments later, tables turned when that "asshole" Lareby stormed out of his market and threw Drake off his property.

He saluted Lareby with his customary middle digit and drove off. Drake would survive. There were dozens of construction sites in the area. The problem he faced was the beaches. If he could somehow combine profits from worksites with beaches, he'd have one hell of a summer.

But back in May, Selectman Oliver Kempton (another prick) denied him a beach vendor's license, stating that the ice cream trucks had that covered. That was a blow to business, but now more and more beachgoers were tracking him down. It had become the "in thing" to do.

The canteen's popularity rose after he made a deal with the owner of Pilgrim Diner to keep a large sign at the entrance. On it, he listed the worksites and times of where the canteen would be.

Zach Goodrich may've owned the diner and was also trying to develop Samoset Woods, but he still wasn't much of a businessman, Drake thought, since it only cost ten bucks and one lobster roll a day for Drake to steal customers from him. The sign was a double whammy, indirectly informing patrons that Pilgrim Diner wasn't quite the place for "World Famous" lobster rolls.

The hungover college kids shoveling their pancakes got that point, showing up at the designated sites and stocking their coolers before lazy days on boats or sand or both.

Even brown baggers working those sites were now leaving their lunches at home. The lobster rolls were such a hit that no one noticed the slight price increase on the extras — sodas, chips, candy, etc.

That increase dented the register when the canteen hit bar parking lots after last call. He'd also hand out pamphlets to the drunken zombies of where he'd be the next day, and like flies on shit, the shitheads showed.

One of those shitheads, a self-described techie vacationing from Silicon Valley told him about the power of mass text messages from cell phones. It was "the wave of the future" and suggested he do it for the canteen.

Drake was skeptical, but he taped a sheet to the counter and the drunks wrote their numbers. The first time he got sixteen numbers and sent a text the next day. Twelve of them showed up. He was onto something. And since then, the new technology of text messaging had lifted his business to profits he could only have dreamed of.

He laughed, thinking about his good luck while his skiff hummed along, jumping the waves under a full moon.

Life was great, but he had to keep it going. And that was getting more difficult by the day considering what he was doing wasn't legal.

He had kept costs down because the lobsters were free — free for him at least — because he was raiding recreational fishermen's traps. It started out as only a couple of them here and there, but it had now turned into a fully organized system. He kept a notebook filled with dates and times, so he'd spread out the times of when he'd hit a spot for a second time. He also made sure that he would find out as much as he could about who owned the traps and what their schedules were. This wasn't a problem in a town that had a bar called The Angry Fisherman.

To avoid suspicion, Drake owned a few traps, and he told anyone who would listen all about them. It always opened the door for the other fishermen to vent about their trials and tribulations and they always ended up handing him a verbal map of where their traps were located.

He couldn't keep the game going forever, but money was so damn good, at least good in his world. He was already looking to buy a second canteen. But it was getting riskier because he was now breaking his own rules, starting with the first one: Never poach under a full moon.

It may've been 3:15 in the morning, but the water glowed like fresh snow on a January night making him visible within fifty or so yards. And to top it off, he was out on the water on a Saturday.

Normally, this was beyond stupid, but the spot he was headed for he hadn't poached in thirty-six days. He also knew the owner didn't check his traps in the dead of night. There were twenty pots a few hundred yards from the beach. That was extremely close, but he didn't fear getting caught by residents. No homes lined the eroded cliffs of Samoset Woods, and the beach was only accessible by boat — unless someone trudged through the poison ivy filled woods in the middle of the night.

If there was ever a place to poach lobsters under a full moon, this was it.

Just to be safe, he cut the engine, then he shotgunned a beer before grabbing an oar and paddling the last twenty yards to the spot. He anchored and was about to put on his rubber gloves but stopped when a faint sound cut through the still night.

"What the hell is that?" he whispered to himself, straining his ears. He heard it again. It sounded like music.

He waited.

Again, it came.

It sounded more like someone was trying to play music. It was harsh and unsatisfying to his ears. He couldn't resist turning on his headlamp and directing it toward the cliffs.

"Stupid!" he scolded himself. The lamp barely threw enough light to see a few yards in front of him.

He switched it off and listened.

Silence.

But just when he figured his ears had played tricks on him, the harsh screeching sound echoed again from the cliffs — this time louder. More constant.

It was definitely a violin, he decided, and whoever was playing it had no clue what they were doing.

Why the hell is someone up in Samoset Woods? And why are they playing a violin at three in the morning? And why does it sound like shit?

Curiosity was too much. Drake pulled up anchor, grabbed the oar, and, directed by the faint glow of his headlamp, paddled toward the beach.

NERO

Nero came to his Silent Place (as always) to gain perspective on his situation. When he was convinced he was dying of cancer, he was ready to unleash his full wrath on Sandy Point, but now everything had changed. He wouldn't call it fear that he was experiencing because he didn't fear anyone or anything. He just didn't want the amazing story that he was literally writing with blood to end so tragically. To Nero, tragically meant having some incompetent idiot stumble onto evidence like DNA or fibers or some other *CSI* bullshit and catch him. That person would then become *the* story — the hero who saved the day. The thought was nauseating, and it would most likely lead to Nero getting shanked in a cell by some inmate also trying to make a name off his coattails.

That was not how this remarkable tale should end, but it was definitely a possibility if he continued down the path he was on. It had to finish on his terms, and for that reason, he knew he had to slow down. Maybe not stop, but he couldn't kill for a very long time. That was easier said than done. His urges weren't like some sort of switch he could turn on and off at his leisure. They controlled everything he was and everything he did. And they were stronger now that he had added another element to his game — people knew someone in Sandy Point had been hunting them.

The challenge excited him. He wanted to continue, but again, he knew he had to change his philosophy. He spent the night forcing his mind to coach away the urges.

Won't it be far more terrifying for these assholes if I disappear for a while? They'll start pointing fingers at one another and I can just sit back and enjoy the show. And just when they think it's safe, I'll strike again.

His justification for taking a break was taking hold, but there was only one true way to calm his urges and that was viewing his trophies.

Tonight, the feelings were pounding his chest and pulsating his pants. He didn't want to experience them like an animal below in the dark shelter. It was risky to be above in the summer, but he couldn't help himself. He had to have some kind of freedom. He stripped naked and picked a jar. After climbing up the ladder, he shook and then placed his trophy on the small wooden table and lit three candles. The golden flames danced around the glass, illuminating the two lifeless eyes slowly bobbing around.

He mouthed the inscription on the tape several times and smiled before settling on the grass and picking up his bow. He was ready. He struck the strings while watching the full moon suspended above the treeline.

Stopping for a minute, he pinched his dick hard. Then he slashed the bow across the strings again. Just as the bloody images of the kill appeared, raising his penis to life, a strange uneasiness stabbed his gut. Something didn't feel right. He lowered the violin and picked up his night-vision goggles.

After he put them on, he headed toward the cluster of trees and brush before the cliff. He maneuvered around the open claws of four bear traps, or as he called them, "coyote traps," continued a bit, and then hopped over the ankle high, clear fishing line. Walking a little farther, he stopped at the edge of the cliff where thirty more yards of fishing line were strung across, but this was chest high — an unofficial DO NOT ENTER sign for anyone who ever decided to climb up the cliff. And if they did, they would find a laminated sign (not visible from below) reading: Beware of Deer Ticks and Poison Oak.

It wasn't a challenging climb if someone set his or her mind to it. A boater actually had, a few years back.

Nero watched from the cover of twilight while the boater shouted to his buddies that he wanted the privacy of the woods to take a shit. After he spotted the sign, the shitter didn't go any farther and retreated down the cliff after he did his business. Nero wished the guy had been alone, so he could give him a private tour of his Silent Place.

Back in the moment, his ears perked. All he could hear were the humming of crickets, but his sixth sense was still controlling him, so he patiently waited.

Then he heard it — oars slapping water.

Adrenaline bubbled. He licked his upper lip.

If I can hear that so far away that means…

He peered through his goggles to make out a yellow halo on the water moving slowly but heading to shore.

Holy shit! Someone did hear me!

His mind screamed but he remained in control. He had been successful over the years by never panicking. He wasn't about to begin now.

Deep breaths! Remember, Nero, this could be fun!

The silhouetted figure rowing a skiff broke through the darkness. The moon quickly illuminated a man — a man trying to land on shore like he was Samoset trying to sneak into his own woods.

But now the woods are mine!

Nero glanced at his watch: 3:33.

There is probably no chance in hell he'll climb up here but if he does…

DRAKE

Just before closing in on the shallow water, Drake stopped rowing, remembering to pull up his engine so it wouldn't get stuck in any muck or sand. He went back to quietly pumping the oars but at the same time wondering if he was now wasting his time since he hadn't heard anything in a while. But that fact kept him just as intrigued. If he could only hear it again, maybe he could distinguish the sound, realize it was nothing, and be on his way. It was the *not* knowing that drove him on.

Finally, the nose of the skiff cut through the sand and slid to a stop a few feet from shore. He grabbed the anchor and tossed it gently. It landed with a thud, spearing the beach.

Drake felt in his shorts pocket for his bait knife then switched off his lamp before flicking on a flashlight. He aimed the beam at the gentle waves curdling the shore. When they retreated, he hopped out onto the sand, so his sneakers stayed dry. After inspecting his skiff, he tugged on the anchor chain, pulling the entire boat's belly onto land.

Now what?

It was obvious. The violin had been coming from above, over in the woods. He moved closer, shining the beam up the side of the eroded cliff. He estimated that it was only thirty or forty feet to the top. It didn't look particularly challenging. A bit steep, but it reminded him of the big dunes down Cape he had scaled as a kid. And like those dunes, the worst-case scenario would be if he stumbled, the sand would cushion his fall.

But then Drake remembered he wasn't a kid. He was a thirty-five-year-old chubby guy with a slight buzz who had been out breaking the law in the middle of the night. And to top it off, other than the crickets (that reminded him of the night setting on his alarm clock) he hadn't heard a peep for the last ten to fifteen minutes.

He no longer had desire, energy, or even the buzz for that matter to continue his little adventure. Those damn singing crickets gave him visions of his comfortable bed back home. That was far away. He still had to pull the traps and then hawk breakfast sandwiches in a few hours.

It was probably just some high school kids partying where they shouldn't be.

Drake turned and headed for his skiff, but then he was paralyzed by the screeching sound. It was back. It was a violin, and just like before, it was crude to his ears. But this time it wasn't in the distance. It was definitely coming from above, not far beyond the cliff edge.

What should I do?

NERO

With the naked intensity of a parking lot floodlight, the white moon revealed the figure at the foot of the cliff — Drake Underhill.

Nero didn't know which jumped first — his heart or his dick. It didn't matter. Both were working hard. He had fantasized for many years of torturing and killing Underhill and now he was within reach. It would be so easy. He had to weigh his options.

I kill him, and another search begins.

But then he thought of the big plus. Underhill had shown up in his boat. That meant if he went missing the search would be on the water. Not the woods. All Nero had to do was dump the skiff. That would be a hell of a lot easier than the time he maneuvered a car ferry in the middle of the night.

If I let him go, he will probably tell someone he heard the violin. That will raise questions and there is a good chance someone will come looking.

He was going to let fate provide the outcome but then Underhill turned around. He was going to leave. That was not the answer Nero was looking for.

It is for times like this that I keep that scuba gear below. I'm always prepared!

His naked figure scampered through the woods, jumped over the fishing line, dodged the traps, and grabbed his violin. With fierce excitement, he violently struck the bow against the strings.

Drake was a big and powerful fat man, but Nero wasn't worried. He was excited and vowed to make sure he would never see God. Visions of his youth came to him. The former high school football star reminded him of another Sandy Point legend — the one who screwed his mother.

I will imagine that it is him! It will be so much fun! I can even use my new toy tonight!

He smiled and played on. Now it was only a matter of time.

DRAKE

Sweat ran a marathon along Drake's brow and was accompanied by a wheezing whistle while he stood at the top of the cliff trying to catch his breath. Luckily, no one had seen his pathetic display. He had stumbled more than a few times in the sand. The realization struck him as he hunched over, hands on knees, gasping for air. He had to stop kidding himself. He wasn't chubby. He was fat.

That Thanksgiving game when I ran for three touchdowns against Silver Shores is long gone. And it's not coming back… Okay, okay, I'll get my shit together and go back to the gym after the summer.

That would never happen, but his lie satisfied him for the moment, and he was able to focus back on the matter at hand.

The violin.

It was nearby. Somewhere between twenty and fifty yards away. The sound was so massively abrasive that an eerie chill shot up his spine. There was something seriously wrong. He had expected to hear drunk and high college kids laughing, ribbing the violinist with barbs like, "Quit your playing, man. You sound like shit!"

But other than the violin, the woods were silent.

Yep, something seriously strange is going on.

He walked forward a few yards, but something slapped his stomach causing him to jump back. He flashed the light down and saw fishing line. It was strung like an invisible fence along the cliff. Attached to it was a sign that warned of deer ticks and poison oak.

That's bizarre. Why would the town use fishing line to make a fence? That doesn't look right at all.

Drake took out his knife and pressed the blade on the line, instantly snapping it. He kept the knife in his left hand and with the other stuck out the flashlight. Despite growing apprehension, he moved into the woods. Just as he entered, it became silent again. But he did spot yellow flames behind a cluster of trees.

Why am I so nervous? It's probably just some drunk camping out?

"I'm probably just worried that I might get poison oak," he softly joked to himself and stepped forward but then almost tripped. He swung his light to the ground and saw ankle high fishing line — literally a trip wire.

What the fuck is going on?

He cupped his hands and hollered. "Hello! Who's in there?"

No answer.

"I said, 'Hello!'" He stepped over the line and continued on.

A quick rustling movement came from the lit area. Any other time he would've thought it was a scared animal, but not this time.

"Look," he lightened his voice, "I'm not going to sell you out for camping in the town's woods. I was just boating and ran out of beer and heard the violin. That is a violin, right? Anyway, I was just hoping I'd stumbled onto a party or something." Drake waited for a response.

Silence

He briefly thought about retreating but then looked at his bait knife. He moved it to his right hand, trading it for the flashlight.

For Christ's sake, you're a grown man and you're armed. Grow up!

"I said, 'Hello!'"

Still nothing.

"Alright, asshole, I'm coming in there!" He barreled forward, pushing his way through trees and brush until he broke through to an open area. The first thing his light caught was the well-manicured lawn.

It looks like the goddamn PGA in here!

"What the..." He began but moved the light over to three lit candles on a small wooden table. Something was on the table.

What the hell is that?

He shifted his head back and forth but walked closer until the object came into view.

"Holy shit," he barely breathed, realizing it was a jar exactly like the one found in the time capsule.

He swung his head around, his eyes wildly searching, but no one was there.

What the fuck!

"Hey fuckface! I'm fucking armed! So, you better fucking take off!" Drake's grip tightened, sweat dripped down his face, the woods closed in on him, and that strange uneasiness had turned into flat-out fear. He had to get out of there.

Now!

But the label on the jar taunted him. His brain begged him to go the other way, but curiosity pulled him closer.

His eyes pinballed the area before he finally placed the flashlight on the table, its beam shooting to nowhere. He kept his knife alert in his right hand and cradled the jar with his left.

Drake brought it close to him and the moon lit the inscription on the label.

He mouthed the words: "Rutger Nelson Summer of 2004."

The moment they left his lips, terror shot through his hands causing him to drop the jar, shattering glass and spilling liquid everywhere. Two human eyeballs lay at his feet.

He turned to run, but a door in the ground sprang up followed by a dizzy, red strobe light. Behind it came a calm voice. "I wish you hadn't done that."

Drake then heard a crackling zap and couldn't comprehend what he was seeing. It looked like an electric snake flying in the air straight for him but then it suddenly died before his eyes, falling to the ground.

"Ah, fuck!" the voice came from behind the flashing red light.

Drake put it together. It was a Taser, and it just missed its mark. There was no time to ponder it. He bolted to the right, diving behind trees. Then rising to his feet, took off zigzagging toward the cliff, his face whipped by branches and brush.

"Don't run, Drake!"

He knows my name!

The shock caused Drake to slacken his pace for a few seconds and then realized he had. He picked up the speed, even though he was gasping for breath again. This time worse. It was only twenty yards or so to the cliff, but it seemed a lifetime away.

If I can just get down the cliff and get to my boat! My cell phone is in the lockbox. If I can get there...

He had a vision of that Thanksgiving game, catching the toss and turning the right corner and seeing that end zone in front of him. He could do it. He pushed on, but suddenly he felt himself flying through the air and then crashing hard to the unforgiving ground.

The ankle high fishing line — he had forgotten about the trip wire. Now he was lying among rocks and sticks and a hot, white pain throbbed from his ankle.

"Fuck!" the word escaped from his lips when he realized not only was his ankle sprained, but he had also lost his bait knife in the fall. His frantic hands felt the ground around him but found only grass and dirt.

"Oh, did Randy get tackled at the goal line?"

How can he read my mind like that? And why is he now calling me Randy? And why does his voice sound so familiar?

As quickly as the questions came, Drake pushed them away. He didn't have time to process what was going on. He had to get out of there. Fear and adrenaline lifted him. After pulling himself up, he limped on. Open space was ahead, he was getting closer to the cliff... He winced and stared down at his ankle.

Holy shit!

One more step and he would've had his leg snapped off by a bear trap. It was just another thought that drained what little energy he had left. But then an idea came to him — an idea that might save his life.

His bugged-out eyes searched, and he couldn't believe his luck. There was a long heavy stick lying beside him. He picked it up and shoved it against the trap causing the claws to spring to life, snapping the stick in half with a loud crack.

"No! No! Ahhhhhh!" He screamed louder than he ever had in his life, but then he quietly tried to move on.

"Randy, it sounds like you found one of my traps. I'm sorry about that!" The voice chuckled in the distance.

Randy? He called me Drake before. Why is he calling me Randy?

Drake knew he didn't have time to think about it. He had just bought himself precious seconds. He used them wisely. He limped on and finally emerged from the woods. When he got to the edge of the cliff, he dove forward, rolling down the sand and landing below at the water's edge.

He heaved for breath while trying to fight the searing pain that had now completely overtaken his ankle. He tried to get up but could only prop himself enough to see something truly terrifying.

The man was coming down the cliff. He was naked except for some strange mask he was wearing. He was also holding something in his hand. Like a snowboarder, the man casually rode the sand down the cliff and then walked over.

Now Drake could see what was in his hand — a massive silver blade that glistened under the moon.

Get up! Get up!

But he couldn't get up.

The man sauntered toward him and hovered over.

"Well," the man paused, "It looks like you ruined my fantasy."

"Please! No! Please!"

"With daylight coming, there's no way I can get your fat ass back up there. Looks like it will be a burial at sea for you. Take a good look, Randy. 'Cause you won't be seeing God or anything else ever again."

"It's a mistake!" Drake waved his hands in front of him, "My name isn't Randy!"

"I know that! That's why it was a fantasy. Drake, you always were a dumb fat fuck." The man pushed his goggles to his forehead revealing his face.

Drake couldn't believe it and was only just registering the unfathomable fact as the heavy blade rained down on him, over and over.

That face would be the last thing to ever go through his brain.

Well, not exactly…

CHAPTER 36
JULY 31, 2004

9:32 A.M.

SATURDAY

J.T.

The last few weeks had proven to be very interesting in all aspects of my life. Socially, I found myself becoming more and more attracted to Echo.

What began as a futile fantasy to bed her had now turned into something much more, dare I say, deep?

God, the crew in Southie would've been all over my shit if they heard me describe it that way, but I had to admit to myself: I was falling for her. And of course, it scared the hell out of me, especially as she gave no signs that she wanted anything more than friendship.

The shift from lust to like had already been forming but really took hold the night we brought David to the Red Sox game. For nine innings of eating, laughing, and cheering on the Sox (who tromped the A's), we were a pseudo family. And, unlike being with my own family, I loved every minute of it.

I was also getting attached to David and had gone fishing with him twice. A part of me questioned if I hung out with him for purely good intentions or was it to get points with Echo? I hoped it was that I liked the kid, but I couldn't honestly say for sure. The experience was new to me. It made me want to be a better person.

When it came to the *Sandy Point Standard Times*, something truly bizarre had just occurred. An unlikely ally to my book project emerged, and his name was Norman Chadwick.

At first, I couldn't believe it. A guy who thought I was barely qualified to deliver newspapers never mind write for them had just puckered up and kissed my ass.

It was Saturday morning, and I was trying to get a leg up by finishing up a puff piece about a charity quahog eating contest. Then I planned on heading down to the morgue to do research on the real stories that had everyone sleeping with their eyes wide open. I was excited to put some quality time in since I didn't have to bartend till 4:30.

But during my haste, I forgot my notebook in the break room and Norman found it. He held on to it, admitting to rifling through it, and wanted to have a meeting. I followed him into his office.

Here we go!

I expected him to go off on me for working on a book during company time, but what followed completely shocked me.

"Look, J.T., I know you're not a big fan of mine," he paused as he settled behind his desk, "and you don't have to guess that I'm also not a big fan of you. You have that Irish sarcasm thing going that can be rather annoying. Quite frankly, it ticks me off."

"Norman," I laughed, sitting in the subservient chair, "Don't hold back now. Tell me how you really feel."

"You just made my point." He leaned back, looking smug.

Damn, he's right.

"Anyway," he continued, "due to that fact, what I'm about to say will likely surprise you. I've enjoyed your articles, and I see a bright future for you here."

Okay, what's the deal here? Why are you BS-ing me?

But for once I kept my thoughts in my head and my trap shut while he went on.

"I have a question. Is the reason you're working on a book because you're frustrated with Greg?"

"That would be a big yes. But there's also another reason."

He slapped the air with his palm interrupting me. "I know what it is. All the TV news stations are scooping your scoops, and you're thinking 'why even write articles since they'll be old news by the time they come out.'"

"You hit the nail on the head. These have been some of the craziest stories ever on Cape Cod, maybe even Massachusetts, and we should be the ones breaking them, especially when technically we *are* breaking them. But instead, the TV people are beating us to the punch every time followed by the dailies. It's friggin' ridiculous, man."

"I totally agree. And that's why I asked you in here. J.T., I think we can help one another."

"How's that?"

"Well, for one, if you continue writing a book and, by some slim chance it actually gets published, it would be great publicity for the paper. So, I have no problem with you using all of our resources here at the paper as long as it doesn't get in the way of your day-to-day assignments." He gave me the first smile ever and handed over my notebook.

"O…kay." I nodded.

I'd love to give a quick jab to that condescending face. Hold your temper, O'Rourke. Let him talk. See where he is going with this.

"But wouldn't it be great if you could write your stories and update them whenever something broke, unlike now when they are just stolen from you?"

"Of course. Norman, what are you getting at?"

"I just returned from a three-day conference in New York City that focused on the future of the newspaper business. I came to one, simple conclusion. My uncle either has to wake up or get out."

"Oh, here we go. The old take over the newspaper plot. I knew you had something up those silk sleeves." I pointed at his Guido style, lavender-colored nightclub shirt.

"Just hear me out for a second, will you? I think you'll like what I'm going to say."

I nodded him on.

"Do you know that within ten years almost all newspapers will be online? They'll be daily and constantly updated throughout the day."

"Yeah. I've heard some stuff, but they always spout that George Jetson 'technology of the future' business about everything."

"Great, I'm dealing with a reporter who references cartoons." He looked up at the ceiling before moving his focus back to me. "J.T., I beg you not to be as ignorant as my uncle. You see, the whole process has already begun. And if we don't get ahead of this now, we'll be out of business in a few years."

"Okay, fine. But even if you're correct, it sounds like you're meant to have this conversation with someone else. Not me." I braced my hands on the arms of the chair, preparing to rise, but he halted me again with a gesture.

"That's the problem. My uncle doesn't listen to anything I tell him. Actually, no one here listens to what I have to say."

"If you don't mind me saying so, it's not what you say but how you say it. If you could lighten up a bit, I'm sure people would relate better with you."

He sighed, and I could actually see him bite his lip.

"Look, you could be right about that. But even if I 'lighten up,' as you say, I'll still never get through to my uncle — especially if I can't get through to the staff first. They've already made up their minds about me, and they all bow down and never challenge him. Someone should challenge him on some of his ridiculous decisions."

"What do you mean?"

"Take Echo as an example."

"What does she have to do with it?" I asked.

"The rest of the world has gone digital, and she's still using an outdated camera and working in a darkroom. And the reason she does that is she loves," he stopped and flashed air quotes, "'Crockerman,' and doesn't want to muddy the waters. She's no dummy. She knows digital is the way to go, but she won't change 'cause he doesn't want her to. It's pure insanity. You see, we need a whole shift in thinking here, and I need someone with some influence to be on my side. I see you as that person."

"Me? I'm still new. I mean, I'm not even from here. They're not going to listen to me."

"My thinking is: if I can get you behind this then we can reel in Echo. Obviously, she likes you. If she gets on board, then I know the others will follow. Then my uncle will have to at least grant me a staff meeting… Here's my promise. If you can help me convince him, you'll have your own online column and a job here for as long as I'm here. And you know I plan on being here long after he's gone. This is a great job if you ever decide to get married and have a family." He let that sink in.

It did. My mind went to that place for a moment and then Norman brought me back.

"Well, what do you say, will you help me?" He put his hand out.

I studied it, realizing all I needed was a cigar and I'd be George Bailey about to team up with Mr. Potter. The irony didn't escape me. Crocker talked about George Bailey during my first day, and now here I was, sharpening a knife to put in his back.

But unlike Bailey, who changed his mind after a puff, I shook Norman's hand knowing I was going to try and make this thing happen. He was right. Times were changing and, for the good of the paper, Crocker had to change with them. Of course, I was probably just rationalizing my "Et tu, Brute" moment.

"Great. I'm really happy to have you working with me on this," he smiled.

"Enough, Norman. I'm not into cuddling and smoking cigarettes after the deed. In fact, I feel a bit dirty about all of this and need a shower. But since I am feeling that way, I want your word again that I can still work on a book on the side."

"You have my word. As I said, your success would only help the paper. And so you won't have any second thoughts, remember this fact. If you have an online column, you'll garner a following so when the book comes out, you'll already have people lined up ready to buy it."

"So, now it's 'when' the book comes out, not 'if'?" I said.

"Well," Norman laughed, "maybe I'm changing already."

His over-friendliness made me feel a little sick, so I got up and headed down to the morgue to do some research for the book. It reminded me of the massive warehouse at the end of the first Indiana Jones movie, except instead of thousands of crates there were literally thousands of file cabinets. I took a deep breath and pondered what I was doing. I had three problems facing me:

1.Time: Between bartending and working on my regular assignments it had been difficult to carve out any quality time. The good news for me (not good news for the town) was that no one had broken anything new in a few weeks. There was still no identity for the eyes in the jar. And no one had a clue who the hell Nero and The Fiddler were.

2.Which story would make the best book?

Since Rutger Nelson's license being attached to Fishy Bryden's bench showed some kind of a connection, I had spent what little time I had for research focusing on both those cases. The dismal result: I was still at stage one. All I really learned was what everybody already knew — Fishy Bryden was a kid everyone loved, and Rutger Nelson was not. There didn't seem to be any connection as far as age, looks, or temperament to link the victims. One was murdered, and one was missing. Other than the license, no one knew for sure that Rutger Nelson was actually dead.

Of course, I was trying to base it on Prichard's theory that someone set up Pop Tucker. He could've been completely wrong, and whoever stuck Rutger Nelson's license on Fishy's bench may've heard the story and was just screwing with the cops. Another part of Prichard's theory was that there had been a child molestation ring sharing or selling pictures and that one was a cop. Why else would evidence go missing?

Thanks to Echo, Officer Jensen had snooped around old files at the police station but hadn't found anything that might point a finger to any shady officers, past or present. So, with no real information, I thought long and hard on no. 3.

3. Do I write a fiction or nonfiction book?

My initial thought was just to take notes and decide later, but that thought had changed. Since there were some major unproven allegations to levy, especially at the police department, I thought those stories could easily be weaved into a good old-fashioned fictional mystery. Seriously, did I really want to piss off the Sandy Point Police Department by accusing some unknown police officer(s) of being a possible child molester(s)? Then I thought of the disappearance of Officer Michael Devlin at the hands of ex-convict Larry Tadmor. That story was a no-brainer. It would make one hell of a true crime book, and I decided I better look into it before it resurfaced. Vic Hauser had already touched on it briefly in news reports. I could only imagine some true crime queen like Ann Rule hearing about it and churning out another bestseller in a matter of months. I decided I'd spend my time looking into the night Devlin disappeared, but in the back of my mind, I knew that if I went in that direction, I would eventually need Sunshine's cooperation. There'd be no book without her account of being the grieving widow, and if I could get her to go on record, then I'd really have something. I felt dirty again but pushed the thought aside.

"Well, no use thinking about that now," I said to myself, opening my notebook and checking my notes of when Devlin was last seen.

May 18, 1977, Officer Michael Devlin is kicked out of the Angry Fisherman for being drunk and causing a scene.

"Okay, put on the Bee Gees and let's go back to the seventies." I humored myself and scanned the area.

The cabinets were divided into rows. Above, red-colored placards hung like supermarket aisle signs. I headed for the one that read: THE '70s but stopped when my eye caught an isolated group of cabinets tucked away in a corner. The sign above those read: SANDY POINT BUSINESSES.

I hadn't noticed it on my previous trips to the morgue and thought: before I do anything, why not look up Pop Tucker's place. Maybe there were articles or pictures that mentioned town kids, i.e., possible victims of his abuse = possible suspects in Fishy's death. Again, Prichard's theory.

Like every other section of cabinets, it was in alphabetical order. My eyes skimmed but stopped quickly on The Angry Fisherman.

Pop Tucker's place can wait.

I opened the cabinet and for the next half hour picked through several stories about The Angry Fisherman ranging from fundraisers, fishing contests, to entertainment.

One was about the one-year memorial of Davis Lawson, Sr.'s death. In his honor, seven local bands were going to play and raise money for the Sandy Point food bank. I got the impression he was well loved by the town and by doing some quick math in my head I realized that my boss Davis Jr. would've been between 10 to 13 years old when he lost his old man.

For half a second, I thought of my own father and wondered if I should call all of his haunts in Boston to check up on him but then something hit me. I hadn't been this content in my life ever and the reason was simple. I hadn't talked to the bastard in almost three months.

Let sleeping dogs lie.

I continued flipping through the folders seeing stories on entertainment at The A.F., and as I got closer to May 18th of 1977, a morbid thought ran through my mind.

I wonder if there was a band playing the night Michael Devlin went missing. If so, what was the last song he heard?

From out of nowhere, a childhood memory of when I was four or five flashed. I could see my oldest sister Erin, who was around eight at the time, tell me that the last thing you hear on the radio is what goes with you to heaven. I had never recalled that memory before, but it was now so vivid.

What bizarre beliefs we have as children.

Back in the moment, I couldn't help but wonder: if Tadmor murdered Officer Devlin, what was the last song Devlin ever heard?

I found a manila folder labeled in boldface type: April-Aug. 1977. My intention was to quickly leaf through the contents to get to May 18. I was doing just that when my eye passed over an ad for The A.F. and one word leapt out like a red light. And stop I did. It was just a few lines, but I could feel my pulse quicken as I read it.

JOHNNY THE BULL VISITS THE POINT TO PLAY AT THE ANGRY FISHERMAN
Johnny the Bull blends his classical violinist training with his unique passion for blue-collar fiddling. He is going to shake the sand from your sandals while you dance the night away. Narragansett Beer 2-for-1 Happy Hour from 6 to 9. Show starts at 10 p.m. $1 cover.

I stared at the word fiddling for several seconds. It could be just a coincidence but something inside told me it wasn't. I knew the 1977 Sandy Point High School senior class buried the capsule on May 1st of that year. Not only would the idea of using the time capsule be fresh in "Nero's" head, but so would the soil be for him to dig up.

I wrote that fact down and read the ad out loud again. This time two other things stuck out. The word "visits" and the performer was advertised under a stage name: Johnny the Bull was visiting The Point. He wasn't from here. Johnny the Bull obviously was not his real name.

So, if he was a traveling musician and put on a show and then went missing, there's a good chance no one would know to report it. Everyone would've assumed he had left town for his next gig.

"Oh my God. I think I just found The Fiddler," I said to no one as I scribbled it all down.

My cell then buzzed, jerking me from my trance.

Echo's name raced across the screen.

I picked it up. "Ec, I was just going to call you."

"So, you... ah, heard?"

"Huh? Heard what?"

"About Drake." Her voice sounded off like it was cracking.

339

"The canteen guy?"

"Yeah. About... he, ah..."

Yep, she was fighting tears.

"Echo, are you okay? Did Underhill do something to you?"

"No, ah, not ah..." She stopped. The dam burst and she sobbed for several seconds.

"Please tell me what's wrong?"

"Jamal just told me the Coast Guard found Drake's boat. But they can't find Drake. They think he drowned last night. I just... Can you come get me?"

I was already out the door.

CHAPTER 37

AUGUST 1, 2004

SUNDAY

J.T.

Having nightmares wake me at ungodly hours always provided me with a hell of a lot of time to reflect. I never considered that a good thing. In fact, I tried to avoid it at all costs. But as I woke from one of my "boiling rain" terror dreams, I viewed the latest interruption as a blessing in disguise. I decided from now on I'd use my insomnia to my advantage. I'd get up and work on my book project(s) and then go for a run.

Rising, I stretched and wiped the sweat from my brow. I had no sense of time. All I knew was that even the foghorn that moaned earlier in the evening had given up and gone to bed.

I looked over at my alarm clock: 5 a.m.

"Great," I sighed, realizing I had only slept for about an hour and change, but still long enough for the nightmare to jump back into my head.

I got up, grabbed some OJ from the fridge, went into the other room, and flipped ESPN on in time for the replay of SportsCenter's top story. Like many bartenders, it was my third viewing in five hours. But I felt justified watching it again since the moment was so historic.

The intro theme played in the image of Red Sox highlights of Nomar Garcia-parra transitioning into him wearing a mocked-up Chicago Cubs uniform.

Third time watching, and the sight still stunned me. The trade deadline arrived the day before and the Sox beat it by unloading Nomar ("Nomah" as the Fenway bleacher creatures worshiped) to the Cubs.

In return, they received a shortstop that, on paper, had a glove but not much of a bat, and a first baseman with a name no one could pronounce.

Around water coolers and beer taps the trade was destined to be the number one topic for dissection for the rest of the season. Sandy Point was probably the only town in New England where it would take a back seat. People here had much more serious things to talk about.

With that thought, I fired up my laptop with the goal of transferring my notes, but before I did that, I knew I should write down what I had learned at the Angry Fisherman a few hours before.

"Focus," I said to myself, but the problem was I couldn't.

My mind was on Echo. I may've been stunned about Nomar's departure, but it was nothing compared to how I felt about Echo's reaction to Drake Underhill's probable drowning. I was completely flabbergasted.

When I picked her up, she was sobbing uncontrollably like she had just devoured a trunkful of Nicholas Sparks' novels. It was a flippant observation considering she was crying over a guy who had drowned, but that guy was Drake Underhill, the biggest jerk in town. And that's why I was so shocked. I knew they had been a couple or hooked up or something in high school, but that was high school and again, the guy was an asshole. Women all love the bad boy, but most grow out of it. I just didn't get her deep pain for the situation. It seemed like there was something else she was crying about, but of course, what did I know? Men are from Mars and women are from out of this solar system.

After she jumped into the passenger seat she told me, "I don't want to talk. Just drive anywhere. Please just drive."

I did. I looped through town over and over (passing the harbor that for some unknown reason caused even more tears) before stopping at Dairy Queen.

"Grape, right?" I asked.

Having calmed down, she nodded in the affirmative. I hopped out and got us two Mistys. After I handed off hers, I switched on the radio for the first time that ride to Dave Matthews singing about his damn ants again.

"You can't escape my Dave, huh?" Echo managed a smile.

"I guess not. I thought this song got killed a couple of years ago. Your boy Dave is getting as bad as Billy Joel."

"What do you mean? Please don't tell me you also don't like the Piano Man."

"Okay, I won't. My bigger point is it doesn't matter where you are, Billy Joel will find you. His music stalks people." I laughed, "Okay, Ec, where to now?"

"I know you bartend soon so I'm good to go home."

"You sure? I can still drive around a bit."

"Positive."

"Okay," I said about to start my engine.

"J.T.," she interrupted.

"Yeah."

"Thanks, ah, for ah, not asking."

"No problem. But know I'm here for you if you ever need to talk or just drive around town listening to bad music."

She playfully punched me with her left hand while equally playfully sucking from her straw and then sticking out her purple tongue. If we were a couple, it was one of those moments where a kiss would follow, but we weren't a couple, so the time just hung in the air.

"Um, there's something I've been wanting to tell you," I began hesitantly and noticed that she moved back ever so slightly. It dawned on me that after our moment, she perceived what I was about to say as something totally different. The comfortable silence I offered her earlier was now downright awkward.

"J.T., I ah... am not... ah..." she faltered, zapping my energy. I wasn't going there at all, but if I ever did want to tell her my feelings, I now knew what her response would be.

"No, it's ah not... Jesus, Echo, what I'm trying to tell you is I think I may've figured out who The Fiddler is."

She wasn't expecting that.

"Huh?"

"Or who The Fiddler was."

"What? How? What's his name?" Totally back in the moment, she fired off the questions.

"Well, when it comes to his name, that's the tricky part."

"J.T., come on, I want to know everything."

I spent the rest of the ride filling her in.

Now thinking about my time with Echo, I realized there was one positive

343

from the big negative. Since she had no interest in me, why waste any more time? I was a full-blooded man living on Cape Cod who every night got to pour stiff drinks to hot girls who also liked stiff other things. Davis had advised me that finding the perfect woman on the Cape was a lot like fishing, "Don't use a hook. Use a net."

I was now going to put all of my energy working on the book and whatever energy was left I'd use on whatever woman or women that wanted to swim into that net.

With new conviction, I began to type: *July 31ˢᵗ (technically August 1ˢᵗ since it was 1:42 a.m.) at The Angry Fisherman. My conversation with owner Davis Lawson, Jr., the best I remember it. These notes will capture the main elements that will later be filled in with better description, dialogue, and character development.*

The bouncer Gonzo ushered local car salesman Murray Philbrick, the last straggler, out the door, while Vicki and I restocked the bar. I told Vicki I'd finish cleaning up, so she could get home to her fourteen-year-old daughter. Gonzo declined his shift drink too, (although, I had already tilted some Captain into his Coke cup more than a few times) and headed out since he had to get up in the morning for his day job — he was a prison guard about forty minutes over the bridge.

Davis, who had been in the back room making copies of the next day's specials then appeared.

"Remember that movie One Crazy Summer with John Cusack and Demi Moore?" Davis asked.

"Yeah."

"You know they filmed a lot of that movie over in Falmouth. I like Cusack but that was a pretty shitty movie."

"Really? I didn't know they filmed it on the Cape. I haven't seen it since I was a kid, so I have memories of it being pretty good, but why are you bringing it up?"

"'Cause this summer has that one beat. This is beyond one crazy summer. Rich kid goes missing. Time capsule with eyeballs is found. And now Drake Underhill falls off his boat and is all dead up somewhere." Davis grabbed the soda gun and poured himself a Sprite.

I went over and drew my half pint of Guinness and let it sit.

"Is that what you think happened?" I asked.

"You saw it. It's no secret the dumbass liked his tea. That and being alone on his boat in the middle of the night, not smart. Believe me, it doesn't take much when it comes to the ocean."

I leveled my pint off and let it settle for another minute before taking a sip.

"Davis, I've got a question for you."

"Shoot."

"When did you start working here?"

He laughed, "Shit, as soon as I could piss standing up. I'd walk around with a basket and sell potato chips to the drunks. And when I was about ten, my ol' man promoted me by handing me a bucket of Lysol and a mop. I'd have to clean this place every morning before school. Father of the year that guy..."

"So, when your father passed away, your mom ran this place?"

Davis stopped mid-sip and stared at me.

"What's this about, J.T.?"

"Well, I've been looking into all of the old stories and also the new ones trying to find something. A connection."

"What does my mother have to do with this?" Davis's tone sharpened.

"I was just curious if she hired the entertainment back in '77?"

"And again, what the hell does she have to do with anything?"

"Okay, clearly, I'm pissing you off, so I'll get to the point. I found an ad in the paper from May of '77 that a guy named Johnny the Bull played here and..."

"Johnny the Bull," he interrupted.

"Yeah, he was a —" I began.

"A fiddler," Davis jumped in and then snapped his fingers, "Oh my God. I see where you're going!"

"So, you remember him?"

"Of course, I do. I hired the bastard. It was also the first press release I put together. I had just turned eighteen and my mother put me in charge of hiring the entertainment. So, this guy comes into the bar and tells me he plays a mean fiddle. I tell him to play, and he was amazing. Not a bad singing voice either. So, are you saying Johnny the Bull is The Fiddler?"

"I have no idea. I'm working on a wild hunch, but I could easily rule him in or out if I knew his real name."

"I can't help you there. He only went by Johnny the Bull. Said he called himself that because Johnny was a regular guy's name and the Bull part was a tribute to some famous violinist named Bull. It's strange you brought this up — I remember all of that because only a month ago I was watching Jeopardy and one of the questions was about a violinist named Bull — I want to say Ole Bull? Anyway, there's Trebek talking about Ole Bull, 'cause he acts like he knows everything, and then I had a flashback of those

days and Johnny the Bull. That was only a few weeks ago. God, so strange you bring this up."

To my surprise, Davis went over and poured himself a Newcastle.

"Want another?" He pointed at my pint that was almost empty.

Davis never drank at the bar and also never allowed more than one free beer a night, so I knew his interest was sparked.

"Sure. Davis, maybe your mom might remember his real name from paying him?"

"We paid him cash. And my mother can't even remember her own name. She's got emphysema and Alzheimers."

"Oh, wow."

"Yeah, she's in a nursing home down in Florida, or as many call it, 'God's Waiting Room.'"

"I'm really sorry to hear that."

"Don't be. She didn't have the best life so maybe it's good that she gets to forget everything. Anyway, what's your game plan on finding Johnny the Bull's real name?"

"I don't know. But on a completely other topic, were you working here the night Officer Devlin went missing."

"Jesus, you're really pulling out all the old skeletons, huh? What does Devlin have to do with this one?"

"Nothing really, but as I say that, let's pretend that Johnny the Bull was The Fiddler, and his eyes are in that jar. Officer Devlin did go missing after being in The Angry Fisherman. Two people go missing who were connected to this bar. Actually, three when you put Rutger Nelson into the mix."

"Slow down! I don't like where this is going."

"I'm just saying that..."

"No, I'm serious. Shit talk like that can kill a place."

"I'm not saying The Angry Fisherman is involved but maybe someone who comes here."

Davis threw his hands up. *"I don't even want to hear what you're saying, and you better stop if you want to keep your job."*

I had gone too far too quickly. I had to learn to tread lightly when getting information and also to stop speculating out loud.

I forced a smile. *"Davis, I'm just talking crazy talk with you. Don't worry. I'll shut up now. You enjoy your beer. It's my job now to get that bucket of Lysol and wash those floors. 'Cause I love working here."*

I stopped typing, cracked my knuckles, and decided to go for a run. Three miles stretched into five and I was feeling pretty good about myself when I got home. I had every intention of making a smoothie for breakfast, but when I got out of the shower, I noticed I had a text message.

I opened it: "I'm just learning how to text. I hope this works. I need to talk to you. Do you want to meet at Pilgrim Diner?" — Sunshine

I looked at the time and it had only come in four minutes before.

I texted back: "Sure. Half hour?"

The screen flashed: "Okay. Thanks."

A few minutes later, I was out the door and soon after in a booth huddled over a cup of coffee. I sipped and studied an elderly couple quietly eating across from me. Not one word spoken. Comfortable silence. Or was that the only way they could coexist? Had life been good to them, or had they suffered unspeakable pain like Sunshine?

"What's your fascination with Frank Williams?"

"Huh?" I turned to the voice, "Oh, hi."

I must've zoned out because I hadn't noticed that Sunshine had slid into the other side of the booth.

Now recovering I asked, "Who?"

She nodded over at the couple. "Frank and Claire Williams."

"Oh, since you know them, you can answer this. They're not talking, so I was wondering if they are happy and quiet or miserable and quiet?"

"Well, you see, frail ol' Frank over there used to be quite handsome," Sunshine stopped and ordered a cranberry juice from the waitress before continuing. "People thought he looked like Paul Newman. I never could see it. For many years, he was stepping out with someone. Actually, it's someone you know."

"Who?"

"Lillian Dumas."

"Lillian as in the woman with the missing dog. My first assignment?"

She smiled. "Yep. She was quite a looker herself at one time. Anyway, Frank promised Lillian that he'd leave Claire someday, but he never did. I swear living with that hope has turned poor Lillian a bit batty. As for those two, I think Frank and Claire just tolerate one another. What's the other choice when you hit that age?"

"That's depressing," I said, signaling to my cup for the waitress.

The ambidextrous server did her magic, pouring a refill while also handing off the cranberry juice. She gave us the "one minute" finger and headed over to freshen Newman and Woodward's cups.

"There's a lot of opportunity for depression in life," Sunshine said in a low voice but then shifted to upbeat, "and speaking of that, word is you're thinking of writing a book or something and you might include my late husband's murder."

It caught me off guard.

"Who told you that? Norman?"

"It doesn't matter who told me. Just tell me: is it true?" She took a sip and waited for my answer.

"Well, I've been taking notes on all the cases, and I thought I'd put something together. I don't even know if I want to write fiction or nonfiction. There are so many bizarre stories in this town. But I swear to you, Sunshine, I was going to talk with you before I did anything that involved Officer Devlin. Please know that."

"Here's what I think," she leaned over the table and then whispered, "If you decide to do fiction, promise me one thing."

"What's that?" I whispered back.

She paused for a long time looking me straight in the eye.

"Give me bigger breasts." Tilting her head back, she howled with laughter.

After a second of registering it, I joined in. The tension was broken.

"Seriously, J.T., you're not the first reporter after the grieving widow story, but I'll tell you what. You may be the last reporter. I'll do it. I'll answer any questions you have."

"Really? Are you serious?"

"Yes, I'm serious. It's time I tell that story. I can trust you. I know that."

"Not to be devil's advocate, but how do you know you can trust me?" I asked.

"It's just a strange feeling of knowing. I can't explain it."

"That's good enough for me." I suppressed a grin.

"I'm sure you noticed that I said my 'murdered husband' even though no one really knows for sure what happened to Michael. I do, though. He was murdered. No question about it. I loved him, and he loved me. Sure, we had our problems, but I know if he were still alive, we'd be at a table in this diner right now, and it would be comfortable laughter we'd be sharing. Get what I'm saying, J.T.?"

I nodded.

"Good. So, I'll answer any questions you have as you research his life. But I think you should write it as nonfiction. When it comes to his story, the truth is stranger than fiction."

"That's fine with me, 'cause I don't want to change anything about you. I think you already have perfect breasts." I smiled.

"There you go with that Irish blarney again," she chuckled.

"Or bullshit." I smiled.

"Yes, bullshit, indeed."

"Now that we settled that, there's something about the paper I need to get your thoughts on," and I launched into Norman's idea of getting the paper online and how we had to convince Crocker to jump on board.

"I agree with Norman. It's time we all start living in the now and also think of the future." A coy smile crossed her lips, "And leave Greg to me. I'll talk to him. And when I'm done, I doubt we'll need a staff meeting. He's part of my thoughts of living in the now and the future."

She followed with a wink and got up from the table.

"Where are you going?"

"I have to fly. A.A. meeting. We'll talk later about any questions you have about my Michael." She exited.

I was feeling pretty good about everything, so I decided to treat myself to a Portuguese omelet. A couple of minutes later a man's voice brought me up from my note pad.

"Here you go, J.T."

I looked up and it was the owner, Zach.

"Oh, hey, thanks Zach." I put my pen down and took the plate. I was ready to devour it, but then he slid into the seat across from me.

"So, have you or your colleagues found out any more about Drake's drowning?" he asked.

I cut into my omelet, releasing steam and an aroma that told my stomach it was "go time" but then realized I was being impolite, so I put down my knife and fork.

"No. From what I heard it was pretty clear-cut. He fell off his boat, and you know the rest."

"Yeah, I guess," Zach looked off.

"You sound skeptical."

"Well, it's just that Drake went out that night to pull his lobster traps, and they found his boat not even close to his spot."

"That is interesting."

"It's also kind of ironic where they found his boat, considering..." Zach trailed off.

"Considering what?"

"You know, since it was only a couple of hundred yards away from Larry's Ledge."

"Larry's Ledge? What's Larry's Ledge? And why is it ironic?"

"For a news guy, you sure need to be clued in. Larry's Ledge is what the locals named the spot where that scuba diver from Australia found Michael Devlin's police car."

"What?"

"Yeah, the fishermen named it that after Larry Tadmor, you know the guy who killed Devlin? I would never say the name in front of Anna," he pointed to the door, "but it is ironic."

"Yeah, okay. I think I get that. But I'm still confused about the ledge thing?"

"Come to think of it, I guess, you wouldn't know about the ledge. You're a city boy, not a local. You see, about a quarter-mile out from the harbor, there's a point where the ocean floor suddenly drops off 180 feet or so. That's where the cruiser was found back in '89. Larry was pretty smart to dump it there. Hence, Larry's Ledge. It was pure luck back then that it was found. Now with advanced equipment, people make those dives like a dip in the pool, but back then with the depth and a very heavy current? No way! Some crazy vacationing Aussie diver only found it 'cause he went in blind that day."

"Blind? Like he couldn't see?" I asked, and Zach burst into laughter.

After a good belly laugh, he continued: "Not Stevie Wonder blind, blind as in not looking at charts beforehand. He just kept going deeper and deeper. He actually almost didn't survive that dive especially when he wandered onto the cruiser. Shit, finding something like that would take anyone's breath away."

"Wow. My God. And you're saying they found Drake's boat in the same location."

"Yep. Just about. But no Drake. I wouldn't be surprised if he was down at the bottom of the sea with Devlin."

"Weren't you friends with Drake?"

"As best you can be with a guy like him. The man had a lot of enemies. I

350

heard the day he went missing he actually had two run-ins: one with Jeremy Bryden and one with Jared Lareby. But that's actually a slow day for him as far as getting into scuffles. That's why it makes me wonder. He may've pissed off the wrong person this time... Now eat your omelet before it gets cold." Zach got up from the table leaving me with an empty stomach to fill and a full head to empty.

CHAPTER 38
AUGUST 4, 2004

WEDNESDAY

ECHO

Echo was dressed and on schedule for her meeting, but then she walked past her computer.

She looked at her watch: 10:15 a.m.

11:15 p.m. in Tokyo.

The time conversion was now second nature.

He's probably still up and getting ready for tomorrow.

She knew she should keep going, but that computer held a power over her that she couldn't resist. She stopped in her tracks and contemplated sitting down. After Drake's "probable" drowning she also needed to feel something good. Her computer could do that.

Lately, when she logged on, it brought her back to those times of trading wine, tentative pecks, and snuggling under a blanket. They'd watch *Harold and Maude* (a rite of passage for any eccentric high schooler) holding one another while trapped in constrictive clothing.

But after Cat Stevens sang away the credits, it all changed. Their glasses empty. Their kisses full. Their clothes off.

She thought of how his long, deep kisses turned into nibbles and licks, wandering from her full lips, down her neck, and over her rigid nipples, igniting a steady flame that coursed through her as his lips and tongue continued on, exploring every inch of her.

She'd lie on the couch, her eyes locked on him, watching that truly beautiful, gentle, teasing tongue continue on its journey. Finally, it would stop, fluttering inches from where she wanted it to be, where she needed it to be, sending spasms of longing up her spine.

But he never rushed. His tongue whispered its want above, his hot breath teasing, coaxing her desire almost to the point of agony. And just when she couldn't bear her own wanting, that's when he'd slip it in, that steady flame exploding into a bonfire of ecstasy.

He'd continue. Over and over. Hands clasped until she begged for the rest of him. And then, only then, he'd give her what she truly needed.

What a romantic lover, always pleasuring me first.

"Yep. I'll just log on and, if he's around, just say hi," she laughed, fanning her face, aware this could be good trouble. Their instant messaging from over 6,500 miles away had recently led to her pouring glasses of wine at 10 in the morning followed by her underwear strewn under her desk.

God, I can't wait till October when he's back. I need to feel the real thing again.

Echo logged on but could see that Tobias was not online.

"Damn, I got all worked up for nothing." She decided that if she was going to be late for the meeting with J.T. and Sunshine, she should at least check the message boards.

That way she'd have something to tell J.T. — even if it was nothing, which had previously always been the case.

Echo had written posts on several music message boards hoping that someone might know the real identity of Johnny the Bull. She had done the same thing over the years with hippie message boards hoping someone could tell her what Rainbow's — her biological father's — real name was.

She never had any luck with that line of inquiry and wasn't too confident that she'd have any luck with this current investigation. But the hope was either to rule out the thought that Johnny the Bull was The Fiddler or to confirm that it was just a coincidence that some guy no one knew was playing a fiddle around the same time.

After ten minutes of checking the message boards and her email, she decided it was time to go.

An instant message icon then popped up.

It was Tobias:

"Hey baby, what's up?"

She could feel the smile burn her face as she typed:

"Nothing, I was just thinking about when we used to watch *Harold and Maude*."

"Oh God, I remember once we both had massive hangovers at school from all that Pinot from the night before, but it was worth it!"

"God, yes!"

Echo stopped when a new instant message appeared from someone else on the screen.

"Damn, Kathy, not now," she said, thinking it was probably her best friend but then realized the screen name was unfamiliar.

She clicked on it.

"Why do you want to know Johnny the Bull's real name?"

Echo stared at the flashing cursor for a long minute and typed.

"How did you get my instant message account?"

"You left your email address on the message board and it's the same as your instant message account."

"Duh! Of course, it is," she scolded her stupidity while glancing over at Tobias's instant message chat that now had three question marks in a row. She wrote back quickly to him that she had to go, and he sent a smiley face before logging out.

She returned her focus to the other instant message. But then another one popped up from the mystery messenger.

"Are you still there?"

"Yes. Sorry. My bad."

Echo waited.

"Can you answer my question? Why do you want to know Johnny the Bull's real name?"

A swirl of thoughts went through Echo's mind.

Do I answer it straight up?

Finally, she typed back:

"I'd rather not answer that online. Why do you want to know anyway? After all, I was the one who asked the question on the message board, not you."

The screen was blank for a long time. She rubbed her brow wondering if her evasive behavior had backfired, but then a new message appeared.

"My brother has been missing since 1975 and I think Johnny the Bull may be him. Please tell me what you know. I'm begging you!"

CHAPTER 39
AUGUST 4, 2004

WEDNESDAY

J.T.

We sat around a table on my deck. Anna Walsh sipped lemonade from her glass and gazed out at the ocean before continuing on about her life as Anna Devlin. For the past hour, I had said nothing. I just listened while my digital recorder captured her emotional recollections of a time gone by; one that she yearned for but was also still haunted by.

At first, I escaped with her to the past, enjoying her account of meeting Michael Devlin and their romantic dates. They would be perfect stories to incorporate into the book to build that emotional connection with the reader. But as those romantic stories piled up, I actually found myself getting jealous of their courtship.

Would I ever find the one?

My real agitation was that I felt I *had* found the one.

I loved her smile, her laugh, her killer body, her sarcasm, her bad singing voice, her devotion to David.

I loved everything about Echo Landers. And it was getting beyond frustrating. As much as I tried to tell myself to stop thinking about her, she was constantly on my mind. But it was clear I wasn't on hers. And the prime example was today.

She was more than an hour late, and she still hadn't showed. It was pissing me off and Anna read it on my face.

"I'm sorry if I'm boring you," she said.

"Oh, no, I'm sorry, Sunshine. You're not boring me at all. It's just Echo. She's late."

"This is a book you're working on? Not an article?" Anna asked.

"Why are you asking me that? You know all of this is for a book... Hopefully."

"Then, J.T, if she can't take my picture today, she can do it another time. It's not like I'm going anywhere."

"Yeah, I suppose you're right." Kicking off my Tevas, I looked down at my list of questions.

"I think you're mad she's not here for other reasons. Am I right?" Her tone was of playful insinuations that opened the door for me to talk.

I avoided chomping on the hook by scanning my notebook.

"Moving on. Did Michael have any run-ins with any of the local kids?"

"Why would you ask that?"

I had learned after talking with Davis that I'd no longer share my theories with people I questioned, even if it was someone I trusted. So I lied to her.

"Professor Kazerian taught me that, when you work on a book like this one, you ask a million questions just for the simple fact that you've asked them. You can then cross them off the list or maybe they'll spark a memory."

"Oh. Well... okay. It's just that I want Michael to be portrayed as the good man he was."

"Right now, I would say that's not a problem, but I can't control where the story takes me."

"True. But..."

"Think about it. If I'm looking for the truth and you believe in Michael, then you shouldn't have any concern."

"Yes. Well then, I know one place it will take you. It will take you to the fact many people loved him, and all the kids looked up to him. They trusted Michael. Sure, he caught a couple now and then skipping school or maybe a shoplifting incident here or there, but he never arrested any kids for anything major. He'd put them on the right path every time."

"Okay, so no major arrests or run-ins with the kids." I made a note and was about to hit her with my next question.

"Wait... Well, there was one thing he told me about but..."

"But what?" I asked.

"It's nothing, 'cause it all turned out alright in the end."

"What was it?"

"Michael caught one of the boys just as he was about to commit arson to one of the Detective's boats."

"Wow, well, that is something big!"

"When I put it that way, yes. But Michael caught him in time, and then Detective Prichard dropped the charges and all was forgiven."

"Prichard!"

"You know of him?" she asked.

"Yes, as I mentioned, I've been doing a lot of research. What was your impression of Prichard?"

"Very by the book. I think he wasn't a fan of Michael. Maybe 'cause of Michael's father and all."

"Okay, so who was the kid?" I asked.

"Murray Philbrick."

"Murray?!"

"Yeah, I know he doesn't seem the type."

"No, he seems like a wiseass who may sell you a lemon but not an arsonist."

"Remember, J.T., he was stopped before he lit the match so technically, he wasn't an arsonist."

"Semantics. So, why the hell do you think he wanted to torch Prichard's boat?"

"Who knows? I know people have asked him over the years but, to this day, Murray will never say why. I know he didn't have the best upbringing, but I really don't know why he wanted to do that." Anna took another sip from her glass.

I wrote in my notebook: Interview Murray Philbrick and call Prichard. I moved on to my next question.

"So, other than the obvious person, Larry Tadmor, did Michael have any enemies in town?"

"You're forgetting Pop Tucker," she reminded.

"Oh, of course. Another given. Other than those two, was there anyone he either didn't like or didn't get along with."

"Yes. Paul Harrison."

"Well, I'm in that club, too."

"Michael despised him, and when Fishy first went missing, Paul Harrison was actually Michael's number one suspect."

I tried to restrain myself, but my juices were flowing.

"Why did he think Harrison would do anything to Fishy?"

"One night while Michael was on duty, he drove by the bike shop and saw the light on in the back. He checked the door and found it unlocked, so he went in. He heard a group of boys talking excitedly so he listened and figured out that they were trading comic books. No big deal. But then he heard Harrison's voice."

"Why would he be hanging out with a group of boys?"

"That's what Michael was wondering. At first, it sounded like Harrison was in charge of their comic book club, so Michael was going to leave undetected. But then Harrison changed the subject and that's what sent Michael into a rage."

"Why?"

"Harrison was showing the boys a comic strip from a *Playboy* of a woman giving a blowjob."

"My God! That's crazy. Jesus, how old were the kids?"

"I don't really know. I know they were young. Michael only told me one boy's name. He said he should keep an extra eye on him because he was so young and naïve. He was legitimately concerned about him."

"Who was the boy?"

"Fishy Bryden."

"Oh my God!"

"Yep. I know. Fishy was around ten or eleven. The whole thing just confused him. Sex is a difficult thing to wrap your mind around at that age."

"So, Harrison, that sick piece of —" I caught the swear before spitting it, "I feel like going after him myself right now. You don't mess with innocence like that."

"That's how Michael felt. What's a grown man doing showing little boys *Playboy* magazines unless he wants something in return? So, Michael stormed in there and —" Anna stopped, laughed for a minute, "Well, let's just say that Harrison never went around any of those boys ever again."

How does that convince me? There's no way we know that for sure!

359

"I'm so confused. How does a guy who hangs out with kids, shows them *Playboys*, was even with the murder victim, get completely cleared? Not to mention why wasn't he seriously looked at in your husband's death?"

"Larry Tadmor killed Michael." Anna said it like she was convincing herself.

"Yes, Tadmor probably did, but man, Harrison still should've been questioned so the cops could dot their I's and cross their T's."

"As I just said, he was looked at both times, and both times he had solid alibis."

"What were they?"

"He was away."

"Where?"

"I really don't know. I know it was overseas somewhere. He takes a lot of vacations."

The screen door suddenly flew open, and Echo came barreling through.

"I'm sorry I'm late. It's just that —" she was catching her breath.

"Just what?" Anna and I asked in unison.

"That…" she took a deep breath, "I think I just found out who The Fiddler was."

"Was?" I repeated.

"Yes, was." Echo nodded her head a hundred times.

CHAPTER 40

AUGUST 4, 2004

NORTH END, BOSTON

WEDNESDAY

J.T.

I t was probably not a good thing when I called Davis and asked if it was cool for me to get Vicki to cover my shift he gruffly replied, "I'll bartend tonight."

Click.

It was clear he was still pissed off about my questions from the previous night.

At least I don't have to track down Vicki.

Oh well, even if I lost my bartending gig, it would be small potatoes compared to what I was now working on. I had serious info that had to be analyzed by a professional, and fast, before Hauser or someone else stumbled onto it. There was no way in hell I was going to trust Detective Gordon.

I was lost. Part of me wished I could call my old man and ask his advice. But I had to stick to my guns. He was out of my life. That was that. My hands were wiped clean.

But I needed to talk to someone who wielded some power.

I spent the middle of the day coming to grips with the fact that I did know one person who had plenty of power. Unfortunately, we pretty much hated one another. I knew he wouldn't take my calls, but I also knew that if I took a solo trip to the city and met him face to face, he'd at least listen. He owed me that.

Well, that's what I was hoping when I walked into the back room of DeLuca's Ristorante.

Much like "Anthony" in the old Prince spaghetti commercials, every Wednesday night was pasta night for FBI Special Agent Salvatore DeLuca at his family's place.

I walked past the faded black and white family tree pictures that lined the wall and continued on to the back table by the kitchen door. There he was in his gray custom-tailored suit, sitting alone, spinning linguine around his fork in one hand and sipping a glass of red in the other.

I hadn't seen DeLuca in about six years but noted that he still had jet-black hair. It was obvious he was keeping Just for Men in business, but not for long. The late forties were winning the hairline battle. He resembled a younger version of LA Lakers' legendary coach Pat Riley all the way down to the slicked back look that I figured was designed to cover-up his hair follicle issues.

DeLuca was tall and strong (and from personal experience) had a powerful right hook. From first glance, it seemed all of that was still intact. He was in surprisingly good shape for someone who still ate pasta by the boatloads and guzzled wine by the goblets. His fork was wandering toward some calamari when he felt my presence. He stopped and glanced up.

"I didn't bring my boxing gloves," he paused, ate his linguine, sipped his wine, and continued, "of course, I didn't bring them that night you jumped me either."

"I hardly *jumped* you."

"Beating up someone who is under the influence might as well be jumping them."

"I was drunk, too."

"Yes, but you're Irish. That's how your kind functions." He sipped again.

I bit my lip and lowered my eyes at the chair across from him.

"Sure. Go ahead. Sit. Why not." He made a grandiose welcome gesture with his left hand.

DeLuca went back to eating and neither one of us spoke for a couple of minutes. I knew why he wasn't talking. He had nothing to say to me. As for me, I was trying to figure out how to begin. I decided I had to shove the elephant out of the restaurant.

"This isn't about Frannie."

I was referring to my best friend Frannie Fitzgerald — the reason we hated one another. Frannie, who had kicked heroin, had met DeLuca after a Narcotics Anonymous meeting in a church basement in Southie ten years before. Frannie was always naïve, and DeLuca befriended him for that simple reason — to use him. No longer did Frannie go to meetings for support. He had been brainwashed to gather "intel" about the drug scene in Southie. My best friend had become a snitch, and I never knew it.

He had been doing it for a few years before he finally broke down and told me one night. I couldn't believe it, and I let him have it.

Yeah, in his mind he was helping the community. I get it "drugs are bad" and "hugs not drugs" and all that other slogan bullshit he bought into, but where I grew up, being a rat is the worst thing you can be.

So, the night Frannie told me, I went off on him. It was so bad that to this day I think I may've been the reason he picked up that needle two days later. That's what I believe on nights when I want to be honest with myself.

But that's not how I had survived the guilt. I did that by believing that the guy sitting across from me was the real reason my buddy was dead. And I know DeLuca had survived the same way. We both admitted those feelings with our fists six years before.

"I know it's not about Frannie," he finally said.

"How do you know that?" I asked.

"I work for the FBI. I keep a pretty good eye on people who, shall I say, I've had conflicts with. It's no secret what you're now doing for a living. I find it ironic that you've become a reporter."

"Why's that?" I asked.

"Well, you judged Frannie for trying to expose the truth and now you're pretty much doing the same thing."

I wanted to cave in his face at that point, but I knew that I needed to hold my O'Rourke temper in check, and also that the asshole was also right.

"Look," I took a deep breath, "If you're looking for an apology for kicking your ass that night, you're not going to get it."

"I think I got a few good shots in, too." He poured himself another glass of wine.

I pushed on. "We'll never agree on whose fault it was that he began using again. I've come to accept that. What I do remember is Frannie told me that, as much as it was immoral to infiltrate N.A. meetings, he felt you were a good man, and you were out to bring people to justice."

"Jesus Christ, O'Rourke, should I get up and turn around, so you can psychically kiss my ass, too." DeLuca laughed. He was enjoying my pandering.

"You're right. I hate you and I'll always hate you. So, now that that's out of the way, I have some major information on the time capsule case. I have no idea if I can trust you, but I don't have much of a choice. I need your help."

DeLuca put his glass down and played with his left cufflink for a minute.

"Why not ask your old man for help? He knows everyone."

"You know the answer to that. He's back on it. From what I hear he is basically homeless."

"Oh, yes, I may've heard something."

"Of course, you have. So, are you going to keep being a dick or do you want to work with me on this?"

"I don't work *with* reporters on anything."

"Too bad," I rose to leave, "This would be one hell of a case for you to break, and I think you could with what I have."

"Wait. Wait. Sit. Sit."

I sat.

"What's the deal?" he asked.

"I want an exclusive on everything you find out. I know someone like you would rather run to the TV lights that Vic Hauser shines, but I'll be the one breaking any stories that result from my info."

"Yeah, okay but don't you write for a paper that comes out once a week?"

"Twice a week."

"Once. Twice. Whatever. My point is I can't make a promise to keep things under the lid for that long."

"I understand you can't, but you can promise me that you'll try."

"Fair enough."

"Shake on it." I stuck out my hand.

"Really?"

"Really."

We shook.

"And DeLuca, if I find out that you gave stories away, I'll crucify you in the book I'm writing, which, I might add, I already have an agent shopping," I lied.

"A book? You really must have something big. So, what is it?"

"I know who The Fiddler is."

DeLuca looked at me and then clapped his hands and waved over the waiter.

"Armand, another bottle and a glass for this gentleman," he stopped and looked at me, "You hungry?"

I nodded.

"And whatever he wants, put on my tab." DeLuca said to Armand.

"But Sal, you don't have a tab."

"Exactly." DeLuca laughed.

I ordered a rack of lamb and for the next ten minutes, I told DeLuca what Echo had found out.

Juan Padilla, a classically trained violinist, took off from his home in Burbank, California, in the summer of 1975 to travel cross-county — to the great displeasure of his parents. His father owned a pool-cleaning business and put much of his earnings toward Juan's training, but Juan didn't want to play in orchestras. He wanted to see the world. So he left a note, and in the dead of night, took off. His sister Marta told Echo it had crushed her father, and they never heard from Juan again. Marta also said a few years back she found a notebook of Juan's with random notes and, scribbled in it: "Johnny the Bull." She had no idea what it meant but when she saw it flashing on the message board before her eyes, she literally got sick to her stomach. She knew it had to be her brother.

When I finished telling DeLuca, he said, "Well, I'll look into it. Is that all you've got?"

"Is that all I got? I just gave you the name of the victim whose eyes are in that jar."

"Well, you may've given me the name. This 'Marta' could easily be playing with your photographer friend. I've seen that happen a million times before. I'll look into it. Do you have anything else?"

I knew he was right. What if it was some big hoax? I felt like I was under pressure to produce something else.

"You probably heard about the guy who went missing on his boat?"

"Yeah, he owned a canteen or something."

"Yep."

"What about him?"

"While doing research for my book I learned that back in 1977 an officer from the Sandy Point Police Department and a local ex-con went missing."

"Yeah, Devlin was the cop. I know that case well 'cause it was big news when they found his cruiser in '86 or '87."

"'89 actually. Well, that canteen guy Drake Underhill's boat was found drifting very close to the spot where Devlin's cruiser was found."

"Really?" he perked up.

"Yeah, it's a place the locals call Larry's Ledge after the ex-con Larry Tadmor who many believe is at the bottom of the ocean. You see, the ocean floor drops about 180 feet or so there. I guess it's not a very easy place to go scuba diving because of the depth and current. I just find it quite a coincidence that in all of the Atlantic Ocean, the boat would be found there."

I could tell this information had DeLuca thinking.

"Okay, I'll look into that, too. Anything else?"

"Yeah, could you do a background check on someone for me?"

"I can't just do random background checks. Does it relate to the time capsule case?"

"I don't know what the hell it relates to. I guess it's just a gnawing feeling I have in my gut. Could you just check out a name for me?"

DeLuca thought for a minute.

Finally: "Alright, what's the name?"

"Paul Harrison," I said and then took a sip of wine.

CHAPTER 41
AUGUST 6, 2004

FRIDAY

NERO

Nero smiled into the bathroom mirror while he reflected on the summer. There was still a month left, but he had already had a banner season highlighted by his most recent killing. After slipping on Drake's Jesus necklace and tucking it under his T-shirt he chuckled.

"Sorry, fat boy. You'll never see God."

His laughter stuttered and stopped when he thought of the mistake he had made when he dumped the body.

The boat.

He had every intention of sinking it and scuba diving back to shore. Unfortunately, he had run out of time. The sun was rising when he got to Larry's Ledge, and a fishing trawler was headed straight toward him.

So, Nero dumped the body and then scuba dived to shore, hoping no one would notice a major clue not in the boat that might make officials think foul play.

So far so good.

It had been several days, and the town gossips had concluded that Drake was probably drunk and fell out of his boat = RIP Drake Underhill.

But as he buttoned up his shirt, Nero realized that was no reason to be so cavalier. He had succeeded in the past by careful planning, attention to detail, and a little luck, but this summer had taught him that he couldn't control everything. And as he aged, it seemed he needed more luck than he used to. It was a hard pill to swallow, so he shifted his thoughts to think about his new project.

Think about the next one.

And that next one was Randy "Runaway Train" Reynolds. Reynolds had been voted into the Sandy Point High School Athletic Hall of Fame. He was to be given a plaque during halftime of the annual Thanksgiving Game.

After reading the story back in May, Nero first had images of Randy with Nero's mother. But then other images appeared — Randy telling his friends about fucking a "colored girl" on the one-yard line so he could score a "sex touchdown" and how Randy expected to get some "Korean pussy" when he shipped off to Nam.

The images turned over in his mind, and Nero had gone straight to his computer and Googled Randy Reynolds. He discovered that the former football star never ended up going to Nam, but instead took a desk job for the Air Force in Germany. He also found out that Reynolds was a rich real estate broker down in Florida and was going through his third divorce.

That's when the images formed into the idea.

Nero would find Randy his "Korean pussy." He'd get an Asian hooker, probably in New York, and pay her to come to Cape Cod. That wouldn't be hard.

Have money. Whores will travel.

The guise to the slut would be that a bunch of Randy's rich buddies had pitched in to play a prank on him. Her job would be to seduce Randy, who most likely would be telling stories while drinking at The Angry Fisherman the night before the game. She'd lure him from the bar and over to the football field. That wouldn't be hard. Nero could envision Randy in the men's room popping a little blue pill before following the gook pussy out of the bar. The "prank" would end when she'd get him naked and then the rich friends would come out and surprise him.

"You won't even have to have sex with him. It will just be a big surprise. A big joke." Nero was talking to the imaginary hooker in the mirror.

In reality, the Asian hooker and Randy would both be getting the biggest surprises of their lives — death.

"Yes, this will be my fall project," Nero said to himself and headed outside.

That's strange.

He noticed the beat-up red Nissan speed up and then screech to a stop in front of his neighbor's driveway. The driver threw something out the window and then continued on.

It wasn't what the driver threw out the window that was strange. It was the time of day he was doing it.

Nero double-checked his watch: 8:06 a.m.

The Nissan usually didn't come by until around 3 p.m.

It makes no sense.

Nero's neighbor was at work, so he walked across the street to the driveway and picked up the copy of the *Sandy Point Standard Times.*

"Special Edition?" he mouthed in confusion.

Then he glanced down at two columns, lined up side by side, both with eye-popping headlines.

On the left: Could Traveling Musician Be "The Fiddler"?

On the right: State Police Divers Called In To Search for Missing Boater

"What the fuck! How the fuck! Who the fuck!" Nero yelled and then realized he was outside in the street for anyone to witness. He looked around quickly and satisfied himself that no one heard him.

He grunted like a bull at the gate while his eyes raced through the print.

When he finished reading, his "fall project" with Randy "Runaway Train" Reynolds was long gone from his mind. There was only one name there now.

It was smack in the middle of Nero's thoughts. It was the name that was also the byline for both stories — J.T. O'Rourke.

He is getting too close. Pretty soon he won't be seeing God.

CHAPTER 42
AUGUST 6, 2004

FRIDAY

J.T.

I had been on the State Police Underwater Recovery Team's boat since 5 a.m. and it was now a little after nine. I was tempted to text Echo and ask how The Point was reacting to the special edition, but I had made a deal with DeLuca: "No calls or text messages while you are on the boat."

It was a fair deal, considering he pulled major strings to get me aboard. A part of me couldn't believe I was allowed to witness URT's search for Drake Underhill, and I wasn't the only one who felt that way.

Detective Gordon's 5 a.m. "F this," "F that," "F him" tirade to DeLuca about me had finally transitioned to just glares and disapproving head shakes from his round orange melon.

I glanced over, and Gordon was literally sneering at me, Snidely Whiplash style, while he and DeLuca talked with one of the divers who had just come back on board.

As far as cartoon characters went, he looked more like one of the Hungry Hippos, and I almost laughed out loud at the thought, but I held it, remembering my analogy didn't work. The Hippos were a game not a show. A quick memory of playing that game with my sisters appeared. I brushed it aside.

Anyway, the bastard should've been thanking me. If it weren't for me, he wouldn't be lead detective hanging out with *real* cops doing *real* investigating.

It all began the morning after my rack of lamb with DeLuca. The special agent had taken a dawn drive to the Cape and looked over Underhill's boat.

I was at the paper and was trying to get a hold of Detective Prichard and Murray Philbrick. Nothing but ringing.

But that all took a back seat when I received DeLuca's call. He told me it took him all of a minute to conclude that something wasn't right about Drake's "apparent" drowning, but he kept quiet and let Gordon describe what he thought had happened. It was the same theory that everyone else in town had been spreading: Drake got drunk and fell out of his boat.

When Gordon was done theorizing, everything turned with one question from DeLuca.

"If he just simply fell out of his boat and everything else is intact then why the hell is the boat anchor missing?"

"What do you mean, missing?" Gordon searched for a couple of minutes before giving in.

DeLuca then "suggested" the URT be brought in to "assist" in the search for remains and/or evidence.

Pretty remarkable. But what was even more surprising was that DeLuca:

A. kept his word and called me with the information;

B. let me run with the story that the state police divers were going to help local law enforcement; and

C. got me on the boat.

The last one was a downright miracle, and I was skeptical about his motives.

"Look, O'Rourke," he had said, "There are rules. I get first look at any story that goes in your paper."

"I don't know about that. That goes against all ethics of reporting."

"Not exactly. If you want a story to unfold for you just like a cop, there are things you have to keep close to your vest. You gotta think of the big picture. I will tell you those things that you should save for the big picture. You see, many reporters hold back on giving info, so they can help the police. They also do it, so they can tell more of the story down the line. I'm sure Hauser knows more info but he's picking and choosing when..." His voice trailed off.

Hauser's name made me visibly cringe.

"Yeah, I know all of that, but I'm still not sure if I want to play ball with you, DeLuca."

"You don't get it. I'm the one letting you on the field. But if you don't want to, no worries, I'll ask Vic Hauser to join me. To get an exclusive, he'll play by my rules in a heartbeat. And sure, we might be out there all day and not find even a goddamn minnow of evidence, but Hauser doing a live remote from URT's boat? Wow, that will show he's the guy getting all the stories. You see, it's all about perception."

I didn't have much of a leg to stand on, so I agreed.

"Alright. I'm in. But I have to ask you why: allow press on the boat? I don't get it?"

"It came from up top that we need some good PR. You know, staties helping out the locals. Sandy Point is a total mess this summer with the missing kid, the eyeballs in the time capsule, and now this. The top brass actually wanted me to use Hauser and his TV camera, but I pushed for you. You see, I keep my word, O'Rourke. Don't forget that."

I didn't buy his B.S. for a second but knew if I pressed for the real reason, he might change his mind.

I moved my questioning to The Fiddler case, and he went on record as "a source at the Massachusetts State Police" that thinks The Fiddler "may" be Juan Padilla and they are doing a rush on DNA tests.

I finished with, "Were you able to find out anything on Paul Harrison?"

DeLuca gave a quick, "Clean as a whistle. Okay, O'Rourke, stay off the Guinness, so you can be ready to go. Tomorrow. 5 a.m. Sharp."

Click.

I had looked at my cell phone clock: 11:09 a.m. It was shortly after that point that the most remarkable thing of all occurred.

I went into Crocker's office to try and convince him to run a special edition for the following morning. I laid out both stories and the importance of us breaking them, etc. etc.

I had expected him to kick and scream, but after I made all my arguments and finally ran out of breath, he just replied, "Okay. We don't tell anyone what your stories are before we go to press. We keep this thing airtight. Our biggest obstacle is our distribution team. I'll put Norman on that. Shit, he's wanted to do that online thing. This will show him how the old school paper business works. You happy?"

"Ah, yes."

"Good. This is going to be a lot of work, but we can make it happen. It's going to be a long night." Crocker symbolically rolled up his sleeves.

And it was a long night. And now it was a long morning. But while I sat on the boat feeling tired and a little seasick, I did have the satisfaction of knowing that everyone back on shore was probably talking about my stories, especially the Juan Padilla one. Echo and I had talked about the strangeness of hoping we were right, and Padilla was in fact The Fiddler. We both wanted closure for his sister, Marta, but selfishly didn't want to be wrong since it could be a career killer, especially for me since it was my name on the byline.

But in our meeting, Crocker felt I had enough circumstantial evidence to run with the story and when he showed me the mockup of the front page he said, "Go get me another one today."

He seemed like a changed man. I didn't know why until I spotted him standing very close to Sunshine, talking and laughing by the water cooler (which had no water). It was clear her powers of persuasion were working on him, but it had also been clear to me that he hadn't revealed that the state police later that day would be diving in the spot where many believed her husband had been murdered.

Getting back in the moment, I watched two more divers strap on their yellow tanks before entering the ocean.

I flipped open my pad and jotted down: *A total of six URT divers searched the area known as Larry's Ledge.*

Then my cell phone rang. I had the volume on low but not low enough.

"Don't answer that." DeLuca hollered over.

"I won't. I'm going to turn it off." I said but then glanced down at the name: Erin.

What did my sister want?

Well, she'd have to wait. I turned the ringer off but a second later a text message appeared. I looked over at DeLuca and he and Gordon were both bent over talking to one of the divers.

Curiosity got the best of me, so I clicked on the message: Call me ASAP. It's urgent.

"Special Agent DeLuca," I shouted over, but he kept his back to me and kept talking to the diver.

"DeLuca!"

"What?" he snapped his head.

"That was my sister and she just texted me that she needs to talk to me and it's urgent."

DeLuca gestured his permission to phone her. I found Erin's name in my contacts, clicked on it, and walked to the back of the boat.

"J.T." She answered out of breath.

"Hey E, this better be good I'm…"

"It's Dad. He was at Gilligan's Pub and…"

"What else is new? I really don't have time for…"

"Can you let me finish?" she yelled.

"Okay, go on."

"He was rushed to the hospital. The doctor says it's bladder cancer."

"Oh… Is it bad?" It was all I could think to say.

"Yep. Could be a few weeks or a few months. He's asking to see you."

"I don't know if I want to do that."

"Look, I understand. I cut him out of my life, too. But he's dying. And he said he needs to tell you something."

"Well… Oh my God!" I blurted as I turned around and couldn't believe what I was witnessing. I didn't have the ability to grasp what my sister was telling me.

"I know it's bad…"

"Not that. I mean. Yes, of course. Holy shit! I'm sorry E. I'm covering a story, and something just happened. I'll call you later." I clicked the phone off.

I hustled over to Gordon and DeLuca who were watching all six divers hoisting what appeared to be the yellow, bloated remains of Drake Underhill onto the deck. He landed face first with a thump followed by the clank of the chains and anchor that was somehow attached to his right hand.

DeLuca yelled, "Help me turn him over."

Gordon and I struggled but eventually rolled the corpse over. Everyone was quiet for a moment, probably trying to find the right words.

Drake's dead eyes had been speared and there were multiple lacerations on his face and head area.

"Probably an ax." DeLuca was the first one to speak.

"Check that out." I pointed to the pair of handcuffs that attached Drake to the anchor.

"I know those." Gordon said and squatted down to take a closer look at the cuffs.

"What do you mean?" DeLuca asked.

"S.P.P. #9," he looked up, shaking his head, "I can't believe it."

"What?" One of the divers asked for all of us.

"My father told me that when he was on the force, they kept losing handcuffs so to make people accountable they had them engraved to match the officers squad car. My ol' man was #4 so his cuffs read S.P.P. #4. So you'll never guess who #9 was."

We didn't have to guess. We all knew. Officer Michael Devlin. And we also knew something else. His killer was not only still alive, but he was still at it.

CHAPTER 43
AUGUST 10, 2004

TUESDAY

J.T.

Echo called the previous night and asked if I would escort her to Drake Underhill's funeral. Trying not to sound excited, I solemnly agreed, and now we were walking down the aisle of Sandy Point First Methodist Church.

I ushered her to a pew. She slipped in before me.

I'm probably going to hell, I thought, after sneaking a peek at the way her black dress hugged her backside as she sat. But then I realized I wasn't the only one checking her out. All eyes were on her, and I knew why.

Echo was part of Drake's history. How much? I still didn't know, but the mascara running down her face told me that the biggest asshole in Sandy Point meant something to her. I didn't get it, but it wasn't my place to get it. I was there for support.

Like a rookie being called up to the majors, I was just happy to be there. And it was for having that kind of feeling at a funeral is why I probably deserved to go to hell.

But I was also destined to go there for a couple of other reasons. I got in a fight with my sisters via emails, text messages, and phone calls, after informing them that I wasn't ready to visit my old man in the hospital.

"Not *ready*?" my oldest sister, Shannon, shouted through the phone, "Well, you better get *ready* because he's ready to die!"

The emotional door flew open for me to unleash my anger for leaving me to care for my old man. After trying to one up one another with creative uses of the f-word we moved on and tried to beat one another in the hang up game.

Shannon won.

The other reason I was going to hell was that I was feeling really good inside. Not about my ailing father. I had no feeling about him, and that alone should've scared me. It didn't. I just put thoughts of him away. As Mark Twain, or was it Stuart Smalley, once said, "Denial ain't just a river in Egypt."

No, I was gloating that my exclusive phone interview with Marta Padilla, sister of Juan "The Fiddler" Padilla, was coming out in today's paper. And beside that article, there would also be my account of how the State Police Underwater Recovery Team retrieved the remains of Drake Underhill and that investigators were looking into it as a "possible homicide."

That would send the town into another frenzy. Vic Hauser, Geraldo, *48 Hours*, *Dateline*, and the rest of them would be on my jock. It would be worse if they knew the full details.

I had promised DeLuca and Chief Harding that I'd keep the handcuffs, anchor, and the corpses' condition a secret until the following Tuesday's edition in order to give my new best friend, Detective Gordon, a head start.

There was no way he'd talk to anyone, considering the flak he caught from the Chief after the last story he leaked. I wondered how much longer Gordon would be heading the investigation, considering DeLuca was staying at a bed and breakfast on the outskirts of town and was breathing down his neck.

God, this is exciting.

If I really analyzed the situation, the truth was I was feeling great because I was capitalizing on other people's pain and for that sole reason a trip to hell was indeed in my future.

I didn't really like myself right now, but I couldn't help it. I felt breaking the recent stories had legitimized me as a journalist.

I even got, "Amazing work," from Norman Chadwick and an even more satisfying growl of envy from Paul Harrison.

I tried to shut it all out and concentrate on the service performed by Reverend

Lewis Wilkinson. I had met the good minister back in June when I did a story on him running some fundraiser to benefit kids in Africa.

At the time, I remembered him as being filled with energy and optimism and looking much younger than his forty-plus years.

Maybe it was the circumstances of the day's event, but he seemed tired and drab and, frankly, a bit unkempt for a minister. His silver buzz cut was now a full head of long gray hair.

And his sermon was by the book. Downright unemotional. Boring. I found my eyelids growing heavy, so to stay awake, I let them wander to the other attendees. No one seemed to like Drake, yet everyone in town seemed to be there.

Two people sitting side by side piqued my interest: Dr. Lindsey Courtland and Murray Philbrick.

Is that a coincidence? Are they friends? Or is she Murray's therapist? Interesting…

Murray hadn't returned my calls. I had planned on tracking him down at his dealership, but the phone interview with Marta had taken precedence. Now I could corner him after the service… But when the ushers rolled the casket past us and out the building, Echo whispered urgently into my ear, "Let's get the hell out of here."

I followed her out and hopped into the passenger seat. But instead of joining the driving-to-the-cemetery line, Echo pulled out the back entrance.

"Aren't we?" I thumbed over my shoulder.

"No. I said my goodbyes. I need a drink. How about you?"

This was no time for me to tell her that I had cut down on my drinking and also I had a major story to chase.

"Yeah, sure."

"Have you ever been to Gunner's?"

"Gunner's?"

"Yeah, it's a clam shack over in Silver Shores. It's a good place to have a couple on a shitty day like this one."

I wasn't sure if she was talking about how she was feeling or the weather since it matched the mood: murky and dreary. In true movie funeral style, it had poured earlier, and now it was a gray blanket stretching across the sky that covered the Vineyard.

The village of Silver Shores was about ten minutes away from The Point along a winding beach road. As we finally roller-coastered up and around a hill and descended the other side, Echo pointed over to an old white building that looked to have been carved into the side of the hill. To the right of that, a couple of hundred yards away, was a lighthouse.

"What a spot!" I exclaimed, admiring the view of the Atlantic surrounding three sides of the restaurant.

"Yeah, you should see it when it's sunny. This was the place to be, but they just sold it to some billionaire who is going to tear it down and build condos. It's a damn shame."

"Interesting you feel that way considering your view on Samoset Woods, which reminds me: there's a selectmen's meeting coming up about that."

"Well, as you've probably guessed, my feeling about Samoset Woods is biased. It's a combination of loyalty to my stepfather and the fear that still haunts me from when I got lost in there as a kid. It's amazing how childhood stuff can make an imprint on you for life."

"I guess," I walked up the boardwalk that ran parallel to the building, hopped the steps, and then opened the door for her.

The hallway entrance was lined with black and white photos of Gunner's Seafood Grille when it once housed a post office, photographer's studio, barber shop, candy store, movie theater, etc.

Those pictures transitioned into colored ones featuring candid shots of customers and staff photos over the years. There were also photos of little league teams and clubs the restaurant sponsored. One that stood out was of the Gunner's Dive Club.

"It must be a prerequisite," I pointed at that picture, referring to an almost identical one at The A.F. that featured Davis and a dozen Pointers.

"I don't get you?" Echo asked.

"Oh, that's right," I laughed, "You wouldn't. Davis has a picture just like this hanging in the Men's Room."

"Really? That's a strange place for it."

"You're telling me. It's even worse since I know half the guys in it. I mean every time I take a piss I feel like they're watching me."

"Davis can be a weirdo." Echo said before continuing beyond the entrance.

Gunner's could fit about 300 people easy, but it was empty except for a half dozen rained-out golfers who were bellied up to the bar.

Echo glanced over at them, grunted, and motioned to a table that was a three-wood shot away and walked toward it.

"I need some privacy," she said over her shoulder.

I nodded, but seeing that the bartender was the only server on duty, I knew he was probably annoyed. I know I always hated when people sat that far away when I was working solo.

I pointed at the dark ocean outside our window. "I know it's a lousy day, but you'd think there'd be a few more people here, with this view and all."

"Well, the locals have been boycotting. They're furious they're going to lose this place. And you know how that works. You piss off the locals, they're going to tell the tourists it's a lousy place. And the result, dead zone."

"So, if you're upset, why aren't you boycotting?"

"Normally I would, but I knew if I came here, we'd have some privacy," she stopped and greeted the bartender who had sidled up to us, "Billy, how are you?"

The bartender pushed his white cowlick aside while delivering a toothy smile.

Of course, his name is Billy, I thought, as a flash of my ol' man came to me.

"Been a while, Ec. Give the good doctor a hug."

He's no dummy. Get that hug when you can old man.

She laughed, got up, hugged him, and he leaned in, lingering for a moment.

He sighed, "Okay now that I got my cheap thrill for the day. What can I get you?"

I liked the guy's candor. It told me a lot. Candor usually equaled good bartender.

"Well, first off, I want to introduce you to J.T. O'Rourke."

He put his hand out. "I could tell you're an Irishman. Billy Dwyer."

"They actually call him Dr. Dwyer, 'cause he's a doctor of mixology," Echo added as I shook his hand.

"Well, I respect a good bartender. Been doing it myself for years," I said.

"Oh, where?" Billy asked.

"Tilt the Jar in Kenmore Square and now I'm at The Angry Fisherman."

"That's ironic. I'm friends with Davis and I just got a call from him today. Since this place is closing down, he's been trying to recruit me. Said something about one of you guys leaving."

"Oh, really?" I said, knowing none of his help would ever leave unless Davis wanted them to leave. Considering he kept cutting my hours since my questions about The Fiddler, I didn't need Sherlock to help figure out that one. It was probably a blessing in disguise since I had more pressing matters these days, but his going behind my back did not make me happy. I tried to hide it but couldn't.

Billy caught my surprised tone and realized he had said too much. "Well, ah... ah. What can I get you two?"

"A glass of bourbon neat," Echo said.

"Bourbon?" Billy and I both said.

"Lately, I've been watching a lot of reruns of *Dallas*, and J.R. is always having a glass of bourbon after a long day of work."

"Yeah, well that's why the real J.R. had to buy a new kidney," Billy laughed. "J.T., what's your flavor?"

"Guinness."

"Sorry. That crew just kicked the last keg. No more till tomorrow."

"That sucks."

"I do have a porter from a brewery in Nantucket. I think you'd like it."

"Yeah, sounds good." I said, and Billy was off.

Echo and I made small talk about who she thought was leaving The A.F., her brother's upcoming birthday, the Red Sox, the weather, but it wasn't until she finished her second bourbon that she shifted to what we were both thinking about.

"Can you take the keys, J.T.? I need to share some serious shit, but I want to get hammered first. God, I love this shit." She wiggled her empty glass.

I was enjoying my second pint and could've easily kept it going too but knew someone had to stay sober. I grabbed the keys.

"With pleasure, since you're almost there," I laughed and pointed at the menu, "Want some food?"

"Nah, not yet. I want another drink."

"Okay, but you're at least switching to beer."

"Lame," she rolled her eyes but agreed.

Halfway through her Miller Lite she finally brought it up.

"Have you asked around town about Drake and me?"

"Ah, no. Why?" I said sipping my ginger ale.

"I didn't think so. I mean you're a reporter. You could've easily asked people what Drake and I were all about. That's why I like you. You respect me."

"Thanks, I guess. I consider you a friend. I figured if you wanted to tell me about you and him, you would."

Echo nodded, looked out the window, and turned to me, "I need to talk to someone, and I think I can trust you, J.T. You won't judge me?"

"I've had such a messed-up life, how could I judge anyone?" I smiled.

She laughed for a minute, took a sip, and was quiet. I didn't say a word. I just waited.

"I'll cut to the chase. My senior year in high school, I got pregnant."

"And Drake was the father?" I blurted.

"No. No way. But the whole town thinks that 'cause we've let them think that."

"I don't understand."

"You see, I wanted to protect the real father."

"The *real* father."

"Well, you know what I mean. The father of the baby."

"Yeah, but what do you mean by protect?"

"That's the part of the story I don't want to get into," Echo's eyes locked on mine, "So, anyway, Drake said he'd tell everyone that he was the father. That way my mother would accept everything, and I could get an abortion."

"Oh, so you didn't keep the baby?" I instantly thought: if *my* mother were alive, she'd be dousing Holy Water all over Echo. She must've been able to read my thoughts.

"Oh, man. That's right, I'm confessing to an Irish Catholic. You hate me now and I'm going to hell, huh?"

"Slow down. Slow down. I don't go by that old playbook anymore. I've seen it ruin too many lives. Echo, I told you, I'm not going to judge you. But can I ask you something?"

"Sure."

"Why would Drake step up to the plate and say he was the father? I don't get it."

"Well... I'm going to tell you something I've never told anyone... I knew Drake's secret."

I nodded for her to continue.

"I was at a party at Drake's house, and everyone had left or had passed out. Anyway, I went upstairs to use the bathroom. Well, I opened his bedroom door by mistake and, without going into specifics, I accidentally saw him "having relations," you might say, with my best friend."

"Kathy?"

"*Kathy?*" she repeated, confused, and then something clicked, "God, no. Oh, man…" She stopped and took a sip.

"What?" I asked.

"I wasn't going to tell you this part. Please promise me you'll keep this to yourself."

"If you haven't realized by now, you're the closest friend I have down here. I'm never going to jeopardize that," I assured her.

She seemed satisfied with my answer. "Drake was having relations with my other best friend. Jamal."

"What?" I almost fell over.

"Yep."

"But I thought you and Jamal were… or sometimes… you know."

"That's what Jamal wants people to think, and I'm fine with that. And how do you think he got that idea of using me as a cover for who he really is?"

"I have no idea."

"That night Drake begged me to keep what I saw a secret. I told him I would never tell anyone, and I didn't. But then I found out I was pregnant, and I wanted to protect the father."

Why did you want to protect the father?

The question was screaming in my head, but I couldn't go there, so I just let her continue.

"So, I went to Drake and did a terrible thing. I told him how I was pregnant and how we could help one another. By him telling everyone he was the father, I was able to protect umm… you know this person, and in return, no one would question his sexuality. So, as much as I didn't like Drake, I do owe him a debt of thanks."

"Wow, that's quite a story."

"Yep. So, what do you think?"

"That's a lot to process. One thing is I can't believe Jamal and Drake. I never would've thought. I really thought my gay-dar was better. Drake was also an asshole."

"Gay guys can be assholes, too," Echo laughed, "I think he was the type who used the false bravado as the ultimate cover. Anyway, what would you know about gay men?"

"My best friend was gay."

"Bullshit."

"I'm dead serious." I said.

"I don't believe you."

"You opened up to me. So, now it's my turn. But promise you won't judge me either?"

"Promise."

"When I was thirteen, I also did something terrible. One night about five of us jumped this kid named Frannie Fitzgerald. We beat the piss out of him 'cause we all knew he was gay. 'Course we didn't call him gay. We called him all the ignorant names we could think of as we punched and kicked him like a goddamn soccer ball."

Echo put her hand on her mouth.

"Yeah, I know. I'm not proud of this story. Anyway, during that beating, Frannie laughed through blood and pain, yelling at us, 'I'm not afraid of any of you. You're all afraid of yourselves. You only make me stronger.' His attitude freaked us out, so we stopped and left him there. I think we broke about five of his ribs and knocked out a tooth."

"My God." The hand hadn't moved.

"Yep. Fast-forward to two years later and I'm walking down the street and who walks up to me but Frannie. But now he's five inches taller and he's jacked. And he gives me the ol' *Good Will Hunting*, 'Do you remember me?' line. And I say, 'Yeah.' And he says, 'Let's do this then.' I get one punch in before he proceeds to beat the piss out of me. But instead of leaving me lying there, he helps me up and brings me to his house where his mother, who was a nurse, cleans me up while telling him she's proud of him for beating me up and teaching me a lesson."

Echo burst into laughter. "I'm sorry, J.T., but good for him. And good for her."

"Don't be sorry. That ass kicking was the best thing that has ever happened to me. You see, that night I asked him how he was able to punch like that. He said his mother made him take up boxing after we jumped him. And to quote Frannie, 'If I wasn't too much of a faggot' he'd bring me and introduce me to his coach."

"He really said 'faggot'?"

"Yep. Said he was allowed to use the word since he was gay. I never called him that word or any other derogatory word after that day. After a few years, I ended up only calling him my best friend. God, he was such a funny bastard."

"So, when is your funny gay friend coming to the Cape?" Echo's question lingered in the air for two reasons.

1.There's never a good segue to why Frannie got into drugs and then ending with him OD-ing.

2.Billy headed over and handed us two more drinks.

I looked down at the pint and then up at Billy. "I thought I told you I was on ginger ale."

"You did, but he demanded I bring you a beer. This round is on him." Billy thumbed over his shoulder, and I saw one of the golfers walking over. It was my father's former partner, Paddy Magill.

Ah, Jesus.

"Hey, Jameson Thomas, small world." Paddy said, plopping down in the chair next to us.

"Sure is," I said, anger rising in my chest, knowing as much as I tried, I'd never escape my hometown.

CHAPTER 44
AUGUST 14, 2004

SATURDAY

J.T.

I t was a strange feeling having a Saturday off from bartending, but I'd have to get used to it. As suspected, Davis had called me into The A.F. and told me that he needed someone he could count on for "every" shift.

The real reason was obvious. What I was reporting was not only giving The A.F. a bad name, but Davis too.

Sure, the cops were looking at him, but the cops were looking at everyone. Davis being a suspect was kind of comical. He was too open with his feelings to be sneaking around town killing people.

Before dropping the hammer on my bartending career, he admitted that he had almost puked when he read that Juan Padilla was probably "The Fiddler."

"At the station, Gordon gave me a picture Juan's sister sent, and I guess I was the first one in town to ID him. He definitely was the kid who played here that summer. I still can't believe it. Terrible shit what happened to that guy, but thanks to your reporting, I ended up spending the next three hours getting questioned by that dumbass Gordon."

"Sorry about that," I offered, lamely.

"Shit, Barney Miller knows more about being a cop than that shithead. Remember that show?"

"Yep," I said.

"And man, Gordon has some serious bad breath. Smelled like the floor mat behind the bar that I was always asking you to clean. Anyway, J.T., back to why I asked you here. I have to let you go. No hard feelings?"

I smiled, shook his hand, and said it had been an honor working for him.

Losing the bartending gig wasn't worth burning bridges.

But my mind was burning with thoughts that actually involved *fire*.

Pointers who had been reluctant to use the word "serial killer" now spouted it to newscasters during live remotes from outside diners to grocery stores. And they were all doing it without knowing the bombshell I was going to drop in Tuesday's edition.

There'd be a full spread on the evidence found at Drake's crime scene — including revealing Officer Devlin's handcuffs.

Of course, Chief Harding and Gordon tried talking me out of our deal.

"Just give us a few more days, pal," Gordon pleaded in one call.

Give you a few more days so you can leak it to Hauser, I thought.

"I know you're new to town, but holding off may help us catch this guy. Think of the citizens." The Chief appealed to my sense of community in another call.

I was thinking of them. They should be warned that a killer has been living among them his/her whole life, or at least the past twenty plus years.

I told both officers I'd consider their request because if it ended up leaked to Hauser, all bets were off with any of my other information.

"What information?" Gordon asked.

"You don't want to find out," I bluffed and hung up.

I had kept my end of the deal and now it was time to inform the good people of my new town that not only was there a sadistic killer out there, but that back in the '70s, he or she most likely killed one of their most beloved police officers and also an ex-convict.

During all of this, I found it intriguing that I hadn't received one call from DeLuca on their behalf or that he hadn't used his power to take over the case. If he wasn't working on the case, why was he still hanging out in town? And why did he pull strings to get me on that boat?

Maybe he was using me and waiting for the Tuesday edition to drop so he could ride in like the cavalry and save the day?

Come Tuesday, Sandy Point would be asking for more than just the cavalry. They'd want the goddamn Indians, too.

This town has seen nothing yet.

On Friday, I suggested to Crocker that we prepare Sunshine for the Devlin handcuff story, and he assured me that he'd be the one to tell her. I wondered if that conversation had taken place.

But my mind went back to why I kept thinking about fire. Now that everyone conceded there was a serial killer loose, that morning I pulled out one of my old psych books. It reminded me that, at a young age, most future serial killers play with fire.

That sent a chill up my spine. I came back to the one person who had been dodging me for several days — Murray Philbrick.

When Murray was a kid, Officer Michael Devlin caught him trying to torch Detective Prichard's boat.

1.Why would Murray do that?

2.Was that a warning to Prichard since shortly after the incident the detective moved?

3.But how and why could a kid intimidate Prichard?

4.Did Devlin put it together and ended up paying for it with his life?

5.Why hasn't Detective Prichard called me back?

6.Why wasn't Murray returning my calls?

Having Saturday night off gave me the upper hand. Murray wouldn't be expecting me to show up at his dealership. I figured I'd wait till the 5 p.m. closing time. That was an hour away.

How do you kill time before confronting a possible serial killer suspect?

I forced a laugh. It wasn't a question I'd asked myself before. I decided to get my mind off it for a while.

I drove to Kempton's Vintage Frames Company to pick up my birthday present for Echo's brother. David's birthday was the following week, but I got a message from Oliver Kempton, the owner and also a town selectman, that my order had been framed and was ready to go.

I pulled up to the family-owned store with the standard sign noting it was established way back when and parked. I sat there for a moment and thought about Echo. I still had a tangle of thoughts and feelings swimming around in my head after what she told me. I meant what I had said that I wouldn't judge her, but her story did leave me feeling conflicted.

She trusted me enough to share her secret and, for that matter, Drake's and Jamal's secret. But she didn't trust me enough to tell me all of it.

Who was the former lover she was trying to protect? And was it a lover? Maybe it was something else. Oh, God, could she have been raped? Maybe that's why she's still living in Sandy Point? She's been afraid to move on.

What she had left out was driving me crazy, but I had to take solace on one point. She was *not* hooking up with Jamal. That was big news. I read that one totally wrong, and for once, I was happy that I did.

She'd shown signs she wasn't interested, but I felt that the more we shared of ourselves, the more likely that was to change. And we had shared quite a bit that day at Gunner's.

"Put her out of your mind," I ordered myself, as I stepped out of my Jeep.

I know I didn't mean it. After all, I was about to pick up a framed picture of Echo, David, and me posing with Wally the Green Monster outside Fenway.

"That's bad ball. You're an asshole, O'Rourke," I chided myself, realizing the picture was more for Echo to see us happy than it was for David.

I decided it was wrong to give it to him, but I had already paid for it, so I went in.

Oliver Kempton, the Bart Simpson look-alike, greeted me. "Well, if it isn't the ace reporter."

"Hi Oliver. You guys called about my order."

"Yes, we'll get to that. Any news? Chief Harding has left me out in the cold."

"Me too. But that's his job. I don't have anything new for you."

"This whole thing is messed up, dog. Just when I think we've seen it all, something else happens." Oliver was doing his Snoop impression again.

"Yep. I know people respect you, so if you ever hear anything let me know. You lead this town and have to stay strong." I said, shamelessly playing on his ego.

"Oh, yes, sure. No doubt. Now let me get you that order."

"Wait a second," I pointed to a bandage on his right hand. "What happened?"

"Oh, this," he laughed, "I had a woman come in here who just got divorced and she gave me her favorite picture of her and her husband. She wanted it framed."

"Huh?" I asked.

"Well, she wanted it framed but also wanted his 'ugly ass' out of it. So…" He picked up a thin bladed knife and flashed it, "I sliced the poor bastard out of it but slipped and cut myself."

"Ouch," I winced.

"Yeah, gouged him and me. Probably the wrong terminology to use these days." Kempton chuckled and headed into the back room.

Moments later, he returned with my picture in a custom frame that had the Red Sox logo on it.

I looked down and my body warmed seeing Echo's face smiling back at me. David was looking off to the side a bit but was also smiling. As for mine, it was probably the biggest smile ever. We looked like a happy family.

"I didn't know you and Echo were an item," Oliver coaxed as he wrapped the frame in paper and slipped it into a bag.

"We're not. Just friends. Great frame, Oliver." I tried to change the subject.

"Yeah, um. Can you do me a favor?" he leaned across the counter and lowered his voice conspiratorially.

"What's that?"

"Off the record, as one would say to someone like you."

"Yeah, okay. Off the record." I egged him on.

"I don't pay the Red Sox a licensing fee to use their logo, so if we can just keep this to ourselves?"

"Sure thing," I laughed, picked up my bag, and left.

I spent the next hour looping town, listening to sports radio rehash the Red Sox loss from the previous night, before pulling up to Murray's dealership. His black Lexus was parked out front.

Perfect.

I tucked my Jeep into a spot behind some hedges in the bank parking lot across the street. I figured when Murray locked the doors to the dealership, that's when I'd run across, and when he turned around, there'd be no escaping me — and my questions.

The plan changed when I saw a gray Honda Accord park in front of the dealership and Greg Crocker jump out.

What the hell is Crocker doing here? I didn't know he was friends with Murray.

Crocker leaned against the trunk of his car and waited for a couple of minutes until Murray appeared. They shook hands, and Murray climbed into the passenger seat of Crocker's car. This was definitely interesting. I fired up the ignition and waited until they were a good forty yards ahead of me before I pulled out and followed.

After about ten minutes, Crocker finally drove up a hill past the Sandy Point Hospital and took a left into a parking lot beyond the hospital lot.

At this point, I was too close to continue unobserved, so I headed up the street and parked near the woods beside the road. I grabbed a pen and jotted – Ran out of gas. Be back in ten minutes.

I slid it under my wiper blade and walked back to the lot entrance. The Accord was parked in front of a brown building adorned with several wooden signs. There was no sign of Crocker or Murray.

They must be inside.

I went in for a closer look. The signs were a directory of doctors and their specialties. I began scanning them, but a female voice stopped me.

"Excuse me. What are you doing here?"

I turned around and was greeted by a scowling Dr. Lindsey Courtland.

I'm busted.

"I ah… ah… Hi, Lindsey!" I grimaced.

"Never mind 'hi.' What are you doing here?"

I had no answer.

The front door of the brown building flew open, and Crocker came out.

"What are you doing here?" he asked.

"I need to talk to Murray Philbrick."

"Murray? Murray's not here." Crocker said.

"Why would Murray Philbrick be here?" Lindsey lamely offered.

"You know Greg, you really haven't made it easy for me working for you when you're constantly stifling me."

"This isn't the place for that conversation. But if we're having it, I don't know what you're talking about. I have handed over the reins for you to write the stories and even break them."

"I know you have. That's why I find it troubling that you're lying to me. I just saw you pick up Murray and I followed you here."

Crocker didn't know what to say.

"I don't know why you two are protecting him. I need to talk to him. There are things about his past that need to be answered."

The door opened again.

Murray walked out shaking his head. "J.T., I used to like you 'cause you made strong drinks but not so much anymore. You're a persistent prick."

"Okay. Okay," Lindsey jumped in, "I think you should leave, Mr. O'Rourke."

"Actually, Linds," Murray interjected, "you want me to talk about it, so I guess it's time to talk. J.T., get your ass in here."

Murray went back into the building and, after some awkward glances, Crocker, Lindsey, and I followed.

We walked past the waiting room and into a room that resembled every TV show therapist's office except it was much larger and there were six, big lazy boys not the standard two.

Lindsey read my mind, "This is my group therapy room."

I nodded and sat.

Murray plopped down. "Not much of a group, though. Just Greg and me are the only ones in town who will admit in here what happened to us."

"So, Pop Tucker raped you?" I asked

"We off the record?"

"Yes, Murray."

"Yeah, that sick fuck raped me... Oh, sorry Lindsey."

"Don't be sorry. We talked about this. Once you get that anger out, you're going to get better," she assured.

"Yeah. Yeah...We'll see..." he said to her, and then turned to me, "What else do you want to know?"

"You tried burning Detective Prichard's boat and..."

"And Devlin caught me," he concluded.

"Yes. So why'd you do that to Prichard? Why were you so angry at him?"

"I was just a dumb kid acting out. I was pissed that Prichard hadn't caught Tucker long ago. I mean the guy owned a candy store and molested half this town. I wanted to make Prichard pay for being a lousy detective. The truth was the poor bastard was as sick about it as I was, if not more. You see, after Officer Devlin caught me, Prichard figured it out. We talked, and he understood. Instead of pressing charges, Prichard actually apologized to me. Like I say, he felt sick about it. He kept my secret and to this day I'm grateful to him."

"That may be true, but as the good doctor will tell you," I nodded at Lindsey, "our secrets are our sickness. I think that's a major problem with this town. If I knew who Pop Tucker's victims were, I'd be able to narrow down suspects of who kidnapped and probably killed Rutger Nelson and probably Juan Padilla and others."

They were all quiet.

"Well, if any of you know any other victims, I promise I will investigate with discretion. Murray, I'm sorry it all came out this way, but you wouldn't return my calls."

"I'm not sorry," he shrugged.

"Why is that?"

"'Cause I have two witnesses here that I told you off the record, asshole."

CHAPTER 45

OCTOBER 16, 2004

SATURDAY

ECHO

"You gotta be kidding me!" Echo yelled after listening to her voicemail. She was scheduled to photograph a 40th wedding anniversary party in two hours and her second shooter had just called in sick. She could still cover the event on her own or get a non- photographer like Kathy Zimmerman to help, so she really shouldn't have had such a chip on her shoulder. But she did.

She clicked off her cell, tossed it on her bed, and headed over to the bureau. She didn't want to analyze why she was in such a sour mood, but as she slipped on her red Victoria Secret underwear, there was no avoiding it — Jameson Thomas O'Rourke.

He had found a way to get into her head and it pissed her off. He is the last person she should've been thinking of.

After all, she had waited too long to reconnect with Tobias, and in another 15 days after years apart, they'd finally be reunited.

But instead of fantasizing about kissing Tobias at the upcoming Halloween party in Boston, she found herself angry and obsessing over what J.T. had told her.

The day before, Lilly Lee, reporter for Channel 9, interviewed him and then handed her card saying, "I'm single. Call me sometime."

When he relayed the encounter to Echo, adding that he was definitely going to call Lilly since she was "smoking hot," Echo's heart sank. She felt sick. And that's why she was so mad. She had no right to be jealous. If she wanted J.T., she could've had him a while ago. He had given her all the signs and she shut him down.

Am I just jealous since he no longer looks at me the way he did when we first met? God, I'm so vain.

That may've been part of it, but as the summer continued, her relationship with J.T. became something more. She had opened up to him about almost all of her secrets and he was the shoulder she had leaned on, never judging.

And when it came to work on the stories, they were partners. They went over thousands of theories of who they thought Nero was and would write them on a whiteboard in J.T.'s place.

I shouldn't be thinking of him.

She should've been thinking of the query she received from a Boston paper. The photo editor had told her, "When you switch to digital give me a call. We might have a job opening up here."

Echo found the courage to make the switch to digital and loved it, but not the courage to make the call.

Maybe fixating on J.T. helps me avoid thinking about placing that call and possibly making the move off Cape?

She thought again about how when they weren't working together, they'd try to outdo one another with their sarcasm. He could be such an asshole, but hilarious at the same time. He also had his own brand of thoughtfulness. She loved how he had given her brother six rolls of colored duct tape for his birthday.

David exclaimed, "This is actually a good gift for once."

Maybe it's not attraction? Maybe I just admire how J.T. has become someone over the past five months?

He arrived in town as an overweight guy with no newspaper experience. And since then, he had broken several stories that rocked Sandy Point. The week before, the paper had even given him his own online column, one of the first in New England.

J.T. didn't disappoint. He already delivered a tearjerker about Rutger

Nelson's mother, Janice, and how she lives day-to-day wondering what has become of her son and how she was now separated from her husband.

The emotions conveyed in the piece had everyone in town talking and demanding justice.

J.T. O'Rourke was a household name, and people speculated that he had a better chance at unmasking Nero than the cops.

He had achieved recognition and respect while also transforming his body and lifestyle, switching from Guinness to Coke to Diet Coke and now to water. Echo's thoughts lingered for a moment on that body. He now resembled the cut boxer he claimed he used to be. She wondered what those strong arms felt like wrapped around…

What the hell is wrong with me? I should be thinking about the love of my life! I should be thinking about Tobias!

She was still angry at Tobias for asking her to wait so he could get "situated" in Boston and his new job before she visited. And of course, ever the romantic, he wanted their first encounter in years to be on Halloween night.

Echo clipped her bra and pulled on some black tights before wriggling into a black pencil skirt and zipping on her boots.

Think of Tobias. Think of Tobias.

Her mind ordered her over and over as she popped her head through the neck of her favorite red top and then tied it all together with a black sweater.

"Think of Tobias. Think of Tobias." This time she said it out loud as she leaned into the mirror and applied candy-apple red lip gloss to her full lips.

But she couldn't see Tobias's face in her mind's eye. She tried visualizing more. No face. Nothing. All she could see was J.T.'s face. It scared her.

She stomped over to her nightstand and picked up her high school yearbook. She flipped through the pages past the sports teams, activities, underclassmen, and senior pictures until she came to the page: FACULTY.

Her eyes scanned down a few rows until she came to ENGLISH DEPARTMENT.

The third picture down. Tobias Russell.

There he was with those piercing green eyes that caught her attention when he called her name during attendance on her first day of senior year. Even in a black and white photo, those eyes still had the same effect on her, and now the memories were back, sending shivers to those places that only he could.

J.T. was gone from her mind. She was happy again.

"Fifteen more days, Tobias. Fifteen more days and we can finally have a normal life together."

She smiled, shut the yearbook, and headed off to call Kathy Zimmerman.

CHAPTER 46
OCTOBER 16, 2004

SATURDAY

J.T.

"Whitford, take it easy man. I'm going to make this thing happen. I'm just waiting for Lilly to call me back." I pleaded with Whitford Leddy, the subject of my soon-to-be latest story on the Juan Padilla a/k/a The Fiddler murder case.

"I don't know. Maybe I should just call another reporter myself. I like watching that Hauser guy. Maybe I should just call him?"

"Trust me. You don't want to do that." I soothed into the receiver while studying the picture Leddy had scanned and emailed to me earlier in the day. It was proof he had known Juan Padilla. It was a picture of Juan from the winter of '76 playing his violin at a ski lodge in Vermont. It was there that Juan befriended the local music shop owner.

"Why should I trust you?" Leddy asked.

"'Cause I can guarantee you things that he can't."

"Money better be one of them," Leddy grunted.

"No, I'm not paying for your info but what I can guarantee is a live remote with Lilly Lee after my story runs."

"Is she as beautiful as she looks on TV?" his voice eager.

"What?" I asked.

"You know what I mean. Is she hot?"

"Oh, yeah. She is a very attractive woman."

"Okay, a live remote with a gorgeous woman... But what else?"

"Well, my paper will pay for you to come from Vermont to do the interview with her here. They'll even put you up for a few days." I didn't know if that was true, considering I had already interviewed him, and it should be Lilly's station footing the bill. Worst case scenario, I'd pony up.

"If my info might help catch that whacko Nero, do you really think I want to hang out in that town? I don't want to be anywhere near that town."

"Good point. How 'bout you do the interview at The Ritz in Boston, and we'll also throw in theater tickets for you and your wife."

Your third wife.

"It sounds like I'm getting a little respect finally. But what else can you guarantee me that Hauser or someone else can't? I'm sure he can get me those things, too."

"I'm working on a book about everything that has happened this summer. I'm going to portray you in a very positive light and, of course, mention your music shop. I'm going to make you a star in this book. You see, Whitford, I've become the face to tell this story. Believe me, you want to stick with me. I know how to get you the exposure you need. People will be traveling to Vermont to your store just to hear your story, and hopefully shop, too. Of course, there'll be no book if we don't catch him, and that's why I need your help. Think of all of the victims. Think of your friend Juan."

There was a long pause.

Finally: "Alright. I want three nights at The Ritz and my wife has always wanted to see Blue Man Group."

Tickets. Note to self: call Fat Pete.

"Done."

"And a dinner at a five-star restaurant."

I thought of DeLuca and how I could bring him into this story. Leddy's info may blow it wide open.

"Does your wife like Italian? I can get you a table at a great place in the North End."

"She loves Italian."

"Good. It's a deal."

"So, now what?" he asked.

Now that I had an online column, I could drop the story anytime — except he told me "Off the record."

I also had ulterior motives. I had to move on from Echo and maybe this was my "in" to get to know Lilly better. I actually didn't need an "in" since she had given me her card the day before when I was interviewed, demanding the state put a rush on the DNA testing for Juan Padilla.

I had learned from Norman Chadwick to publish a piece like this one midweek, that way I could tease it for a few days beforehand. And speaking of midweek, my buddy Seth, night manager at The Ritz, could get me midweek prices for that greedy bastard, Whitford Leddy, and his wife. I also would have everything coincide with Lilly Lee so her interview would follow.

"I still have to talk with Lilly, but Whitford, please be patient. Everyone in the news media will be too busy tonight with the Sox-Yanks playoff game. I'll get back to you when I hear from her. And everything you told me off the record will go on the record when I'm ready to drop the story. Of course, you'll have to say the magic words: 'on the record.'"

"Get me that room, dinner, and those goddamn Blue Man tickets and I'll say them."

Click.

I walked over to the white board and under the 20 or so wild theories and suspects I wrote: Could a Stradivarius be key to this case?

Going over my timeline and what Whitford Leddy had told me, he may've been the last person to talk with Juan Padilla in May of 1977.

Juan had called him from the Sand Dollar Boarding House saying he had been partying with some guy who owned what Juan thought was a Stradivarius, the rarest violins around. The monetary value was astronomical. Juan planned on stealing it and bringing it to Whitford Leddy for an appraisal.

Leddy stressed to me that he told Juan not to steal it but to offer the guy money. This part of his account I didn't buy for a second, but I allowed Leddy to spin his lie.

He went on to state that he never heard from Juan again and since he didn't know Juan's real name, he never went searching for him. He assumed the whole thing was just a drunken joke and forgot all about it until he saw the national coverage and Juan's picture.

This article might slam the final nail in the state's coffin and force them to put in that rush for the lab results so poor Juan Padilla could be positively identified. As strong as all the evidence was, it was still circumstantial. Not knowing was causing more agony to Juan's sister Marta. I talked to her at least once a day trying to assure her that Detective Gordon and others were working to get her brother justice.

As I waited for Lilly Lee's call, I tried to work on my other assignments. I was supposed to be working on a story about an upcoming town meeting on Samoset Woods, and a puff piece about Paul Harrison's retirement, but my mind couldn't go there. This new information was too much. Nothing could take my mind off it.

"Out of all of the suspects up here, who plays the violin?" I asked myself, eyeing the names but got distracted when the phone rang.

I looked down at the caller ID and realized I was wrong. There was one thing that could take my mind off it. It seemed to always take my mind off everything.

I answered on the third ring.

"Hello, Echo. What's up?"

CHAPTER 47

OCTOBER 16, 2004

SATURDAY

J.T.

My plan was to chip away at my Paul Harrison retirement story unless I got a text or call from Lilly Lee. Then I'd have an excuse to shift my focus to a real story — Whitford Leddy's conversation with Juan Padilla.

In a couple of hours, the Sox were playing the Yankees in game three of the playoffs (already down two games to nil) so without much fanfare, I figured I'd also put the game on for background noise. I didn't expect much from my boys. They had taken me down that road of hope too many times. If they lost two more games, it would be another winter waiting for the newscast showing the equipment truck being loaded up for spring training.

Regardless of watching a possible loss, I still had a solid plan for my night, especially since the weather was made for writing — spitting rain and bits of hail tapping against my window.

Everything changed when I got a call from Echo asking if I could be her second photographer, or as she referred to it, "second shooter," at a 40th anniversary party at the yacht club. Her assistant had called in sick and her friend Kathy, who sometimes helped, had scored tickets to the Sox game.

"Are they still even playing considering the weather?" I asked.

"Yep. Weather people say they can get the game in. Poor Kathy is already in her seat. Bad move. Game time is still like two hours away. She just texted me that she's — and I quote — 'freezing her ass off.' You know her. Her idea of roughing it is a day at the spa without a pedicure." Echo laughed.

I held my laughter. "Well... I don't know if I'd be welcomed at the yacht club. Commodore Nelson hates my guts. He still blames me for Rutger disappearing that night."

"I think he hates you even more now that you did that article on his wife, but I have it on good authority that he's away on business."

"Yeah, but other members might be looking at me."

"J.T., any sane person in town including Mrs. Nelson realizes that you did your job that night, and ironically, Drake was the reason Rutger left The A.F. Funny how the universe works. Not ha ha funny of course. Anyway, back to my question..."

"I don't know anything about cameras, so I..."

"Look, I'll give you a very basic one and all you have to do is shoot people on the dance floor. That way when the pics are blurry, we'll just say that was the action technique." She laughed again.

That damn laugh. God, I love it.

"What do you say J.T., can you help me out?"

I should've said, no, but when it came to Echo my spine was made from Jello, and man, did she like to wrestle in it.

So, fast-forward to two hours later and here I was in my "sports banquet attire" snapping photos of old people moving their bodies in ways they shouldn't to Kool & the Gang's "Celebration."

One couple that wasn't as old as the rest but just as dance-challenged caught my attention. They were flailing away, and I loved seeing it. At the D.J.'s request, the couple even threw their hands up in the air like they just didn't care.

"No shit. That's awesome." I smiled to myself and walked over.

They didn't see me coming.

"Well, well... What do we have here?" I asked Crocker and Sunshine while catching them in a full after dance hug and kiss.

They turned around with shocked expressions.

"Say cheese," I laughed, snapped the shot, catching the moment forever.

"What are you doing here?" Anna asked.

"What am I doing here? What are you two doing here? Together, I might add."

Crocker turned to Anna and laughed. "He would be the one to find out first. Should we, Sunshine?"

"Greg, you know I have nothing to hide."

Crocker faced me and smiled. "Well, my ace reporter who keeps getting into other people's lives, you've finally stumbled into some good news. Anna and I are now dating."

"Oh my God! Are you serious? That's awesome!"

"Yeah, we're pretty happy about it, too," Anna said and lovingly brushed her hand across Crocker's cheek.

"So why are you here?" Crocker asked me.

"Echo needed a second shooter."

Crocker smiled. "Well, I'm going to get Anna and me some punch. Do you want some?"

"Sure."

"You people and your goddamn punch!" A guy from behind bellowed, walked over, and placed a pint of Guinness in my free hand.

I looked down at it, contemplating whether or not to drink it. I was trying to figure out if I had known him from The A.F.

He was tall and scholarly looking, wearing blocky brown glasses that he kept pushing back up to the bridge of his nose Woody Allen-style. He sucked on his gin and tonic before he continued.

"Of course, you know I'm kidding with you, Greg and Anna. Sobriety is the path to something. What is it again? Oh yeah, the liquor store."

Everyone laughed.

"Seriously, great to see you two found sobriety and one another. But this young guy over here should be drinking tonight in honor of my 40 years in prison. I mean marriage." He laughed again and added, "Echo said Guinness is your drink."

"It was, but I've been taking a break."

"Well, the break is over. You're the help. I hired you and one of your jobs is to have a drink with me," he chuckled again, "Nice to meet you. Dan Armstrong, and that silver fox coming our way is my wife, Kristen. And in about 42 seconds she'll be shutting me off from G&Ts." He thumbed over to a woman with silver hair wearing a matching silver colored dress.

Anna leaned over and kissed Dan on the cheek. "Congrats to you and Kristen. So happy for you guys."

"A kiss from the never aging Anna Dev... ahm, Walsh. You know, the only reason I agreed to this thing is for the cheap thrills. Hell, why do you think I hired Echo away from her day job? I mean look at her over there."

"Easy, pal. Remember the story you told at your retirement party." Crocker laughed, and Dan almost doubled over from their inside joke.

"Okay, I'm just saying she is a beautiful young woman." Dan gestured with his G&T toward Echo who was now also headed our way.

Kristen arrived first.

"Greg and Anna, thank you so much for being here tonight." Kristen hugged Anna then Crocker.

She turned to me. "You must be J.T. O'Rourke the famous local reporter."

I laughed. "I don't know about that. I do know tonight I'm the second shooter. A shot of you and your husband on the dance floor?"

"Thanks, but maybe later, J.T." She turned back to Anna, "We'll have to have coffee soon. From the looks of things, I think we need to catch up."

Anna smiled, "Absolutely."

"As for my wonderful husband of 40 years," Kristen turned to Dan, "I have to steal him away from you folks. We need to make the rounds." She began to walk off the dance floor.

"Sure, honey," he rolled his eyes at me and whispered. "Definitely, not the rounds I was thinking of. Speaking of that, it's an open bar, J.T. You'd better use it. Someone has to."

I nodded at him.

"Well, off to Shawshank," Dan's voice rose.

"I heard that!" Kristen sniped over her shoulder.

"Guess at least her hearing aid is working," he winked and started off in Kristen's wake but then paused to chat with Echo.

He said something to Echo, she laughed, and punched him in the arm before continuing over to us.

"J.T., Dan just told me to tell you that his wife doesn't really have a hearing aid. A mobility scooter, yes, but not a hearing aid."

I howled, shook my head, and confessed to the group, "He's quite a character."

"Actually, he's usually a pretty quiet guy until you get a few G&Ts in him. And then he's a party machine. But he only does that once in a blue moon, which is probably best for everyone," Crocker said.

"He was one of my favorite teachers. Very cool dude," Echo added, adjusting her lens. "Let's get that first official photo of you two as a couple."

"We're only dating," they said in unison and then laughed.

"Wait a second," I jumped in, "Echo, you knew about this?"

"Some reporter you are. They didn't tell me, but it was obvious that something was going on. Leaving ten minutes before the other to go to lunch. The other signs were there, too."

"What are other signs?" I asked.

"Ahm, hello, you guys are talking about us right in front of us." Anna said.

Echo adjusted her lens and pointed it at them. "Don't mind us, I'm just realizing J.T. can't read signs. That's all. Now Crocker put your arm around Sunshine and hold her like you'll never let go."

"That will be easy," he blurted, and the two women gave the typical "oooh" reaction.

Echo snapped the picture while I stood staring down at my pint wondering was she trying to tell me something or was she just being a tease?

I couldn't come up with the answer. I decided to stop wondering about one thing. I was going to drink that pint. I took a sip from my beer and was confident I could put her out of my mind.

Five pints and a few Kamikaze shots later, and, at the request of Dan Armstrong, I was twirling Kristen around the dance floor. He told me he made his wife a simple promise — he'd stop drinking G&Ts for the night if she started. It worked. She had loosened up considerably, but scanning the room, I noticed everyone else had too, including Echo who was done with her duties and, after two glasses of wine, was twisting and shouting with Dan.

Not having consumed a drink in a couple of months, my tolerance was low, and I had a pretty good buzz going. When the music slowed and "Come Away With Me" by Norah Jones came on, Dan proved to be my new best friend by tapping me on the shoulder.

"Hit the road, O'Rourke. Go dance with Echo. I want to dance with my Silver Fox."

Kristen smiled, kissed him, and took his hand, leaving Echo and me staring at one another during the romantic slow song.

This isn't seventh grade! Screw it. I'm asking her to dance.

"Hey, ah, I, do you wa…" I didn't even finish the sentence.

"I know Dan said I'm done for the night, but I really should get some pictures of this." She pointed over at Dan and Kristen who were lost in each other's eyes.

"Can you hold this?" It wasn't a question. She handed me her half-glass of wine and went over to the corner where her camera equipment was stored.

"Maybe this is seventh grade…" I laughed to myself and gulped down her wine before walking over to an empty table.

As Echo took pictures, I sat down and decided to text Lilly:

Hey Lilly, did you get my phone message or other text message?

I waited, thinking I wasn't going to get anything back, but a few seconds later my phone bleeped.

Hey J.T. Yes, I did. So sorry. Stuck at Fenway doing interviews with pissed off fans. You watching this?

No, I'm at a 40th wedding party. No TVs!

Oh, they're losing bad. Anyway, I'm on board for that interview. Can't believe you're hooking me up! You're a sweetheart!

"Speaking of hooking up," I laughed to myself and typed a mild innuendo.

You're going to owe me.

I waited and then my phone flashed:

I've done my research. You're a boxer. Will this involve grabbing and clutching?

My eyes popped out of my head for a double take. Yep, that's what she wrote.

I instantly felt excited.

"Who needs Echo? And God love whoever created text messaging!" I laughed out loud and continued talking to myself, "Imagine if I had this in the seventh grade!"

"Imagine if you had what?" Echo looked down at me.

"Oh, nothing." I text quickly — You'll see. Gotta go — and sent it.

"Who are you texting?"

"Lilly."

"That Lilly Lee reporter chick?"

Her sharp tone and frown made me smile inside.

"Yeah, I guess you could call her that, too."

"What are you texting her for?"

"Something to do with a story. I'll tell you when we get out of here."

Echo scanned the room and then looked at me.

"Let's go now. I've done everything. I'm starving and I'm dying to know the score of the Sox game."

I was tempted to tell her what I knew but kept quiet and followed her out the door. She seemed genuinely annoyed about something. Was she giving me a sign?

Hell if I knew…

NERO

In the past, Nero feared nothing. Why would he? They had no idea he existed, so for decades it was easy to elude capture. He could've gone on and they never would have known. If only he could've lived with the fact that only he knew he was the greatest. But he couldn't. He had to show them. This whole thing was his fault. He allowed the number one weakness of any taker of life to seep into his bones: cockiness.

He became cocky and began to toy with them. And they all played along, especially J.T. O'Rourke. And now, with every subsequent article, time was running out for the lucky-ass reporter. Nero had launched his backup plan, but with his investigation, O'Rourke kept speeding up the process. Every week a new story exposed another piece, and very quickly those pieces would come together and, before he knew it, a completed jigsaw puzzle of Nero's face would be plastered on the front page of the local fish wrapper. He knew it.

He didn't like this feeling — the fear of being captured. It had grown inside him over the summer, and he decided he couldn't just sit back and let it keep growing. With the rain and the Red Sox playoff game going on, tonight would be the perfect night to surprise O'Rourke. The drunk Mick wouldn't know what hit him. Of course, he knew O'Rourke may be sober, but once Nero struck him, it wouldn't matter.

The night was black, so Nero planned to pull up to the shore in front of one of the empty summer huts and make his way unseen down the beach.

Thanks to an illegal wood stove that was just installed, O'Rourke was the only person still living in one of the beach cottages.

Nero had been tempted to report the illegal stove that night back in

September when he spotted them putting it in, but he stopped himself when he realized it was the greatest gift he could receive.

It assured him that J.T. O'Rourke would stay on in that summer shack long after the other beach dwellers had given up and fled. No one else would be around the night he decided to send J.T. O'Rourke to hell. And tonight was that night.

J.T.

"Should I turn it off?" I asked Echo, motioning to her Jeep radio. Jerry Trupiano had just informed us that the Sox were down 17 to 6 going into the bottom of the seventh.

"Would it make me a non-believer if I said yes?"

"No, not a non-believer, just a realist."

She nodded yes, and I turned the knob to off.

We sat quietly for a minute, watching the rain and heavy hail pound the windshield like they were Yankees bats.

Finally I said, "I'd tell you to pray for rain, but unlike here, it's playable up in Boston, and it's also an official game so rain wouldn't help."

Echo started the engine and began driving. "Let's not think about it. I'm still starving. Those hors d'oeuvres looked so tasty. They were right in front of me, ready for me to devour but so out of reach. That's the worst part of being a photographer at these kinds of events."

"Well, you want to go to The A.F. for a burger?"

She laughed.

"What's so funny?"

"Oh, that's right. You got fired so you wouldn't know that they're on the fall schedule now. Kitchen closes early. The only place at this time of night to get a burger is Mickey D's, and they don't serve wine."

"Bummer."

She drove on for a minute heading toward my road.

"You got any food at your place?"

The question caught me off guard, but I tried not to let it show.

"Ah, yeah. I could make you something from my cookbook of Irish bachelor cuisine."

"Seriously, is that an actual cookbook?"

409

"Not yet, but the way I'm going, it will be." I smiled.

"Okay, O'Rourke, but the bigger question is: do you have any wine?"

"I know I have a couple of bottles of red, but you like pinot grigio."

"You remembered I like my gris."

"Of course." I said, wanting to add, "I remember everything you like."

"I enjoy red, too. That is, if you have any Italian recipes in that Irish bachelor cookbook of yours."

"Yes, I do. But remember: it is bachelor cuisine."

"This should be interesting," Echo laughed.

She continued on and, a few minutes later, pulled into my driveway.

It was now all rain, and it was coming down hard. Inside the Jeep, we counted to three and then made a run for it. I was halfway up the stairs when I turned around and realized Echo wasn't behind me.

I cupped my hands and yelled. "Echo! Echo!"

Nothing.

"Echo! Echo!" I yelled again.

Nothing.

I was getting a little anxious. I hurried up two more steps to set off my motion light, and that's when I saw her — face down on all fours.

"What the hell?"

I raced down the stairs and ran over to her.

"Are you alright?" I asked, turning her over to face me.

She gave me her hand and I pulled her to her feet. She was completely soaked.

"I can't believe I just did that."

"Did what?" I asked.

"I friggin' tripped and fell face first into that huge ass puddle." She pointed over to an area beside the driver's side that resembled a small lake.

"Oh, man. And I thought I was the buzzed one."

"Yeah, I know. Check this out, too," she held up her dripping purse, "I'm sure my cell is ruined."

It looked like if she opened it a fish would swim out.

"Never mind that right now, let's get you inside." I ushered her up the steps and into my house.

I pointed her in the direction of the shower and got busy lighting a fire in the woodstove. Once the fire was crackling, I opened a bottle of red and poured a glass. I walked over to the bathroom door and knuckled on it lightly. Echo opened the door — she was wrapped in a towel and backlit by a cloud of steam.

"This might help," I smiled and handed it to her.

She returned my smile with a laugh. "I'm such an idiot."

"No argument here." I said, and she playfully punched me with her free hand, and I really thought her towel was going to come undone.

"Well," I thumbed over my shoulder, "there's sweatpants, PJs, etcetera, whatever you need in my room. Off to the kitchen."

I lit some candles, put another log on the fire, and twenty minutes later, the place was warm — and I was too when Echo emerged from my bedroom wearing what looked to be nothing but my red flannel shirt.

No sweats or PJ bottoms. What is she doing to me?

"Hope you don't mind, but I borrowed a pair of your boxer shorts."

"Which ones?" I asked just so I could have my own visual for after she went home.

"The clean ones."

We both laughed.

"Seriously, the white ones with the red lips all over them."

She would have to say that!

"Obviously, those are my favorites, but that's fine," I clapped my hands, "Take a seat and prepare to be wowed."

She sat at the table and I served her.

"Is this what I think it is?"

"Yep. English muffin pizzas. I wasn't kidding when I told you that it was coming from the Irish Bachelor Cuisine Cookbook. Don't judge until you take a bite."

"Okay, but more wine."

I poured her a glass and watched her take a bite. I waited for her reaction.

"Oh my God. I have to admit, these are amazing."

"They should be. When I was a kid, I used to make them for my sisters and me all the time."

"No, I'm serious. These are incredible. I mean it's sauce, cheese, and English muffins. But they're really awesome. What's the secret?"

"Maybe I'll tell you sometime."

"Okay, speaking of secrets, you were going to tell me about some upcoming story."

"Yes, and I'll need you to take pictures, but we're going to have to do the interview up in Boston."

"Explain."

I pointed to the white board where the word "Stradivarius" was written in blue marker above about a dozen suspects. I spent the next couple of glasses of wine telling her about Whitford Leddy, and a glass after that we tried connecting that word to one of our suspects.

At this point, we were not making much sense and it was pure drunken speculation even about some of our friends.

"Okay, I just said that Crocker could be the guy so that tells me I've had way too much to drink and it's time for me to change and call a taxi. I think my clothes must be dry by now." Echo got up and felt her clothes that were draped over a chair in front of the stove.

"Yep, dry enough. I'm just going to change in your room." She headed into the other room, and reality set in. The wonderful night with her, like most nights, was about to end.

I wanted to rush into the room, grab her, and hold her in my arms, but instead I began clearing the plates.

Soft music began to filter from my room.

"J.T., come in here for a second."

I put the plates in the sink and headed into the room.

"What is this?" Echo asked.

"Oh, ah, well, it's a picture of you, David, and me at the Red Sox game. I mean what does it look like?" I said embarrassed.

"I know that. But it's framed, and it was on your bureau."

"Well, yeah. The thing is, I got it for him for his birthday and then decided he might not like it. It's just been kicking around. I've been meaning to put it away."

"And I also saw the signed baseball bat," she pointed to the Kevin Millar autographed bat inscribed to David beside my bed.

"Oh, yeah, that. A friend of mine just got me that. I, ah, I knew David liked Millar. Nothing big."

Echo's brown eyes locked with mine and she moved closer. That tangerine scent that I had dreamt about was inches away.

She tilted her head up and almost in a whisper said, "Do you know who this is singing?"

"Of course I do." I managed.

"J.T., I thought you hated Dave Matthews."

"I do."

"Well, then, why do you have one of his CDs?"

"I don't know. I just thought…" I couldn't finish the sentence. My heart was beating too fast. I had never wanted a woman so much while at the same time feeling so intimidated.

Was she teasing me again? Or was this time for real? Was this actually going to happen?

"J.T., did you think that maybe you'd find someone who would help you like this music again?"

I nodded, yes, and watched her undo the first two buttons of the flannel revealing her cleavage.

"This song, 'Lover Lay Down,' is my favorite and, you know what Jameson…" She paused, not wanting an answer but the kiss I finally found the courage to give her. It was soft. Tentative. And her full lips accepted it. The second one was stronger. Longer and sensual.

She gave a coy smile, put her arms around me and pulled me down onto the bed.

"Maybe this can be your favorite song, too," she whispered before kissing me again.

My body was throbbing with joy everywhere and my lips were ready to wander elsewhere when my cell phone buzzed and lit up. I wanted to ignore it. Push it off the bureau. I wanted her. I needed her. This was my chance. But the name that flashed across the screen. I couldn't avoid it.

It was 4:46 in the morning. Why was he calling? I had to make a choice. Echo or the phone?

I chose the phone.

"What do you want, DeLuca?!" I yelled into the receiver.

"Wow. Sorry. I thought you might want an exclusive."

"On what?"

"Two of the biggest arrests in Sandy Point. I'm outside your door so hurry up."

CHAPTER 48

OCTOBER 17, 2004

SUNDAY

J.T.

The blue unmarked van with tinted windows flew down the street, churning up puddles. Two beefy agents sat in the front chatting about the Sox while DeLuca and I argued in the back.

"I still don't understand why Echo couldn't come with us to take pictures. She is my photographer after all."

"Really? She looked more like your girlfriend, which makes me have to say, 'Nice job, O'Rourke.' That's a nice piece of tail you scored yourself. Here, have a stick of gum. Clearly, I got you after another drunken night. You Irish..."

I ignored the jab and took the piece. I wanted to smile and say, "She is hot, isn't she?" but pressed on, "You still didn't answer my question."

"Right now, she doesn't know who we are going to arrest."

"And neither do I."

"Yes, but I'm positive you won't tip them off. That Landers chick, on the other hand, could send a text to warn them."

Her phone is toast.

"And why the hell would she do that?"

"She grew up in this town. Personal relationships. She knows them. And maybe you're right. Maybe she thinks they're scum and wouldn't do any of that. But the bigger reason is that perfect ass I just saw," DeLuca smiled.

"Huh?"

"You see, if anything goes wrong, I have no problem watching a bullet take you out. Whereas for that fine specimen of woman back there, it would absolutely kill me. So, are we going to keep arguing about this or do you want to know what's going on?"

I nodded, "Continue."

He was about to do just that when the van went around the corner on two wheels.

"Jesus Christ, Cirino! Are you trying to kill us?" DeLuca yelled at the driver.

"Sorry, Sal. Just don't want to be late."

"We are way ahead of schedule so just pull that fat foot of yours off the gas a bit. Alright?"

"Fat foot?" Cirino eyed DeLuca through the mirror, "Is that all you got?"

"Yeah, I'm tired," he crabbed, but then turned his attention back to me, "Okay, where was I? Oh yeah, remember you asked me to look into Paul Harrison."

"Yes, and you did, and you said he was clean."

"Yep. That was one big lie." DeLuca laughed.

"Really? Go on."

"I had to build my case before I brought you in and now that it's built..."

"Holy... Are you saying Harrison is Nero?"

"No. No. I wish. No. A guy like him doesn't have what it takes to go to the next level. At least, I don't think he does. But I did find out he's scum. Turns out he's been selling child porn for decades."

"What??" I gasped.

"Why so surprised? You must've had your theories for having me to check him out."

"Yeah, you're right. I heard a story of how he showed a group of boys a *Playboy* once and wondered. It sounded like a big red flag. But how can you rule him out as Nero? Maybe it wasn't Pop Tucker who killed Fishy Bryden? Maybe Harrison also killed Devlin or Juan Padilla or Drake Underhill. Or all of them?"

"W-o-a-h," DeLuca raised his hands and patted the air in front of him, "Slow down, cowboy. Okay, okay. You are correct. I can't completely rule him out of all the murders in this cursed town, but I can rule him out for the Bryden boy's murder and Officer Devlin. Harrison was away, and it was for that reason the ball got rolling for me."

"What do you mean?"

"I checked on all of his alibis. He always told friends he was going to either France or Germany on his trips. Well, turns out the trips he was taking back then — and takes still to this day — are to Thailand."

"Thailand?"

"Yep. He peddles what those sickos like to term 'vintage boy toys' porn to American sickos who go over there to live out their perverse fantasies."

"What the hell is 'vintage boy toys'?"

"Just like it sounds. It's either black and white pictures or old Polaroids of boys doing... well, you know. No need to go into detail. Harrison sells or trades over there and also buys. He brings Asian boy porn back and sells it over here. I've connected the pictures to the Pop Tucker molestation case. Talking with Detective Prichard, he said the old pictures of Tucker molesting kids would make anyone realize that someone else took them. My guess it was Harrison or his friend or maybe both of them."

"Holy shit," I said, "Wait — his friend?"

"Yep, holy shit is right. I said, 'two arrests,' remember? I'll get to the friend in a second. The plan for me was after Harrison's next visit to Thailand to arrest him coming off the plane, but we just found out that he canceled the trip. He's spooked about what's going on in the town and feels someone might be onto him. He plans to dump his computer as well as give away all of his negatives to his sick buddy. He said he was retiring not just from the newspaper but also the side job."

"And how do you know all of this?"

"An email to that friend. In the end, they can't help themselves. Email always gets these bastards. We are headed to his buddy's right now."

"That's his house up there." Cirino yelled over his shoulder to us and pointed to a simple Cape house.

"Pull into that side street." DeLuca instructed Cirino.

DeLuca then took out a pair of night binoculars and peered through them before glancing at his watch. "Perfect. The fish is already swimming to the hook. Harrison is supposed to be here in twenty minutes."

"Who's the fish?" I asked.

He handed me the goggles and pointed.

"That guy. God, talk about anxious. He looks like a kid on Christmas Eve. Probably not the best analogy considering. Goddamn, sick fuck."

I looked through the lens and spotted a man pacing back and forth on the porch.

"Wait a second. I think I know that guy. Someone about him looks familiar."

"Yep. If you're picking up your girlfriend all the time, you know him."

"Huh? Not her stepfather!"

DeLuca gave a pleased laugh. "No. That would be really something. Guy's name is Scott Gallo. He's a security guard where Echo Landers lives, and that's why I didn't want her here."

I thought of the first time I encountered Gallo. He was reading a *Soldier of Fortune* magazine. It now made me sick wondering what kind of magazine was really tucked in the middle of that *Soldier of Fortune*.

"Oh my God," I said for probably the thousandth time.

"Yep. But here's a bigger oh-my-God moment: Gallo used to be a cop. My suspicion is that he sabotaged a lot of evidence of their crimes over the years, including stealing pics of Pop Tucker's victims. And who says they haven't molested kids, too? If we can get them on distributing, I bet victims will begin to come forward." DeLuca said.

"This is unbelievable," I handed back the binoculars. "This all adds up. But you know what doesn't add up?"

"What?"

"Why you keep feeding me great stories when you could have a TV crew in this van ready to storm the house with you?"

He pointed to the two beefy agents in the front seat and placed his index finger on his lips. "Now's not the time O'Rourke, but you know I have my reasons."

No doubt he did, but I let it go. I was too busy imagining the expression on Paul Harrison's face when he was cuffed. Like the slogan on those Mastercard commercials, it was going to be priceless.

. . .

ECHO

Echo pretended she was pissed that she couldn't go with J.T. on his secret rendezvous with DeLuca, but the truth was she was relieved. After a twenty-minute nap, sobriety and second thoughts shook her, now she had time to sift through them and regroup.

What the hell had she just done?

Her relationship with Tobias may've been just cyber these days, but it didn't matter. She just cheated on him.

She could justify it (and knew later she would) by blaming it on being drunk, but if she took a good look into her heart, the truth was she wanted it to happen. She instigated the whole thing and now, as she lay down on another man's bed staring up into darkness, Echo realized something else. Not only had she cheated on Tobias, but she also had just messed with J.T.'s emotions.

Angry with herself, she punched down on the mattress realizing she had become the kind of woman she detested, and she was just about to make it worse.

"I've gotta get the hell out of here." She turned on the bureau light.

She looked over at her wrinkled clothes hanging over the desk chair. She thought briefly about wearing them. Even though she was a grown woman, she still didn't want to do the walk of shame into her parents' house.

They wouldn't say anything but David, being David, would.

Her eyes scanned the room. She spotted the folded B.C. sweatshirt and gray sweatpants that earlier she had decided not to wear. She rose from the bed, walked over, and put them on.

"If I had only worn this earlier, none of this would've happened." She chided herself but again, inside, she didn't mean it. She was confused. She wanted J.T., but she also wanted Tobias. She was never torn between two men before, and it made her feel like a whore.

"Get home and figure it out, Landers," she whispered to herself, and headed into the bathroom. She looked around for her purse but remembered that she had left it on the kitchen counter, but her small bottle of perfume was on the sink.

"This is a clear indication that I am a slut," she admonished herself again, picking it up and putting it in her pocket.

She could've showered and stayed smelling of Ivory soap and worn sweats, but she had decided to dab on her signature perfume and wear his flannel and boxers.

"But if he didn't have that picture of all of us and the autographed bat... And let's not forget the Dave Matthews CD," she said to the reflection in the mirror. Then it dawned on her that maybe she wasn't completely sober since she was speaking out loud into a mirror — and she also decided to place some of the blame on J.T.

Echo was about to turn on the faucet when a strange sensation gripped her. Except for the wind and rain outside, the cottage was quiet.

Something doesn't feel right.

She glanced out the window just in time to see the motion light turn off. She knew an animal could've triggered it, but a sixth sense ran through her bones and told her that she was not alone. Someone was in the cottage.

NERO

When Nero approached the cottage from the beach and saw the blue van with the tinted windows pull up to O'Rourke's, he almost made a run for it back to the boat.

He assumed they were onto him, but that inner voice calmed him and ordered him to take cover behind a dune.

"Survey the situation, Nero," it counseled.

That turned out to be a wise move.

He watched the same agent who had been sniffing around town, DeLuca was his name, get out and talk briefly with J.T. before they both jumped into the van and raced off.

Nero didn't even consider if they were going off to look for him. He was too busy homing in on something he had thought about for years: Echo Landers.

Her Jeep was parked in the driveway. Rumor was O'Rourke was banging Landers, and now that rumor proved to be true. She was probably lying in his bed right now waiting for him to come home.

The thought made Nero's wet suit expand.

He had wanted that slut ever since that night in the woods. Not for sex. But he'd still screw her and release into those dirty brown eyes. Why not?

No, he wanted to take her and display her body parts in a place for all the town of do-gooders to see.

At least, that was the plan back then. With age and wisdom, a better plan had emerged. He thought again of the past.

She was a dumb little kid who got lost in his woods, and because of it, a search party almost found his Silent Place.

He vowed that someday he'd make her pay. He should've just done it that night when he found her wandering around helplessly in his woods. She was right there, ripe for the picking... But common sense prevented him. He knew people would come looking for her, sooner or later. And he was right. It wasn't long before that asshole Crockerman showed up and fed her Kit Kat bars and bullshit stories all night long. He knew he had to wait, it was just too risky...

And it was even more risky now, especially with that goddamn motion light. But he lived his life by fate and fate had given him his ultimate fantasy.

Picking the lock was child's play, but a simple motion light could ruin everything. If she had been awake when O'Rourke left, it would take about fifteen or twenty minutes for her to get back to sleep. Well, at least that's as long as he could wait. The sun would be up in a couple of hours, and he had to be off the water and back in his Silent Place by then. He had a decision to make, but he already knew what it would be. He was going to go for it.

The rain and wind didn't bother him, but the wait did. At fifteen minutes, he decided it was time. He put on the Cinderella mask, the one he had stolen from Pop Tucker's store decades ago, and ran across the sand.

He moved quickly up the stairs, waking the light to life. He ignored it. She was probably sound asleep. It was a major assumption, one that Nero normally would not rely on, but he wasn't listening to his rational voice. He was listening to the one that told him tonight he could take her beautiful eyes.

He picked the lock in seconds and eased into the house. A night-light was on in the tiny living room, barely illuminating a white board. He walked over and flashed his penlight on the board.

There were dozens upon dozens of theories of who Nero was and he wanted to laugh out loud at some of O'Rourke's suspects. The reporter had quite an imagination. Nero wasn't surprised that his birth name was on the board. It was clear O'Rourke had written down every man in Sandy Point, but what surprised him was one word written above all the names: Stradivarius.

How did O'Rourke know about the Stradivarius? Only one person knew about that, and his eyes were just found floating in a jar.

The question confounded his brain and slowed his task at hand. Finally, it came to him. The night The Fiddler made the phone call.

Nero never could track down a "Whitford" but a Whitford must've tracked down O'Rourke.

"That lucky prick," he growled, but allowed himself to smile because he heard her behind him.

He swung his body around, catching Echo Landers who was in mid-swing with a baseball bat.

Nero dodged it easily, pulled out his Taser, and let the bitch have it.

CHAPTER 49
OCTOBER 17, 2004

SUNDAY

J.T.

I t was 7:30 p.m. and I was emotionally and physically drained, but I could see the finish line. I pulled onto my street headed for home. I needed food and sleep, but my mind was still working. I thought of the conversation I just had with Crocker in his office.

"J.T., I want to thank you..." he began, but his voice cracked and he began to cry.

I stood there for a moment and then gave him an awkward hug.

"It's okay. What's wrong?"

"Nothing. For the first time in years, everything is right." He accepted the hug, wiped his eyes dry, and sat down behind his desk.

I waited for him to regain his composure.

He continued, "I need to tell you something, but I don't want any confusion. This is off the record."

I tried to lighten the moment. "Well, even if it were on the record, how could I ever print it? You have the final say."

There was no laughter.

"J.T., I remember your first day when you asked me why I wouldn't fire Harrison. I lied to you. The truth is, I tried firing him years ago, and that's when he gave me a picture. It was of Pop Tucker doing... ah... things to me while I was passed out. Harrison said the picture and others were sent to the newspaper when the case first broke. He told me Pop had sent them, stating if there was newspaper coverage, he would release the pictures to the world. Harrison told me he covered Tucker's arrest in a very limited manner to protect me. Well, I now know that was a lie. He used those pictures to blackmail me. He said he'd hand them over if I agreed that he had a job for life. I did. Obviously, I had no idea that he not only had negatives but that he was distributing them overseas. I literally got sick to my stomach this morning when you told me that. If I didn't buy his story way back when, none of this would've continued. I think of all the other victims. My friends. Jesus, my friends. I should've seen through it."

"I'm not going to let you sit there and blame yourself. You are a victim of sick people. You're also a survivor and you're now dating a survivor. You'll get through this. Look how far you've come."

"Thanks, J.T. But I still should've done something."

"Okay, then. It's not too late. You can talk with Dr. Courtland about this and see what she thinks, too. Don't you find it troubling that you immediately went off the record with me?"

"What do you mean?"

"Well, everyone being silent is what allowed guys like Tucker, Harrison, and Gallo to thrive. Let's be realistic. The paper is going to take quite a PR hit when this story comes out, considering Harrison worked here. But what would make a compelling story is if you did come forward — on the record — as a survivor. By doing that, you'd accomplish three things. 1. Fix the PR problem. 2. Be a role model to sexual abuse victims. And 3. By sharing everything, you'd also be able to let it all go. You could move on. This secret has been killing you. Let it go. Don't let any of them keep abusing you."

Crocker leaned back in his chair and steepled his hands. "You make a lot of great points. I'm not copping out when I say this, but: I need a little time to think. I'm still in shock."

"Okay, you think about it. But here's something that should cheer you up when you go to sleep tonight. When Harrison got busted this morning, he pissed his pants and cried like a little baby. Tonight, you'll be sleeping in a nice warm bed, and he'll be sleeping on a hard mattress in a cold cell."

423

Crocker cracked his first smile. "I will think about that. Thank you."

It was Crocker's smile I was picturing in my head as I pulled into my driveway. I wondered how many other victims were smiling like that right now after reading my online story that had gone up a few hours earlier.

I had received several calls from Lilly, Hauser, and others who wanted to interview me live for the eleven o'clock news. I politely declined and sent them all in the direction of Sal DeLuca. I had found out why he had fed me that story and others.

"I have Sage Stevens, one of the top book agents out of Boston and New York, who thinks my life would make a great story. She's been watching your stories, and we both think you should write it. You see, it's my hope in a few years to run for governor. If I already have a book out there highlighting my accomplishments, I'll have a leg up."

"I'll think about it," I equivocated, knowing full well that having Sage Stevens on my side would not hurt my own literary aspirations. Sage was a regular in the *Boston Herald's* "Inside Track" for her glamor, beauty, and ability to get all of her authors Stephen King level money. I knew I would agree, but I wasn't going to show him my excitement.

It was Crocker's smile I was picturing in my head as I pulled into my driveway. I wondered how many other victims were smiling like that right now after reading my online story that had gone up a few hours earlier. I was also smiling, excited to connect with Echo. It's amazing how not being able to reach someone on a cell phone can make them feel like a ghost. It almost felt like a lifetime ago we almost got intimate. I just wanted to hold her again and share my other exciting news.

Everyone always has an angle, I thought, as I got out of my Jeep, sprang up the steps, and opened the door.

I flipped on the lights. It felt like a hundred years since I had been home. I noticed nothing had been cleaned up from the night before. I kinda thought Echo would've done the dishes, but maybe I had fallen in love with a slob. I laughed. I didn't care. I looked around for a note but found nothing.

In the back of my mind, I did wonder if she had had second thoughts. I knew her cell phone was ruined, but she could've at least stopped by the paper.

"Don't analyze it," I told myself. I reminded myself that she had requested a personal day from the paper to develop the pictures from the Armstrong anniversary party and that tonight she had plans with David.

I went to get a Poland Spring from the fridge and noticed her cell phone on the counter.

That's odd. Why wouldn't she take it with her?

Just then, my own cell chimed and I looked at the screen. It was a random number. I considered not answering but then thought maybe Echo had got a new phone.

"Hello?"

"Hi J.T. It's Officer Jensen."

"Oh, hey. What's up, Jamal?" I asked, looking over and seeing the autographed baseball bat resting next to my TV.

Echo must've picked it up and put it there. Why would she take it out of my room?

"J.T., I've been trying to get in touch with Echo and it goes straight to voicemail. I'm worried."

"Oh, don't be. Her phone fell in a puddle last night. It's fried."

"Oh, thank God. It just seemed really strange with her Jeep and all, and David waiting for her."

"What?" I asked while noticing my whiteboard. Something about it was different. The word Stradivarius had been erased. My heart began pumping as I suddenly understood what was going on, but I asked the question anyway.

"What about her Jeep? And David?"

"Her Jeep was ticketed and towed up the street from you near the bike path. Did she overdo it with the rollerblading again? David is not happy. He's walking home from work as we speak."

"Holy shit. What do you mean he's walking home?" I asked, racing around my place.

"He called me 'cause she was supposed to pick him up from Lareby's. They have plans to go to the movies tonight."

"Where're his parents??" I gave up trying to hide my skyrocketing anxiety.

"They went to Newport this afternoon for some lawyer conference. J.T., what is going on?"

"Oh my God! Oh my God!!" I yelled, finding Echo's wallet and her clothes.

"J.T., talk to me!"

"It's Echo! I think… Oh, God! Nero's got her!"

NERO

Nero watched her. She looked so pretty with the rainbow-colored duct tape across her lips. He was glad he had chosen it for her. She was sound asleep in such a comfortable state. This was one of his favorite parts, and the fact that it was Echo Landers took it to another level of enjoyment.

He wondered what was going on in her mind. Was she dreaming like the slut she was? Dreaming about being gangbanged? Or maybe she was dreaming of beautiful innocent moments like sailing with her mother, stepfather, and that retard brother of hers. Either way, the dreaming would soon end. She'd wake up, and he'd be there to greet her with the ultimate nightmare.

He thought about his plan for her and decided it might be the best one yet. But for it to work best, he should keep her alive a little longer. The truly wonderful thing was — and, as always, fate had stepped in to help him — no one had reported her missing. He still couldn't believe his luck. He was way ahead of them. He ripped the duct tape off her mouth. She stirred to life.

"Hello, Echo!" he yelled from behind his Cinderella mask, and then shined a flashlight on his mask.

Her eyes popped wide open. She began flailing away, but quickly discovered that her arms and legs were bound tightly. She wasn't going anywhere. and when she realized it, her horror was a beautiful sight.

Nero laughed and turned the oxygen tank on before placing the mask over her face.

"This tank was my mother's. When she wasn't smoking cocks, she was smoking cigarettes," he laughed for a long time. "The poor bitch got emphysema and died a very slow death."

Echo screamed, and this only made Nero laugh more.

"Scream all you want. No one is going to hear you. In fact, no one will hear you ever again."

She screamed louder. This time he casually talked over it.

"So, where was I? Oh, yes. A little bedtime story for you. I always wanted to do my mother like I've done the rest of them, but even I knew it was too risky. She was like you — a dirty little birdy, screwing men and women and sometimes both at the same time. She had an abortion just like you. Just to live a convenient dirty lifestyle. So, it's only fitting that I fill you up with her dirty air. You are lucky, though. I usually strangle the sluts right away, or do other things... But I'm gonna let you live a little longer. But then... Well, that's when the fun will really begin. I can see your eyes are trying to figure it all out. Those poor pretty, dark marbles. Do you know who I am?"

Echo shook her head, no.

"Then I will show you." He raised his hand to his face just as a red light flashed in the darkness.

"What the — ?" Nero hurried toward the light and then climbed the ladder.

ECHO

Echo had screamed, over and over, but she knew she had to stop. Screaming wouldn't keep her alive. Using her head might. Although muffled behind the mask, his voice sounded familiar. She tried but couldn't place it. Whoever Nero was, he knew her.

If I can only figure out who it is, maybe I can use psychology on him? He thinks I'm a whore. Maybe I admit that I am and apologize to him. He might see me as his mother. Maybe that's all he wants, for his mother to apologize?

She moved on from her frantic efforts at pop psychology to trying to figure out where she was. She knew a couple of things. She was underground, and she was freezing. That didn't answer any questions. She could be anywhere. She decided to listen for any kind of sounds while at the same time praying in her head.

Nothing.

But then she heard panting, and it sounded like someone was coming down a ladder.

A flashlight blinded her eyes.

"What the...?" A voice exclaimed, and the light quickly went from Echo to around the room, illuminating cloudy jars with masking tape and writing on them.

Echo couldn't hold it in.

She begged, "Please! Please don't kill me!"

"Be quiet! I'm not going to kill you!" the voice whispered sharply then shone the light onto his own face — Chuck Renna from the bike store.

This only caused Echo to yell more.

"Ssh!" Chuck put his index finger to his lips, "He'll hear us! Man, this is so fucked up. I didn't even smoke. Jesus!"

Chuck removed the oxygen mask and began untying her hands and then her legs. That's when it finally dawned on her: He wasn't Nero. He was there to help.

"Echo, take this and this and call 911. I'll go back up there and stall him." He handed her his flashlight and cell.

"Don't, Chuck. Stay here. He's crazy. He'll kill you."

"I'll be fine. I have to buy you time," he put his hand on the ladder.

"At least take the flashlight," she pleaded.

"No, it's okay. I have a smaller one."

"Wait!"

"What?" Chuck paused.

"I don't even know where we are."

"Samoset Woods."

A moment later, she was alone again. She dialed but nothing happened. Again. Nothing. Again. She then realized she was probably nowhere near a cell phone tower.

Her only hope was to make a run for it, but the chances of making a call and possibly running away from Nero at the same time were slim. An idea grabbed her. By now, he'd be looking for her.

"But what's his number?" she whispered to herself.

Then it came to her. "The year before the Sox won the last World Series."

Instead of texting "Samoset Woods" to J.T. she decided to send two words that only he would know. That way if Nero caught her, it would at least buy a little time. Nero would never figure out the code.

At least, that's what she was desperately hoping.

She typed the message and pressed SEND. She knew it would only go to a certain point of sending since she had no signal, but if she made a run for it, the message would continue to send and finish when she got within range of a tower.

Again, at least that was what she was hoping.

She was in so much pain, physically and emotionally. If she stopped to listen to her body, she'd never move. She had to keep listening to the voice in her head that said "If you don't move, you'll die tonight."

NERO

Nero climbed the ladder ready to attack whoever was standing above.

Nobody. What he did make out was a coyote howling in the distance. He knew that sound. He had heard it before. The coyote was howling in pain. It must've found one of his traps. But that wouldn't explain setting off the red light of the motion detector. The light was only triggered when someone entered the confines of his Silent Place.

He flashed his light around the area, and everything was untouched, even his violin. Then it occurred to him: maybe the coyote had run through, set off the light, and continued on until it found the trap.

It made sense. What also made sense was killing the goddamn thing before it attracted more coyotes — or some animal-loving do-gooder trying to rescue it.

He sprinted to the spot and there was the coyote staring back at him. The trap had clamped down on his hind leg. Any other time, Nero would've watched his eyes for a little while and enjoyed the sound of death approaching. Tonight, he didn't have time. He gave the coyote a swift kick in the face and in the same motion pulled out a knife and sliced its throat.

Nero unhitched the trap, pulled the carcass out, and threw it to the side. Relieved that it was only a minor annoyance, he headed back to his Silent Place. He stopped walking when, under the moonlight, he spotted a figure emerging from the trapdoor. The silhouetted figure was too tall to be Echo. His muscles tensed.

He waited for the figure to move closer to him. When the person did, he was fully exposed under the white moon. Nero smiled.

ECHO

Echo kept the flashlight off while she climbed the ladder. It wasn't a long climb, but she stopped when the trapdoor flew open. She turned on the light and flashed it above her.

Gasping but then quickly recovering, she saw that it was Chuck Renna on all fours looking down at her. She went up a couple of more steps.

"What happened? Is he gone?" she kept her voice low. Then she noticed Renna's eyes. They were blank. Distant. And then a river of blood gushed from his mouth onto her.

Reflexively, Echo raised her hands to shield herself and fell, tumbling back to the bottom of the pit. She dropped both the cell and the flashlight when she hit the ground. Echo tried to regain her feet, but Renna's lifeless body tumbled down on top of her. She tried pushing him off her, but it was futile.

Like a wild animal, Nero leapt into the pit and pulled Renna off Echo. It was almost as if he didn't even see her. He was focused entirely on Renna. He continued to stab him in the heart, the stomach, the eyes... blood splattering and painting his Cinderella mask.

"You'll never see God!" Nero yelled over and over.

Echo was in shock at the scene, but her survival mode finally kicked back in. She realized Nero was so fixated on Renna that he didn't care what she was doing. She felt around for the cell phone but kept grabbing dirt.

He straddled Renna's body and continued tearing through flesh. Nero's back was to Echo and the ladder to the trapdoor was in front of her. This was her chance. She stood up and felt her foot kick the cell phone. She grabbed it and climbed the rungs of the ladder in seconds.

When she opened the trapdoor, the cold crisp night awakened her will to continue. She put the cell in her sweatpants pocket and felt something else. It was her perfume bottle. She took it out, opened it, and emptied it on the ground.

At least, they might find my body.

If she allowed that thought to penetrate her brain, fear may've paralyzed her right then and there, but she refused to give up. She sprinted ahead but didn't know where she was going. She was just zigzagging, banging into trees, whipped by branches.

"Get back here!" Nero commanded.

The voice was no longer muffled. It was clear, and it sounded so familiar. He had taken off his mask. But this was no time to think about who he was.

She took the phone out and pressed SEND again. She couldn't stop running. She ran and kept pressing the button.

Her energy was draining.

Gaining. She felt him behind her. She felt his breath. She felt him tackling her. And then she felt nothing.

CHAPTER 50

OCTOBER 17, 2004

SUNDAY

J.T.

"Get in the Jeep!" I yelled at David for the third time.

"No! I can't drive with strangers."

"I'm not a stranger! I'm J.T. You know me!"

"Unless you know the code word, my parents say you're a stranger."

"The code word is: get the fuck in! We don't have time!"

"You're making me nervous." David recoiled. It finally registered that my approach wasn't working.

"I'm sorry, David. Wait one second."

I dialed Jamal. He picked up after the first ring.

"Did you hear from her?" Jamal was out of breath.

"No. It's David. He won't get in my Jeep. Could you talk to him?"

"Jesus. Okay. Put him on."

"David," I handed the phone out my window, "It's Officer Jensen. He wants to talk to you."

David studied the phone for what felt like an eternity before finally taking it.

"Hello, Officer Jensen," there was a long pause, "Yes, but he doesn't know the code word."

An even longer pause and then: "Yes, I understand… I will… Okay… Thank you."

David hung up, but then looked down and inspected the phone again.

Hurry up! Give it back!

"We all set?" I asked him, motioning for the phone. He finally handed it over before walking over to the passenger side. After he settled into the seat, I hit the gas and we were off. After about a mile, I turned to him.

"I'm sorry for yelling at you back there, but I have to be honest with you."

He didn't respond.

"I'm worried about your sister."

"I'm mad at her. She is supposed to take me out tonight. She didn't show up. She always shows up. She said this was going to be our special night."

"I know David, that's why I'm worried. She'd never forget you. She loves you. I'm sure something just came up. I'm going to take you home and then go look for her."

"Where are you going to look for her?" he asked.

I have no clue!

"Around town. When I drop you off, I want you to do something for me. It may help us find Echo."

"Okay. What?"

"I want you to keep calling your parents And the moment you get through to them, I want you to have them call me. Any guess as to why they haven't answered their phones?"

"They were going to the movies after Dad's conference. You're not supposed to have your phone on at the movies. It's rude."

"Oh, that explains it," I said more to myself. I then thought of DeLuca and why he wasn't answering. When last I saw him, he was leaving the station to get some much-needed sleep. He was probably snoring away. I had told Jamal to send a car over to his hotel and wake his ass up. I needed DeLuca's firepower ASAP if we had any chance of finding Echo alive.

From out of nowhere David asked, "What is Cool Hand?"

The name jogged a memory of Lillian Dumas's dog. For a split second, I was back in that warm, early summer memory of my first day of hanging out with Echo. I wanted to stay there.

"Cool Hand. You mean, *who* is Cool Hand. He's a… well, *was* a dog. Why are you asking? Did your sister tell you about him?"

"Cool Hand is a him?"

"Yeah, David. He was Lillian Dumas's dog."

"Oh, I know her. She's not very nice. She always wants me to double bag everything. That's why I like my other job working for the beaches. I can take my time and make the sand nice and smooth, and no one bothers me."

"Yes, I've seen you out there. You do great work. But David, why are you asking me about Cool Hand?"

"It was in the text message."

"What text message?"

"The text message you got when I was on the phone with Jamal."

I grabbed my phone and clicked on the message. It was only two words: Cool Hand.

I scanned the sender. It was just a number, a number I didn't recognize.

"Cool Hand…" I said the words again. "Oh my God!"

I spun the wheel hard, doing a U-turn.

"What are you doing? Where are we going? My house is the other way!" David was nervous again.

"Trust me. We're going to find your sister."

I dialed Jamal.

He answered, "What now?"

"She's in Samoset Woods!"

"Did she call you?"

"No, texted me. Take this down. 555-3160. Have DeLuca, or whoever, trace it. Don't call it. It's clear she sent it as a code to me. Only I would know what she was talking about. If she was safe, she would've just come out and written Samoset Woods."

"Alright. Be careful. We're right behind you."

"Jamal! Wait! No sirens! We know what this… ah… person… is ah… capable of. We don't want to tip off… you know…" looking over at David, I was trying to find the right words. Fortunately, Jamal understood my cryptic behavior.

"I hear you, J.T. No sirens. Wait for us, though."

"Sure."

Click.

There was no way in hell I was going to wait for anyone.

"See. I told you codes are good," David said nonchalantly.

"Yes, David, codes are good."

"Does that mean my sister is okay?"

I pulled up to the main entrance, skidded to a stop, and parked.

"She's going to be fine, but I need you to stay here in case Echo shows up."

He nodded yes and said, "I don't know why she'd be in the woods. She hates the woods. She told me she got lost in there when she was little."

"I know, buddy. I think she just got lost again. That's why I'm going to find her."

I faked a smile before jumping out and sprinting down the main path.

My phone rang: DeLuca.

I clicked on as I kept running down the dark trail.

"Where are you?" he asked.

"Samoset Woods. Never mind me. What about you?"

"Just talked to Jensen. I sent a K-9 unit to your place."

"Why? She's in the woods."

"Yes, but the dogs have to get her scent first and no one's at her house. Your place was the last spot we know of. Not to mention the dogs may get Nero's scent, too."

"Okay," I stopped to catch my breath at a dead end in the trail where I had to decide to go left or right.

"Get here now. Any trace on the number?"

"I'm starting to... lose... you..." His voice turned static.

"You got a name for that number?" I tried again.

"J.T., I... ca... hear... you... Wait... us... Don't go..." DeLuca's voice was now complete static. I clicked the phone off. It sounded like he was asking me to wait for him, but I didn't have time for any of that bullshit. I had to find her, but at the same time, I realized I was walking in circles. If only I had a flashlight, I might have had a chance to at least maneuver or look for tracks or something.

I opened my cell and it lit up. I was hoping to use it as a flashlight, but it was more like a weak night-light. It wasn't much, but it would have to do. My other problem: the battery was about to die.

Do I turn left or right?

I was about to decide when the faint green light illuminated something at the base of a massive briar patch. I rushed over and shined my cell on it. It was a piece of dark fabric and white stuffing. Crouching down to get a better look, I decided it looked like someone had ripped their coat while crawling under the sharp thorns.

Did they see me coming and were hiding behind the briar patch or did this happen earlier?

It might have had nothing to do with Nero and Echo, but I had no other leads. The alternative would be to go left or right. I stopped to think — and listened. I could hear the ocean beyond the cliff and then another memory came to me.

I could see Lillian Dumas smoking her cigarette and telling Echo and me that, on quiet nights, she could hear the lobstermen listening to music out on the ocean beyond the woods. The noise never bothered her, she said, because it sounded like classical music.

I remembered thinking it was kind of odd for lobstermen to listen to classical music, but I was from the city, so I hadn't questioned it.

Oh my God. She hadn't heard classical music on a fishing boat. She heard someone playing a violin in the woods!

I knew that someone was Nero. He was somewhere beyond that briar patch.

NERO

Nero was running out of time. He had spent a few minutes catching his breath, collecting his thoughts, and grabbing more duct tape — when he accidentally stepped on the phone. The surge of satisfaction he felt from knocking Echo out vanished at that moment. He picked up the phone and read the message: Cool Hand.

He quickly identified it as belonging to Chuck Renna.

What a hero!

Nero checked the time it was sent — fifteen minutes ago. There was no turning back.

They may already be looking for me!

His Silent Place would no longer be silent. The world would soon know. He always knew this day would come, and he had prepared for it, but the reality made him reflective.

So much fun! So many killings… So many eyes…

He didn't have time for sentimentality.

Stop it! Get moving!

He had to execute his exit strategy. Fast.

He carried Echo's unconscious body down to the beach, and, like a sack of potatoes, dumped her into his boat. He stood over her, watching her. She was quietly dreaming again.

The dumb bitch probably thought she was so clever. It's too bad she didn't know that I was the one who cut the annoying dog's head off. Her horrified eyes will be so beautiful when I tell her that!

He trudged back up the dunes and sprinted through the woods back to his Silent Place. After going down the ladder and stepping on and over Renna's body, he grabbed the first of three canisters of gasoline.

The plan was a simple one. He'd saturate his Silent Place, and like his hero and namesake, he'd torch it. All of it.

His violin was stored in the hollowed out tree from his youth. It was waiting for him. Nero planned to play it while watching the flames engulf his Rome.

Yes! Tonight, my dream will come true. Tonight, I will truly be Nero!

Having already replaced his Cinderella mask with his night-vision goggles, he made his way with the drum back up the ladder. He rushed about, dousing the bushes around the base of his camp. He repeated the procedure and just as he was finishing with the last canister, he stopped.

He had heard a voice.

Then nothing.

Silence.

Rustling.

It was coming from the side of the briar patch closest to the main path. Nero strained his ears.

"Ahhhh."

Someone was grunting in pain. The thorns were ripping into whoever was crawling into his Silent Place.

Nero moved closer. The figure was squirming like a worm under and through the bush. The figure finally broke through. It was about to rise, completely unaware that Nero was inches away.

But Nero knew who it was. He checked Renna's phone — it had one bar on it. It was just enough to make a call.

This will be fun!

Nero smiled and dialed the number from the text message. The night below him lit up green.

"Shit," the crawler whispered.

"Aren't you going to answer it?" Nero laughed then drew back his steel-toed boot and kicked J.T. O'Rourke directly in the face.

O'Rourke tumbled over, and Nero laughed again.

A second later, Nero's knife was out, ripping through jacket and clothing and striking flesh. It was in O'Rourke's back, just above his right shoulder blade.

O'Rourke's scream awakened the night.

Nero pulled the blade out quickly and plunged it into the same spot, this time twisting it.

The scream that followed brought pleasure to Nero's loins. He pulled it out again, took another lunge, but this time missed and struck dirt.

O'Rourke had rolled away, but Nero could see him.

Nero laughed. He was caught up in the moment and had strayed from the reality of the situation. He had to be quick, but he wasn't thinking that way. He was thinking about fun. And he was having it. He sauntered over, raised his blade, but suddenly felt his body falling to the ground.

"What the hell?" Nero was in shock.

His eyes took in the new information. Someone was on top of him.

"Stop hurting people! Stop it!" The voice repeated over and over, punching Nero as he yelled. The blows delivered more shock than pain. Then he figured it out.

The goddamn retard brother is trying to play hero! Shit! Two of them! This is too risky! Go! Go now!

As soon as it registered, Nero pushed the retard off, got up, and ran. He would've loved to collect their eyes, especially O'Rourke's, since retards are God's mistake so there was no way the 'tard was going to heaven.

But Nero didn't have time. He sprinted beyond the ring of gasoline, turned around, lit a match, and dropped it.

The fire erupted in a perfect circle, surrounding not only his Silent Place, but also O'Rourke and the retard.

It was comical watching them realize that they were about to burn to death.

Nero strolled over to the hollowed out tree, grabbed his violin, and began to play. He had never felt so much peace, listening to them scream in unison, but reality hit and punched Nero in the head again.

A fire would bring sirens and sirens would wake the slut on the boat.

437

He had to go. He thought about bringing the violin but decided to put it back in the hollow tree.

Soon his Rome would be ashes, and he would no longer be Nero to the world. As he raced down toward his boat, he decided he would start fresh.

I need a new name. What will my new name be? How I kill the slut on the boat might help me come up with one.

CHAPTER 51

OCTOBER 17, 2004

SUNDAY

J.T.

I couldn't believe it. It didn't seem real. It was like one of my nightmares. Everything went from slow motion to high-speed action.

Let me back up.

After struggling with the constant jabbing of multiple thorns finding my face and legs, I finally made it to the other side of the briar patch. I emerged onto thick grass, like you might find on a golf course, and tried to collect my thoughts — then my cell rang.

I reached to turn off the ringer but was surprised by a male's voice. He was standing above me. I couldn't see what he looked like, and I have no idea what he said, but whatever it was, he sure thought it was funny because he laughed.

My face then felt like it had been struck with a vicious uppercut, and I had that familiar salty taste of blood in my mouth. I spat it out and realized it had come from a boot.

Seconds later, I heard ripping. Something dug into the back of my North Face jacket. I couldn't figure out the noise, but it was followed instantly by what felt like an electric shock to my system.

439

Suddenly a flashback of being a kid and getting ready to watch the Red Sox play the Reds in the World Series came to me.

Why am I thinking about that?

As quickly as the flashback appeared, it left. The shock turned into a cold steel numbing near my right shoulder blade. Then the frigid sensation became a constant throbbing pain. That's when I figured out what was going on. I was being stabbed.

I rolled over and turned my head just in time to see a knife blade strike dirt. The realization of being stabbed seeped into my brain and slowed my movements. What had begun as an electric shock now felt like a thousand killer bees had just invaded my right shoulder. I surveyed the damp area on my back with my left hand then brought it up to my face. Blood. And lots of it.

I was bleeding, but I had to force my mind away from thinking about that and focus on what was happening. Nero was going to stab me to death.

I raised my head and saw the night-vision goggles framing his face. He looked so familiar. My mind was processing it. If I studied him a little longer, I knew I could figure out who he was... But that's when I also realized my slight hesitation was about to kill me.

The blade came down on me. I knew it was over.

But my real-life nightmare turned from slow motion into fast-paced hell on wheels. A body flew through the air knocking Nero to the ground. It was David.

He just saved my life!

Before I could process anything, a wall of flames shot up, encircling us.

"He hurt you with his knife. Are you okay?" David asked.

"Yes! We have to find a way out." I pointed at the orange ball of fire closing in on us.

My burning eyes searched frantically, but found no exit. The smoke and heat built, choking our lungs, and we coughed for air. But what really choked me, and any hope of survival, was the harsh sound of a violin being played beyond the flames.

Even if we escape, he will be there waiting to end us.

I couldn't let that hopeless feeling defeat me. I had been on the ropes before and had come out the winner. I immediately turned on my boxer's brain, looking for Nero's mistake.

"We're going to burn to death!" David yelled.

"No! No, we're not! Stay calm!" I hollered.

Where is Nero's mistake?

And then I saw it. It brought another flashback of my youth. Jumping on the T with my buddies and going to see *Red Dawn*.

It was right out of *Red Dawn* — a trapped door cut into the grass.

There was no way I would've seen it any other time, but Nero had made a mistake. He had forgotten to shut it.

Thank you, Nero!

"Over there!" Using my left hand, I grabbed David and ushered him through the billowing smoke.

"You first!" I ordered.

"What if it's a trick?"

I hadn't thought of that. We have no other choice...

"He didn't have time to think up tricks. Go down there! Go now!" I knew if I went first there was a chance David wouldn't follow.

"I don't know if I want to..." he hesitated, but I nudged him forward. Either he was going to climb on his own, or I was going to push him down into that black hole.

David put his foot on the ladder and slowly began his descent. As soon as there was room, I started down after him. I pulled the trapdoor shut above my head, plunging us into complete darkness.

"I'm scared."

"We'll be okay." I tried to sound reassuring.

I continued down the ladder, but then David gave a horrific scream.

"What's wrong? What's wrong, David?"

"A body! It's ah!! It's a body! I tripped over a body!"

Oh Jesus! Oh, no! It's Echo! Oh my God!

I scaled down the last few rungs but tripped and went sprawling on all fours. Like a blind man, I furiously felt around on the dirt floor — until I touched a lifeless hand.

"Is it my sister? *Is it?*" David began to cry.

"Do you have your cell phone?"

"Yes."

"David! Turn it on!"

The small green glow dimly illuminated the area around it. David was across from me. Our eyes met for a moment before we both had the courage to look down.

One of the strangest feelings I have ever experienced came over me then. The sight was absolutely grotesque — a man riddled with stab wounds all over his body, even his eyes. There was no way anyone could identify him.

The natural reaction should've been screaming in fear, but instead, in unison, we both uttered the same phrase, "Thank God."

"Echo, are you here?" David yelled.

"Echo! It's David and me!" I followed.

Silence.

"David, I need your phone."

He handed it to me — no reception.

"I think that's Mr. Renna," David said quietly.

"Why do you think that?"

"He always wears a light blue winter coat like that one."

I took another look and the features seemed to fit.

"I am scared J.T. Did the bad man kill my sister?" His quiver was coming back.

"No, he didn't. I promise. I think he has her, though."

Why did I say that? I have no clue what he's done.

"What are we going to do?" he stammered.

I shined the light around and saw glass jars on a shelf in the distance. I knew what they were — trophies. I flashed the beam away quickly before David focused on them. Then I spotted an air tank next to a chair.

"Follow me."

We went over to the air tank. There was also a full replacement next to it. Beside that were several bottles of spring water piled up.

"David, we have oxygen and water. We're going to be okay. We can stay here until the firefighters come."

"But what about Echo! He's going to hurt her!"

"I won't lie to you. I know. We have to think about who that man is. We must know him, somehow. What do you remember about him? Did anything stand out?"

"I don't remember anything! I'm scared! He's going to hurt my sister!"

"David, I need you to stay calm." I directed the green light toward his eyes before shining it on my own face, "We have to stay calm for Echo."

"What's that?" David's tone softened as he pointed to something hanging off my jacket.

I looked down, "It looks like duct tape."

"I know. It's rainbow duct tape. That is very hard to get around here. You know, I've made a couple of rainbow duct tape wallets." There was glee in his voice, and he clapped.

Jesus H. Christ kid!

"This is good," he said.

I couldn't believe it. A dead body was only feet away, and his sister could be next if she hadn't already been killed, and here was David talking about making rainbow wallets.

I pulled the duct tape off my coat and handed it to him. He inspected it like it was gold.

"Where did you get this?" David asked.

"Jesus, I don't know. I must've rolled in it after I tripped over the body. Remember, there's a dead body down here!"

"Oh, yes, this is good." He smiled.

Nothing was getting through to him.

"David, we don't have time! I need you to focus! We need to figure out who he is!" I pointed emphatically to the space above us.

David smiled again. "I just did. I know who the bad man is. That is why I'm happy."

NERO

Orange flames engulfed Nero's woods. He paused to take it in before guiding his boat into the water, hopping over the incoming surf. He was regretting his decision to leave his violin behind in the hollow tree. He thought long and hard about going back for it. His life story was in that tree and, due to his impulsive act, it would never be told. He knew he'd never tell it. The end was near, and there was no way in hell he was going to let them take him alive. Not only had he been impulsive, but he had also been sloppy.

His fingerprints, DNA, and handwriting were all over his Silent Place.

Surprise! It's me!

After discovering the charred remains of O'Rourke and the 'tard, they'd find the trapdoor that led to Renna, and once that door was opened, the evidence would reveal Nero's true identity.

He only had a couple of hours before they'd come for him. He had to use that time wisely. He opted to go full throttle. His boat raced just beyond the jetties of several beaches.

The wind whipping his face and the serenity of the moment calmed his mind. He found himself back in a memory.

It was that night long ago, moments before he killed his father.

He was Junior again, sitting cross-legged on a throw rug, listening to his drunken father.

"Remember, boy, how I told you I lost these two fingers in Korea when a grenade exploded?" Senior leaned forward, flashing the stubs on his left hand.

Junior nodded.

"Well, I lied to you. I never even served in Korea. You know how I really lost these?"

Junior shook his head, no.

"Of course you don't. You see, when I was six years old my ol' man bought me a cheap violin and paid for lessons. He thought music would be good for me. It was. I loved the goddamn thing. My teacher, Heidi, said I was a natural and that I could be something special. That made my ol' man search everywhere for the perfect violin.

Sure enough, his friend, an antique dealer, told him he had a replica of a Stradivarius. No one would know the difference. There was only one problem. It was stolen. And also, it was made by the Nazis."

Junior's eyes bulged and Senior laughed.

"I know, huh, the Nazis. They were quite good at forgeries, and they made a couple hundred Stradivarius knockoffs. My father's friend warned him that it could be cursed. My ol' man laughed, bought it, and gave it to me. He never told me any of this, mind you. My bitch of a mother did, years later." Senior was fading into his drink.

"So, ah, what happened then?" Junior found the courage to ask.

"It *was* cursed. My ol' man died of a heart attack two days later. The weak S.O.B.

A year later, my mother remarried, and my life changed for good. Her new husband was vicious. He told me I had to help him at work. I refused and told him I wanted to play my violin instead. So he handed it to me and made me play it fifteen hours straight, until my hands bled. He yelled, 'Had enough yet? Do you want to stop??' and I begged him, 'Yes, please! Please!' So he said, 'Give me the violin, then.' I handed it to him and he was about to smash it, but my mother

444

at least had the decency to take it from him and put it away, never to be seen again."

Nero paused his flashback to dock the boat. He hoisted Echo up and slung her body over his shoulder. He hurried to his car and shoved her into the back seat.

Nero fired up the engine and began humming "Goodnight, Irene" and was back in the flashback listening to his father.

"It was shortly after that I had to go work for my stepfather. I was eleven years old and working every day for him after school. One day when my mother wasn't around, I told my stepfather to 'fuck off' and that I would never work for him again. I said I was going to be the world's greatest violinist, and do you know what he did?" Senior asked, but again Nero had to stop the flashback.

He parked the car, pulled Echo out of the back seat, and carried her into the unlit back entrance of the building. He walked over to the new elevator and, with his pinky, pushed G for "ground floor."

Sighing, he went back into the memory.

"No, what did he do?" Junior asked the safe question.

"He wanted to know which hand I used to play the strings. I showed him my left one. Before I knew what was happening, he grabbed my hand and chopped two of my fingers off. He yelled, 'Now you'll never play the violin ever again!' In pain and shock, I slumped to the floor in a heap, but he hauled me up and said, 'Now I'm going to teach you how to kill and how to become strong!' And, as much as I hated the bastard, he did. He gave me a cleaver and pointed to Old Heidi. I butchered her that night. I felt such a great sense of power. I still do."

"You *killed* your violin teacher?" Junior asked in disbelief, and Senior roared with laughter.

"No, no..." he was still chuckling, "Do you think I'm crazy? Old Heidi was our milk cow that I had named after my violin teacher. You see, he taught me to be who I am today, and that's what I was doing with you that day on the beach. I was teaching you how to kill. I'll tell you what, though... I wish I had never made you burn that violin."

After that moment, Junior admitted he hadn't burned the violin. It was safe and waiting for his father. And that's when his father spun out of control. That old memory now took control of Nero.

He slammed Echo onto a stainless steel cart, grabbed a filet knife, and in lightning-fast speed, cut off her clothes. He lifted her up and let her clothes fall to the floor. Then he flopped her limp body back onto the cart, tying her arms and legs, spread-eagle, to the four steel supports at the corners.

This is going to be the best one yet!

He went over to one of several fish tanks lining the wall. This one held dozens upon dozens of lobsters.

When he realized his Silent Place was to be no more, he wanted to honor his father. After all, with age, he had gained a far greater appreciation for his father. It occurred to him how he could both pay homage and offer an apology to his spirit, so he had taken two of Chuck Renna's fingers.

He pulled the fingers out of his pocket and held them over the tank for a few seconds before dropping them in. It was fitting. Renna was always walking around in his woods half-baked. He knew sooner or later he'd have to kill him.

He just wished he'd had the time to make it so that stoner loser wouldn't see God, he thought while watching the lobsters make a mad dash toward the fingers. Being banded, the poor bastards could only bat them around.

"I know the feeling," he said and plucked one out. He took the bands off and plopped it back in. He did this with two others and watched as the tug-o-war began.

"That's more like it." He smiled but suddenly felt empty. He had to face what was going on in his head.

Next to the tank, on another steel cart, sat an old record player with a long extension cord that was plugged into the wall.

He looked at it. In his rash decision to leave his violin behind, he hadn't fully considered how much he still needed a bit of Nero in his soul. He turned on the player, and the sound of beautiful violin music followed.

You can enjoy the music, but remember: you are no longer Nero. Embrace who you really are!

The music made Echo stir. Soon she'd be awake.

Embrace who you really are.

He smiled and walked over to the pristine white lab coat hanging on the wall. He pulled it off the hook, looked down, and momentarily fingered the stitching that spelled "Jared Lareby."

Junior was no longer Nero.

He was now simply Jared Lareby — the Butcher of Cape Cod.

J.T.

"*Jared Lareby* is *Nero*? What the hell are you talking about?"

I was trying to make sense of what David had just told me. Logically, it didn't seem possible, but when I heard his name, my gut danced with apprehension. There was always something about the guy that I never could pinpoint.

"The rainbow duct tape."

"I know, David, you keep saying that. Explain."

"When I was working at Lareby's the other night collecting shopping carts, I noticed one had rolled behind the market. After I grabbed it, I walked by Mr. Lareby's Mercedes. He always parks in the back. The back door wasn't shut all of the way, so I opened it and was about to shut it again. But then I saw some really cool rainbow duct tape. There were four rolls of it."

The hairs on my neck came alive. I nodded for him to continue.

"Well, you know how I like to make duct tape wallets. I... ah, ah, ah, I took one roll of tape. I didn't think he'd notice. But maybe he did. Oh my God, do you think he found out that I took it and that's why he took Echo? Oh my God is it because of me that my sister is going to get hurt? It's all my fault!"

"No, David! Listen to me! This has nothing to do with you. I promise you. That guy is crazy. Remember, he hurt Mr. Renna, and that has nothing to do with the duct tape. None of this is because of you. You've actually done great work figuring out who Nero is!"

"But he's going to hurt Echo. How can we save my sister?"

If he hasn't already killed her!

I tried to push the thought from my head and think of a plan. An idea struck.

"He's not going to hurt Echo 'cause I'm not going to let him. But David, do you want to know how you can really help your sister?"

"How?"

"Wait here a minute and then I'll tell you." I felt my way through the dark until I was at Chuck Renna's body.

I had to get Renna's winter coat off. I tried respecting the remains by gently pulling at it while keeping his head upright, but it wasn't working. The nauseating stench of death inflamed my nostrils. I thought I was going to puke. Also, there was the throbbing pain from the knife wounds in my shoulder and I had to constantly open and close my right hand to keep blood flowing.

"I'm sorry, Chuck," I whispered and let his lifeless head fall. I used both hands and yanked as hard as I could, and when I did, his head banged around like a bobblehead.

Finally, the coat slid off both arms, and I tumbled to the ground in the process.

"This might work," I said to myself as I got up and inspected it.

I was fortunate Renna had essentially overdressed by wearing such a big winter coat. I slipped it over my head and torso but kept the arms free, like a person protecting their hair from a sudden downpour.

This might be the perfect shield from the fire.

I headed back to David.

"Why do you have Mr. Renna's coat over your head?" He flashed his cell phone light on me.

"You'll understand in a moment. David, see all of that spring water?"

"Yes."

"I need you to pour as much of it over me as possible? I need to get completely drenched. All of my clothes need to be soaking wet."

"Why?"

"Please just do it and then I'll tell you."

David opened and poured bottle after bottle over me, causing me to start shivering uncontrollably, which was ironic considering what I was about to do.

"Okay, that's good. Now, David, do you know how you can help your sister?"

"No. But I also don't know why you put Mr. Renna's coat on, or why you made me pour water all over you."

"Fair enough. It might seem kinda crazy, but it's all part of you helping Echo. You see, I need you to be strong and stay here. If you put that oxygen mask over your mouth, you will have air to breath until the fire is out."

"Are you going to run through the fire?"

"I have no other choice."

"That's dangerous."

"I know. And staying here is also dangerous. But we both have to do dangerous things to help your sister. Don't worry, I will get you help first." I tried to be calm and break it down the best way I could, but I still expected resistance. After a minute of processing, he surprised me.

"I don't need help. I can stay here. I am a big boy. But J.T., you have to help my sister. I knew Mr. Lareby was a bad man. He was too nice to me. It was strange. No one is that nice in life. Go save Echo from the bad man."

"I will." I nodded, made my way up the ladder, I stopped for a moment. In this den of stench, a sweet smell faintly penetrated my nostrils. It was Echo's fragrance. At first, I was dizzy with memories of her smile, but then my blood boiled realizing what Nero probably had done to her. I knew I'd kill him. I pushed the trapped door open to be greeted by the roar of flames. The fire was still in a ring around the clearing and was beginning to catch on some trees, but it hadn't made its way across the grass yet. That was a good sign. I'd have enough space to get a running start. I popped the trapped door open to be greeted by the roar of flames. The fire was still in a ring around the clearing and was beginning to catch on some trees, but it hadn't made its way across the grass yet. That was a good sign. I'd have enough space to get a running start.

I pulled myself up and let the trapdoor fall back into the ground. I draped the dripping, fur-trimmed hood over my head and stared in front of me.

A wall of flames was standing between me and hopefully Echo. I couldn't waste another second since the heat was already causing steam to rise from my clothes. I felt sweat streak across my brow and my heart rate rise with the temperature.

"Let's do this!" I yelled to myself, closed my eyes, and sprinted as fast as I could into the flames. They instantly attacked, like Nero's knife, stabbing all around me. I opened my eyes and could see a cloud of steam forming around me. The strangest thought followed. I look like Pig Pen with his dust cloud in *Peanuts*. The thought must have helped my mind detach from the event because, before I knew it, I had made it completely through to the other side. Like a drag racer unleashing his 'chute, I let go of Renna's coat, which was engulfed in flames, and hit the ground. I rolled back and forth on the ground like I had been taught in grade school. I glanced at the coat. The flames from it had caught on to the branches of a nearby tree.

"Fuck! Fuck! Fuck!" I yelled in pain, looking down and realizing my left leg was still on fire. I grabbed a handful of dirt and leaves and slammed them over and over against the leg until the last flame was out.

I was breathing heavy and knew I couldn't let the excruciating pain win. I needed to use my mind. I was briefly grateful for all those times in the ring when I got the shit kicked out of me. I had lived with pain before and now, with the burnt leg on top of the bleeding shoulder, I had to trick my body.

You're not in the woods. You're in the boxing ring and you still have a few more rounds to go.

I rose from my canvas and continued on. The farther I got away from the fire the stronger I felt and the faster I ran.

Where does Lareby live? I have no clue! Why didn't I take David's cell? How could I be so stupid?

I was cursing myself, but as I left the woods, I saw Jamal's cruiser and felt instant relief. I rushed to the car, but it was locked, lights off.

Shit! He's probably in the woods looking for me! What do I do? What do I do?

Memories flashed of when I lost my keys at parties behind radiators and stereos that also resulted in lost girlfriends. All of this rolled through my mind as I ran toward my Jeep.

Where the hell is my mind going? What was I thinking about?

The severe needling pain in my back and leg caused my brain to wander back to K Street. I had to get a grip. I wasn't eighteen back in Southie doing Jello shots wondering if one of the Delaney sisters was going to let me unhook their bra.

"Wow, they had some party balloons."

It was a bizarre reaction and even stranger to laugh at that moment, but I did, and that's when I confirmed something to myself: I was getting loopy.

The keys! Do I have my keys??

"Keep your shit together, O'Rourke!" I yelled and felt my left pants pocket — the keys were still there. I got in my Jeep, started it, and headed out.

Where the hell am I going? Go to the police station!

I was feeling dizzy and confused. I had to stay in the moment. I couldn't keep drifting.

Think about Lareby! Where would he take her? Where would he have room to hide her?

For anyone else, it would've been obvious, but I wasn't running on full mental capacity. It took me a minute before it finally hit me.

"Lareby's Market!"

The market was closed. Lareby would have all the privacy in the world to do whatever he wanted to do to Echo.

"Fuck the police station!"

I spun my wheel and hauled ass for Lareby's. I hoped I was right. Time was running out.

CHAPTER 52

OCTOBER 17, 2004

SUNDAY

ECHO

Echo sighed in comfort. She felt warm water wash over her breasts and continue down to her belly. Was she taking a bath? Or was she dreaming about taking a bath?

Maybe I'm at the spa? Oh, goody, a day at the spa!

She loved the thought. It soothed her, along with the classical music that played in the background.

Embracing the pure relaxation that settled into her body, she gave a contented moan.

Opening her eyes, she was brought back to reality. Blinding white lights bore down and fear awoke within. The memory of Nero replaced her previous thoughts and her chest immediately heaved with terror.

Was she dead? Were the white lights and the voice beyond them calling her to heaven? If so, shouldn't there be a sense of peace, not fear?

She figured it out. She had to leave the terrifying thoughts of Nero behind and focus on the voice, so she could go to heaven and find serenity.

"Sponge baths can be so very pleasant. Don't you agree?"

Echo nodded yes, but her eyes were finally adjusting to the light. She looked to her right and then swung her head to the left. She couldn't move her arms; her hands were tied. She stared down at her chest and could see her naked breasts. The warmth from the water was now a cold steel table numbing her buttocks. She tried to move her legs, but they were tied, too, and she felt air between them. She was not dead. She was bound — spread eagle — to a metal table. She was completely exposed, wide open, and there was nothing she could do about it. Fear heated her blood, and it raced through her system.

"I thought I'd clean you up, especially that dirty clam of yours," the voice laughed mirthlessly. "A fitting statement considering I have you in this room."

Echo screamed.

"Actually, I probably should've done this over by the crab tank. Get it? Crab tank." He laughed again, and she answered him with more screams.

"Do you know who I am?"

"No! And I don't care! I swear I won't tell anyone anything! Please let me go!"

"Oh, you won't tell anyone? Okay. I guess I should let you go, then." He paused for a beat or two, pretending to be serious — and then he laughed in her face, "I honestly love how people beg for their lives. Do you think I'd go through all of this trouble just to let you go?" He turned off one of the lights and his face came into focus.

It was Jared Lareby.

"Jared?"

"I guess I *am* Jared now."

"But you're so nice. I don't believe it. This is not you. You don't do these things. You wouldn't hurt a soul."

"Shut up!" He slapped her across the face with his left hand and then flashed a knife inches from her eyes that grew wide.

"Now, Echo, I don't want to hear another word. If I do, I will make it worse than it has to be. Right now, it's actually going to be quite pleasurable for you. Well, at least for a while. I know you're weak and tired, but you have to stay with me if you want to be part of the fun. Okay?"

He straightened his coat but took off his pants while he kept talking. His penis dangled loosely, inches from her face. She turned her head away in disgust.

"I know you're not shy, but you can play that game. First a gift." He took a necklace out of his coat pocket and put it around her neck, "I used to wear this when Lillian Dumas would pick up her groceries. She had no clue."

Echo strained to see what was attached to the necklace but could only make out some sort of tag.

"I suppose you can't read it from there. Let me help you." He held it up where her eyes could focus on it. "It says 'Cool Hand.'"

Echo's heart began to shut down. There was no hope of a rescue.

"Yes, I saw that little trick you tried to pull with the text message. It didn't work. It's funny, 'cause I knew Cool Hand quite well. He tried interrupting me one night and two days later he was burger meat for poor grieving Lillian. I remember her complaining that she got sick from the hamburger. Apparently, she didn't love him as much as she claimed." He laughed for a long time before he continued.

"You see, I know everything about everyone in this town. Especially you. I could give you a Kit Kat and tell you stupid stories," he taunted, "but I'm not going to. I'm going to give you what you really want — a nice hard cock from an older man. I know you like hard cocks on older men because I used to watch you back in high school. I remember one day when you should've been in school but you were in the market instead. I watched you from my office as you walked up and down the aisles."

Lareby started fondling himself in front of her as he continued talking. She was almost beyond feeling fear at this point. She had no plans. She had no hope.

"Then I noticed that young English teacher, Tobias Russell, in another aisle. I watched as the two of you met. You thought you were so sneaky. You thought no one else could see. But I could see. I watched as he grabbed your juicy ass and kissed you."

Echo begged her mind not to care that Jared knew her secret.

"Yes, Echo, I have always known you're a slut. You remind me so much of my mother. And now, just like her, I'm going to show you what a real man is all about."

"What do you mean 'just like her?'" Echo managed.

"I told you not to talk!"

Echo felt the blade burn through her cheek; blood splattered on his white coat. She was completely helpless while blood flowed, running down her cheek and into her mouth.

"Look what you made me do! I wanted you to look pretty for me, but now you look like any other whore that will feed the worms. They'll probably even spit you out. You are just like my mother. Did I show *her!*" His voice dipped into a singsong, "Yes, she died in her sleep and yes, I was a good son and let her see God. But to be honest, I had no choice in the matter. If I did her like I did the rest, I would've been caught. But I couldn't let her go to heaven and not know what she did to me. She found out what it was like to be fucked by her little boy, and to gasp for breath wanting more and knowing it was just out of reach."

She couldn't believe what she was hearing. He was totally deranged. How could she not have known all this time? She squeezed her eyes tight against the hot tears that spilled down her cheeks to mingle with the blood.

"And now it's your turn."

Echo felt the table shudder as it received his weight. The warmth of his body near her exposed flesh made her skin crawl, a wave of panic and nausea gripped her. "No, no. Please no. Oh God, oh God..." she begged silently.

Jared rubbed the tip of his dick on her thigh and she felt him press closer, preparing to enter her.

"Please God..." the words escaped her lips. The pain and fear were shutting down her body. A black curtain descended over her mind. She gave up resisting, she was passing out... No! She thought of J.T. and then she thought of Tobias. She had such a past with Tobias. She decided to let him stay in her mind during her last moments of life.

"You'll need more than God to..." Jared didn't finish the sentence. A loud crash shook the building. A blaring alarm followed.

"Fuck!" He jumped off her and ran to a table on the far side of the room.

Echo summoned the last of her strength to lift her head up. Jared was looking at a video monitor, "Everyone wants to be a hero."

He dressed quickly, cursing at the top of his lungs.

Echo wondered briefly who he meant by "everyone," before finally passing out.

J.T.

I was about to downshift and park, but then I spotted the blue Mercedes tucked behind the market.

Do I park and try to sneak in there somehow? There's a good chance I'd trigger an alarm.

A sick vision flashed into my head — Lareby torturing Echo.

If he hasn't already killed her! God, I wish I had a phone.

"Wait, the alarm! That's it!" I yelled and stepped on the gas. It was obvious. The sooner I triggered the alarm the sooner I'd get help, either from the police or even the security company. If I was wrong and Lareby was not in the market, the police would still have just cause to enter the building and look for evidence to track him down. I was going by David's story about rainbow duct tape, after all, and there still could be a logical explanation, but there was no time to worry about being wrong.

I drove straight for the massive window and aimed for the Lareby's Market logo. It didn't go as planned. The left side of the Jeep popped the curb while my right tire caught the lip of the handicapped-ramp crosswalk. The Jeep twisted through the air and crashed through the window, glass shattering everywhere.

I rubbed my eyes. I felt like I was in a cave.

Am I dead?

The alarm blared and all the lights flashed on, telling me that I wasn't dead. But I did feel strange, like I was dangling in the air... Then I got my bearings. I was hovering a few feet over the floor.

Wow! Thank God for my seatbelt.

My Jeep had landed upside down. Wheels spun while gas gushed out, and its unmistakable odor stung my nostrils. It was flooding the floor.

How was I not crushed?

I unbuckled my seatbelt and crashed to the cement surface. I crawled out from under the Jeep and straightened up. Now it made sense. The Jeep would've crushed me if it hadn't landed in between two conveyor belts. The checkout counters kept it from hitting the floor.

If I had landed a few feet either way I would've been knocked out or killed on impact. I had no time to dwell on my good fortune.

Jared Lareby was sprinting toward me.

"You want to go!"

I wasn't going to back down. As much as my right side was paralyzing me, I knew I could take him. I headed his way with full fury, but then saw an object in his hand.

Lareby smiled as he raised it.

Oh, shit!

I turned around and ran back toward the Jeep. If I could get around it, I'd be shielded long enough to head for the aisles and try and find a place to hide. I knew I should keep my head forward and try to get as much distance from him, but I also knew he could shoot me right in the back. I had to be ready to try and dodge the bullet, so I cocked my head back.

He was pointing his gun but not at me. He shot something, but it wasn't a bullet. It was an electrical spark.

Taser?

He aimed at the gas puddle. The spark ignited the puddle like a flame on charcoal. Lareby took off in the other direction.

The liquid turned into a ball of flames in less than a second and in even less time continued to the Jeep.

Oh my God!

It sounded like a tsunami approaching. I knew what was coming would have the same impact. I had no time to run. I race-dived into an aisle just as my Jeep caught fire. Moments later, it exploded.

This is it!

Debris rained down on me, and, for a moment, I had the same feeling of death approaching before realizing it was hundreds of boxes of tissues, napkins, and other paper goods.

I had picked the right aisle, but that feeling only lasted for a second. Hungry flames were consuming everything in sight as they headed down the aisle. Headed for me.

Black smoke hindered my breathing, but adrenaline helped me to my feet. Trying to outrun the fire, I pushed on until I was at the back of the market. Turning the corner, I hopped over the meat and poultry section and took refuge in the refrigerated area.

I coughed for a minute, but the cold air refreshed my lungs and helped me catch my breath. I could've stayed in there to regroup, but then I thought about Echo.

Where is she?

I had to keep operating on the assumption that she was still alive and that she was somewhere in the market.

Where would he hide her?

A memory flashed into my mind — the day Echo and I were shopping together and I met Lareby.

Walking into the market, I had seen two guys with jackhammers. I remembered telling Lareby that I'd do a story on his renovation after it was done. His reaction had been odd, and he quickly changed the subject.

Months later, there was no sign of a renovation, but maybe it had been done under the market.

"Just like his place in the woods," I said to myself, headed for the swinging doors. I looked out and saw that the fire was still on one side of the building. Fortunately, from noticing it while shopping, I knew the elevator was on the other side.

I pushed the doors open, jumped back over the meat and poultry case, and zigzagged to my left. Fatigue and pain weren't going to beat me because another force beyond adrenaline was driving me now. A force I had never known before. Love. I loved Echo, and I couldn't lose her.

I got to the elevator and pressed the down arrow. The doors swished open. Inside, I had only two choices, 1 and B, plus another up or down arrow.

I was already on 1 so I pressed B. Half a minute later, the elevator made a ding sound. I had to be ready. Lareby could be on the other side.

I cocked my left fist. Ready to go. The door opened. No one was there. I walked around carefully inspecting the room. It was filled with endless crates. There was an office, too. I checked it out. Nothing. It also didn't look like it had been renovated.

There was a warehouse, but it wasn't attached to the building... *Maybe that's where he put her?*

I hurried back into the elevator and was about to push the 1 to go back up but noticed something strange about the panel.

Why have an up and down arrow when there's already buttons for 1 and B? Why so many buttons for only two floors?

I pressed the down arrow.

Nothing.

The elevator didn't even budge.

So much for that hunch.

I was about to press 1 again but stopped.

Why have a down arrow when it doesn't even work, unless...

This time I pressed the B and the down arrow at the same time. The elevator door shut.

"Holy shit," I muttered.

I felt it going down another level. It took almost a minute. I could no longer hear the blare of the alarm. It was almost churchlike, but that changed when the doors opened.

I heard music. Violins. There were torches illuminating a long corridor, like a scene in a movie — a movie with castles not supermarkets. I followed the long hall. The farther I went, the louder the music got.

A door. I opened it and saw a candlelit room, the naked figure of a woman tied to a metal cart.

Echo! Is she alive? Please God!

My eyes ricocheted around the room.

Where is he?

But there was no sign of him. I rushed over to Echo and felt for a pulse.

"Echo! Wake up! Please wake up."

Her eyes opened to slits, "Tobias? Tobias is that you?"

"No, Echo. It's J.T. Wake up. Please wake up."

"J.T. You're here. Thank God." Her arms strained against the bindings, "Oh my God. My clothes. What's going on?"

"Jared Lareby. He's…"

"Yes! Yes! We've got to get out of here!" Echo began crying.

"Hold still. Let me untie you. It will be okay."

It took me a minute, but I got one hand untied.

"He almost raped me. I feel so…" she sobbed, but stopped and screamed, "J.T., watch out!"

Before I heard her scream, I felt his presence and I was able to duck just in time. A hatchet clanged down, denting the metal cart exactly where Echo's hand had been.

I jabbed upward with my left elbow, aiming for his groin. I heard him grunt and drop the hatchet. This gave me enough time to turn around and lunge on top of him. I quickly realized this was a bad move — I was a boxer not a wrestler — and he surprised me. He squirmed around and, before I knew it, he had wrapped his legs around my neck and was squeezing my windpipe shut.

"You'll never see God! You'll never see God!" Lareby yelled in a distorted voice. I was beginning to think he was right. Air was leaving me, and I was on the verge of passing out.

With her free hand, Echo was able to untie her other hand and then her legs. She jumped off the cart, ran over to us, and began stomping her bare foot on his face.

This caused Lareby to loosen his grip just enough. I was able to slip out of his grasp and get to my feet.

"Ahhh!" Echo howled in pain as Lareby locked his teeth on to her toes. He let go when he saw me coming, and Echo fell to the floor, clutching her bleeding foot.

I grabbed his collar and hauled him to his feet. I hit him with a weak right, and we started trading blows. As painful as the punches were, they gave me strength. Using fists was my world, and there was no way in hell he was going to take me from it. I had a secret weapon. I held on to the thought of that weapon and let him hit me in the face over and over until we were moving dangerously close to a fish tank.

"You'll never see God! You'll never see God!" Lareby shrieked, hitting me for the third time, blood and snot from my face flew. He was laughing now. And this was good. He was letting his guard down.

"Please let me live. I promise to tell your story." I faked sincerity and Lareby paused.

That hesitation was all I needed. My cocked left hand was ready to go. Being a southpaw, I surprised him with a powerful uppercut, and his body crashed against the tank.

I followed up by quickly horse-collaring him and shoving his head deep in the tank. I held his head down for a long time before pulling it up.

"My... story..." he spluttered, choking on water before I pushed his head down again.

I pulled him back.

"In... tree... woods... my... story..." Lareby managed in between choking on more water.

"J.T.! Stop! Don't kill him!" I heard Echo, but I wasn't listening to her voice.

I was listening to another voice, one that gave me a surge of power.

I pulled him up again and screamed at him, "Guess, who's never going to see God!"

After shoving his face in the water again, I looked over at the record player on the metal cart.

That fucking violin music is driving me crazy!

With all my rage, I kept his head down, his desperate flailing hands reached back, grabbing for anything. I was enjoying his desperation and found myself laughing.

"Stop it! Stop! Stop now!" Echo continued.

I waited until the hands went limp before releasing him. I studied his body. Lareby lay hunched over in the tank and was seconds from slumping to the floor. I propped him forward a bit so he wouldn't do that. He was probably dead, but I wasn't finished. Something compelled me to go over to the record player.

"Stop J.T.! Please!!! Stop it!!!" Echo pleaded.

I didn't.

"Listen to your fucking music in hell!" I hollered at him.

I rolled up my wet sleeves, dried my hands on my pants, picked up the player, and heaved it in the air. The tank suddenly looked like boiling rain as the sound of violins splashed into silence, electrocuting any possible chance for Nero to tell his story.

I turned to Echo. She looked away.

EPILOGUE

OCTOBER 20, 2004

WEDNESDAY

J.T.

Having been down three games and one out away from elimination, the Red Sox were about to make history. They were nine outs away from beating the Yankees in four consecutive games and going to the World Series.

The atmosphere in The Angry Fisherman should've been jubilant, but the town was still numb over losing Chuck Renna and also in shock from learning "the man everyone loved," Jared Lareby, was Nero.

Davis sensed the mood and did something he never did. He handed out free shots.

He took two Mind Erasers off his tray and put them in front of me.

"Here, drink up. Jesus, man, you look like the stunt double for all of the *Rocky* movies."

"Thanks."

"Thought a couple of shots might help dull the pain. How's the shoulder feeling?"

"Feeling like it could use that whole goddamn tray. Appropriate shot by the way," I said, grabbing one of the glasses with my left hand.

He nodded and whispered, "Thought you'd appreciate the symbolism."

I did. There was a lot I wanted to forget, starting with my conversation that morning at Echo's house.

She had told me that she had a job offer up in Boston and was going to take it.

"It's temporary for now. I told them I couldn't commit to anything long term. I have to get out of here and clear my head." She gently fingered the healing gash on her face.

"But what about us?"

"I can't think about us right now. If there even is an us. My feelings. My mind. Everything is so scattered."

"Ec, you know we were moving toward something."

"Maybe we were. I don't know. All I know is when I go to sleep, I see that horrible man about to — you know..."

"I know. That's why I'll be here for you."

"But that's not all I see. And it's not what scares me the most."

"Well, what then?"

"I see you killing him — and enjoying it."

"I was in the moment. It had to be. I was saving you, for Christ's sake. You know that's not the real me."

"You don't get it. I may've looked away at the time, but ever since then, I keep playing the scene over and over in my head and..."

"And what?"

"And I enjoy it. I enjoy the memory of seeing that monster get fried. You see, J.T.? That's not me, either. At least, it didn't *used* to be me. I feel like that night has changed me. I just need to go up to Boston and escape from all of this for a while."

"Okay, I get that. Nothing is holding me here. I can come with you. I mean, I just scored that big-time agent. I'll write the book about all of this and..."

"You're still going to write a book?"

"Of course I am. The whole country is waiting for my story. Sage thinks it could be a bestseller. She sees a future for me in true crime novels."

462

Echo's eyes filled with tears and then she slowly walked over and hugged me.

For that brief moment, I thought it was our beginning, but then she whispered in my ear, "Good luck, but I can't be a part of this."

I wanted to punch the memory out of my head, but instead, I downed the second shot before ordering an Irish Car Bomb from Billy.

Echo was out of my life, so I decided to think about someone else — Lilly Lee. She had been blowing up my phone ever since I got out of the hospital.

Maybe I should just get hammered and drop her a text message.

That wouldn't numb my feelings for Echo, at least not tonight. Echo owned my heart, and I had to figure out a way for her to see we were meant to be.

I looked up at the TV and the Sox were now eight outs away.

Billy handed the drink to me, and a voice hollered from across the bar, "That one's on me."

I glanced over and saw my father's old partner Paddy Magill raising his pint to me. He was already seeing triple.

I nodded and whispered to Billy while he leaned over the counter, "Can you tell him thanks for the offer, but I'm all set."

I took out my new red and white duct tape wallet that David had made for me as a "Thank you for saving my sister" and threw a ten on the bar.

"Okay. Good. 'Bout to shut him off anyway so you don't have to play the 'you buy me a drink; I'll buy you a drink game.'"

"Well, can I buy you a drink then?"

I looked to my other side to see Selectman Oliver Kempton sitting down.

"Sure."

"Can I ask you something?" Kempton asked.

"Yeah, what?"

"I heard a rumor that I was on your white board as a suspect. Is that true?" Kempton's bug eyes danced.

"Who told you that? Detective Gordon?"

"Yes, how did you know?"

"That day at the frame shop, I figured he must've been feeding you info."

"So, was I up on your board?"

"The cut on your hand. You used the word 'gouge.' Yes, you were on the board. Sorry about that."

"Are you kidding? That's so cool. Anyway, thanks for saving this town." Kempton patted me on the back and went over to brag to his table of nerds.

Seven outs away and another Mind Eraser handed to me.

I turned my thoughts to the voicemail message I received from book agent Sage Stevens. She wanted to set up a lunch date.

"Hi, J.T. I know Agent DeLuca has told you about me. I'm not calling about his book project. I'm calling about yours. Come up to Boston and let's talk. I think I can make you a superstar."

Six outs away and another Car Bomb.

I thought about the violin. They never found it. Did he leave it to burn in the woods? Was it really a Stradivarius? I'll never know.

Five outs away and a shot of Jägermeister.

At least Crocker and Anna and even Norman Chadwick were grateful for what I had done. They had thrown a ginger ale and subs party that afternoon at the paper to celebrate. The extended hug from Anna told me that she didn't care if I had overkilled Lareby! It was good to see Crocker and Norman getting along. Crocker also said he was ready to go on record as being one of Pop Tucker's victims.

Sobriety is a good thing. It makes you strong.

We also decided to have the bench across from Fishy Bryden engraved "In Memory of Chuck Renna."

Four outs to go and a shot of tequila and "fuck the salt."

I glanced at the text from Erin begging me to come to Boston.

Dad wants to say goodbye. Doc says any day. Dad is proud of you. Please J.T.

I wrote back: Maybe.

I pushed off the bar rail, steadied myself, and walked to the bathroom to take a piss. I looked around and saw the empty spot where the Sandy Point Dive Club picture used to be. I knew why Davis had taken it down. Jared Lareby had been one of the members.

I passed Magill on my way back to my stool.

"What's the deal, O'Rourke? Too good for me?"

"Save your money, Paddy." I continued on my way.

"Maybe *you* should. Your ol' man sure didn't." Magill laughed to his entourage

Three outs to go and my blood boiled.

"What did you just say?"

"I'm not afraid of you. Sure, you can kick my ass. But you forget, Jameson, I know your family. I knew your *imaginary* friend, Owen." He smiled.

Owen. The name almost knocked me over. When I was little, I would talk about my friend Owen. My mother would beg me to stop talking about him.

"He's imaginary and he is gone. He's not coming back!" she'd cry and run to her room and stay in bed for days. I never understood why she got so upset. I finally stopped talking about him and stopped wondering.

The way Paddy Magill had stressed the word *imaginary* and was looking at me made me dizzy with anger.

"Outside." I ordered.

"The game," he pointed to the TV, and they were two outs away.

"Now!"

"Paddy, you want us to come with you," one of them said.

"I'll be fine. We're just going to have a little chat about the old neighborhood. Remind the young man of where he came from." He laughed and followed me out the door.

The moment we got out of view from the windows, I grabbed him by his coat.

"What were you saying to me back there?"

"I've been wondering if you still believed that story."

"What story?"

"The one your parents told you after Owen died."

"What do you mean 'died'? He was an imaginary friend!"

"Wow, their ridiculous pop psychology actually worked on you."

"Start making sense!"

"I will, but let go of me first."

I did.

"When you were four years old, your ol' man and me got a call to your house. He was really worried because your mom had been suffering from postpartum depression."

"But I was four."

"Yes, but your baby brother, Owen, was nine months old. Your dad was worried that she might neglect him. And when we got there, well, what we found was worse than neglect. Your mother had thrown a radio in the bathtub and electrocuted him."

The nightmare. The boiling rain. The spaceships were on the wallpaper of the baby's room. I could see it all. I had witnessed my mother killing my baby brother, and that's why I did the same thing with Lareby.

They lied to me. My whole life was a lie. They covered up her murder telling me that Owen was an imaginary friend.

"How come she wasn't arrested?" I could barely form the question.

"Back then, there were a lot of people who did favors for your father. He had a lot of power and knew people on both sides of the law. I was in his debt, but most importantly, so was the medical examiner. He put down SIDS on the death certificate and life moved on."

But life hadn't moved on. It broke at that point, and it was never put back together for my family. My miserable childhood now made sense.

"Be a little more civil to me next time, Jameson." Magill walked back into The A.F.

I stood there for a moment and thought of my sister Erin. She knew. She had to have known.

I took out my phone and texted: Tell him I'll be up tomorrow to hear the truth about Owen.

It chimed back immediately: You remember?

Yes. I remember everything. We need to talk.

I'll tell him.

I could hear a loud roar from The Angry Fisherman. The Sox had "cowboyed up" and done it.

I was in shock. My childhood was a lie. I didn't know what I was going to do next, but I did know it would involve another drink. It would be the first of many.

ACKNOWLEDGMENTS

I'd like to thank Gerry Hagerty for his law enforcement knowledge, Andrea Norris for her fashion sense, and Sarah E. Murphy for her keen eye and being my first editor.

I'm grateful to E-Murph, the St. A's boys, Shane McWeeny, Scott Etler, Jay Oliveira, Kenny Kozens and Craig Kozens for being my early readers who pushed me on.

A big shout out to Seton Murphy, Bob Gallagher, and Larry Palmucci for helping me land one of the coolest agents, Murray Weiss.

I want to thank my Dark Waters Book team of Mary Petiet, Eugenia Nordskog and Janet Edmonds. You made the editing process painless with your thoughtful suggestions.

I want to thank Mark Penta for being Penta.

Finally, I want to thank Jennifer A. Murphy for being the most supportive person in my life. I am lucky every day to have you as my wife.

ABOUT THE AUTHOR

Devlin Rush is the pseudonym of an accomplished author who has received numerous awards for his other work. *Macabre Trophies* marks a profound break from his previous offerings. Rush lives in a seasonal town in Massachusetts.

ABOUT THE PRESS

Dark Waters Books is an imprint of Sea Crow Press dedicated to mystery, thriller, fantasy, fiction, and crime noir. The home of unsolved mysteries and things that go bump in the night, Dark Waters Books offers traditional storytelling with a thrilling modern edge.